Pony Stories

Patricia Leitch

The Summer Riders
Night of the Red Horse

This edition published in 1995 for
Parragon Book Service Limited
Units 13–17 Avonbridge Industrial Estate
Atlantic Road
Avonmouth, Bristol BS11 9QD
by Diamond Books
77–85 Fulham Palace Road
Hammersmith, London W6 8JB

First edition published 1992 for Parragon
Book Service Limited

Printed in England

Contents

The Summer Riders

First published in a single volume in paperback in
1977 in Armada

CHAPTER ONE

Jinny Manders woke with the thought quite clear in her mind that today was the first day of the summer holidays.

"The summer holidays," Jinny said aloud and shivered with excitement.

She jumped out of bed and padded on bare feet across her bedroom to the window that looked out to the rolling hills and high, rocky crags that surrounded Finmory House. Nothing stirred in the grey summer dawn. Then, as Jinny stared out, the glistening golden disc of the sun began to slip up from behind the hills. The high, cloudless sky shimmered into blue.

"Going to be a smashing day," thought Jinny. "I'll go for a ride now," she decided. "Before anyone else is awake. Nobody to spoil it. Just Shantih and me."

Jinny somersaulted back across her room, past the mural of a red horse charging through a jungle of white flowers, past her own drawings and paintings pinned to the walls, under the arch that separated the two halves of her room and did a floppy cartwheel over her bed to reach her other window. It faced in the opposite direction, looked over Finmory's garden, down to the ponies' field and on to Finmory Bay and the glittering reach of the sea.

Jinny opened the window wide and leaned out, her long, red-gold hair swinging over the sill.

"Shantih," Jinny called. "Shantih."

Punch and Bramble, the two borrowed trekking ponies that Jinny and her younger brother Mike had ridden to school, went on grazing, ignoring her, but the third horse looked up, instantly alert at the sound of Jinny's voice.

"Shantih," Jinny breathed, and the Arab horse whinnied in reply, her nostrils dark pits in her delicate, dished face. Her ears were pricked above her silken forelock and her dark, lustrous eyes looked up at Jinny from under long-fringed lashes. She was a pure-bred Arab, red-gold with a white blaze and four white socks, and Jinny loved her completely, totally.

Jinny had first seen Shantih in a circus. Then she had

9

been 'Yasmin, the Killer Horse', being lashed into rearing viciousness by the ringmaster. But now she belonged to Jinny and was Shantih, which means peace. Ken had chosen the name, saying that names changed people and that it would help Shantih to forget the circus.

Almost a year ago, Jinny and her family—Petra who was now fifteen and Mike who was ten—had all left the city life of Stopton, where Mr. Manders had been a probation officer, to come and live at Finmory House. It was a large, grey, stone house in the Scottish Highlands. Their nearest neighbour was Mr. MacKenzie, whose farm supplied the Manders with milk and eggs, and then there was nothing but moorland until the tiny village of Glenbost where Mike and Jinny went to school. Now Mr. Manders made his living as a potter, helped by Ken, who was seventeen and was staying with the Manders.

They had first got to know Ken Dawson when he had been on probation in Stopton, charged with other boys for breaking into a warehouse. At the end of his probation he had said to Mr. Manders, "I'd nothing to do with it." "I know," Mr. Manders had acknowledged.

Although Ken's parents were rich enough to send him a monthly cheque, they wanted nothing further to do with him. "Just so long as they know I'm not starving," Ken had mocked when his first cheque had arrived direct from the bank, and he had laughed, stuffing it into the pocket of his jeans. But Jinny hadn't thought it was funny. Your own parents not loving you. She couldn't even bear to think it might be possible.

"We want you here," she had assured Ken. "I care." And Ken had smiled directly at her, his green eyes bright in his thin, tanned face. He had pushed back his long, straw-coloured hair and looked down at her from his bony height. "Thank you," he'd said and gone out to the vegetable garden he was creating, with Kelly, his grey, shaggy dog padding at his heels.

Jinny wasn't quite sure what was the best thing, Ken living with them or owning Shantih. She could never make up her mind.

Shantih whinnied again and walked towards the hedge closest to the house, her stride neat and precise through the dew dark grass.

"We're going for a ride," Jinny told her. "I shan't be long. Stay there."

A few minutes later Jinny was flipping down the steep flight of stairs that led from her attic bedroom. She ran along the corridor, down the wide staircase to the hall, and into the kitchen. She was the first, there was no one else awake. She paused for a second to choose two apples, one for herself and one for Shantih, then she opened the heavy back door, hearing its creaking echoing through the sleeping house, and she was free. In the back yard she whirled round and round, her long hair flying out about her skinny body.

"Summer," she yelled. "Summer, summer, summer." And thought of galloping over the moors, swimming Shantih in the sea, camping by Loch Varrich—if she could find a tent. Days and days of being with Shantih. "And it was summer; warm delightful summer," said Jinny slowly.

The Manders stables had once been crumbling outhouses. Now there was a place for tack and the horses' feed, two stalls for the Highland ponies and a loose box for Shantih. Jinny took down Shantih's snaffle bridle. Beside it, polished and gleaming, was the tack belonging to Bramble and Punch. Jinny swallowed hard and tried not to look at it. It wasn't that she had forgotten that tomorrow Punch and Bramble were going back to Miss Tuke's trekking centre, just that she wasn't allowing it to come up to the surface of her mind. Tomorrow would be time enough to think about Shantih being alone in the field and Miss Tuke taking back both saddles which meant that Jinny would need to ride bareback all the time. Jinny didn't mind riding bareback but she had to admit that without a saddle Shantih would be able to throw her off more often than usual.

"Nobody, absolutely nobody, could possibly say that Shantih wasn't improving," Jinny thought. Only last Easter Jinny had spent most of her rides flying through the air while Shantih bucked or reared but now she managed to stay on top most of the time.

Jinny counted on her fingers as she walked down to the ponies' field. Last week she had only been bucked off six times and Shantih hadn't really reared at all. Not what you'd call rearing. There had been rather a nasty moment

11

when they had met Mr. MacKenzie's tractor, but she hadn't actually reared, Jinny decided, just tipped up a bit, and it had all been Mr. MacKenzie's fault, coming charging round the corner when he knew he might meet them. "He does it for kicks," thought Jinny darkly. "Lurks and pounces on us."

Shantih was waiting at the field gate and whickered when she saw Jinny.

"Horse," said Jinny lovingly, "are you in a good mood or can you smell the apples?"

Jinny slipped the bridle over the Arab's head and led her out of the field. She shared the apples with her, feeling Shantih's velvet muzzle lipping her hand.

"Finished," Jinny told her. "That's all." Shantih pushed at Jinny to make sure. "Come on," said Jinny. "We're going down to the sea."

Jinny sprang up onto Shantih's back. There hadn't seemed much point in dirtying a saddle for one day, not after Mike had helped her to clean the tack. Now that Punch and Bramble were going back to Miss Tuke's trekking centre Jinny didn't suppose she'd be seeing much of her brother round the stables. Mike was easy-going and cheerful, with brown eyes and curly hair. Jinny liked being with him but she knew that although Mike was fond of Punch he wouldn't really mind not having a pony to ride. Mike's summer holidays would be full of his own things—fishing and helping Alec Clark on his father's farm, hoping that this summer he might just be allowed to drive the tractor.

Petra was even less horsy than Mike. When it suited her she didn't mind sitting sweetly on a horse with a headscarf knotted at just the right angle over her curls, but most of the time Petra wasn't in the least interested in Shantih. Really, Jinny was quite glad. Whenever Petra was around, Jinny seemed to make more of a muddle of things than usual. Sometimes Jinny thought that her sister was made up of all the opposites to herself. She was sharp and efficient and organised; her curly hair was always tidy and her clothes always looked clean and smart. "And bossy," thought Jinny darkly. "Very bossy indeed." Later in the summer Petra was going to sit an important music exam and all her spare time would be spent practising the piano. Jinny knew

12

she would pass. Passing exams was one of Petra's things. Reading teenage fashion magazines was another. "But not helping me with Shantih," Jinny decided.

It wasn't that Jinny wanted anyone else to ride Shantih but she couldn't help thinking that it would be nice to have a friend. Someone to ride with her. None of the other children at the village school was the least interested in ponies. They thought of them as things they had kept around the crofts before the tractors came.

"What I would like," thought Jinny, "is another girl who has her own pony and knows a bit about schooling. Someone who could tell me what I'm doing wrong. Someone to help me to lunge her . . ." Jinny stopped in mid thought. Last Easter holidays she had tried to make Clare Burnley help her with Shantih and things had gone disastrously wrong. It was not something that Jinny allowed herself to think about too often.

"All past. Utterly past," thought Jinny, and she gathered up Shantih's reins and urged her into a canter. Shantih bucked. Jinny sailed over her head, landed on her feet and sprang back up, almost in one smooth circle.

"Get on with you," shouted Jinny, sitting tight and close. "On you go." And the mare was cantering smoothly, towards the beach. The sea breeze flicked back her mane and lifted strands of Jinny's red hair. Jinny laid the palm of her hand flat on Shantih's shoulder, feeling the power of the Arab's stride. "Faster," urged Jinny and the mare stretched her neck and raced over the rough grass.

Jinny brought Shantih back to a walk before they reached the beach. She slowed down reluctantly, snaking her head and jangling her bit, curtseying suddenly sideways, her tail kinked over her back.

"Don't bother showing off," said Jinny severely. "There's no one to see you. Walk now. Steady."

Shantih strode down the path between the massed boulders and out into the dazzle of the shore. On the sands Jinny stopped her and sat staring over the water. Gulls searching for an early breakfast looped the sky or squabbled at the edge of the surf, a pied squadron of oyster catchers flew low over the sea.

"Cor!" thought Jinny, glutted with the blue and silver and gold. "Just think, you might still have been in your

13

piggy circus and I might have been stuck in filthy old Stopton. You remember, Shantih Manders, how lucky you are and stop bucking me off."

Shantih flickered disinterested ears and dug impatiently at the wet sand until Jinny let her walk on along the beach.

At the far side of the bay, on the grass above the barrier of sea-smoothed boulders, was something that looked to Jinny like a bright yellow sheet hanging out to dry. She peered at it but couldn't make out what it could be, then trotted Shantih towards it, thinking that it might be some sort of shelter that Mr. MacKenzie had put up. Then suddenly she stopped Shantih and stared in disbelief at the sands in front of her.

"It can't be!" thought Jinny. "Yet it is!"

Someone, but Jinny couldn't imagine who it could possibly have been, had been schooling a horse. The wet sand was pitted with hoof prints. Circles, figure eights and serpentines were tracked out on the sand. For a moment Jinny wondered if Clare Burnley might have been riding on the shore; but Jinny knew the Burnleys were still in Sussex and their house, Craigvaar, was still empty. And it couldn't have been Mike or Petra or Ken. Even if one of them had taken a Highland for a ride they would never ever have brought him down here to school.

"Man Friday," thought Jinny, and jumped down to examine the marks more closely.

They were certainly hoof prints. Someone *had* been schooling a horse there and not so very long ago. Then suddenly Shantih jerked her head into the air, almost snatching the reins out of Jinny's hand. She whinnied with a blast of sound and was answered with a high, squealing neigh. Almost invisible against the boulders a girl in jodphurs and a yellow tee shirt was riding a skewbald pony.

Jinny threw herself back up on to Shantih, knowing that if the Arab got too excited she might not be able to get up on to her again. With neck arched and tail high, Shantih pranced across the sands towards the skewbald. The girl had seen them. She waved and walked her pony to meet them.

The brown and white pony was thick-set and cobby, with a shaving brush mane and a placid, two-colour expression. His rider looked about twelve years old, about

14

the same age as Jinny. She had short, brown, wavy hair, a tip-tilted nose and wide-set, hazel eyes. She wasn't fat, but rather like her pony, Jinny thought, sturdy and reliable-looking.

They were within a few yards of the girl and her skewbald when Shantih reared violently, hung poised in the air, balanced on her hind legs. Jinny clung round her neck helplessly until she touched down again.

"It's the strange pony . . ." Jinny began, her face scarlet from being scrubbed into Shantih's mane. She looked defiantly across at the girl, expecting to see her laughing at Shantih's bad manners and Jinny's rotten riding, but on the girl's round, freckled face was an expression of total admiration.

"She is absolutely super," said the girl. "She's an Arab, isn't she? Is she yours? I've always wanted an Arab. And a chestnut too! Oh, she is beautiful!"

Jinny's sharp features spread into an ear-to-ear grin. It wasn't often she met someone who said the things that she herself thought about Shantih.

"Super horse," repeated the girl, still gazing at Shantih. "Oh, how I'd love a horse like that."

"She gets a bit excited," apologised Jinny. "She used to be in a circus where they treated her badly."

"Not that I don't think Pippen is the mostest pony and I wouldn't change him for anything. But an Arab . . ."

"I'm Jinny Manders," said Jinny. "And this is Shantih. We live at Finmory House."

"You don't! We saw it last night when we arrived. Dad said he'd give anything to live there but Mum said there'd be mice. I'm Sue, Sue Horton, and this is Pippen."

"Are you staying here?" asked Jinny.

"Camping," said Sue. "All summer. Normally we have a fortnight in a stuffy hotel but with things being so expensive we bought a tent and more or less at the last minute we were able to borrow a trailer and bring Pippen with us. Thought we were going to have to leave you behind all summer, didn't we?" said Sue, ruffling the skewbald's mane. "Would you look at it?" she said. "Every spring I swear I'm going to let it grow and it goes on growing up and up and up. Then every autumn I give in and have it clipped again. Still, perhaps this time . . ." She grinned, then said, "You are lucky living here. Can you ride all over the hills?"

"More or less," said Jinny. "You have to watch out for boggy bits on the moors but there are lots of places where it's quite safe to gallop."

"Shall we go for a ride together?" asked Sue. "That's if you'd like to. I don't want to be tagging on."

"Like to!" exclaimed Jinny. "Honestly I was longing for someone to ride with. I'm the only one who's keen on horses in my family."

"Well, I'm the only anything one," said Sue.

"This morning?" asked Jinny. "We could go for a ride this morning if you like."

"Not at all today," said Sue regretfully. "We're all going to Inverburgh to stock up and Dad wants some new fishing gear—but every day after that."

"Sue! Sue! Breakfast's ready," called a voice, and Jinny, seeing a woman standing by the bright yellow sheet, realised that it was part of an elaborate tent.

"How about tomorrow?" Sue asked.

"This time," said Jinny. "Very early." And she explained about having to return Punch and Bramble to Miss Tuke.

"See you here, then. Tomorrow at seven."

"Right," said Jinny, sitting very tight on Shantih in case she reared again when Sue rode Pippen away. "'Bye."

Riding back to Finmory, squeaks of delight burst out of Jinny. "And a friend for you," she told Shantih. "Dare say Pippen can share your field. Will that be nice?"

Jinny's family were all sitting round the kitchen table having breakfast when Jinny burst into the kitchen.

"There's a family camping on the beach," Jinny told them. "And there's a girl called Sue, 'bout my age I should think, AND SHE'S GOT A PONY!"

"Oh, I'm glad," said Mrs. Manders. "She'll be company for you. I've been worrying about you riding Shantih by yourself all summer."

"Well, you don't need to now," said Jinny. "I'll be riding with Sue." All the things Jinny had been planning to do were suddenly warmer, more exciting, now that they were to be shared with someone else. "We're going for a ride tomorrow."

16

"What about the sad returning?" asked Mike.

"Hadn't forgotten," said Jinny, making herself toast. "We're going to ride early."

"The Thorpes come tomorrow," said her father.

"Tomorrow!" cried Jinny. "But I thought they weren't coming until the end of August!"

"That was changed weeks ago," said Petra, crimping at her crispbread with her front teeth. "You never listen to anything, do you?"

"When was it changed? No one told me," said Jinny indignantly.

The Thorpes were two children Mr. Manders had known in Stopton. The boy, Bill Thorpe, was thirteen and had been on probation for shoplifting. Since the Manders had been at Finmory, Bill had spent six months in hospital with lung trouble. Mr. Manders had heard from a colleague that they were trying to get Bill away from Stopton for a holiday in the country but were having trouble fixing it up because the boy's younger sister wanted to go with him. "Send them to us," Mr. Manders had offered, and the visit had been arranged.

"Well, everyone else knew," said Mike.

"I didn't. And I think someone could have told me," grumphed Jinny, sitting down beside her father with her plate of blackish toast. The very last thing she wanted was two unknown Stopton children coming to stay just when she had found a friend. Jinny hacked at the butter and spread it thickly on her toast. She gulped the coffee that her mother had poured out for her.

"Having a tiny tantrum, are we?" asked Petra.

"Well . . . I didn't know they were coming," said Jinny. "Still, I don't suppose I'll see much of them. I'll be riding Shantih with Sue."

Ken got up from the table, pushing his chair back with a sharp sound of disgust. He went silently out of the back door, his bony shoulders hunched.

Jinny ignored his departure.

"What's the sister's name?" Mike asked.

"Marlene," said Mr. Manders. "She's ten. Both lived in Stopton all their lives."

"Isn't the girl lame?" asked his wife.

17

"Lame?" said Jinny. "Then she won't want to ride, will she?"

"She was knocked down crossing the road when she was about six," said her father. "Her leg was badly broken and never set properly. Now she walks with a very bad limp." Mr. Manders went to get a sheet of paper out of his desk.

"Meant to show you this," he said to Jinny, handing it to her. "Marlene's teacher gave it to Tim Lawrence, the social worker who's working with the Thorpes. I must have mentioned Shantih to him and he must have told Marlene about her. Anyway this is what she wrote. Normally her compositions consist of one or two words. Read it."

Jinny looked suspiciously at the folded page that had obviously been taken from a school exercise book. She took it from her father unwillingly. The writing was uneven and sprawling and even Jinny could see that the spelling was terrible.

"This sumer I am to ride a arab hors. We will gallopp. When I am on the hors you wont see me leg is wonky. It wont mattar. I think the hors will be ok with me. He is spesull. I will lov the hors. When I am on the hors we will go fast as flames."

When Jinny had finished reading she kept her eyes on the paper. The girl must be daft thinking she could come and gallop Shantih. No one who hadn't been on a horse before could just get on a horse and gallop off.

"She could have had a ride on Bramble if he hadn't had to go back to Miss Tuke," Jinny muttered. "Or perhaps Sue would let her have a ride on her pony. He looked pretty quiet. But not on Shantih."

Mr. Manders took back Marlene's composition.

"I think the hors will be ok with me," he read.

"Well, I don't think Shantih will be O.K. with her," stated Jinny. "She can't ride. She can't arrive here and expect to go galloping off on Shantih."

"Fast as flames," said her father.

"Not fast as flames on my horse," muttered Jinny sullenly.

18

CHAPTER TWO

The next morning Shantih and Jinny careered down the track to the beach. Jinny had slept in and was still feeling cross and gritty. Shantih, catching her irritation, was playing up. She would bound forward then jerk to a sudden halt, wait with her neck arched and every muscle tensed—totally ignoring her rider, who was perched insecurely on her bare back—then with a half rear she would spin round and plunge back to her field.

"Oh, come on then," said Jinny furiously, when she had been carted back to Punch and Bramble three times. "I'll just have to lead you or Sue will be back in her tent."

Jinny dragged the reins over Shantih's head and, tugging on her bit, set off for the beach.

"Might as well be pulling a rhinoceros," thought Jinny as she plodded towards the sea. Her book on horsemanship said that you should never look back when you were leading a horse. "'Spect she has changed," Jinny decided. "Wonder what Sue will say. Expect she'll be polite. 'What strange horns your horse has got,' she'll say, and I'll say, 'All the better to charge you with'."

From the direction of the beach came a shrill whinny. Shantih froze, her eyes goggling. Just in time, Jinny lassoed her reins over her head and managed to scrabble on to her back before Shantih, with an answering whinny, was galloping down the track.

Jinny fell off when Shantih did a four hoof, emergency stop in front of Pippen and Sue.

"Hi," said Sue as Jinny picked herself up off the sand. "Wish I'd had a ciné. She looked fantastic galloping like that."

"Huh," grunted Jinny. "She wouldn't leave the Highlands. That's why I'm so late. She must have known they're going away today."

"I've been schooling him," said Sue. "Would you watch for a minute and see if he does change legs when we do a figure eight?"

"I'll try," said Jinny, who wasn't too sure what it looked

like when a horse did change legs, although she knew it was the correct thing to do.

Watching Pippen cantering round, Jinny grinned to herself as she imagined his legs dropping off and reassembling themselves at the centre of the figure eight.

"No good, was it?" demanded Sue when she rode back to Jinny. "He trotted."

Jinny thought it best to agree.

"Would you mind if we stayed here and schooled? It's after eight so we haven't much time for a ride."

Jinny didn't think Shantih was in the mood for schooling but she had promised Mike that she would be ready to set off for Miss Tuke's before ten.

"Even leaving at ten we won't get there much before twelve," Mike had said. "Dad's meeting us there with the car. We've to take his pots in to Miss Storr's shop and then be at the station to meet the two-thirty train. You be late to start with and the whole day will be a mess."

"That's right," Jinny had replied. "Make it all my fault. And we haven't even begun."

But Jinny knew that if they went for a ride now she wouldn't be ready to set out at ten and it would be her fault.

"Flippin' time," thought Jinny, already seeing how the day was going to be full of people telling her to hurry up.

"Well, all right," she said to Sue, "but Shantih isn't very good at schooling."

"Walk her round in a circle," suggested Sue and Jinny rode Shantih out in a wide circle.

It took all Jinny's concentration to keep Shantih going round at a walk, and each time they passed Sue and Pippen the circle bulged towards them.

"Try a trot," called Sue.

"Well . . ." said Jinny, but closed her fingers on Shantih's reins, tightening her legs against the Arab's sides.

Shantih leapt forward into a raking trot and there was a moment when Jinny felt all the pride and gaiety of her horse as she flowed round the circle, but the next minute Shantih was fighting to get to Pippen. Jinny shortened her left rein and kicked with her right heel.

"Get on," she shouted. "Get on with you," as Shantih began to buck, her head tucked between her forelegs, her quarters and hind legs soaring skywards. Clinging to a lump of hairy wither, Jinny clamped her knees against Shantih's hard shoulders and fought to stay on. Sue was shouting to her but Jinny couldn't hear her, could only see her mouth opening and shutting and Pippen's bland, brown and white face as he knitted his brows in disapproval at such behaviour.

Shantih managed to work a twist into her fourth buck that sent Jinny sprawling towards her ears. Arms linked round her mare's neck, Jinny slithered to the ground.

"Gosh," said Sue. "Is that what she did in the circus?"

"She is much, much better than she used to be," stated Jinny firmly. "She didn't feel like schooling. It was my fault. I should have known better. She hardly ever mucks about when we go for a ride. I don't blame her for bucking. If I wanted to go over the moors and some stupid human tried to make me go round in circles I'd buck them off." Jinny rubbed Shantih's neck and stroked her hand over her muzzle. "She gets excited, that's all. I don't mind."

"She looked terrific," said Sue. "All mane and tail and hooves. I'd be scared stiff to ride her. Bit of a coward, that's me."

"Me too," said Jinny in surprise that anyone should think of her as brave. "Only it's different with Shantih."

"You don't use a stick, do you?" asked Sue. "Mrs. Ross at our Pony Club would say that she needed to be taught a lesson."

"Clare Burnley thought that too. But it's no use. The ringmaster at that circus whipped her. It only makes her go mad."

"Well, I think I'd ride with a saddle."

"Well I did," said Jinny. "Haven't got one now. I used one of the ponies' saddles but it goes back to Miss Tuke today." And guiltily Jinny remembered about the time. Her watch said ten to twelve which Jinny considered unlikely.

"But I can lend you one!" said Sue. "I thought you were improving your seat. Come up to the tent and we'll see if it fits."

"Oh, but I couldn't take that," cried Jinny when Sue, after a car key sortie into the tent, unlocked the boot of their car and took out an almost brand-new saddle. "It's far too good."

"Try it on," said Sue, ignoring Jinny's protests.

Sue fitted the saddle on to Shantih's back. "There," she said, tightening the girth. "Seems perfect. Get up. I must look under it while you're sitting on it to make sure I can see daylight under the channel."

"Perfect," said Sue, squinting under the saddle when Jinny was mounted. "Not touching her spine."

"But I can't just take it," gasped Jinny. Her knees were tucked against the knee rolls and she sat with a new sense of security in the deep seat of the saddle. "It's too good. I mean, you don't really know me. And it's such a smashing saddle."

"Please borrow it," said Sue. "I'd be glad to see someone using it. Perhaps it will stop Dad moaning. My cousin, who is completely spoiled, thought she wanted to ride. They bought her everything, including a beastly show pony. Of course she fell off, broke her arm, and that was that. No more ponies. Screamed if she saw one. They had to sell the lot. I persuaded Dad to buy the saddle for Pippen. And he's too broad for it. 'Course I really knew that, didn't I, but I so wanted to have it. It gave Pippen a sore back and I can't use it. We brought it with us because Dad thinks this holiday will slim Pippen down. If it doesn't he's going to sell it. Now if you were using it you'd be doing me a favour. It upsets Dad when he sees it lying around."

"He didn't buy it for me to use," insisted Jinny. "Perhaps seeing me using it would upset him more." She couldn't believe that a more or less complete stranger was offering to lend her the kind of saddle that she had always dreamed about but known she could never afford.

A stoutish woman with long, dark hair came out of the tent.

"Mum," called Sue. "Here. This is Jinny who lives at Finmory House."

The woman pulled a heavy sweater over her head and came towards them.

"Hullo," she said, smiling with Sue's smile and holding her hand out to Jinny. "Just crawled out of our burrow. Shocking lying in bed until this time on a camping holiday."

"Time!" remembered Jinny.

"I'm lending Jinny *the* saddle," said Sue.

"Grand," said Mrs. Horton. "Glad to see someone using it. Gave poor old Pippen a bad back, didn't it, son? I'm about to brew up. Will you two have a cup?"

"Is it nine o'clock yet?" Jinny asked, wondering desperately if she could just ride off with Sue's saddle; just turn round and ride off with a brand-new saddle or whether she should offer to sign some sort of agreement or even leave a deposit—not that she had any money.

"Twenty past," Mrs Horton told her.

"Oh no," cried Jinny. "I'll need to go."

"You will," said Sue. "I'd forgotten all about the time."

"They'll be mad with me," said Jinny, already beginning to turn Shantih towards Finmory. "Are you sure it's O.K. for me to take the saddle?"

"Certain," said Mrs. Horton.

"I told you," said Sue.

"Well, thank you very much indeed," said Jinny. "I mean thank you isn't enough but I will need to go."

"Then go," said Sue, giggling. "Don't keep on telling us."

"See you tomorrow," Jinny shouted back as she cantered off. "Come up to Finmory."

Half-way across the field, Shantih's head went down and she began to buck.

"Ah, no you don't. Not this time." And Jinny, bracing her knees against the knee rolls and sitting deep in the saddle, was able to pull Shantih's head up and send her on.

"This saddle," Jinny told her horse as they cantered home, "is going to make a great deal of difference in your life. See if it doesn't." And she thought that she would do some drawings of Pippen and give them to Sue. As Jinny rode home she could see quite clearly how she would paint the skewbald pony. She knew the way his hooves had to be round and settled into the ground, his neck bulky and his ears thickly rooted into his head. She could feel how she would draw the corners of his smug lips. Jinny didn't understand how she knew these things. They came welling up inside her and then she was able to draw them.

The ponies' field was empty, and as Jinny took off Shantih's tack and turned her loose, she supposed that Mike must have taken both Highlands in to their stalls.

"You're late," shouted Petra's voice.

"Surprise, surprise," shouted back Jinny, running up to her bedroom and setting the new saddle carefully in a corner. She paused for a second of utter disbelief and then ran out to the stables.

"Thought you were going to be back before nine," said Mike, who was grooming the white Punch. "I've brought them in and given them a last feed. We don't want to arrive at Miss Tuke's with them covered in sweat. She'll think that's the way we've been treating them all year."

"Well, we haven't," said Jinny, grabbing a dandy and starting to groom Bramble. Under the strokes of the brush Bramble's summer coat gleamed like jet, dapples spangled his quarters and broad barrel. Jinny ran her hands down his flat knees and strong-boned legs. She brushed out his feathery fetlocks and tipped his haystack mane from one side of his neck to the other as she tried to brush it flat.

"I shall miss you terribly," she whispered to the pony, remembering all the wild gallops they had shared, all the journeys to and from school. Jinny buried her face in Bramble's mane. She wanted to keep him, wanted to find her parents and try to persuade them to buy Bramble. Punch could go back to Miss Tuke's, but Bramble belonged to her.

"No time," said Mike. "Don't start to cry. You should have been earlier if you wanted to go on like that."

Reluctantly Jinny supposed so. She put on Bramble's tack and went inside. Her mother caught her and made her drink a cup of coffee and gobble down a bacon sandwich.

All the family came to say goodbye to the ponies.

Ken, his hands encrusted with clay, held his face out to them and breathed in their nostrils. "Been nice having you with us," he murmured, rubbing his face against their fumbling lips.

"He'll be back in September," said Petra, seeing her sister's red eyes. "You'll still need him to take you into the village."

Next term Jinny was to go to the new comprehensive school that was still being built in Inverburgh. She would ride Bramble into Glenbost, leave him there and catch a school bus. Jinny was sorry to be leaving the village school. Trailing in and out to Inverburgh every day wouldn't leave her much time for Shantih. But it was so much better than going with Petra to Duninver school where you had to spend the week in the school hostel that Jinny had hardly grumbled at all.

"But I don't want him to go," said Jinny obstinately. "Couldn't we keep Bramble, even if we have to pay for him? He would be just right for this Marlene to learn on."

"I'll be at Miss Tuke's for half-past twelve," Mr. Manders said, ignoring Jinny. "We must be away from there before one if I'm to get my pottery delivered."

"Oh, O.K.," said Jinny. "Don't go on about it. We're going."

But they had to wait in the farm yard while Mr. Mac-Kenzie found a bit of turnip for the ponies, said they had been like hairy vacuum cleaners when it came to the oats and that it hadn't taken Jinny long to be scrounging her way down to the tent.

"Scotland Yard needs you," said Jinny. In all the months she had known Mr. MacKenzie she had never managed to discover how he managed to know about things almost before they happened.

By the time they had waited for the ponies to scrunch their way through the turnip they were even later.

"Come on," said Mike, when they had escaped from the old farmer. "We're not even going to be in time to meet Bill and Marlene at this rate."

"Fuss, fuss, fuss," said Jinny. "You're growing up just like Petra," but she urged Bramble on along the road to Glenbost.

They clattered through the village, past the school, the garage—encrusted with wrecked, rusting cars—Mrs. Simpson's sell-everything shop, past the crofts and the two churches and turned left to jog on towards Ardtallon.

At last they reached the track that took them over the hills to Miss Tuke's.

"Remember the day we brought them home?" asked Mike. "They kept on stopping dead and we had to shout, 'Trek forward,' to make them move."

"I expect they'll be as bad when we get them back in the autumn," said Jinny despondently.

About a mile from Miss Tuke's Bramble's head went up and he began to walk out excitedly. By the time they'd reached the drive that led to the trekking centre he was bouncing along, whiffling to himself and making sudden dives to smell the piles of droppings on the hoof-pocked ground.

"They don't half know where they are," said Mike. "I've never felt Punch like this before."

Miss Tuke was waiting for them. She opened the yard gate and the ponies bustled through.

"They are looking well," she said. "You've done them proud. I shall need to find two trekkers who can ride to take them over for next week."

"They're pleased to be home," said Jinny while Bramble clomped around her, whinnying to a bunch of ponies standing at a gate leading on to moorland.

"Right," said Miss Tuke when they had taken off the ponies' saddles. "Here we go. Be heels and teeth," she warned, as Mike and Jinny led Punch and Bramble through the gate on to the moor and unbridled them.

"Look out!" she warned, as Bramble plunged away from Jinny.

"But I'd got an apple for him," exclaimed Jinny, staring in dismay as the mob of Highlands went hightailing off up the hill.

"Too late," said Miss Tuke. "That's one of the things I like about native ponies. Independent little blighters," and she laughed as she shut the gate tightly.

"Your Dad says you'll be wanting them back in September."

"There is just a chance that I might be riding Shantih to school next term," said Jinny, admitting it to herself now that she had seen Bramble happily reunited with his mates.

"That red squib you had at the show?" demanded Miss Tuke. "I shall reserve Bramble for you."

"Has Dad been here long?" asked Mike.

"Quite a wee while. Seems in a hurry. Not his usual self."

They thanked Miss Tuke again for lending them the ponies and went to find their father. Seeing his face, Jinny got into the back of the car and thought hard about her saddle.

It was two o'clock before they reached Nell Storr's craft shop. Jinny and Mike helped their father to carry in the crates of pottery.

"Oh, lovely," cried Nell Storr, bearing down on them from a cloud of chiffon that seemed to be floating around her rather than being worn by her. "Thought you weren't going to make it. I've to be off in a min. with someone who's starting up a weaving centre on one of the islands. Free trip to inspect the goodies. As you can see, your shelves are nearly empty again, so fill them up and I'll take another lot as soon as you like."

"Bless you," said Mr. Manders. "You do realise that you are the mainstay of all my family."

"Nonsense," said Nell. "I do it for the money. These matching mugs and plates have been madly popular. I know a bod who's branching out into Europe. Shall I send him samples?"

"They're Ken's," said Mr. Manders. "Do send them."

"Wonderful glazes he gets," said Nell, picking up one of Ken's mugs that they had just unpacked and rubbing her hands over the scarlet glaze as she spoke to Mr. Manders about special orders.

"Now, Miss Manders," she said, turning to Jinny. "What about you? Have you brought me some more drawings?"

Jinny hadn't. Since Easter Nell had been buying Jinny's drawings and selling them in her shop.

"More of that Arab horse. She's their favourite."

"Well, maybe one lot more," said Jinny grudgingly. "I still need more money for my lungeing rein but now I've got the use of Sue's saddle I might buy a martingale."

"Live dangerously," encouraged Nell. "Bring me more drawings and buy both."

"I'll see," said Jinny. At first it had seemed a wonderful idea selling her drawings to Nell, but when it actually came to parting with them Jinny wasn't so sure. Sold to Nell they had gone forever. "I'll see," she said again.

It was half-past two before they reached Inverburgh station.

"Platform six," Mr. Manders shouted, running across the crowded station. Jinny and Mike sped after him, dodging in and out between luggage and trollies, passengers and rooted, old men.

They reached platform six just as the Stopton train came in.

"Too late. Here they come," said the ticket collector, so

27

they had to wait by the barrier, craning their necks to see if any of the people flooding out of the train looked like Marlene or Bill.

"That's them," cried Jinny. "Bet you."

"It is," said her father, recognising Bill, and then they could all see that the girl beside Bill dragged her left leg as she walked.

Both children were wearing jeans and black nylon anoraks. They were both pale with thick, white, city complexions and spikey, short, brown hair. The boy was slightly taller than his sister. His lower lip stuck out in a defiant, down-turning pout, and even walking along the platform his thick brows were clamped into a scowl. His sister was looking about her anxiously, her face working and her lips twisting as if she was carrying on a conversation with herself.

Mr. Manders waved. "Bill," he shouted. "Bill."

The boy heard him. He looked up, glowering under his fringe of greasy hair, and without changing his expression he spoke to his sister. She dumped the large, tartan shopper she was carrying on to the platform and waved with both hands. Then, clutching the bag in her arms again, she began to half run, half limp, towards them.

Marlene reached the ticket barrier and produced two tickets from her shopper, "I ain't half glad you're here. Didn't know what we'd do if you weren't. Them's two tickets, one for me and one for him." Marlene pointed out Bill to the ticket collector, then she pushed her way through the ticket barrier, holding her shopper well clear of the turnstile.

"Me Mum would have us bring a bag each. Said it wasn't decent unless. One each, like. Pleased to meet you," Marlene said, holding her hand out to Mr. Manders. "I'm fair dying for a cup of tea. Parched I am with that train. And I need the toilet. Didn't fancy going on that train."

Mr. Manders shook Marlene's hand. "I'm Mr. Manders," he said. "And this is Jinny."

"Pleased to meet you," said Marlene again.

Jinny grasped the small bony hand with its gnawed fingernails.

"How do you do," said Jinny distantly, her voice sounding cold and polite.

28

Marlene's black eyes beetling up at Jinny were hard as chips of flint. Her thin lips over her decayed teeth were laughing at Jinny. Jinny tried to make her mouth smile but it stuck in a half grimace and she stared across the busy station trying not to show what she was thinking—that already she didn't know how she was going to stick living with Marlene for a fortnight.

"Glad you could come, Bill," said Mr. Manders and introduced Jinny and Mike. Bill grunted, standing behind his sister, not looking up.

"Eh now," said Marlene, "now that we've got the la-di-dahs over how about the toilet and a bite of food?"

She grinned round, her eyes plucking at each person's face until she made them respond to her.

"Then it's me for the rodeo, ain't it? I'm proper churned up about it. Me on that fancy horse," and Marlene clutched up her tartan shopper and slapping her hand on her thigh she limped off to the Ladies.

"Better go with her," said Mr. Manders.

Cold with embarrassment, Jinny turned to follow Marlene, trying not to see the people who were staring as she gave Wild West whoops and hirpled her way through the crowds.

CHAPTER THREE

"Have you seen Marlene?" Mrs. Manders asked Jinny when she came down for breakfast the next morning. "We thought she must be with you."

"Well, she's not," said Jinny, glancing quickly round the table and realising that there were only two empty places—her own and Marlene's.

"We thought you might have been out with Shantih," went on Jinny's mother.

"You were wrong. I haven't seen her."

Yesterday, when they had got back to Finmory, Marlene had demanded a ride on Shantih.

"I'm not taking her out again today," Jinny had stated. "I was riding her this morning. She's not a bicycle, you know."

"Never thought he was," Marlene had replied. "Ain't never seen a bicycle that looked like that. Don't see why I can't have a ride now. He's walking round the field, ain't he? Why can't I sit on him?"

"Because," said Jinny finally and took herself off to her bedroom to clean her saddle.

"Bill, have you seen your sister?" persisted Mrs. Manders.

"Naw," said Bill, a slice of thickly-buttered toast in one hand a forkload of tomatoes and bacon in the other.

"Jinny, go and see if she's in her room."

"Why can't Petra go?" complained Jinny automatically but without hope.

"Marlene," Jinny called as she ran upstairs. "Marlene." But there was no reply. Jinny knocked on her bedroom door, then opened it. Marlene's bed was neatly made, her tartan shopper sitting on top of the quilt. Propped up on the dressing table was a blurry photograph of Marlene, Bill, a thin woman with a wintry face and a large, bleary man. Jinny looked at it intently, then, remembering what she was meant to be doing, went back down to tell her family that Marlene wasn't there.

"Try the garden," said her mother.

"I haven't had my breakfast and Sue's coming up to ride."

"It won't take you a second," said Mrs. Manders.

"Jinny," said her father, and Jinny went.

"Some holiday this is going to be," she thought rebelliously. "I'll bet she's with Shantih. I'll bet they make me give her a ride and when she falls off and hurts herself it will be Shantih's fault."

There was no sign of Marlene in the garden and Jinny went on past the stables, down to the ponies' field.

Marlene was sitting on top of the field gate. In the middle of the field Shantih was standing, watching her warily. Marlene looked quickly over her shoulder at the sound of Jinny's approach, then dropped down into the field. She landed on her hands and knees, scrambled up and began to run towards the Arab.

"Look out," yelled Jinny. "She'll kick you. Don't run at her like that."

Marlene paused to scowl at Jinny then went on limping across the field towards the horse.

30

Shantih's front feet were planted close together, her neck stretched out, her pointed ears nearly touching. Jinny knew that when she stood like that, she could swing round and whirl away in a split second, hooves flying as she galloped off.

"Be careful," shouted Jinny, but Marlene paid no attention to her. She was holding out a sugar lump to Shantih. Half limping, half running she blundered towards the Arab.

"Stop running," Jinny shouted. "Walk!" But Marlene went on stumbling and tripping in her haste to reach Shantih.

"Have a sugar lump," Marlene was saying. "Sweeten you up so it will."

As Jinny reached the field she paused uncertainly, knowing how Shantih's hooves could flash out quicker than lightning when she was frightened, and not wanting to risk chasing Marlene.

"Oh, slow down," she cried.

"Shut up. I'm giving him a sugar lump, ain't I," Marlene yelled back.

"Her," said Jinny, and to her horror she saw Marlene's lame foot catch in a tussock of grass, saw her go falling, sprawling towards Shantih, her arms outstretched, catching at the Arab's shoulder and legs as she fell.

The shoes on Shantih's hind feet glinted in the sun as she lashed out, missing Marlene's head by inches as she lay in the grass.

Jinny vaulted over the gate, ran at Shantih, shouting, chasing her away, but already the mare had thundered off to the far corner of the field, where she waited, quarters turned against the girls, the whites of her eyes rolling wildly.

"Are you all right?" demanded Jinny, helping Marlene to her feet. "I told you to stop running at her. That was enough to frighten any horse."

Marlene shook herself free.

"Get off me," she muttered. "I only fell, didn't I? Where's me sugar? I'm going to give it to the horse."

Jinny picked up the sugar lump. "You've to come in for breakfast," she said.

"Give us me sugar," said Marlene. "I'll just pop it in first," and she set off again towards Shantih.

Jinny grabbed hold of her arms. "You were nearly

kicked," she exclaimed. "Don't you realise that if Shantih had got you she could have killed you? You can't treat a horse like that."

"Give over," said Marlene, "pulling at me."

"You've got to come in to breakfast NOW," said Jinny, keeping her hold on Marlene's arm.

"What about the old horse? Got to get his sugar lump, ain't he?"

"She doesn't care whether she has a sugar lump or not. She doesn't want your sugar."

Marlene's black eyes bulleted into Jinny.

"Let me go," she demanded. "I got to give the horse his sugar. Like it says in the papers—'Be kind to a little donkey' —well, I'm being kind to a little horse if you'll only let off holding me."

"But she doesn't . . ." words failed Jinny. She let go of Marlene. "Well, wait there till I get a halter," she said.

"Halter?" said Marlene.

"Rope," said Jinny, "to hold her with while you give her your precious sugar lump. Now promise, stand there till I get back. Promise?"

"Get a move on then," grinned Marlene.

Jinny caught Shantih with a handful of oats and led her towards Marlene.

"Hold your hand out flat," said Jinny irritably. "And put the sugar lump on it."

"Bit dirty that," said Marlene, holding out the sugar lump between finger and thumb.

"No," said Jinny. "Not that way."

Shantih made a grab at the sugar. Marlene dropped it and Shantih snuffled it up and crunched it.

"Now," said Jinny. "Let's go and have our breakfast while you are still in one piece. She nearly took your fingers off that time. Not that you'd notice."

Jinny took Shantih's halter off and the horse walked beside them to the gate.

"See, I was right," said Marlene. "He right enjoyed that sugar. He's after more."

Mrs. Manders suggested that Marlene should wash her hands before she started on her cornflakes.

"They don't need it," said Marlene sitting down. "I held the sugar lump out ever so dainty. Old horse didn't muck me up at all. If I'd done it the way she told me I'd have been in a right mess then."

Jinny, sitting slumped in her chair, groaned to herself. Already Marlene had nearly been kicked to death and almost had her fingers bitten off. "And whose fault would it be?" thought Jinny. "It would all be Shantih's fault."

"And what are you doing this morning?" Mrs. Manders asked.

"Mike and I are going for a walk up the hill," said Mr. Manders to Bill. "Some wood to chop first. How about helping and then coming up the hill?"

"Naw," said Bill.

"Not after being in hospital he ain't. Doctor wouldn't have it," Marlene explained. "He can come and watch me riding. Be some fireworks when I get up on the old horse, I bet."

"Will you stop calling Shantih an old horse," cried Jinny.

"Didn't mean no offence," said Marlene. "Bit touchy, ain't she?" Marlene winked at Ken.

Jinny took a deep breath and another slice of toast.

"I'm just telling you," she said. "Just so that you'll all know, that I don't think Marlene is fit to ride Shantih. I think she'll get hurt. And it won't be my fault when it happens."

"Don't listen to her," said Petra. "She's got this thing about Shantih. Has to keep her all to herself."

"I've told you," repeated Jinny. "It will not be my fault when she hurts herself."

"I'll come and help," offered Petra, smiling at Marlene. "I'll hold you on. You'll be quite safe."

"That," said Jinny, "is all I need. Two of you who know nothing about horses."

When Jinny had groomed Shantih and put her tack on she led her down to the field with Petra and Marlene walking beside her. Mike, Ken and Bill were waiting at the gate.

"I'll ride her round first," said Jinny, mounting, and easing her fingers on the reins she let Shantih walk forward. The Arab was uneasy about the group watching from the gate and still troubled by the strange disappearance of Punch and Bramble.

"There's the horse," murmured Jinny. "Gently the good horse."

33

Shantih mouthed at the snaffle and Jinny let her trot on. They crossed the field and trotted round in the other direction. Riding Shantih, Jinny was aware of nothing but the rhythm of her horse; the brightness and freedom of riding her.

Jinny sat down and asked Shantih to canter. She was ready when the mare plunged and shied. Sitting deep in her new saddle, Jinny gathered her together between seat and fingers and sent her on, flowing round the field at a steady canter.

As they passed the gate Petra shouted that it was Marlene's turn, distracting Jinny, and at the same moment Kelly emerged from the hedge. Shantih reared. Jinny, secure in her saddle, hardly moved. Shantih reared again, without much enthusiasm, and Jinny sent her on to canter for a last time round the field.

While Shantih had been rearing, Jinny had caught a glimpse of Marlene's face. It had been clenched tight with fear. "Why does she want to ride when she's afraid?" thought Jinny. "And with her leg!"

"Are you sure you do want to ride?" Jinny demanded when she got back to Marlene. "You don't have to, you know."

But already Marlene was limping towards her.

"Thought you weren't never going to give me a shot," she said as Jinny dismounted. "Poor old thing'll be worn out by the time it's me turn."

Petra had brought a length of rope from the stables and was knotting it efficiently through Shantih's bit ring.

"Better put the stirrups down," she told Jinny. "Now, reins in your left hand and face her tail," she instructed Marlene.

Marlene grabbed a bundle of reins with a shaking hand.

"Left foot into the stirrup," bossed Petra, "and spring up into the saddle."

"She can't . . ." began Jinny, who was holding Shantih's head.

"Me wonky leg," said Marlene. "No use this side," and she ducked down under Shantih's neck and before Jinny had realised what was happening she had pulled herself up on the off side and was sitting astride Shantih.

34

"Eh, he ain't half high," squeaked Marlene. "When we going to get moving, eh? Gee up, old horse."

"Don't hit her," cried Jinny desperately as Marlene flapped Shantih's reins on her neck, but her warning was too late. Shantih, terrified by anything that reminded her of the circus master's whip, had flung away from Jinny in bunching, twisting fear.

"Hold the saddle," Jinny yelled and grabbed at the rope to help Petra to control Shantih.

"Whoa. Steady, steady," Jinny soothed as she caught at Shantih's bridle. "Steady now. It's all right."

At last Shantih stood still. She was tense and shivering, her nostrils wide, her eyes bulging from her head and, somehow, Marlene was still on top.

"What did you have to go and do that for?" Jinny demanded. Her hands gentled Shantih as she glared furiously at Marlene's white face. "Giving her a fright like that."

Mike had come dashing across to help. Only Ken still leaned on the gate, his face calm, his eyes unconnected to the turmoil in the field.

."How was I to know I shouldn't hit him? You want to see them on the telly. They wallop them good. Thought I was doing it right."

"Well, you weren't," snapped Jinny.

"I think you were wonderful staying on like that," praised Petra. "Wonderful. I'd have been off."

Marlene beamed. "Perhaps it's going to be me thing, this horse-riding. Got to get him moving though, ain't we?" And for a horrible moment Jinny thought she was going to slap the reins down again on Shantih's neck.

"Don't," cried Jinny.

But suddenly Marlene seemed to have lost interest in Shantih.

"Where's our Bill?" Marlene demanded, straining forward. "He ain't there."

They all looked at the gate and realised that she was right. Bill wasn't there, only Ken.

"Gone off somewhere on his own, I suppose," said Mike.

Marlene slithered to the ground and limped to the gate.

"Our Bill," she said. "Where's he off to?"

"Why?" said Ken.

"You know," said Marlene.

Ken eased himself off the gate. "I'll find him," he said.

"Proper decent of you," said Marlene. "It's O.K.," she said to Mike, "Ken'll keep an eye on him." And she ran back to Shantih.

There was the sound of trotting hooves, Pippen's squealing whinny, and Sue rode up.

"Morning," she said, smiling round.

"Come on," said Marlene. "Let's get on with me riding. We've been mucking round here long enough."

"Honestly!" exclaimed Jinny in disgust, wanting to introduce Sue to her family, not wanting any more to do with Marlene's riding. "Can't you wait a minute? Perhaps Sue will let you have a ride on Pippen. He'd be much more suitable."

"Ride that fat old thing?" said Marlene. "I wouldn't have it at me funeral." And she hoisted herself determinedly back on to Shantih. "Gee up, then," she said. "Gee up."

CHAPTER FOUR

Pippen snorted, digging his toes into the peaty hillside, bumbling along as he tried to keep up with Shantih's long stride.

"Look at that!" exclaimed Sue, turning to gaze back the way they had ridden. Rolling moorland fell away beneath them, hummocked with sheep and jagged with rocks. Finmory House and Mr. MacKenzie's farm were toy buildings standing in patchwork fields. The sea crinkled between the black jaws of Finmory Bay, then stretched out, a shimmering, flickering blue, to the far horizon.

"Uh huh," agreed Jinny. Normally a day like this made her frothy with delight at living surrounded by such wide freedom; at riding Shantih over the moors; at having escaped from the dirt and traffic of Stopton, but today she hardly noticed it. She had Marlene on her mind.

"There's our tent," pointed Sue.

Jinny supposed it was. Marlene had had two more rides on Shantih and was becoming bored with being led round the field. "We've been stuck in this old field for two days," she had said to Jinny earlier that morning. "Might as well be on a roundabout. When we going to go a proper ride?" she kept demanding.

"Can't you see I'm having a job keeping her quiet enough for you when we're in the field? If I took you on to the beach and she started playing up there I couldn't hold on to her, what would happen then?"

"How about Petra? She could hang on too."

"You seem to think that everyone should spend all their time running after you. How about Bill helping for a change?"

"Not with his lungs," warned Marlene. "Doctor wouldn't have it."

Jinny had not been surprised to hear that. It seemed to Jinny that the only thing that Bill was allowed to do was to sit around reading his pile of American comics under Marlene's protective eye.

"And," Jinny told Sue, "she won't leave Shantih alone. Keeps on wanting to give her sugar."

"Marlene?" asked Sue. "She's O.K. I like her."

"You don't know her," retorted Jinny indignantly. "It's not your horse that she's messing about with. When she falls off and breaks her back they'll say it was because Shantih is wild and uncontrollable, and it won't be that at all. It will be all Marlene's fault."

Sue laughed at Jinny's expression of gloom. "Shantih hasn't bucked once today," she said, hoping to cheer Jinny up.

"Pollyanna," said Jinny scornfully and she glowered over the bright sunlit moor, seeing nothing but Marlene annoying her horse.

"We can canter here," Jinny called back when they reached a flat stretch of moor, and she let Shantih plunge forward into a gallop.

Pippen's hooves drumming behind her filled Shantih with a sudden excitement. She stretched her neck and raced forward. Jinny felt her hair banner out behind her with their speed, the whole moorland blurred as Shantih scorched over it. Jinny crouched forward, her knees secure against the knee rolls, her knuckles digging into her horse's shoulders. Normally when Shantih took off like this Jinny was completely out of control, being carted wherever Shantih cared to take her, but now, with Sue's saddle, Jinny had the purchase to collect her horse and feel her respond to the bit's pressure even at a flat out gallop.

They reached the end of the canter, where normally Jinny had to fight Shantih, turning her uphill into the boggy hillside to steady her up. But today Jinny sat down deep into the saddle and was able to use her reins and seat to bring Shantih back to a trot. Within a few strides they were walking again.

Exultant, Jinny turned to see Pippen rocking sedately along at a collected canter.

"Did you see that!" Jinny cried.

"She's like a racehorse," exclaimed Sue, catching up.

"Oh, not that," said Jinny. "She can go faster than that. I mean the way we stopped. And it's all your saddle."

With Sue telling tales of her Pony Club at home, they rode towards the standing stones.

"Wish there was a Pony Club here," said Jinny.

"Don't be daft. We just make up things to do," said Sue, "because we don't have anywhere real to ride. I'd swop all Mrs. Moss's instruction for even the littlest bit of this moor."

And Jinny knew that what Sue said was true.

They dismounted at the standing stones and, holding their horses' reins, sat down in the sun to share a bar of chocolate.

Jinny shuddered as she looked at the sun-glossed moorland and the floating, mauve-shadowed mountains, remembering how it had been in the winter—a terrifying desert of snow.

"What's up?" asked Sue.

"Some day," said Jinny quickly, to drive the snow ghosts away, "I'm going to ride up here and camp." She imagined herself curled up, warm and safe, in her sleeping-bag while Shantih grazed close by.

"Oh yes!" agreed Sue.

"That is," said Jinny, "when I can find a tent. *If* I ever can find a tent."

"But I've got one."

"You're all sleeping in it. You can't expect your mother and father to sleep in the car while we take their tent!"

"Not that one, stupid. We've got a small one. Plenty of room in it for us."

"Could we?" said Jinny. "Now, while the weather's good?"

"Why not?"

"Yes, let's. Let's."

"Tomorrow," suggested Sue.

"We wouldn't need much," said Jinny.

"A kettle and a pan," said Sue. "We could have a camp fire and cook our food on it. Pippen can be a pack pony."

The two girls grinned at each other.

"If we camp here we can ride further into the hills," said Jinny. "Further than I've ever ridden before."

"Pippen's been to Pony Club camp," said Sue. "He's used to being tethered."

Jinny wasn't so sure about Shantih, but she pushed the doubt hurriedly to the back of her mind.

"We can camp for as long as we like," said Sue. "We'll send up smoke signals to let them know we're surviving."

"Go wooding," said Jinny. "There's plenty of dead branches from the pines round Loch Varrich."

Then suddenly Jinny thought about Marlene. Marlene would want to come with them. Jinny got up to make sure that Shantih's girth wasn't too tight, which she knew it wasn't because she had just loosened it a minute ago. Whatever happened Jinny didn't want Marlene spoiling their camp. She fiddled with the girth buckles, trying not to think how Marlene would stand watching them ride off to camp in the hills. "I don't care," Jinny thought. "She's not coming with us," and she sat down again beside Sue.

"What about Marlene?" asked Sue, knowing Jinny's thoughts.

"Oh, she wouldn't want to come," cried Jinny, defending herself. "She couldn't possibly come all this way when she's lame. And I don't suppose she'd want to sleep in a tent."

Sue twisted the buckle on Pippen's reins, not looking at Jinny.

"I'm sure she wouldn't want to come," insisted Jinny. "She can't come, anyway, and that's that."

Sue didn't answer and for a moment there was only the sound of their horses cropping the short moorland turf, the high, twittering lark song, and, far off, a curlew's liquid, bubbling notes.

Jinny jumped to her feet.

"Come on," she said. "If we're camping tomorrow we'll need to get a move on. I think Mum's going to the shop this afternoon so she could buy some tins for us."

"Couldn't we each put a pound into the kitty and buy our own food?" Sue asked as they remounted. "I can afford it because I've got my holiday money."

Jinny thought of saying that she couldn't afford a pound and that she'd bring some food from home, but it sounded so much more independent going to Mrs. Simpson's to buy their own food. She would need to open the tin box where she kept the money she was saving towards a lungeing rein for Shantih.

"And I've some money from the drawings I sold to the craft shop," she admitted.

"We'll need to make a list," said Sue as they rode home.

"Bread, dried milk and butter," said Jinny.

"A raspberry jelly," suggested Sue. "To eat not make."

"Dried apple rings. They swell up inside you in case we're starving."

"And marzipan," said Sue.

Sue's parents were quite agreeable for her to camp at the standing stones but felt that it would be rather nice if she spent the rest of the day with them, so Sue gave Jinny her pound, telling her to be sure to buy marzipan if she could possibly manage it.

When Jinny got back home she tipped some oats for Shantih on to the grass and left her eating them. She hung her bridle on its hook and carried the saddle up to her bedroom.

"Had a good ride?" asked her mother, who was vacuuming the landing. Jinny said she had and went on up to her room. She stood on a chair to reach the top of her wardrobe and lifted down her cash box. Originally it had belonged to Petra, but when the lock had broken she had abandoned it to Jinny who swathed it in sellotape to stop herself getting into it.

Hesitating, Jinny thought of asking her father to give her the money, then jumped down off the chair and ripped off the sellotape in a scrumpled, sticky mess. "You are getting too mean to live," she told herself. "You'll be hiring out Shantih next." And she opened the box and took out a pound.

The sellotape was too messed up to be used again. Jinny considered putting the box back as it was, but she knew that if she did the money left in it would soon be spent.

"Need to find some more," she thought. "Better stick it up again." And she remembered seeing a roll of sellotape in the pottery room.

Ken was working at the wheel.

"Hi," he said, looking up at Jinny and smiling his slow smile that seemed to light up his green eyes and spread easily over his whole face. He set you before him, making space for you to be yourself. Not the quick, half-afraid twitch that most people made at you. "Bit of a stranger," he suggested.

" 'Spose so," agreed Jinny, looking round for the sello-tape, "and you'll be seeing less of me. We're going to camp at the standing stones."

"We?"

"Might camp for nights and nights if the weather stays fine."

Jinny's eyes flicked over the bats of pots waiting to be fired, over the glowing rows of glazed pottery and the plastic bins of clay. She searched the mess of the window-sill with its frosting of powdered clay, jars of glaze and bits of broken pots. The table, too, was littered. Jinny moved things about, searching.

"Have you seen that roll of sellotape?" she asked.

"We?" said Ken again.

"Well, you're bound to find out," said Jinny in exas-peration. "We means Sue and myself and *not* Marlene. She couldn't come all that way. Not with her lame leg."

"You have to camp as far away as the standing stones?" said Ken, treadling the wheel, doodling the clay between his long, gentle fingers, but Jinny could feel his eyes on her.

"Yes," she said. "We have to camp at the standing stones. We've arranged it." And to her relief she spotted the sellotape.

"Feel free," said Ken. "Do what you like."

"Will do," said Jinny, already half way out of the door. Jinny told them at lunchtime that she was going camp-

41

ing. Eating stew and potatoes gave her hands something to do while she was telling them.

"What about water?" asked Mr. Manders, and Jinny's mother wondered about warmth and having enough to eat.

"I'm coming with you to Mrs. Simpson's this afternoon," said Jinny. "I've got a list of supplies and we're only camping while it's fine, so we will be quite all right."

"What'll we take for the old horse?" asked Marlene. "Won't be much grass up on them mountains for him. I'd better take him plenty of sugar lumps."

For one moment Jinny hadn't been able to stop herself looking up at Marlene. Just long enough to see her face brighten with expectation at the thought of going with Shantih over the moors.

"Oh, we'll take oats for the horses," Jinny said, staring down at her plate. She was being polite and brisk. Not using her own voice. For that was the way you dealt with situations like this. You were polite but firm, and then everyone knew where they stood. "I'm going with Sue. We'll only be away for a night or two. It's too far for you, I'm afraid."

"Oh, Jinny!" cried Mrs. Manders in dismay. "Of course Marlene can go with you. Of course you can, dear."

Jinny forced herself not to look up.

"Don't 'Oh Jinny' her for me," shrilled Marlene. "I wouldn't want to go trailing up them mountains, not for nothing. I just pity that poor old horse, that's all."

"There you are," said Jinny. "I knew she wouldn't want to come." But she kept her eyes clamped tight on to her hands, gripping her knife and fork until her knuckles shone through her skin and her nails bit into her palms.

Mrs. Manders cornered Jinny as she finished washing up.

"I am thoroughly ashamed of you," she said. "Really I am. How could you be so cruel?"

"I'm being kind," said Jinny. "If she goes on making me give her rides on Shantih she's going to fall off and hurt herself. So I'm being kind to her, taking Shantih away so that she can't ride her."

Mrs. Manders turned her back and walked away. Every bit of Jinny ached to run after her and try to explain how it really was true; that Marlene really would be hurt if she went on riding Shantih; that it was dangerous; that Shantih wasn't a pony like Miss Tuke's trekkers who would plod along with beginners on their backs not caring what their riders did. Shantih was a highly-strung Arab horse. You couldn't mess about with her. She could so easily be frightened and then it would be too late, Marlene would be injured.

But Jinny couldn't make herself move. She stood fiddling with her hair.

"When are you going to Mrs. Simpson's?" she called after her mother, her voice flat as if she was speaking to a stranger.

"About three," replied Mrs. Manders without stopping.

Mr. and Mrs. Manders, Jinny and Marlene, taking an unwilling Bill with her, all packed into the car.

"After we've done the shopping we'll drive on for a bit. Let you see the country round about," said Mrs. Manders to Bill. "We'll go round by the Crawlin rocks. Fantastic scenery there. Black gaping caves. You can stand on the cliffs and hear the sea booming under your feet."

Bill didn't bother to reply. Since he had arrived Jinny had hardly heard him speak at all. The only time he showed any enthusiasm was when Mrs. Manders called him for his meals and whenever he had stuffed the last bite in his mouth he went back to reading his comics and scratching his head.

"Anything special you'd like to do, Bill?" Mr. Manders asked. "We're open to suggestions. There's a wildlife park about thirty miles away. We could go there for the day? Or a sail?"

"Doctor wouldn't have that," said Marlene. "He's O.K., ain't you, Bill? He's better taking it easy like. Doctor said he wasn't to strain himself. Couldn't go pulling up anchors and all that."

"Not a yacht," Mr. Manders assured her. "A sail on a steamer. Bill could sit in an armchair as we sailed along."

"Naw," said Bill.

"Better not," said Marlene.

"Perhaps Mrs. Simpson will have some comics you haven't read," suggested Mrs. Manders.

"He likes the ones he's got, thank you all the same," said Marlene.

Mr. Manders trod on the accelerator and wondered what they were doing wrong. He knew what Jinny was doing wrong—smuggling Shantih off to the hills so that she didn't have to share her with Marlene. Part of him was furious with his daughter for being so selfish, part was standing back waiting to see what would happen next and part of him wasn't even surprised. To possess a loved one; to possess completely and absolutely, so that you didn't care what you did as long as you could say MINE, seemed to be deep at the centre of every human being. Except the few. The very few.

"Tom!" shouted his wife. "Look where you're going. We were right off the road then."

And Mr. Manders remembered he was driving.

"Come away in with you now," Mrs. Simpson said, as they all crowded into her shop.

Mrs. Simpson's was the only shop in Glenbost and it sold everything. Slippers and paraffin heaters, cheese and liqueur chocolates, pork chops and cabbages, men's long winter drawers and women's Sunday hats, stamps and pensions were all to be had at Mrs. Simpson's. Some of her stock had taken up more or less permanent residence, some had lodgers. Petra had found a dead mouse in a net of oranges. "Wasn't that the lucky thing now that the wee fellow died in the oranges," Mrs. Simpson had said when Petra pointed it out to her. "And them done up so tidy in their skins. I'd have been worried myself if he'd been living in with the sausages."

Mrs. Simpson leaned over her counter and examined Bill and Marlene with a hard stare. She had almost accepted the Manders as harmless lunatics but she was still suspicious of any of their visitors. She feared that the families she referred to as heathen hippies, who had lived at Finmory before the Manders, were still lurking in the hills ready to make a comeback.

"It's the beautiful day," she admitted grudgingly. "But I'm thinking myself it won't last much longer."

"See you've been branching out into a new line," said Mr. Manders.

"Indeed I have. Not new because we were having them before, but perhaps you wouldn't be here then."

Jinny couldn't think how her father could possibly notice

44

whether Mrs. Simpson had anything new or not since all her stock was scrabbled and jumbled together. Then she saw what he meant. On the counter was a smart perspex case with about a dozen watches in it. On top of the case, displayed in its own box, was a man's gold watch. Mr. Manders picked it up.

"Very nice," he said.

"Now there's the coincidence," said Mrs. Simpson. "When the traveller showed me that very one, it was yourself I saw walk into this shop, Mr. Manders, put it on, and walk out a man with the pride about him."

"Joke taken," said Mr. Manders. "How much?"

"To you, eighty-two pounds. It has the wee bookie with it to tell you the value of it. Jewels like Aladdin's cave and the everlasting calendar so that you need never be wasting your money on the paper rubbish ever again."

"Yes. Well," said Mr. Manders putting the watch back in it's box. "How much do I owe you for looking at it?"

"Eh, give us a see," said Bill, snatching the watch from Mr. Manders. "That's what I call a watch, that is. I'll have one of them. You'll see."

Mrs. Simpson swiftly removed the watch from Bill, put it back in its box and replaced it reverently on top of the case.

"How much did you say?" demanded Bill.

"Who will ever buy that here?" exclaimed Mrs. Manders. "It's a beautiful watch," she added quickly, in case Mrs. Simpson should take umbrage and plunge the Manders into sudden famine. "But eighty-two pounds!"

"Goodness yes," stated Mrs. Simpson coldly. "It's five hundred pounds they're paying for them in the cities."

"It's a tourist trap," guessed Mr. Manders.

"You could be saying that, but if there's not a tourist in my trap by October I'm thinking eighty-two pounds is about the exact sum the congregation will be giving to the Reverend James when he comes to the retirement in November. And him poor man without a watch to his name."

Mr. Manders burst out laughing.

"Laugh you may," said Mrs. Simpson, not even smiling, "but that's the good business sense." And she took the

45

watch away again from Bill. "Leave it be," she said sharply. "Keep your fingers to yourself in my shop."

Quickly, Mrs. Manders began to read out her order.

When her mother had finished Jinny fished out her list.

"I want some things too," she said, and began with the bread and butter essentials.

On the wall behind Mrs. Simpson was a mirror hung round with pairs of wellington boots on a string so that there was only a small space left to reflect the front of the shop, but enough for a movement in it to catch Jinny's attention. In the mirror she saw Bill reaching up for the watch again, saw Marlene catch hold of his hand and snatch it away from the case. There was a tightness at the corners of Marlene's lips. a pinched, indrawn shadow at her cheeks and nostrils, her black, bead eyes were narrowed and her brows knotted down. Jinny hadn't seen her looking like that before but she had seen that look somewhere, that cold, defeated, bitterness.

"You'll be setting up your own establishment with all this food?" said Mrs. Simpson, waiting to be told why Jinny was buying it.

"We're going camping on the moors," said Jinny.

"With that terrible wild horse?"

"And a friend," said Jinny.

From the mirror, Marlene's indrawn mask stared straight at her and suddenly Jinny knew where she had seen that look before. It had been on the woman's face in the photograph on Marlene's dressing table.

CHAPTER FIVE

Just after ten the next morning, Sue led Pippen towards Finmory, and Jinny, watching from the stable doorway, thought that he looked like the original clothes horse or the White Knight's horse from Alice.

"Even the kitchen sink," Sue yelled, waving a plastic bucket. "Did you get the supplies?"

"Couldn't afford marzipan," Jinny told her. "Anyway, the lump Mrs. Simpson had looked mousley. She'd had it since Christmas. But I got two jellies. A lemon and a raspberry."

"Same to you," giggled Sue. "Are you nearly ready?"

"I've brought Shantih in," Jinny said, "and I've packed all the things in a rucksack. I think she'll let me tie my sleeping bag on to the front of the saddle but not much else. Just need to hang them on to myself seeing Pippen is fully occupied."

"Isn't he?" said Sue lovingly. "Took me ages to pack him. It's times like this, when he's so totally obliging, that I try to remember when we're last in races. Mummy says they will be coming up the mountain to borrow back their stuff."

"You've even brought a kettle," said Jinny, examining Pippen's load more closely.

"Do not look down the spout. It has white furry knickers all over it."

"Yuch," said Jinny. "Thanks for the warning."

She put Shantih's tack on, then, very cautiously tied her sleeping bag to the front of the saddle. Shantih rolled her eyes back suspiciously, but apart from this didn't object.

"She was O.K.," Jinny announced to Sue, who didn't seem to care. "I expect it's being used to Pippen," Jinny thought. "If she'd known Shantih last autumn she'd realise what it means being able to put a saddle on her, never mind a sleeping bag.

"I'm going for my hat," Jinny said to Sue. "And then I think we're ready."

"I haven't got a pan," said Sue. "Could you bring one?"

"Frying?"

"That's all we'll need, isn't it? Be mostly sandwiches."

"Cordon bleu," said Jinny, "but between bread." And she ran up to the house.

"A frying pan," said her mother and found an old one.

"Matches?" asked her father, and Jinny said she thought Sue would have some because she seemed to have most things but in case Sue hadn't any she'd take some.

"Come straight home if the weather changes," warned Mrs. Manders.

Jinny said they would. Then there was a pause when her family should have been telling her to enjoy herself, planning to join them for a camp fire sing-song or giving her a

47

surprise food parcel to be opened at camp. Jinny would even have welcomed one of Petra's comments, but she could hear the piano and knew that Petra must be practising. Jinny hadn't seen Ken that morning. In a way she didn't mind. She didn't particularly want to see him.

"Well," Jinny said, sitting her hard hat in the frying pan and holding it as if she was entering for an egg and spoon race. "I'd better fry."

Nobody even smiled.

" 'Bye," said Jinny, not really looking at her parents, more taking them in as she glanced round the kitchen, before escaping back to Sue.

Marlene and Bill were standing at the stables.

"Oh no!" thought Jinny. "As if they haven't caused enough trouble already. Why can't Marlene leave our horses alone?" Jinny stomped down the path pulling her hard hat down over her eyes.

"This you off, then?" asked Marlene. "Going to give us a last shot before you go?" Her black eyes clawed at Jinny's face forcing her to answer. "Better have a ride now, eh? Old thing'll be worn out when he comes back from them mountains. Won't be fit for me to ride, he won't."

"She," retorted Jinny furiously. Her temper surged up, making her want to run at Marlene and shake her by the shoulders, yelling that she couldn't ride Shantih because Shantih was hers and Marlene was to leave her alone.

"Round the field, like?" said Marlene. "Go on, just once before you go off?"

"No!" shouted Jinny. "No! No! No!"

"Look," suggested Sue hurriedly, "I'll take Pippen's saddle off and you can have a ride bareback."

"Naw," said Marlene. "He's all hairy and he's too fat. I'd be split up me middle sitting on him."

"You see," said Jinny smugly. "It's no use trying to be nice to her."

But Sue didn't seem to mind. She was laughing at Marlene.

"Perhaps you're right," she said to Marlene, and then to Jinny, "Give her a ride round the field. It won't take a minute. I don't mind waiting."

48

"Well!" said Jinny. "Well honestly." And she banged down the frying pan, making Pippen jump.

Muttering to herself, Jinny led Shantih down the path to the field.

"Bill," shouted Marlene. "Come and watch me. I'm for the riding again." And Bill followed them down to the field, still reading his comic.

"This is bad enough," thought Jinny, "but it would be much worse if he wanted to ride too." And she imagined Bill sitting slumped on Shantih, scratching his head and reading his comic.

"Here we are old horse," said Marlene. "Up and over."

Despite her lame leg, Marlene could mount from the off side without any difficulty. She swung her leg over Shantih's back, taking care not to touch the horse's quarters with her foot, found her stirrup without looking down and gathered up her reins, holding them correctly.

"Walk on," Jinny said to Shantih and led the Arab forward by the halter rope she was wearing underneath her bridle.

"Wait on me there, Bill," Marlene called, casting one last, quick look at her brother before she gave all her attention to Shantih.

Jinny walked at Shantih's side paying no attention to Marlene.

"How about some speed?" asked Marlene.

Jinny clenched her teeth and pretended not to hear. She thought hard about camping with Sue, of sleeping in the tent and riding out tomorrow to discover what lay beyond Loch Varrich. Mr. MacKenzie had told her that before the clearances there had been a village in the hills. Perhaps they would discover the ruined crofts. Jinny stepped over the moss-covered stones that had once been the walls of the crofts. Her eye caught the glint of silver and she pounced on a brooch that had fallen from a woman's shawl when she was being driven out to the ship that had waited in Finmory Bay to take the crofters to America.

Jinny had completely blocked out Marlene.

Suddenly the halter rope scorched through her hand as Shantih leaped forward at a ragged trot. Just in time, Jinny managed to hold on to the tail end of the rope and to dash forward beside her. For a second Jinny thought that

Shantih had bounded forward by herself, and then she saw Marlene's face. She was grinning with delight, her bullet eyes sparkling, her mouth laughing. "Gee up," she shouted as she bounced enthusiastically up and down in the saddle.

"Right," thought Jinny. "I'll show her. I'll teach her a lesson." And instead of trying to slow Shantih back to a walk she went on running at her side, keeping her trotting, urging the Arab to go faster.

"Eh, watch out, I'll be off," gasped Marlene.

"Good," thought Jinny. "Serve you right."

Marlene grabbed at the pommel of the saddle. Her shrill sounds of alarm coming out in sudden jerks as she bumped about.

Back at the gate Jinny checked Shantih to a sudden halt.

"That's it," she said. "Get down."

Marlene slithered to the ground.

"Did you mean to trot?" Sue asked. "Marlene nearly fell. She'd no idea how to post."

"She wanted to go fast so I let her," said Jinny.

"Oh," said Sue.

Jinny ran up Shantih's stirrups, took her reins over her head and swung the loaded rucksack on to her own back. She knew what Sue was thinking but she didn't care. Jinny hoped that she'd given Marlene a fright. She hoped it would stop Marlene wanting to ride Shantih. Or, better still, make her want to go back to Stopton so that Jinny never needed to see her again.

"Gracious," exclaimed Mrs. Manders. "Are you two still here?" She looked from her scowling daughter to Marlene, who had collapsed flat on the grass.

"Jin was giving Marlene a last ride," explained Sue. "We're going now."

"We hope," said Jinny. "That is *if* we can get away."

"Marlene and Bill," said Mrs. Manders, paying no attention to Jinny's grumbling. "We're going down to the shop. Would you like to come for the drive."

Bill stuffed his comic into his trouser pocket with untypical haste, pushed the hair out of his eyes, and said, "Come on then if you're going."

"What d'you want to be going back to that shop for?" Marlene demanded, sitting up. "You was there yesterday."

"I forgot the sugar," said Mrs. Manders.

50

"Me and Bill, we don't need sugar. We don't want it. No need to fetch it for us."

"Afraid Tom does," said Mrs. Manders. "You can stay here though. Just as you like."

"Naw," said Marlene. "I've got to go if our Bill's going."

Jinny shrugged her rucksack impatiently. She was ready to go. She wanted nothing so much as to get away from them all. To get away from her family and most of all to get away from Marlene.

Jinny stared at Marlene resentfully. The enthusiasm that had lit up Marlene's pale face when she had been riding had vanished. As she struggled to her feet, Jinny could see the pinched, withered expression clamped at her mouth and eyes.

"Wait on me, Bill," Marlene shouted and limped after Bill, who was already striding up the path. "Wait on me."

Mrs. Manders, speaking more to Sue than to Jinny, hoped that they'd remember to brush their teeth if not their hair and that the sun would go on shining for them.

"The moon will be shining if we don't get a move on," Jinny muttered as Shantih pranced impatiently at the full length of her reins.

Mrs. Manders said goodbye and went up the path after Bill and Marlene.

"At last," said Jinny. "At flippin' last." And, leading the way, she turned Shantih towards the moors. "We could have been away an hour ago if it hadn't been for her. I don't know what she thinks Shantih is. Some kind of seaside donkey. Always wanting rides on her. Always going on at her the way she does. Stupid nuisance!"

"Marlene's O.K.," said Sue, leading Pippen behind Shantih. "She's just keen. And you never hear her complaining about her leg."

Jinny snorted. "She complains enough about Shantih. Always wanting to ride her. Wanted to stand in the field holding the halter. Just stand there holding the halter!"

"I was like that about Pippen."

"That's different. That's quite different. Shantih could have kicked her or anything. Reared up and kicked her. Marlene wouldn't even have noticed until her head was rolling on the ground. And then what would have happened to Shantih?"

51

Jinny's bad temper was set, hard and furious. She had to keep on telling Sue how impossible Marlene was, how incredibly stupid, how she had absolutely no right to even touch Jinny's horse.

"Cooee, cooee. Wait a minute. You two wait on me. Cooee. Wait on me."

"Oh no!" exclaimed Jinny. "What does she want now?"

Marlene was running after them, her arms swimming through the air to help her to keep her balance. She limped right up to Jinny.

"Here you are," she said, tugging at something in her pocket. "Nearly forgot, what with all that banging about you made me do. Bashed me brains. Them's for the old horse," and she thrust a paper bag full of sugar lumps into Jinny's hand, and before Jinny could say anything she was hirpling back to Finmory.

Jinny stared at the sugar lumps in disgust.

"What did she want to give me these for? Shantih doesn't want them," and Jinny almost threw the sugar away, but something in the way Sue was looking at her made her keep them. "Stupid thing," she declared and marched on with Shantih jogging at her side.

The sun blazed down and the flies zooming round Jinny's head made the day seem hotter than ever. The metal frame of the rucksack hurt her back, its straps gnawed into her shoulders. It seemed to grow heavier and heavier at every step she took. She tried balancing it on Shantih's saddle and holding it there as they walked along, but the Arab sprang away and the pack went crashing to the ground.

Sue stood watching, without offering to help, while Jinny tried to hoist the rucksack on to her back again and hold on to her skittering horse at the same time. Sue waited without speaking until Jinny had reorganised herself and then followed on behind her.

"Not going to be much of a camp if Sue's going to be like this," thought Jinny. She'd given up trying to make conversation. No matter how often she'd pointed out to Sue how hopeless Marlene was, Sue hadn't joined in. As she plodded on, Jinny could feel the bag of sugar lumps in her pocket and hear Marlene's voice telling her to give them to the old horse.

"Old horse, indeed," thought Jinny. "She is just so stupid.

It's a good job I'm taking Shantih away from her," and she wondered if they could possibly go on camping until the Thorpes went back to Stopton.

As she trudged on, Jinny's mind bubbled and boiled, full of all the things that made her hate Marlene. She had to keep on telling herself how dangerous it was for Marlene to be near Shantih, telling herself over and over again that Marlene was too stupid to ride Shantih, for no matter how hard she tried to block it out she kept seeing Marlene's white pinched face. She couldn't stop herself remembering the dirt and noise of Stopton and the decaying slums where Marlene and Bill lived. Worst of all was the thought of Marlene's delight when she had started to trot, the way she had lit up with excitement.

"You could have steadied Shantih. Held Marlene's leg against the saddle. Shown her how to post. And what did you do? You tried to make her fall off."

"But she knows nothing about horses!"

Jinny shouted the words inside her head. But it was too late. She had allowed herself to listen to the voice.

"How could she know about horses?" demanded the voice that was her parents and Ken, and Jinny herself, really. "There's not many Arabs in Stopton."

"I'm telling you she could hurt herself," yelled Jinny in silent self-defence.

The voice that couldn't be silenced now that Jinny had started listening to it laughed scornfully. "Is that so?" it said. "How convenient." And resentfully Jinny knew what she was going to have to do.

"Pippen is sweating like anything," Sue called. "Can we have a stop?"

"O.K.," said Jinny and collapsed on to a handy boulder.

Sue sat down on the grass. Neither of them spoke. The silence was filled with waiting for who was going to speak first.

"Go on," urged the voice in Jinny's head. "It's all your fault. Sue would have brought Marlene with us." Jinny drew in her breath and said, "We can't, can we?"

At the same moment Sue looked round. "Let's go back for Marlene," she said.

CHAPTER SIX

Shantih and Pippen trotted back side by side to Finmory. The two girls had unloaded Pippen and deposited the rucksack, frying pan and Jinny's sleeping bag on the ground.

"May as well camp here," Jinny had said. "It's not too bad a place. Quite close to the burn."

"It's great," agreed Sue. "A wall to shelter us and that old sheep pen to tie the ponies to. And a smashing view. We could never take Marlene all the way to the standing stones."

"This isn't really very far from Finmory," Jinny had said regretfully. "There's a short cut through Mr. MacKenzie's yard, but the last field gate is sometimes locked, then you have to trail back and come round this way."

As Finmory came into sight, Jinny said, "I expect they'll all come and visit us, now that we're camping so close to the house." She wasn't looking forward to telling Marlene that she was sorry for being so mean, and was trying to keep her thoughts on other things. "Your parents could come to."

"They'd like that," said Sue. "Mum plays the guitar. She'd bring it with her."

And Jinny imagined them all sitting round a blazing camp-fire, singing, while the horses listened, ears pricked, eyes glinting in the firelight.

"I'll hold Shantih," Sue offered when they reached Finmory. "You go and find Marlene."

"Say she doesn't want to come?"

"You know she does."

"Oh well," said Jinny and went off to look for Marlene.

There was no one around the stables, no one in the garden, and then Jinny noticed that the car wasn't there. "Can't be back from Mrs. Simpson's," she thought and drew in a gasp of relief. It would be a few minutes at least before she had to apologise to Marlene. She thought of going back to tell Sue to put the horses in the stable and come in for lemonade but decided not to bother. If she could manage to speak to Marlene without Sue listening Jinny felt it would be easier.

She leaned against the back door, the sun burning down on her. "Jinny Manders," she told herself. "You very nearly ruined your summer holidays too. Just saved yourself in time." And she went over in her mind what she would say to Marlene.

There was a noise in the kitchen. Too definite to be Kelly or one of the cats. It was a person. Jinny heard them draw back a chair and sit down at the table.

"Ken," thought Jinny. "May as well tell him first." She pushed open the back door and ran inside.

Bill was sitting at the table, hunched over something he was holding in his hands. Blinded by the dark kitchen after the bright morning, Jinny couldn't see what it was.

Bill jumped up when he heard her come in, fumbling to hide what he had been looking at behind his back.

"What you want?" he demanded, glaring suspiciously at Jinny.

"Sorry," said Jinny. "I didn't mean to give you a fright. I'm looking for Marlene."

"She ain't here."

"I can see that," said Jinny. "Is she still at Glenbost?"

"Naw. She's out at them vegetables with the hippie," Bill told her as he backed away.

"Thanks," said Jinny and went off to Ken's kitchen garden.

She made herself walk steadily—left foot, right foot. Her mind too full of apologising to Marlene to leave any room for wondering why Bill had looked so guilty.

Just before she reached the kitchen garden, Jinny hesitated behind a screen of rhododendrons. She could hear Marlene's high-pitched voice rasping at Ken.

"We had a little pup once but me Mum got sick of it, messing the floor and eating all her good things. She was having a tea party for her friends, like, and she had it all laid out nice with a fancy cloth covering it all and when her friends came they lifted up the cloth and there were only the pup there. He'd eaten all the cakes and things. Didn't take me Mum long to get shot of him after that. But he were a nice little thing. He were brown with a bit funny

55

tail. Used to push him round in a pram, all tucked in proper nice."

"Oh no," thought Jinny. "Days of listening to that; of listening to her talking nonsense and having to watch her ride Shantih." Then Jinny thought of going back to tell Sue that she had changed her mind. "Bear up," she told herself. "It's only for a day or two," and she stepped out from behind the bushes.

Marlene was making a daisy chain. Kelly, lying beside her on the grass, was already wearing one round his neck. Ken was standing between his rows of vegetables, the hoe he held in his hands seemed almost to be working by itself, moving slowly but rhythmically. He looked up, saw Jinny, but didn't speak.

Jinny swallowed hard and marched on towards them.

"Well, look who's here," said Marlene. "You'll be in that book for records, you will. Shortestest camp in the world, that's what you'll be."

"We've come back for you," said Jinny. "Come and camp with us. I'm sorry I didn't ask you before. I thought it would be too far for you."

"Eh, get her," said Marlene. Her black eyes glistened without expression in her whitish-yellow face. "Want me to come running now do you? What's up? Can't neither of you do the cooking?"

"We were going to the standing stones but it was too hot," lied Jinny. "So when we decided not to go as far as that we came back for you."

Marlene went on with her daisy chain.

"Sue wants you to come," said Jinny.

"May be," said Marlene. "But what about you? You think I'm not posh enough for your horse, don't you?"

"She doesn't," stated Ken. "Things have just got a bit twisted between you."

"I'm asking you," said Jinny. "I wouldn't have come back for you if I hadn't wanted you to come."

"That'll be it," said Marlene.

"Go on," said Ken. "Don't hold on to that nonsense."

Marlene grinned quickly at Ken.

"What makes you all so sure that I'd want to give up me comfy bed to sleep on dirty old ground, eh? I ain't daft."

56

"It'll be fun," said Jinny. "An adventure. Something new. Exciting."

"Exciting!" scoffed Marlene. "Reckon that's the last thing our lot needs. Anyway, can't go all that trail with me leg."

Jinny stared at her in despair. She was sure that Marlene could walk over the moor if she wanted to. Jinny wanted to shout, "All right, then, stay where you are," but heard her own voice saying, "You can ride Shantih."

Marlene's mouth twitched, she kinked a quick look out of the corner of her eye at Ken.

"Need to get me bag," she said, scrambling to her feet.

"You won't need it," said Jinny.

"That I will," said Marlene.

Jinny went to find Mike's sleeping bag for Marlene to use, then she waited in the garden for Marlene to return with her shopper.

"Didn't they go with Mum and Dad?" Jinny asked Ken.

"To the shop? Yes. They've all been to the village. Think your parents went in to the farm and the kids came on here."

"That's me," said Marlene, clutching her tartan shopper to her stomach. "Now mind," she said to Ken. "We made it a promise. You keep an eye on him or I ain't going."

"All the time," confirmed Ken.

"What?" said Jinny.

"Me brother. Ken there'll watch him while we're up at the camp. We arranged it."

"You did, did you?" said Jinny, realising that if Ken and Marlene had arranged it they must have been expecting her to come back.

"Knew it wasn't you," said Ken.

"Nearly was," Jinny said to Ken. She told Marlene that Sue had been waiting ages for them, and they all went down to join her.

"Right pleased you came back for me," Marlene said to Sue.

More than she said to me, thought Jinny darkly.

"Where is the camp now?" Ken asked. "Dare say your mother will feel safer if she knows."

"Not far," said Jinny. "By the old sheep pen. That's where we've left the stuff so that's where we'll camp. If

57

you go up the hill for a bit, you'll be able to spot the tent."

"Bright orange," said Sue. "So that helicopters and St. Bernards can spy us out."

"Mind and tell Bill where I'll be," said Marlene. "In case he wants me or anything, like. I've told him I won't be gone long."

"Only a day or two," said Jinny, taking Marlene's bag while she mounted. "No. I'll hold it while you're riding. No, I shan't drop it."

"Take joy," said Ken, and went back to his hoeing.

"What about the short cut you were talking about?" Sue asked.

"It's much quicker," said Jinny, seeing herself battering through bogs and bracken, trying to control Shantih and keep Marlene on top. "But no," she decided. "The gate might be shut and it's so maddening when you have to turn round and come all the way back."

"Couldn't we jump?" asked Sue.

"On Shantih?" demanded Jinny, feeling her stomach tighten—half nerves, half excitement. "But I've never jumped Shantih!"

"First time," suggested Sue.

"No chance," said Jinny. "It's a five-bar gate and the walls are built up to keep Mr. MacKenzie's cows in. It is HUGE."

"In that case," agreed Sue, turning Pippen round the way they had come, "old man Finnigin begin agin."

After ten minutes of trying to answer Marlene's questions, Jinny stopped listening to her and Marlene went on chatting to Shantih. Jinny had made a rule. Hold on to the pommel with one hand. She had used her father's no nonsense voice and Marlene was doing as she had been told.

Jinny smiled to herself as she plodded along behind Pippen's brown and white bottom. She could see the moorland again, the shimmer of the sea; the black cliffs, the hazy, summer mountains. They were all part of her again. Instead of hating Marlene she was alive again, and Jinny glanced up at Marlene to make sure she hadn't abandoned her firm hand hold.

"Eh, this is smashing," beamed Marlene. "Even the old horse is enjoying hisself, ain't he?"

Jinny agreed.

58

Sue pulled Pippen back to ride beside them.

"Have you ever jumped?" she asked Jinny.

"Once," said Jinny. "On Clare Burnley's showjumper."

"Not on Shantih?"

"No! I'm just reaching the stage where I can control her at a canter."

"There's lots of places here where you could jump," said Sue, pointing to the low, broken-down walls that criss-crossed the moor. "We could easily clear away the fallen stones and make a place for jumping. Shall we?"

"Now?" said Jinny in alarm.

"Why not?" challenged Sue.

"Not with me on horse," cried Marlene and instantly began to dismount. Shantih shied, depositing Marlene on the ground. "Getting as bad as you," Marlene said to Jinny. "Neither of us much good at this old riding."

"Really!" said Jinny in disgust. "You've got some cheek!" Then she realised Marlene was laughing at her.

The thought of jumping made Jinny curl up inside. She had read books about training horses to jump and none of them had suggested just suddenly starting to jump over stone walls.

"I don't mean great enormous jumps," declared Sue. "Well, if you don't want to jump, I do. Here," she said to Marlene, "hold his reins." She jumped down from Pippen and walked across to the wall.

Jinny, on Shantih, and Marlene, being led by Pippen, followed her across.

"This would do," said Sue, lifting fallen stones out of the way. "Good landing. No holes. And that couldn't be too high for anyone."

Jinny regarded the wall with a measuring eye. If she thought of having to jump Shantih over it, it looked about three feet; if she saw it as just an old wall, it probably wasn't even two feet high.

"Shouldn't we start with a pole on the ground and things like that first?"

"Oh, come on," said Sue. "This is fun. Not Hickstead. I'll go first."

"If she gets too excited I'm not jumping," said Jinny, feeling her mouth go suddenly dry. She certainly wasn't afraid, but . . .

Sue gathered up Pippen's reins, trotted him in a circle, turned him to face the wall and cantered him straight at it. With a gay flick of his tail, Pippen bounced over.

"Now me," thought Jinny as she eased Shantih into a slow sitting trot and took her round in a circle. She turned her horse to the jump, and Shantih, her ears pricked, raced at the wall. Jinny was only conscious of a sudden blur of speed, Shantih's neck arching in front of her, her mane blown back; and then, long before Jinny expected it, Shantih had taken off. Jinny jack-knifed over her shoulder, caught a vivid glimpse of Shantih's white legs tucked up close to her body, and then they had landed, far out on the other side of the wall.

"Whee!" exclaimed Sue.

Marlene clapped her hands above her head and stamped her foot, making Shantih shy and whirl round. "Nice one old horse!" she shrieked.

Jinny was too delighted to care. Her face had almost disappeared behind its ear-to-ear grin.

Pippen bounced back, popping obediently over the wall, and Shantih cantered behind him. Again she spread herself over the wall in a flowing arc.

"Jump back over again," said Sue, "and then we'll try something higher."

At the other side they searched for a higher bit of wall that was safe to jump.

"That's enormous," said Jinny in delight.

"Might be two foot six," deflated Sue. "Watch her this time. Be ready for her 'cause she'll really need to jump." Sue sat down in her saddle and rode Pippen determinedly at the wall. He cleared it with hardly an inch to spare.

Shantih plunged to follow him. Jinny checked her, trotted her in a circle, then, controlling her between her seat and hands, cantered her at the wall. She felt her horse rise up and over, then they seemed to come soaring down as if they had just cleared a steeplechase fence. Jinny was thrown forward when Shantih landed, lost a stirrup but stayed on top.

"That was super," she cried and threw herself over Shantih's neck, arms outstretched round her, praising her horse.

"Has she really never jumped before?" asked Sue.

60

"Not with me," said Jinny. "She flew over that. I didn't have to make her jump. She wanted to."

They went on jumping low bits of the wall until Marlene said to give the old horse a chance and when were they coming to this tent because she was starving, so they said now and went on to the camp site. Marlene led Shantih by the reins because she thought she needed a rest and Jinny held on to the halter rope in case a sudden grouse flew up under Shantih's nose or she saw an tiger lurking in the bracken.

As they walked up the hillside Jinny was suddenly aware of walls. They had always been there but she'd never really noticed them before. Now she was looking for places where she could jump; thinking of bringing a can of paint up the hill with her and marking suitable places with splodges of white paint so that she could canter over the moors and jump the walls without stopping to check whether they were safe to jump.

The tent, sleeping bags, rucksack, pan and their other things that had been stacked on Pippen were still lying obediently where they had left them that morning. It seemed to Jinny as if she had left them there in another life. Then she had been thinking about nothing but Marlene and now Shantih could jump. Jinny was lost in a dream of taking Shantih over Badminton-sized fences, over drop jumps and even possibly round the red and white show jumps at the Inverburgh Show next year.

"First thing," said Sue, "is to get the tent up."

Reluctantly Jinny abandoned the applause that followed her out of the ring after Shantih had jumped her clear round.

"Shall I tie him to the fence?" Marlene was asking, and Jinny realised that Sue had taken Pippen's tack off and tied him up to the most solid-looking bit of the sheep pen.

"Aren't you going to tie her up?" Sue asked.

Jinny looked dubiously at the sheep pen's rotted wood. Shantih would never stand tied to that. In fact, Jinny wasn't too sure that Shantih would stand tied to anything in the open.

"Think I'd better hold her."

"You can't hold her all the time," Sue said. "Who's going to help me with the tent?"

"Me," said Marlene.

"Well, I can't just let her go," said Jinny, seeing Shantih careering back to Finmory or running wild with Mr. MacKenzie's herd of Shetlands.

"What about tonight?" Sue asked. "You can't hold her all night."

"But I'll hold her just now," said Jinny.

CHAPTER SEVEN

Sue and Marlene put up the tent, arranged the sleeping bags and laid out their food while Jinny, leading Shantih, brought a bucket of water from the burn and gathered dried bracken and heather. She found flattish stones and laid them in front of the tent to make a fireplace.

"We'll need to go wooding to Loch Varrich," Jinny said. "We could light a fire with these bits but we'll need branches to keep it going."

"What d'you want a fire for?" demanded Marlene. "Right hot up here. We don't need a fire."

"For the water," Jinny told her. "You can't drink it unless it's boiled."

"I can," said Marlene. "Bit brown, but it's not that bad."

"Further up the hill," said Jinny, "there might be a dead fox or a dead sheep lying in that burn and all the water that flows past here has been over it—that's why we need a fire. You can catch terrible diseases drinking burn water if you don't boil it first."

"Should think I've had them all," said Marlene, unimpressed by Jinny's warnings. "You want to see our water. Real green."

Unwillingly, Marlene agreed to stay at the tent while Jinny and Sue went wooding on their horses.

"You be back before it's dark," Marlene said. "Don't want them wolves eating me, do I?"

Jinny rode Shantih as fast as she dared to Loch Varrich, galloping over any flat stretch of moor, keeping at a steady trot even when her horse was stumbling into holes and over hidden stones. Jinny could hear Sue urging Pippen on as they tried to keep up with Shantih but Jinny didn't slow down. She closed her legs against Shantih's sides and forced her on.

"One minute mile?" asked Sue crossly, when they reached the pines above the loch. "What was all the hurry for?"

"In case the wolves eat Marlene," replied Jinny, not looking at Pippen's bellowing sides and sweat-streaked neck and trying not to notice Shantih's gulping nostrils Jinny was planning to make her horse so tired that she would be glad to stand tied for some of the night at least.

They gathered dead pine branches, tied them into bundles and took them back to camp. Sue rode Pippen and dragged her bundles behind her. Jinny clutched Shantih's reins with one hand and the string tied round her branches with the other. She had fallen off twice before Sue had decided that it would be quicker if Jinny walked. As the bundles of wood bounced along, Shantih pirouetted and shied, high trotting in panic at the terrible creatures bounding behind her.

"Good," thought Jinny. "After all this carry-on she'll not have the strength to break loose."

Marlene was watching out for them.

"Where you been then?" she demanded. "I've been that scared, left here on me own. There weren't no noise. Thought it was a trick you were at. Taking the horses and leaving me here. Been much longer I'd have been for off."

"Gosh," exclaimed Sue. "We couldn't have been much quicker."

"I got a bit bothered about our Bill," said Marlene. "Should I go down and look at him, like, and see how he's doing?"

"You can't go back to Finmory tonight," said Jinny. "Bill's O.K. He's with Ken."

Marlene looked blankly at Jinny, as if she hardly heard what Jinny was saying, or if she did hear knew that it didn't matter, and Jinny recognised the look. It was the way she had looked at people when Shantih had been starving on the moor and they kept telling her that the Arab would be all right.

"Just nip down?" pleaded Marlene.

"Goodness," said Sue, taking Pippen's tack off and leading him to the sheep pen. "He's older than you, isn't he? I should think he's perfectly all right."

Jinny hesitated, torn between admitting to herself that she knew what it was like to be worried about something and surrounded by people who didn't understand, and because she knew this knowing that she had to try and help Marlene; and the more pressing need of deciding whether she could risk tying up Shantih.

"Tie her up here, next to Pippen," Sue called. "This bit here is strong enough. You can't hang on to her all night."

"I could scoot down," said Marlene.

"Of course you can't," Jinny snapped, worried about Shantih. If they'd camped at the standing stones Jinny had been planning to tie her up to a tree that grew close by. Shantih might have pulled against the tree but she couldn't have pulled it up by the roots. Looking at the grey, weather-gnawed wood of the sheep pen, Jinny knew that Shantih could drag herself free from it in seconds. "I'll wait until later in the evening," Jinny told Sue. "She'll settle better then."

Jinny took Shantih's tack off, rubbed her down and fed both horses from the bag of nuts and oats that they'd brought with them. She would decide later what to do with Shantih. Later was always easier.

Sue was organising Marlene into opening tins and filling the kettle while she blew at the flickering tendrils of flame that bloomed along the dried bracken.

Jinny crouched on the grass, holding Shantih, the Arab looming above her. Shantih's head with its delicate bones, silken skin, great liquid eyes and flimpering muzzle swooped down for a mouthful of oats, then up again, silhouetted above Jinny as her horse stared out over the pearly-grey, luminous space.

"Must be quite late," Jinny thought. The sun that had blazed above them all day had sunk into a neat, glowing disc touching the distant glint of the sea with one golden finger. The cliffs were smudgy black and the reaches of moor had softened from their sun-chiselled enamel into pastel shadings that glowed more warmly than the greying sky.

Sue placed branches carefully over the core of fire. Tongues of flame licked greedily, crackled and bit, and Jinny smelt the itchy wood smell at the back of her nose. The flames spawned shadows. Suddenly it was almost night. One minute grey, stretching evening, the next minute night. Shadows had crowded Sue, Marlene and the tent into a centre of golden security. Jinny moved closer to the fire.

"Beans?" said Sue as she tipped baked beans into the frying pan. "With sausages and, when Marlene finds them, eggs."

"Gone proper dark, ain't it," said Marlene. "Better get me torch." She burrowed into her tartan shopper.

"Forgot!" said Jinny.

"Never thought," said Sue.

"You see," said Marlene. "Can't do without me." She shone the torch to and fro in the dark. "It's me mum's. She'd have a canary if she could see me sitting out here with her good torch."

Marlene began to laugh and suddenly they were all laughing—infectious giggling that brought them together and made them all forget that only a few hours ago they'd left Marlene behind.

Still giggling, Marlene found the eggs.

"One day at school," Marlene told them, "we had this student teacher and we all had to take a turn round the class at being Noah, getting them all into the ark, like. We had to say, 'forward the elephants', or 'forward the horses', but you hadn't to say an animal any of them others had said. Well, when it were my turn they'd had all the animals I knew, so I said . . ." Marlene doubled up at the memory. "I said . . . I said, 'forward the eggs!' "

"Forward the eggs," choked Jinny in delight. It seemed the funniest thing she had ever heard.

Outside the circle of firelight, Pippen clattered the sheep pen, disturbed by the din and Shantih pricked curious ears, staring in uneasy suspicion at the three girls rolling on the ground shouting, "Forward the eggs!"

Sue ate her nosh out of the frying pan because she'd only brought two bowls and there were three of them now. They ate jelly cubes as they waited for the kettle to boil and when it did they drank tea bag tea and ate wedges of Sue's mother's fruit cake.

Sue held Shantih while Marlene and Jinny washed up in the burn.

"My hands!" cried Jinny, flapping her frozen hands as she tried to bring them back to life. "I've got burn bite."

"What a fuss," said Marlene. "Where we lived once we only had the one tap and it was always right freezing."

"But you could boil kettles," said Jinny.

"Not likely," said Marlene. "Them rotters had cut us off."

"You'd no electricity?" asked Sue incredulously. "Or gas?"

"We'd bloomin' candles," said Marlene. "Didn't even give enough light to scare off them rats." She flashed quicksilver glances at Sue and Jinny, mocking them.

"Well, anyway," said Sue a shade too quickly, not believing Marlene, "what are you going to do with her ladyship? Is she coming into the tent with us?"

"Is there a sleeping bag for her?" countered Jinny. She had seen the Stopton slums. In her mind she understood that people who lived there had rats in their houses. But she didn't know it. Couldn't believe it really possible. To open a door and see rats in your house.

"Better to tie her up now," decided Sue. "While we're still up. She will be all right. Pippen'll keep an eye on her."

Reluctantly, Jinny led Shantih across to the sheep pen. It was really dark, now that she was away from the fire. "But there'll be a moon later," Jinny thought as she tested the wooden bars, trying to find the strongest place. She imagined herself lying warm inside her sleeping bag and being able to look through the flap of the tent and see Shantih.

"Stand quietly now," Jinny murmured, clapping Shantih's sleek neck. She ran her hand over the mare's withers, stretched her arm over Shantih's back to clap her hard side and quarters, waited a moment leaning against the warm, safe bulk of her horse, then she tied her up with a quick-release knot to the strongest part of the sheep pen. "You've got Pippen," Jinny told Shantih. "You're perfectly safe. Stay there till the morning. I'll be in the tent. You don't need to be afraid."

Jinny took a few steps away from Shantih and waited. Pippen went back to his dozing, his round bulk tipped to one side by a resting hind leg, his head hanging. Shantih's neck was arched, her head high, sniffing the breeze from the night moors, and Jinny wondered if she might be smelling the Shetlands, wondered if she remembered when she had roamed the hills with them. Shantih stepped back, testing the rope that held her. She whinnied—a shrill, sudden sound—and Pippen wuffled back to her.

"He's telling her not to be so silly," Jinny thought, as she saw Shantih relax.

"There," said Sue, coming over to inspect. "She'll be all right. Stop bothering her. Come back to the fire. Marlene's making cocoa for us. We'll need to get more wood tomorrow, we've nearly used up the lot we brought today."

Jinny shivered, realising how cold it was away from the fire. She shone the torch beam for a last look at Shantih, trying not to notice the rusty nails sticking out of the planks of wood or the sheets of corrugated iron that still clung loosely, here and there, to the pen. It wasn't the place to tie up a horse and Jinny knew it. Maybe all right for Pippen but not for Shantih.

"Come and get it while it's hot," shouted Marlene, and Jinny went unwillingly over to the fire.

"You're the old cow's tail so you'll need to have the bowl," said Marlene, handing Jinny a bowl of cocoa. "But you can have all the sugar you want, nobody here won't be counting." Marlene gave Jinny the bag of sugar with a spoon stuck in it. "We're right comfy here, ain't we? Once you brew up you can make any old hole proper nice. That's what me mum says." Marlene beamed at Jinny. "Guess I'll be for the old horse again tomorrow, won't I? Can we do some more of that trotting bit?"

Jinny nodded, hardly listening. Her ears were tight to hear the least movement from Shantih. Drinking her cocoa, Jinny was ready to spring up and run to Shantih, ready to grab the tail end of the rope and set her free.

"That bloke Ken—reckon he'll watch our Bill?"

"I'm sure he will," said Jinny and far below them she heard the wind moan with a low movement of sound.

"It were strange the way he knew you'd come back for

me. I were crying a bit when he found me, bit lonely like being left, and he said you'd come back for me."

Jinny heard the wind again. It came blowing in from the sea, lifting the tent flap, scurrying paper bags they had left lying about, gusting the camp fire.

"It's proper knacky that trotting," said Marlene. "Guess me wonky leg won't help."

Sue told her she had known a man with an artificial leg who had hunted, never mind posting.

"Wouldn't want none of that rubbish, killing them little foxes, but I guess I'll need to get this, what d'you call it?"

"Posting," said Jinny. "Stops you bumping about." But she was listening to the wind, hearing it surging up from the sea, a sudden, howling voice gathering strength as it roared at them over the moors.

"What a wind," said Sue as the fire smoked and flamed. "We'll be blown away. And what about Mummy and Dad? They'll be afloat."

Shantih trampled restlessly back and forward. "If it's going to be a wild night I'll need to sit up and hold her," Jinny thought. She zipped up her anorak and stood up to go to the horses.

There was a sudden clattering rattle of corrugated iron, a stampeding panic of hooves and Jinny, running flat out to the horses, saw the whitish gleam of the corrugated iron sheet lifted by the wind. Sue had snatched up Marlene's torch and was running behind her. By its light Jinny could make out the frantic shape of Shantih fighting to escape— her head wrenched upward, the rope taut, her eyeballs white glisters in her head, the skin of her face drawn tight with terror. Her forelegs were splayed out and she pivoted from her crouching quarters as she fought to free herself.

"Pull the end of the rope!" Sue yelled, but already Jinny had ducked past Shantih's straining chest and was tugging at the end of the rope. The pressure of the struggling horse held the knot tight as Jinny jerked it helplessly.

"Can't get it loose," she screamed, as the sheet of corrugated iron was caught by another gust of wind and flung up again to rattle and crash above their heads.

With a rending, splintering crash, the bar to which Shantih had been tied broke. The mare plunged back, and the rotted lump of wood, still attached to her halter rope, whammed past Jinny, hitting her behind the knees and knocking her down.

"Catch her," Jinny screamed as she fell. She had seen the rusty nails sticking out of the lump of wood and in her imagination saw the wood entangled in Shantih's legs, the nails ripping and tearing. "Catch her! Get hold of her!"

As Jinny fought back to her feet she saw Sue grab at the halter rope, miss, and duck away from Shantih's plunging hooves.

"Shantih," cried Jinny in despair, "Shantih stop! Stop!"

Then, black against the camp fire, Jinny saw Marlene crouch close to the ground, leap up and throw herself at the jolting, leaping, jagged chunk of wood—not thinking of herself first, the way Sue had done, but with a movement so concentrated and direct that she seemed dragged on to the lump of wood as if it had been a magnet. Splayed over the wood, grasping at the rope, Marlene hung on while Shantih plunged above her.

In seconds Jinny reached her, grabbed at the rope, and struggled to calm her horse, to bring sanity back into Shantih's nightmare of terror.

At last the Arab stood still, her flanks heaving, her belly curded with sweat, eyes rolling and her ears pinned back to her neck.

Blood was running down Marlene's face. "Eh," she said, "that were a right to do. Poor old horse, he don't much fancy being tied up."

Jinny stared at her, speechless. It was Sue who came to worry about Marlene's cut face; demanding to know if she was all right; to praise her for holding on to Shantih.

"Weren't you scared?" demanded Sue. "I was. I thought she was going to kick me."

"Scared? Me?" said Marlene, dabbing at her face with a grubby ball of paper hanky. "Not likely. That don't stop me."

Jinny had unknotted the wood from Shantih's halter and was looking in horror at the twisted nails sticking out of it.

"If she'd gone galloping over the moor her legs would have been torn to ribbons," Jinny said. "If you hadn't caught her . . ."

"Eh, but I did, didn't I," said Marlene and told Sue to stop fussing about the scratch on her face, that it were nothing.

Jinny couldn't speak, couldn't find words to thank Marlene for what she had done.

They all had another cup of cocoa while the wind gusted about them and Pippen, hardly disturbed by all the commotion, returned to his doze.

"I can't tie her up again," stated Jinny. "I'll stay up and hold her."

"We'll take turns," said Sue.

"No," said Jinny. "I'll be O.K. She is mine. There's no reason why you should have to sit up." Sue watched Shantih, who was standing, still fleer-nostrilled and wide-eyed, the wind scattering her mane into wisping strands. Jinny's stomach tightened with love for her horse—the beauty and fire of her. Not for all the world would she have exchanged her for the placid Pippen. But as well as love there was fear, fear that one day Shantih would really hurt someone or damage herself. Jinny imagined her horse's legs torn and bleeding, or Marlene's face if she had fallen against the nails in the wood. "No," said Jinny again. "I'll hold her."

"Don't be silly," said Sue. "Of course we'll take turns. Nothing can happen if we're holding her."

They argued but Sue won. She held out two blades of grass to Jinny.

"The shortest bit holds first."

"What about me, then? Suppose I don't matter no more, eh? I'm the only one that was quick enough to catch her. Don't that matter now?"

So they had three pieces of grass. Jinny was first.

"Guess what time it is?" Sue asked when she'd looked at her watch to arrange shifts.

"One o'clock," guessed Jinny, whose own watch, as usual, wasn't going.

"Quarter to one," said Sue.

So Jinny took Shantih for the first shift from one to three o'clock. Marlene had drawn second and then Sue was third.

Wrapped in her sleeping bag, her hands inside her anorak sleeves, Jinny held Shantih while the mare grazed.

70

High above them, a wind-scoured moon darted in and out behind billowing clouds. The voices in the tent stopped. The torch was switched off. Jinny and Shantih were alone. Soon it was too cold for Jinny to even think. She waited, frozen, for the hands of Sue's watch to reach three o'clock. At first Jinny decided not to wake Marlene, but Marlene had made her promise and now Jinny wouldn't have cared who she woke as long as she could get in from the cold.

Just before three o'clock Jinny thought she heard someone moving quite close to her. Shantih, too, had looked up suddenly. Jinny swung round, the skin on the back of her neck prickling, but there was no one there. She couldn't see anyone. She tried to listen but the wind made it impossible to make out any movements.

At three, Jinny hobbled on numb feet to wake Marlene. A touch on her shoulder made Marlene spring upright.

"What's up?" she cried. "What's the matter?"

Then remembered where she was.

"Gone proper perishing," Marlene said as she wriggled into the extra clothes she had brought in her shopper.

Jinny waited until Marlene was settled with Shantih, then went back to the tent, too cold to do more than hope they would be all right.

She squirmed down into her sleeping bag, pulling it over her head. Sue was snoring and what felt to Jinny like a force ten gale seemed to be blowing into the tent. She waited, hoping she would fall asleep, but the ground was knobbly and most of the gale seemed to be finding its way into her sleeping bag. Reluctantly Jinny poked her face out into the cold. The flap of the tent was gaping open.

Jinny reached out to tie it together again. Then she looked out for a last check on Shantih.

Her horse wasn't grazing but standing with her neck stretched and her ears sharply pricked. Marlene was holding her halter but paying no attention to her. Jinny had been right. She had heard someone else on the moor and whoever it was they were standing talking urgently to Marlene.

CHAPTER EIGHT

For a moment Jinny wondered if she should wake Sue. She thought of horror films and night attackers and getting to Pippen so that she could ride for help. But Marlene didn't seem to be afraid. As far as Jinny could make out it looked as if Marlene was holding on to the stranger's arm.

Jinny wriggled out of her sleeping bag and crept out of the tent. Keeping to the pools of shadow by the side of the wall, she moved silently towards Marlene. Shantih saw her. She swung her head round to watch Jinny but Marlene didn't notice the horse's movement. Jinny edged her way closer and realised that the second figure was Bill.

Instantly Jinny felt as if she were spying. Whatever it was that had brought Bill out on to the moors to find his sister had nothing to do with Jinny.

"Say they see me," Jinny thought. "They'll think I've been standing here listening to them, that I'm the kind of fungus who would want to watch other people when they think they're alone." Jinny screwed up her face in total disgust. "Yuch," she thought and half turned to go back to the tent. A branch cracked beneath her foot. Jinny froze as both Marlene and Bill looked sharply round in her direction.

Jinny waited, her heart leaping in her throat, to be discovered. But although they both seemed to be staring straight at her they obviously couldn't see her and after a moment went back to their discussion. Jinny couldn't make out what they were saying, only the sound of their urgent whispering.

She eased her foot over the ground again, trying to get away before they found her; again the dried heather twigs crackled under her weight.

Jinny held her breath but this time only Shantih heard. Bill was trying to make Marlene take a small, flat parcel and Marlene was pushing it back at him. They were both too involved to have heard Jinny.

Suddenly Bill threw the parcel on the ground, spun

round and was off down the hill. Marlene had grabbed at his sleeve but he had been too quick for her. Left alone, she stooped to pick up the parcel and Jinny thought she could see tears glistening on her cheeks.

Marlene walked across to Shantih and stood whispering to the horse, as she looked down uncertainly at the parcel in her hand.

"Right bloomin' idiot," she was muttering. "Stupid bloomin' nit." Then she scrubbed the sleeve of her anorak over her eyes and began to lead Shantih towards the sheep pen.

For a second Jinny thought Marlene was going to try and tie Shantih up again.

"I'll need to pretend that I've just come out to see how she's managing," Jinny thought, watching anxiously.

But Marlene didn't tie Shantih up. She stopped by the wall at the side of the pen and began lifting down the stones.

"Now's your chance," Jinny told herself. "Get back to the tent now."

Jinny took one last look at Marlene working at the wall, then satisfied that, whatever she was doing, she wasn't going to tie Shantih up, Jinny crept back to the tent and crawled into her sleeping bag.

"Is it my turn?" Sue asked sleepily.

"Not nearly," said Jinny.

"Are you O.K.?"

"Yes."

Sue grunted and curled back down. "Wake me when it's time," she said and almost before she had finished speaking was asleep again.

Jinny lay flat on her back trying to sort out what she'd seen. She was almost certain that the parcel that Bill had left with Marlene was the same one as he had hidden behind his back when she had surprised him in the kitchen that morning. Why had he brought it to Marlene? What was in it? Why was it so important that he had come over the moors at night to give it to her? Jinny couldn't find the answers.

Before it was Sue's turn to hold Shantih, rain was drumming on the canvas. Marlene's voice woke Jinny. "Proper pouring," she said.

73

Jinny switched on the torch and saw Marlene's rain-sodden hair and pale, wet face looking in at her.

"Better get the old horse home, eh?" stated Marlene. "No point in hanging about in this?"

Sue emerged to organise an extended halter rope for Shantih made up of stirrup leathers, so they could sit inside the tent holding the end of the halter while Shantih grazed outside.

"Pippen is a very no-trouble pony," said Jinny, feeling guilty about all the fuss that Shantih was causing.

"Isn't he," agreed Sue. "And the thing about him is that he really doesn't mind. He's not just putting it on." Sue gazed contentedly at Pippen still dozing by the sheep pen, his tail plastered flat over his hocks and quarters by the driving rain.

It was nearly morning and they were all crouched inside the tent, saddles and bridles, rucksacks and food packed in around them.

"I'm asking you," said Marlene. "When are we going back down?"

Neither Jinny or Sue were answering.

"We're going to have breakfast soon," Sue said, consulting her watch. "Nearly six. We'll have breakfast at six."

"Then back down?" insisted Marlene.

"It's only a shower," said Sue irritably.

"Some shower," said Marlene, and Jinny, looking out at the louring, grey sky and the visible sheets of rain gusting over the moors, had to agree with her.

Pretending to be checking on Pippen, Jinny had taken a quick look at the wall where Marlene had lifted down the stones during the night. At first she hadn't been able to see any signs of Marlene's activities. Whatever she had been doing she had built up the wall again so that no one could tell that the stones had been removed. Then Jinny had noticed several long hairs from Shantih's tail caught between the stones just where Marlene had been standing. "So I didn't dream it," Jinny thought and went back quickly to the tent in case Marlene should be watching.

At six they had breakfast—bread and butter, cold baked beans and a tin of peaches. They drank the peach juice instead of water because Jinny refused to let anyone drink unboiled burn water.

74

"No chance of lighting a fire in this," said Sue.

"So no one drinks it," said Jinny flatly.

"When are we going down?" demanded Marlene every few minutes.

"You don't go running home just because it's raining," Sue told her.

"Do what I bloomin' like," said Marlene. "Only loonies sit out in the rain."

But Jinny didn't think it had anything to do with the rain. She thought that even if the sun had been shining Marlene would have wanted to go back to Finmory to find out what Bill was doing. Jinny hadn't told Sue about Bill's night visit. She wished that she had never seen him herself.

By nine o'clock, Marlene's patience had worn out.

"I ain't waiting no longer," she announced. "I got to get back. No use sitting here." Before Sue or Jinny realised what was happening Marlene was out of the tent.

"Poor old horse," she said, pausing to clap Shantih's spongy side. "You ain't half drowned." And Marlene limped off over the moor.

"Come back," yelled Jinny. "You can't go off like that. Come back!"

Hunched over her tartan shopper Marlene didn't even look round.

Sue ran after her. They stood in the grey downpour arguing with each other until Sue, her arm round Marlene's shoulders, began to steer her back to the tent.

"Oh well," thought Jinny. "Home we go."

She didn't mind. Rain had seeped through her jeans, her feet were sodden, her hair heavy with the rain and her stomach hadn't thought cold baked beans and peaches were the ideal breakfast. To be dry and warm in Finmory kitchen would be quite pleasant, Jinny decided, and with numb hands she began to fumble things back into her rucksack.

"She says she MUST go back NOW," announced Sue. "So I suppose we may as well pack up. Looks as if it's going to rain all day. And I don't fancy another night holding Shantih."

"Next time," said Jinny, "we'll need to find something solid to tie her to."

Shantih's chestnut coat was darkened with the rain.

Dark streaks of water ran down her white stockings. It was bad their camp whimpering out like this but it would have been much, much worse if Shantih's legs had been torn by the nails; if Marlene hadn't held on to her. Jinny shuddered at the thought. She looked at Marlene standing in the rain holding Shantih. If Marlene hadn't been there . . . Hadn't . . .

"If you'd not caught her last night . . ." began Jinny, desperately wanting to thank Marlene.

"What?" demanded Marlene. "Eh, don't start on about that now. Come on. Let's get on down quick."

Marlene's black, bullet eyes glinted in her pàle face. She was tense as a coiled spring. Her whole self set on one aim. Last night it had been to hold Shantih. Now it was to get back to Finmory as soon as possible.

Sue loaded up Pippen, tying the soaking tent, sleeping bags, bucket, pans and kettle on to his saddle. Jinny heaved her rucksack on to her back and stared round their campsite, making sure that they hadn't left tins or plastic bags lying about. She scuffled the ashes of their fire, knowing it wasn't really necessary. They were cold and dead with the rain.

It had been good in the evening when they were all sitting round the fire. That had been really nice. But it was over now.

"Eh, come on," said Marlene.

"Do you want to ride?" Jinny asked her, pulling down Shantih's stirrups, soothing her restless fretting.

"Might as well. Be a bit quicker." Fingers slipping on the wet leather, Marlene pulled herself into the saddle.

"Thought you'd want to ride," said Jinny.

"Don't mind. Be quicker."

"But I thought you wanted to learn to post?"

"Eh, well. Don't matter now. Too late for that. Got to get a move on." Marlene's knuckles shone through her skin as she gripped the pommel, and from Shantih's back she looked tensely over the moors. "Gee up," said Marlene. "Gee up, old horse."

Jinny led Shantih down the hillside. pushing with all her strength against the mare's shoulder, fighting to control her as she plunged forward, bounding downhill in great leaps that splashed peaty water into Jinny's face. Jolting

76

back and forward in the saddle, Marlene stared straight ahead.

"Don't fuss on about me," she said. "Let him hurry up if he wants. Best get out of this rain, ain't we?"

"Doesn't it get boggy?" Sue shouted as Pippen suctioned soup plate feet through the mire.

"It's the green bits that are dangerous," Jinny shouted back. "Suck you down and drown you."

"Eh, hope our Bill didn't get stuck in one of them," said Marlene. "I mean if he were out for a walk, like. He's not used to all this nothing."

"Hot coffee," said Jinny as Finmory came into sight.

"Glad to see our tent's still there," said Sue, looking at the fluorescent patch of colour still perched by the shore.

"Do you want to come up to Finmory?" Jinny offered. "All of you, I mean."

"Not likely," said Sue. "Dad's got it all fixed up for rain. More like a caravan really than a tent."

Excited by the sight of home, Shantih broke into a pounding canter. Jinny dug her elbow sharply into her shoulder, yelled at her to behave, grabbed her bit ring and pulled up her head to stop her bucking.

"Stop fussing at him," ordered Marlene. "Doing his best to get us back, ain't he?"

So Jinny, splodging at Shantih's side, let the mare surge forward. Marlene's hands were welded on to the pommel and her eyes fixed on Finmory. "Even if I let go," Jinny thought, "she'd still be on top when Shantih reached home."

As they came closer to Finmory, Jinny thought there seemed something strange about the house. No lights in any of the rooms although the morning was dark; no one in the yard or about the stables; no sign of smoke from a fire; not one of her family watching their approach from a window.

"Odd," thought Jinny, and even as they reached Finmory there was no one to be seen. "Must be the bad weather," she decided, but knew that couldn't really be the reason. The Manders had lived long enough at Finmory to have stopped staying indoors when it rained.

Down past the ruined outhouse they went and into the yard. Still no one opened the door to welcome them. Even when Jinny called, announcing that they were back, there was no reply.

"I'll go on to our tent," Sue said. "May as well dump all this clobber. See you later."

"Right. Come over whenever you like," Jinny said, but she was thinking how strange it was that all her family should be away from home in the morning. It certainly wasn't the day for a picnic or a drive.

"Let me off here," demanded Marlene.

"Wait," said Jinny, "until we get to the stable."

"I got to get off now," cried Marlene, but Jinny ignored her and let Shantih jog on down to the stables.

The second Shantih reached the stable door, Marlene dropped to the ground. She snatched her shopper from Jinny and began to run back to the house.

"Good job," said Jinny to Shantih, "that you've got me to look after you."

In the loose box Jinny's numb fingers couldn't unbuckle the girth. She put her hand in her mouth, blowing to bring her fingers back to life and then tugged at the buckles again and managed to loosen them. She took Shantih's tack off, fetched an armful of hay for her and then stood pulling the mare's cold, wet ears through her hands to warm her.

"Jinny! Jinny!"

Marlene's voice made Jinny dash out of the stable. It linked with her own uneasy feelings about the strange emptiness around Finmory.

"He's not there," Marlene cried. "There ain't no one there. And our Bill's gone. He's taken his case and done a bunk. I shouldn't never have left him to go with that horse."

Marlene wasn't crying but her face under her rain-flattened hair was peaked and drawn, her mouth twisted into a lipless knot.

"There must be someone in the house," said Jinny. "Or a note to say where they are."

"There ain't," said Marlene. "He's gone."

CHAPTER NINE

"We're back," Jinny shouted as she ran along the landing. There had been no one downstairs and no note to say where they had all gone to. "They wouldn't be expecting us," Jinny thought, trying to reassure herself. "That's why they haven't left a note." But she knew that whenever her mother saw the rain she would have been expecting them to come home.

"Anybody there?" called Jinny, her voice echoing through the empty house.

"No need to panic," Jinny said when she was back in the kitchen with Marlene. "They've just gone somewhere for the day, that's all."

"I'm telling you, our Bill's taken his case. That means he's off. And his old books. He ain't coming back, not when he's got his books."

"There's nothing we can do," said Jinny. "We'll just need to wait until someone comes home. I don't suppose Mike is with them. He hates going for drives. Or Ken."

"I got to find Bill," said Marlene.

"How?"

"I don't know, do I? I don't know where to look, not here. I'd know in Stopton. Know all the places he goes there. I'd find him there. I think he's gone back home. That's where he's gone."

Jinny thought it likely. Perhaps that was what Bill had told Marlene last night—that he wanted to go back to Stopton.

"There's nothing we can do until the others come home," repeated Jinny. "You can't go off to Stopton by yourself. We'd better change out of these wet clothes and have some coffee. Shall I lend you a pair of jeans?"

"Got me good ones," said Marlene, and they went upstairs to change.

When Jinny got back to the kitchen, Marlene was wearing black velvet trousers and a lacy, lurex jumper. She had brought her tartan shopper down with her.

"When's this rain goin' to stop?" she demanded as if

79

Jinny were in control of a rain tap. "I got to get going. Can't muck about here when Bill's off on his own."

"Have a cup of coffee," said Jinny. "You'll look daft if you go tearing off to Stopton and Bill's only away for the day. Then you'll be in Stopton and he'll be here."

Marlene considered this while Jinny made the coffee.

"How we going to find out?" she cried. "I got to know."

"Don't worry," said Jinny. "Bill wouldn't go without you."

"Not much," said Marlene. "Not bloomin' much."

There was a sound of footsteps outside. Marlene rushed to the door and flung it open. Ken came into the kitchen, his hair sleeked back, his oilskin dripping.

"Hi," he said.

"Where's Bill?" demanded Marlene. "Thought you was keeping the eye on him? You let him go off, didn't you?"

Ken hung up his oilskin, asked Jinny if there was a cup of coffee for him and sat down at the table before he answered Marlene.

"Mr MacKenzie phoned up this morning about seven, said he thought we should check up that Bill was O.K. He was up with a sick cow and saw Bill going past his farm at about four o'clock. Said he had a case with him. Wondered if we knew."

Marlene's black eyes stared unblinkingly at Ken as she chewed at her nails.

"We checked Bill's room but he wasn't there. Your Mum and Dad have gone into Inverburgh. Tom thought he might have hitched a lift, trying to get the train back to Stopton. I've been up the moor. Petra and Mike have gone down to the shore, just in case. He might have fallen and hurt himself."

"Thought you promised," Marlene accused bitterly. "You ain't no better than the rest. Thought you understood. I'd have heard him. I'd have stopped him. It's me that's to blame. Shouldn't have gone off with that old horse."

The sound of a car interrupted Marlene's reproaches.

"That be them?" she cried. "Think they've got him, then?"

Jinny knew that it wasn't their car. It was too powerful. "Might be news," she said.

There was a heavy banging at the front door. Jinny went to answer it. A policeman stood there with Mrs. Simpson standing behind him.

"Good morning," said the policeman. "Is Mr. Manders in?"

Jinny said he wasn't.

"We'll be coming in to wait on him for it's the urgent word I'm for having with him," said Mrs. Simpson, and, pushing past the policeman and Jinny, she walked into the hall.

The policeman took off his hat, stroked down his sandy hair with a calloused hand and followed the shopkeeper into the kitchen.

"Would you be looking at the state of that one," said Mrs. Simpson, meaning Ken. "I tell you, Donald," she said to the policeman, "they're all tarred with the same brush. Nothing but layabouts has there been in this house since the last of the MacCraes was taken."

"It's your brother I'm wanting," she said to Marlene, "though I daresay you'd be having a hand in it yourself. Be telling me now where's the boy?"

Jinny saw Marlene's shoulder stiffen, her hands clench under the table.

"Do you mean Mike?" Ken asked.

"I mean that one's brother, as you know very well. The one that stole the watch from my shop yesterday."

Events linked together like jig-saw pieces in Jinny's mind—Bill in the shop holding Mrs. Simpson's eighty-two pound watch; Marlene snatching his hand away from it; their second visit to the shop; the flat parcel Bill had hidden in a guilty fumble when Jinny found him in the kitchen; the same flat parcel he had left with Marlene at their camp.

"And she buried it in the wall," thought Jinny and sat down suddenly, pretending to tie her shoelace, so that she could keep her head down and stop the kitchen sliding about.

"You ain't got no right to say that. Our Bill never touched your old watch."

But Jinny knew he had. She felt sick at the thought of

81

it. What good was a gold watch to Bill? Bill would be charged with stealing it but Marlene would be hurt as well. She would feel that it was her fault because she had left him to go camping.

"You could be had up for saying those things about Bill. You ain't got no proof. You're just saying lies to get him into trouble. When me mum hears she'll sort you out. 'Cause our Bill, he didn't never touch your watch. He didn't have nothing to do with it."

Words sputtered out of Marlene. Her back eyes darted hate at Mrs. Simpson.

"You leave our Bill alone," Marlene threatened. "You leave him alone."

"Would the boy be in the house?" the policeman asked Ken. "I could be asking him a few questions."

Ken said no Bill wasn't and the phone rang in the hall. Jinny's feet took her to answer it over a floor that felt as soft as sponge rubber, past walls that breathed in and out.

"Hullo," she said.

"Jinny," said her father's voice and Jinny felt tears prick in her eyes, wanted to tell him what had happened but didn't know how to begin.

"Were you washed out?" Mr. Manders asked but didn't wait for a reply. "Tell the others we found Bill at Inverburgh station. Sudden bout of homesickness. He wanted back to the city but he missed the train so he's coming back with us until tomorrow."

The sound of pips interrupted Mr. Manders' voice. "Sorry, no more change," he said and the line went dead.

Jinny went back to the kitchen. They all looked round at her, their faces turned on her. She had to tell them.

"Bill was at Inverburgh station," Jinny said. "He's coming back with them."

"Did you hear that, Donald?" Mrs. Simpson demanded of the policeman. "Is that not his guilt clear now! Off to England with my watch." She stroked her flowered nylon overall down over her knees with both hands. "And we will be staying here, I'm thinking, until he walks through that door."

"If you think Bill took the watch yesterday morning," Ken asked. "Why weren't you up here yesterday?"

Mrs. Simpson regarded him coldly. "It's no business of

82

yours," she said, "but I'll be telling you. Mr. Simpson was away on the wee visit to his brother and I was thinking he had the watch with him."

"He didn't?" asked Ken.

"He did not," said Mrs. Simpson.

Petra and Mike came in and stared in amazement to see Mrs. Simpson and a policeman in the kitchen.

"Not surprised," stated Petra when she understood what was happening. "He'd been in trouble before, you know. I think it was shoplifting then, as well. Dad ll know. If you ask me they get away with these things once and they just go on doing them."

"You wait," thought Jinny, glaring at her sister. "You wait till something like this happens in our family. You'll not be so sure then."

"Is that a fact, now," said the policeman, and Ken said that if it was true it was over and done with.

"I'll be telling you this," said Mrs. Simpson. "I knew there was bad in that boy the minute I saw him. Couldn't keep his thieving hands off that watch. Up to no good. Nothing but a yob."

"We'll soon be at the truth," said the policeman soothingly. "I have the questions ready. Wait now until we see the boy."

Since Jinny had told them that Bill was coming back to Finmory with her parents, Marlene had sat silently hunched into herself, nibbling at her fingers and picking at a thread in her jumper.

"You don't need to do no more waiting," she announced suddenly. "Because I told you, didn't I? It wasn't Bill who took your old watch. It were me. I took it. Me you got to get at. Not our Bill. Me."

A moment of absolute silence followed Marlene's words.

"I don't doubt you'd the hand in it," declared Mrs. Simpson.

"Where is the watch?" asked the policeman.

"But that brother of yours, he was the one taking it from my counter," said Mrs. Simpson, not believing Marlene.

"You never saw him," stated Marlene. "And he don't know nothing about it 'cause I took it, see. You come back up them moors with me and I'll get you the watch.

I'll show you where I hid it." And Marlene stood up, hitching at her good velvet trousers, dragging the kirby grip out of her short hair, opening it with her teeth and jabbing it back more securely. "Come on with me and I'll get your bloomin' old watch for you."

Jinny's voice that had been stuck in her throat came out in a croak.

"You didn't take it," Jinny cried. "I know you didn't. I saw . . ."

Marlene's hands gripped the edge of the table. For a moment, as she realised that Jinny must have seen Bill giving her the watch, Marlene's face lost its mask and Jinny saw her as she really was—desperately vulnerable, powerless against them and terrified that Bill should be charged with stealing a second time.

For that moment it seemed to Jinny that they were alone in the kitchen and Marlene's true face made the false things vanish. Because she had seen Bill, Jinny had the power to break Marlene, to tell them all how Bill had come up to their camp at night to leave the watch with his sister, how Marlene had nothing to do with stealing it. This time Bill might be sent to a remand home.

"If it were Shantih," Jinny thought. "If they wanted to take Shantih away from me and shut her up . . ."

Jinny couldn't bear to look at Marlene, yet there was nothing else she could do. To see Marlene as she was now was to know what it was like to live in the Stopton slums; what it was like to come to a strange place and be treated the way Jinny had treated Marlene. "Oh no," cried Jinny. "No! I didn't mean it." But the moment was naked. The easy words of polite apology weren't there to cover it up. Jinny had been rotten to Marlene. Words couldn't change that. And Jinny saw Marlene throw herself at the bar of wood ripped from the sheep pen, grab Shantih's halter and hold on. "Oh no," cried Jinny, but the words had no sound.

Then the mask slipped back into place. They were back in the familiar kitchen.

Marlene turned furiously on Jinny.

"Shut up!" she shouted. "Shut up! Don't you come messing me up. This ain't got nothing to do with you, Miss La-di-dah Manders. So you shut up."

84

"Officer," said Marlene to the policeman. "Come on with me up them hills. I'll show you where it is."

"And what would a watch be doing out on the hills?" asked the policeman suspiciously.

"They were camping up there," Petra explained. "Where were you? By that old sheep pen?" Jinny nodded. "But Marlene can't walk all that way," continued Petra. "She's a bit lame."

"I ain't a bloomin' cripple," spat Marlene, putting on her soaking anorak. "That's me ready. Come on."

The policeman hesitated.

"Have I to be going myself?" demanded Mrs. Simpson.

"Hadn't you better wait until Dad gets back?" suggested Mike.

"Naw," said Marlene. "Come on with me now."

The policeman settled his hat back on his head. "Does the lassie know the way?" he asked.

"I'll come with you," said Ken, but Jinny, catching his eye, shook her head at him. She had to tell Ken what had happened. There must be some way of stopping Marlene taking the blame for Bill's stealing. And if anyone could help her Ken could.

Realising that Jinny didn't want him to go with the policeman, Ken asked Mike if he would go and reluctantly Mike agreed.

"A wee bitty thing her age," clucked Mrs. Simpson with satisfaction when the policeman, Marlene and Mike had set off. "Who would have thought it. Though I'm telling you that nowadays the lassies are as bad as the boys."

"I know," agreed Petra. "The things some of them do at our school."

Jinny hurried Ken out of the room.

"The pottery," he said, and impatiently Jinny followed him into the pottery. Its window looked out on to the hills at the back of the house. The rain had changed to a smirring drizzle and through its grey mist Jinny could see the three shapes walking up the hill, heads down, shoulders hunched against the rain. Mike was taking them up the hill the way they had ridden to their camp.

"It wasn't Marlene," Jinny told Ken. "It was Bill. He brought the watch up to her during the night. She hid it up there. She's only saying she took it to protect Bill."

Ken listened to the details.

"We've got to get the watch back to the shop," he said. "Make the Simpsons believe that it wasn't stolen."

"But how? If Marlene takes the stones off the wall and the watch is there, they'll never believe that it wasn't stolen. We've got to take it away before Marlene gets there. But how?" Jinny cried.

She didn't really know about courts or Children's Panels but she pictured Marlene, in her lacy jumper and good trousers, standing in the witness box telling the jury how she had stolen the watch, her bitten fingers clutching the rail of the box, her bullet eyes defying them—not caring what they did to her as long as they left Bill alone.

"They'd guess what you were up to if you rode past them."

"Marlene would," said Jinny, and suddenly she thought of the short cut, the way through Mr. MacKenzie's farm yard, on over his fields and out on to the moor. *If* the gate wasn't padlocked.

"I could try the short cut," Jinny cried. "I'd make it that way." And she knew she had to try. The gate had to be open. That way she could take the watch out of the wall before Marlene got there.

"Right," said Ken. "I'll go after them and do my best to slow them down."

They raced out of the house together. Ken turned to run up the hill. Jinny tore through the garden and down to the stables. She grabbed up her tack from where she had left it to go with Marlene. Shantih clattered her box door, expecting to be taken out to her field.

"It's for Marlene," Jinny explained as she put her bridle on, slid the saddle on to her back and tugged up the girth. "We've got to get there first."

In the yard, Shantih flung herself away from Jinny as she tried to mount.

"Whoa, steady, stand still," Jinny pleaded.

She sprang up, threw herself over the saddle and wriggled upright. Shantih plunged and reared but Jinny hardly noticed. She turned Shantih's head towards the path that led to Mr. MacKenzie's farm, kicked her heels against the mare's sides and sent her on at a splattering canter.

86

Shantih caught Jinny's urgency, knew that this was no ordinary ride, and Jinny felt her respond willingly, with a gay eagerness that matched her own determination to reach the wall first.

Sprays of muddy water flew up from Shantih's hooves as she galloped down the path to the farm. Jinny swung her round into the farmyard and saw to her relief that there was no sign of Mr. MacKenzie. Only his wife pulled aside the lace curtain of the farmhouse window to see what was causing the disturbance, but by the time she came hurrying to the door Jinny was across the yard and out of sight.

The gate into the first field stood propped open. Jinny crouched over Shantih's withers as they galloped through and flared over the field. She didn't know where her own body ended and her horse began. The piston beat of Shantih's hooves was the beat of her own heart.

"Let the gate be open," cried Jinny, mouthing the words. "Oh please, please, let it be open."

CHAPTER TEN

Shantih galloped across the last field before the gate. The ground was more broken here and Jinny eased her horse to a steady canter as she rode towards a rise in the land. From the top of the slope Jinny would be able to see the gate.

"It must be open. It MUST," thought Jinny desperately. She hadn't allowed herself to consider what she would do if the gate was shut.

As Shantih cantered the last few strides to the crest of the hill Jenny screwed her eyes shut. At the top of the hill she opened them. For a split second she was still sure that the gate was open, she had seen it so clearly inside her head, but instantly she knew that it was shut. She made a gulping, strangled noise in her throat and thought, "Don't let it be padlocked," as Shantih plunged downhill towards it.

The padlock was made of whitish, blue-grey metal. It

held together the links of a stout chain that encircled the gatepost and the gate, and it was locked.

In front of the gate Shantih whirled and fretted. Excited by her wild gallop, she refused to stand still. Jinny had gone cold inside. Had stopped feeling anything. She just didn't know what she could do now.

The gate was a strongly built, five-bar gate. On either side was a four-foot stone wall. At intervals, upright iron bars had been driven into the top of it and three strands of barbed wire strung through them. There was no way for Jinny to get Shantih through to the other side. If she left her horse here and ran to the sheep pen Jinny was certain she would be too late. All the time she had been galloping she had felt the approach of Marlene, the policeman, Mike and Ken; had tried to guess where they would be; how far on they were; had thought of the gold watch lying inside the wall, drawing the others and herself towards it as if it were a magnet; and now they would reach it and she wouldn't.

But there was one way. One way she could reach the watch before Marlene. Jinny hadn't dared to think about it until now. She could jump the gate.

Jinny sized up the jump. The gate was about four and a half feet high but appeared lower because of the high barbed wire on either side.

"Shantih could jump it," Jinny told herself.

"But she's never jumped anything like that height. She's hardly ever jumped anything. Nor have I. Not really," Jinny pleaded with herself. She had done her best. It wasn't her fault the gate was locked. She'd tell the police how Bill had left the watch with Marlene. They'd question Bill, find out for themselves and nothing would happen to Marlene. But Jinny knew that if they sent Bill to a remand home it would be worse for Marlene than anything they could do to her.

She had to jump the gate. There was no other way.

"We've got to get to the other side," Jinny told her horse. "You've got to jump it. You can do it easily, easily."

She cantered Shantih in a circle. Her legs seemed loose against the saddle and a hard choking lump somewhere inside her was stopping her breathing properly. "I'll hold on to her mane," Jinny thought, "and then I'll be all right."

She turned Shantih and rode her at the gate. To Jinny's magnifying eye it seemed to have grown to an enormous size. She crouched stiffly in the saddle, a lump of mane knotted between her fingers.

"Jump!" she shouted at Shantih. "Jump!" But Jinny's mind was filled with the thought of Shantih hitting the gate, crashing down and lying unable to get up because her leg was broken.

"Jump," cried Jinny again as she clung nervously to Shantih's mane. "Jump it!"

Shantih slid to a halt in front of the gate. Her eyes rolling, her tail switching, she swung round and charged away. Jinny grabbed up her reins, hauled her round and rode her at the gate for a second time.

Jinny's voice said words that were meant to urge her on but Shantih only heard her nervous, high-pitched tone. Jinny's clinging hands and rigid body held her back. Shantih stopped dead in front of the gate and Jinny went on thumping into it.

"We're going to be too late," Jinny thought as she remounted. "Are you afraid?" she asked herself and knew that the answer was yes. She was afraid.

"Then be afraid," said the voice in Jinny's head. "Be afraid but don't let that stop you." Jinny remembered the look on Marlene's face before she had ridden Shantih for the first time. Marlene had been afraid then but it hadn't stopped her. "And now," Jinny thought, "telling them she stole the watch, she's afraid of what they'll do to her. And she was afraid when she caught Shantih but it didn't stop her."

Jinny took off her hard hat, shook her hair back and settled it more firmly on her head. This time she would jump the gate. This time Shantih wouldn't refuse.

Jinny gathered up her reins, steadied her horse, cantered in a circle then rode her at the gate for a third time and this time Jinny wasn't thinking about holding on to Shantih's mane, or of Shantih falling. The only thought in Jinny's head was to be on the other side. Sitting tight in the saddle, Jinny drove the Arab at the gate, left no doubt in Shantih's mind about what she was to do. Jinny held her together, waited for the moment when Shantih must soar into the air if she was to clear the gate safely, kicked her on at that exact moment and Shantih leapt from her hocks, struck upwards, sailed high over the gate and landed far out on the other side.

"You did it!" cried Jinny. "You jumped it! Oh horse! Horse! Horse!"

As they galloped on, Jinny glanced back once to see a rather low gate just being there between the walls, totally unperturbed by all the commotion, then she set herself to ride as fast as she could to the sheep pen.

Tensely, Jinny searched the moor, knowing where the others would first come into sight, but there was no sign of them, no crows flew up, cawing a warning of their approach.

Jinny reached the sheep pen, threw herself off Shantih and searched the wall for the chestnut hairs from Shantih's tail. She found them and began to topple the stones to the ground. She had to remove about a dozen stones before she found the parcel. A plastic bag was wrapped round the box, but the long, flat shape of the box was unmistakable. Jinny grabbed it up and stuffed it into the pocket of her oilskin. She lifted the stones back on to the wall, scraping her knuckles in her haste to rebuild it and be away. A gull rasped the moorland silence with a harsh cry. Jinny froze. What would she say if they caught her? Then she realised that it was only a bird and went on struggling to make the stones balance on top of each other.

"You could tell," Jinny thought, surveying the wall, "but you couldn't be certain it had been a person. A sheep could have rumpled it." She jumped back on to Shantih.

Jinny didn't stop galloping until she was absolutely certain that she was well out of sight of the sheep pen, then she stopped Shantih and sat slumped in the saddle, took her feet out of the stirrups, dropped her reins. They had done it! Shantih and herself.

"My horse without peer," quoted Jinny, achievement overflowing in her. "Leaned, patted her ear, called her my Shantih, my horse without peer," she cried, throwing herself over Shantih's neck, clapping her, praising her.

When Marlene got to the wall there would be no watch for her to find. Mrs. Simpson and the policeman would be annoyed, thinking she had tricked them, but Marlene would be safe.

Jinny sat up and took the watch out of her pocket. She put one arm through Shantih's reins to stop them vanishing over her head while she was grazing, and then Jinny unwrapped the box. She opened it and looked at the watch. It seemed to Jinny a clumsy lump of metal, a single handcuff. She shivered, closed the box, wrapped it up again and put it back into her pocket. Now she had to get it back into Mrs. Simpson's shop where it belonged.

Without a second thought, Jinny rode Shantih at the locked gate; grinned with delight as her Arab soared effortlessly over it and cantered on to the farm.

Jinny avoided the farmyard. Even if Mr. MacKenzie wasn't there, Jinny felt that Mrs. MacKenzie would be more prepared to pounce. She walked Shantih down the edge of a sown field, by the side of a wall that bounded a hayfield, and then trotted her out on to the road to Glenbost.

She had to get the watch back before the policeman had the chance to question Bill. From what Jinny knew of Bill she had no confidence in his being able to outwit even the Glenbost police force.

As she rode she eased the watch out of its plastic wrapping. Jinny wasn't too sure how she was going to get it back to the Simpsons but there was a chance that if she lingered over the shop's pile of paperbacks, Mr. Simpson, who would be in charge of the shop while his wife was at Finmory, would leave her alone while he attended to another customer.

"Need to find someone to hold you," Jinny told Shantih as the shop came into sight.

Dolina, who had attended the village school and was going with Jinny to the new Inverburgh Comprehensive in September, was standing in front of the garage.

"Is it the mud pack you've been giving her?" Dolina asked, coming to meet them.

Jinny dismounted. "Looks like it," she agreed, seeing Shantih's mud-splattered legs and sides. "Could you hold her for me? I've got to go into the shop."

91

Dolina regarded Shantih warily. "If she's at her nonsense I'll let her go," she stated.

"She'll be fine," said Jinny. "She'll eat the grass. Don't think I'll be long." She handed Shantih's reins to Dolina and hurried into the shop.

There were two women at the counter. Jinny knew them both by sight, the way she knew everyone in Glenbost. They both looked round at Jinny who was sure that they could see into her pocket and would think that she had stolen the watch.

"And what can I get for you?" Mr. Simpson asked in a distant polite voice. Normally he teased Jinny about her red hair.

"I want a book," Jinny said. "Can I have a look at them?"

"Don't be soiling them, now," Mr. Simpson cautioned and went back to his other customers.

Jinny rubbed her dirty hands down her wet oilskin, then dried them on her jeans.

There were about twenty children's paperbacks sitting next to a pile of murders, westerns and romances. Jinny looked through them slowly. Mr. Simpson resumed his conversation with the two women and Jinny, pretending to be reading one of the books, let her gaze wander round the shop. In front of the counter, quite close to the perspex case of watches, was an open crate of apples. It wasn't absolutely underneath the watches, but close enough to make it possible for the gold watch to have fallen in amongst the apples from the top of the case.

"But," thought Jinny sharply, "the apples would have had to be there before Mrs. Simpson noticed that the watch was missing or it couldn't possibly have fallen amongst them."

Jinny tried to remember if the apples had been there when she had bought their camping supplies. At first she wasn't sure. She could picture them there, or not, whichever way she chose. Then she remembered her father filling a bag with apples from the crate before Mrs. Simpson weighed them. The apples had definitely been there on Thursday.

Jinny slid her hand into her oilskin pocket. The box was closed. When it had been sitting on top of the case

92

the lid of the box had been fitted on to the back of the box to display the watch. Still pretending to read her book, Jinny opened the box in her pocket and fitted the lid on to the back.

One of the women went out, making Jimmy start guiltily. "I should have fixed the box before I came in," Jinny thought and wondered what other stupid mistakes she had made.

When the box felt all right Jinny palmed it up into her sleeve; holding it there, secret and hidden by her oilskin, while she waited for her chance to put it into the box of apples.

Another woman came in and Mr. Simpson began to serve her. She asked for butter and Jinny knew he would have to go into the back shop to take her pound of butter from the great mound that was kept there.

Still reading her book, Jinny moved across to the counter. Mr. Simpson went into the back shop, leaving the two women gossiping together. Jinny balanced her book on the very edge of the counter, put her right hand into the right hand pocket of her oilskin and help out her un-buttoned coat so that the women couldn't possibly see what she was doing with her other hand.

Jinny tipped the book so that it fell to the floor. The women glanced in her direction then paid no more atten-tion to her. Jinny crouched down, still shielding her left hand with her coat as she placed the watch delicately amongst the apples. Then, without looking at the women, she made sure that the fruit was covering the watch. She picked up her book and stood up. Her hands were shaking so much that she had to let the book flop on the counter and bury her hands out of sight in her pockets.

Jinny let her eyes flick down over the crate of apples. The watch was almost completely hidden. Only a tiny patch of its red box was visible. Yet to Jinny it seemed the most obvious thing in the whole shop, as if anyone coming in would instantly stop and point to it, asking what on earth a gold watch was doing in a crate of apples.

"Now to make Mr. Simpson find it," Jinny thought. Everyone must know that the watch had been recovered before the policeman had a chance to question Bill. Jinny drew in long slow breaths, let the air flow slowly out of her nose, as she tried to calm herself.

"Have you decided, then?" demanded Mr. Simpson when the two women had left the shop. "Is this the one you're taking?"

"Yes please," said Jinny. "And could I have a pound of eating apples?" To her relief her voice sounded as it always did; as if it was an ordinary day and she was just shopping for her mother.

"You'll have heard about that boy you have with you stealing the gold watch from us," said Mr. Simpson, coming to the front of the counter to fill a paper bag with apples.

Jinny said yes she had.

"It's the sorry day when you've strangers on your door-step bringing thieves into your shop."

Mr. Simpson had put three apples into the bag and was going back behind the counter without noticing the watch.

"Do I only get three?" cried Jinny in alarm. "Could you make them small ones, please? Could I have four or five small ones, please?"

Mr. Simpson glared at her sourly but he tipped the three apples back into the crate and began to hunt around for smaller ones. The movement of the apples pushed the watch to the surface.

Mr. Simpson swore in gaelic as he grabbed it up.

"If it isn't the very watch the boy stole," he exclaimed. "Was it yourself put it there?"

"If you say Bill stole it, how could I have put it there?" Jinny said indignantly, hoping she was looking sufficiently surprised. "It must have fallen. Dropped down and got mixed up with the apples."

Mr. Simpson's eyes totally disbelieved her.

"Gosh, I bet you're jolly glad to have got it back. Is it O.K.?"

As Jinny left the shop, Mr. Simpson was on the phone to Finmory, telling his wife that the watch had been found.

When Jinny got back to Dolina and Shantih she couldn't stop shaking. She leant over Shantih's withers and shook. Her teeth chattered and her hands twitched.

"Are you feeling fit?" asked Dolina.

"Having one," said Jinny.

Her legs weren't strong enough to get her back on to Shantih.

"I'll walk beside her and lean," Jinny said, refusing Dolina's offer of a hoist on.

Gradually, as she walked back to Finmory, Jinny began to calm down. She shared the apples with Shantih as they went along.

"Shoplifters should get medals," Jinny thought. She was feeling as exhausted as if she had been galloping for hours on a runaway Shantih.

First the police car, with Mrs. Simpson sitting next to the policeman and staring straight ahead, passed them, and then the Manders' car, with Bill in the back, drove up and stopped beside her.

"Jinny," said her mother in a surprised tone of voice. "Are you all right?"

"Perfectly," said Jinny. "We were rained off so I thought I'd go for a ride."

"But you're not," said her mother. "Where's Sue and Marlene?"

"Her tent and our kitchen, I should think, and I am having a ride, only at this particular moment I'm not."

"I see," said Mrs. Manders. "'Bye then," and they drove on.

It wasn't until her parents had driven up and Jinny had seen Bill slouching in the back seat that she had given a thought to the rights and wrongs of covering up for Bill when, after all, he had stolen the watch. Until that moment all Jinny had been thinking about had been stopping Marlene taking the blame.

Jinny knew that Ken would think that for anyone— Mrs. Simpson or Bill—to own a watch that cost eighty-two pounds, when human beings were dying because they hadn't enough to eat, was so disgusting that it didn't matter who took the watch. But Jinny wasn't so sure what her parents would think. Her father might feel that Bill shouldn't get off without some form of repayment for all the trouble he had caused. It was, Jinny decided, one of the things that it might be better for her parents never to know about.

It was easier to think about Shantih. Jinny swung herself back into the saddle and, letting Shantih walk on at her own pace, she relived the thrill of sailing, high, wide and handsome over the gate. The more she thought about it, the higher the gate became.

"Next autumn the White City and then the Olympics," thought Jinny, wondering what she would call Princess Anne when they were riding together in the British cross country team, and she laughed aloud at herself.

They were all having a late lunch when Jinny got back. Ken looked up when she came into the kitchen, and Jinny signalled to him that she had managed it. Marlene, as silent as Bill, was bent over her plate of tomato soup.

"Where have you been?" cried Petra. "Mrs. Simpson and I thought another one of you had run off."

"Mrs. Simpson said you were in the shop when her husband found the watch," Mike said, wanting to know the details.

"It had fallen into a crate of apples," said Jinny. Marlene's beady eyes chiselled into her, but twitched away if Jinny tried to look directly at her. "And I was buying apples for Shantih, so he found it."

"You'd think they'd have found it before today," said Petra. "Lots of people must have bought apples before you."

"It had sort of worked its way down between them," said Jinny, and her father said that one thing certain was that they wouldn't leave it on top of the case again.

When she had finished her lunch, Jinny went up to her bedroom. She shut the door firmly behind her. She felt like being alone. She took out a drawing pad and pencil and sat on the floor opposite her mural, thinking that she might do some drawings of Pippen for Sue but she couldn't even start. The pencil in her hand was a dead lump of wood and lead.

Jinny stared up at the mural of the red horse. It had been on the wall before the Manders had come to Finmory and often Jinny wondered who had painted it. The horse's yellow eyes blazed light. It was a nightmare that came charging through the blue green foliage of Jinny's wondering.

"What could it be like?" she wondered. "To love

someone else so much that you said, 'do it to me, not to him'."

Footsteps came along the landing towards Jinny's attic stair. She heard them pause, then limp slowly up towards her. Marlene's clenched fist banged on the door.

CHAPTER ELEVEN

Jinny opened the door and Marlene limped in. She stood staring round the room.

"Eh," Marlene said. "You're a lucky thing, having a place like this for yourself. You ain't half spoilt, you ain't." Marlene sat down on Jinny's bed. "'Spect you took it. Come on, tell us."

"I rode Shantih round by the short cut," said Jinny. "And took the watch out of the wall. Then I put it in the crate of apples when Mr. Simpson wasn't looking."

"What you want to do that for? Wasn't none of your business."

"It was," cried Jinny. "I saw Bill bring it up to you last night. "I didn't mean to spy on you. I thought he was a stranger and I was coming to see what he wanted and then I couldn't get away. That's how I knew you hadn't done it."

"He was scared they'd find the watch on him. That's why he left it with me. Thought they wouldn't search me. Said he'd tell them that he knew nothing about it. But see our Bill, he's proper soft. The minute they started with those questions he'd be in a mess."

"I couldn't let you take the blame for something you hadn't done. I'd have told them it was Bill, only I knew you didn't want that either. The only thing I could think of was to get there first and take the watch back to the shop."

Marlene was fiddling with the fringe of Jinny's bed-spread, plaiting it into little pigtails which sprang out as soon as she let go of them. "Thanks," she said without looking up. "They might have put him away this time."

"I didn't do it for Bill," said Jinny. "I just didn't see why you should say you had stolen it when he did it."

"Like I love him," suggested Marlene. "Not what he does, not what he looks like—same as me, bit of a mess. But he's O.K. He's Bill. Me mum's right fond of him too. Thinks the world of him, she does. She don't believe he does any of these things. Thinks he wouldn't steal nothing, not if you dropped a thousand pounds at his feet. She thinks our Bill would hand it in."

"I bet he would," said Jinny sarcastically.

"What do you know about it?" demanded Marlene, turning on Jinny. "You just keep your mouth shut because you don't know nothing about how it really is, you don't."

Jinny felt her skin creep, a cold shiver run over her scalp. It was true. She lived wrapped round in layers of cotton wool. It had all been an adventure to her. If Bill had gone to a remand home it wouldn't really have made any difference, not to her, not to her safe, secure little world.

"So you keep shut up," warned Marlene again.

"Of course," said Jinny. "I wouldn't tell anyone."

"Not that sister of yours."

"Ken knows."

"Argh, that don't matter. But mind, no one else." Marlene stood up. "Best be going to say goodbye to the old horse," she said.

"Goodbye?" echoed Jinny. "It's only Friday. You've got another week. Don't you want any more rides?"

"Naw," said Marlene. "Too late. We're for off tomorrow."

"Not you," exclaimed Jinny. "Bill's going but you don't have to go."

"Not much," said Marlene scornfully. "I'm for Stopton tomorrow. Can't let him go off without me."

"But can't your mother meet him?" argued Jinny. "You can't spend all your life looking after Bill."

But Marlene wasn't listening to her.

"Just say tarrah," she said as she went towards the door, "and that'll be that." Then she stopped and looked through the archway into the other half of Jinny's room.

"Proper art gallery you got here, ain't it," said Marlene and she went through to look at Jinny's pictures that were pinned on the wall opposite the mural.

Reluctantly Jinny followed her through. She hated other people looking at her drawings. Couldn't bear the things they said, even when they were trying to be pleasant. Once, years ago, her mother had made her show some of her drawings to a friend, the friend had said how nice it was for Jinny to have such a happy hobby. The phrase had stuck in Jinny's mind—always there when Jinny made a mess of a drawing.

"Did you do them? The big one and all?" demanded Marlene.

"Not the mural on the wall," said Jinny. "But the rest."

"Eh-h-h-h!" Marlene let out her breath in slow admiration. "That's Shantih, ain't it? That's smashing, that is. Eh, that's proper smashing." She stood staring at a painting that Jinny had done for a competition.

"See, d'you know what I'd have done if I'd been like you?" Marlene turned her bright face on Jinny, her eyes sparkling, her mouth smiling. "Like you've drawn Shantih, well I'd have written it. Did a composition about the old horse. Before I knew, like, and it made me feel real happy. As if I was going in on a Saturday night and finding them all settled round the fire. Me dad there too, and Bill, and me mum cooking something up for us all."

And suddenly Jinny remembered Marlene's composition that her father had shown her before the Thorpes arrived.

"You see," went on Marlene, "I didn't know then about all the fuss you have with this riding business. I thought you just sat on like a chair and that were it. Eh, didn't know much then, did I? Thought me leg wouldn't matter, that I'd just sit there and gallop off. Fast, like I can't with me leg."

"But it is like that," cried Jinny. "Once you've learned."

"I were scared at first, but once I was on it were O.K. Felt like I knew the old horse, somehow. Having written about him and all."

"But you've done very well," cried Jinny. "Lots of beginners would never have gone near a horse again after the way Shantih bucked with you. You only need a bit of practice."

"Don't have time for that," stated Marlene. "Got to go back to Stopton."

99

"You don't!" raged Jinny. "Of course you don't! You can stay and I'll teach you to ride. I will. I promise. Just because Bill wants you to go back you don't need to. They can't do any more about the watch now."

Marlene shook her head. "Be proper good," she said, "but I ain't staying."

Jinny listened as Marlene's footsteps limped down the stairs.

"But it's not fair," she thought. "Why shouldn't Marlene stay? She can't spend all her life looking after Bill. If he wants to steal things, that's what he'll do. whether Marlene is there or not." Jinny wondered if she should follow Marlene down to Shantih's field and try again to persuade her to stay, but reluctantly she supposed that it wouldn't make any difference. If Bill went back to Stopton Marlene would go too.

Jinny sat down, picked up her pencil and got on with drawing Pippen.

"Happy hobby," she thought when she had finished. Her drawing might have been any plump, skewbald pony. It didn't look the least bit Pippenish. Jinny tore the sheet off her pad, screwed it into a ball and threw it furiously into the corner of the room.

"It's so unfair," she thought. "Why shouldn't Marlene stay if she wants to." But Jinny knew that if Bill left, Marlene would go too.

"I've got to make Bill stay," cried Jinny. She jumped to her feet and clattered downstairs in search of him.

Petra said no she hadn't seen him but had Jinny tried Mrs. Simpson's?

Mr. Manders and Ken were loading their kiln and were not pleased at being disturbed. They hadn't seen Bill either.

"Well, I can't tell you where he'll be," said her mother, "but I can tell you what he'll be doing. He'll be reading his comics. When we found him at the station he was sitting in a waiting room reading them. What did you want him for?"

"Just something," said Jinny.

She met Mike carrying full cans of milk from Mr. MacKenzie's.

"Seen Bill?" she asked him.

100

Mike shook his head. "What were you up to this morning?" he asked.

"Getting back from our camp," said Jinny, wondering suddenly if it should have been her turn to fetch the milk.

"I mean after that," said Mike. "While I was having to trail over the moors with that policeman and Marlene. What were you doing then?"

"Went for a ride," said Jinny, edging away from her brother. "I didn't want to stay with Mrs. Simpson and Petra."

"And," persisted Mike, "I think it's very odd the way you just happened to be buying apples when Mr. Simpson found the watch in amongst them. That's what I think."

"Don't think too hard," warned Jinny.

"Tell me," said Mike.

"Some day," said Jinny, grinning at her brother, knowing that he would leave it at that, wouldn't go prodding and prying. Some day she would tell him. Show him the gate that Shantih had jumped.

"Look for Marlene, if you want Bill," Mike suggested as he walked on to the house.

"Of course," thought Jinny and ran down to the ponies' field.

Bill was standing by the gate with a comic in his hand. Marlene was in the field feeding bits of bread to Shantih.

"Come and help me clean Shantih's tack," Jinny called to Bill.

"Naw," said Bill.

"We're going to clean Shantih's tack," Jinny called to Marlene. "We'll be in the stables."

"I'm not," said Bill.

"I want to talk to you," said Jinny, lowering her voice so that Marlene couldn't hear.

"What you at?" asked Bill.

"Come on," said Jinny and led the way back to the tack room. Bill followed her, unwillingly.

Jinny hung up Shantih's bridle from a hook, found a sponge and a bucket half full of oldish water and began to wipe down the bridle. Through the open door Jinny would be able to see Marlene approaching.

"What?" asked Bill, leaning against the saddle horse. "What?"

Jinny tossed back her hair, dragged the sponge down the leather with all her strength.

"You're not going back to Stopton tomorrow," she said. "Marlene wants to stay until your fortnight's up. She wants to learn to ride. If you go she'll go with you. She won't stay here and let you go. So you're not going."

"Am that," said Bill.

"Please," said Jinny. "For Marlene. Don't be so mean. You can easily stay for a few more days, only another week."

"Naw," said Bill and opened his comic again.

Furiously Jinny snatched it from him and threw it on the ground. Bill swung his fist at her. Jinny ducked and felt the rush of air over her head as he missed her.

"Listen," she threatened. "Listen to me. If you go back to Stopton tomorrow I'll tell the police you stole the watch."

Bill took a step back from her.

"What you talking about? What watch?"

"I saw you giving it to Marlene last night. I found it in the wall where she had hidden it and I took it back to Mrs. Simpson's shop this morning."

Bill's normal putty-coloured complexion had turned dark red.

"Marlene will be here in a second," said Jinny, "and she's not to know anything about this. Nothing. So listen, so that you know what to do. You've to tell Dad at teatime, when we're all there to hear you, that you want to stay. And there's to be no more stealing, see? Not while you're here. You've to stay with Ken. In the pottery with him. Be keen on pottery so that Marlene doesn't worry about you. See?"

Bill didn't answer.

"That's Marlene now," warned Jinny. "You know what to do. Tell them at teatime. Or I'll tell the police. And don't think I don't mean it because I do." Jinny scrubbed at Shantih's bridle.

"He didn't half eat up that bread. I don't think you feed him proper. It's hens you feed on that old corn and he ain't no hen."

"You can send her food parcels," suggested Jinny.

"Eh, O.K., I'll do that," said Marlene. "What's he been at?" she asked suspiciously, looking at Bill.

Jinny thrust a sponge into Bill's unwilling hand. "He's helping me to clean tack," she said and gave Bill Shantih's grass-encrusted bit to clean.

Marlene, planning ways in which they could posh up Shantih, helped Jinny to clean the saddle.

"Them old brushes don't get at the deep down dirt," she said. "You got to get with it. Try the Hoover on him. Or like they do with cars—a horse wash."

"Set the table for tea," said Mrs. Manders when they got into the house. "What did Sue do with all her wet clothes?"

"Took them back to their tent," said Jinny, taking knives and forks out of the drawer.

"She should have left them here," said Mrs. Manders. "You could go over and ask her if she wants to bring them up here to dry off."

"O.K.," said Jinny. "Though she didn't seem very keen on charity. I offered them all instant Dr. Barnardo's when it rained but she didn't want it."

"I won't see the fat horse again," said Marlene. "Eh, it were that podgy. What she wants to stick with that old dough ball for when she could have one like yours?"

"Bet she wouldn't change Pippen for Shantih," said Jinny.

"Like she loves him," said Marlene, grinning.

When she went to tell Ken and her father that their tea was ready, Jinny paused by Bill's side. "O.K.?" she said. "I mean it." She went on to the pottery.

There was only Ken there.

"Tea," said Jinny. "Where's Dad?"

"Bathroom," said Ken. "You managed it this morning?"

And Jinny told him about Shantih jumping the gate and how she had hidden the watch in among the apples.

"Marlene wants to stay," said Jinny. "She wants to ride Shantih. So Bill's got to stay too or she won't. If he stays, can he be with you in here? I told him that he's got to tell us at teatime that he wants to stay."

"Does he want to?"

103

"He can make clay monsters," suggested Jinny. "That's what his comics are full of—monsters from the dawn of time, monsters from the centre of the earth, deep sea monsters, space monsters—I had a read at some of them. Well, he can make them in clay. Be a bit of a relief seeing them solid rather than just reading about them and having them prowling round in your head."

"*If* he stays," said Ken, and suddenly he crashed his clenched fist down on the table, filling the air with white, clay dust. "The mess we've made of a kid like that! Where's he going to go? What's he going to do now? Back to Stopton with his monsters until he picks up some more of their trashy bits of obscene rubbish and then they'll shut him up and we'll all be able to forget about him."

"Well it's not *my* fault," said Jinny.

"You reckon?" said Ken. "Not your fault?"

"Well, it's not!" repeated Jinny indignantly. "I don't make him steal things."

"What a nasty thought," said Ken. "Tuck it away out of sign. Got nothing to do with you, has it?"

"Oh, come on for tea," said Jinny. "I don't know what you're talking about." She pushed the thought to the back of her mind that in any way she, Jinny Manders, might be responsible for Bill Thorpe.

Bill was sitting at the table having a pre-tea slice of bread and jam. Jinny gave him another hard look as she sat down but didn't risk saying anything more in case she aroused Marlene's suspicions.

If he didn't tell them that he wanted to stay would she phone the police? Jinny knew she wouldn't, but she knew that Bill couldn't be certain of this.

Jinny smiled at Petra, asking her when her music exam was, how long it would last, whether she would need to stay overnight in Inverburgh when she sat it. When Mike put down her plate of grilled tomatoes and ham pie, Jinny thanked him sweetly. This was the way someone would behave who was the sort of person who would phone up the police and tell them that Bill had stolen the watch.

Jinny stared hard at Bill, hoping he was noticing her.

They had reached the cake and second cup of tea

stage. Ken had finished. Since he never ate anything that was connected with animals, not even cheese or milk or eggs, Ken's meals, mostly of raw vegetables, fruit, wholemeal bread and brown rice had their own timing, didn't fit in with the Manders' pattern of meat and veg., chips and eggs. Quite often Ken had days of not eating—to make him aware of the gift of food, he said. He was watching Jinny now, knowing that she was up to something.

Bill took his fourth piece of cake and Mrs. Manders removed the plate.

"Need to leave proper early tomorrow?" asked Marlene. "Best not sleep, eh?"

Petra said she would set her alarm, and as she always heard it, she would wake Marlene.

"But you're not going," Jinny thought desperately and glared at Bill. She had tried kicking him under the table but had kicked Kelly instead, making the dog remove himself with wounded dignity to the far corner of the room.

"Tell them! Tell them! Go on, tell them," Jinny thought at Bill, but Bill was stuffing the last piece of cake into his mouth.

"That policeman who was with Mrs. Simpson," Jinny said, "does he live in Glenbost?"

"Police cottages at Ardtallon. There's two of them," said Mr. Manders.

"Could you phone him there?" asked Jinny.

"Oh yes," said her father. "It's really the police station."

"Is the number in the book?" asked Jinny.

"Will be," said Mr. Manders.

"Whatever do you want to know that for?" asked Petra.

"Handy," said Jinny. "Handy to know."

"What you on at?" asked Marlene suspiciously.

But Bill pushed his chair back from the table. Before he stood up he looked across at Jinny, mocking her. He knew she would never phone the police. He knew that Marlene cared more about him than learning to ride. And he knew that Jinny knew this. He wanted back to Stopton and he was going.

"Beast," thought Jinny helplessly. "Selfish, pigging beast."

105

He'd called her bluff. She wouldn't phone. There was nothing more she could do. Marlene wasn't going to get her chance to go fast like flames on Shantih. It was all hopeless.

Ken stretched out a long arm and caught hold of Bill.

"Sit down," said Ken. "No hurry." Jinny saw Ken's bony fingers biting into Bill's wrist as he forced him to sit down again.

"I was having a chat with Jinny," said Ken, and Jinny saw the red flush creep up Bill's neck and redden his ears. He shifted uneasily in his chair.

"Jinny said she'd had a word with you." Ken's green eyes had set as hard as stones. He forced Bill to look at him. There was no softness in Ken. He was contained in himself. Independent. Lived from his own centre. "Jinny said you'd something to tell us."

Everyone was looking at Ken and Bill, wondering what Ken was talking about. But no one interrupted. Not Mr. Manders, or Marlene.

"Now," said Ken, and they were all waiting for Bill to speak.

"I changed me mind," said Bill. "We ain't going to-morrow."

"Oh, grand," said Mr. Manders. "Great."

"More food," thought Mrs. Manders and hoped that Mrs. Simpson wouldn't hold the matter of the watch against her.

Marlene had sat without moving, so drawn into herself that she hardly seemed to be breathing.

"That what you really want?" she asked Bill.

"Yus," said Bill and Marlene exploded from her chair like a rocket. Stamping her lame leg, clapping her hands, she danced round the kitchen.

"Eh, ain't that right smashing?" she cried. "That's right proper smashing, that is! Jin's going to learn me to ride the old horse, ain't you? To sit on him proper so we can go galloping off, him and me, for miles and miles. Eh, I'm right pleased, Bill. I'm right proper pleased you want to stay!"

Jinny blew her nose hard but didn't feel so bad about it because her mother had suddenly found it necessary to start and collect up the tea plates.

"Come into the pottery, now," said Ken, "and I'll show you round. You can try the wheel."

Bill went with him.

"When we going to start?" Marlene demanded.

"Ride down to Sue's," suggested Mrs. Manders. "See if we can dry out anything for them."

"Want me to wipe up first?" asked Marlene.

"Don't think you'd be safe," laughed Mrs. Manders.

"It's Petra's day," said Jinny. "We'll go and find Sue."

"Take the old horse?"

"But of course," said Jinny.

"Got to start and learn how to do things, ain't I? Now that I'm going to be doing the proper riding."

CHAPTER TWELVE

"Give us the halter thing," said Marlene the next morning. "I'll do the catching bit."

"Well, take care," said Jinny, handing Shantih's halter to Marlene. "Don't rush at her."

"Eh, give over fussing. Here, how's that then?" and Marlene placed a sugar lump on the palm of her hand and tucked the halter, more or less out of sight, behind her back. "That do? Like you showed me?"

"A scoop of nuts would be easier," suggested Jinny. "Then there'd be more than one mouthful. You could put her halter on while she's got her head down munching."

"He's right fed up with all those old dried things you're always giving him. Enjoys a sugar lump he does. I've got more in me pocket." Marlene set off confidently across the field.

Jinny watched, biting her tongue to stop herself interfering, as Marlene advanced on Shantih.

"Here you are, horse," Marlene said and let Shantih lip up the sugar from her hand.

"Now for this rope thing. Let's be having your head down. End of that rope round your neck and that's me got you. Now this bit round your face."

Marlene struggled to get the halter over Shantih's ears

107

then announced triumphantly, "That's the job," and remembered to knot the halter rope. "That deserves another sugar lump, that does."

Marlene produced her bag of sugar lumps, and was just placing one correctly on her outstretched palm, when Shantih snatched it up. Without a second's hesitation, Marlene smacked Shantih hard across the muzzle. The Arab sprang back to the length of her rope, rearing away from Marlene. But Marlene hardly noticed. "You need sorting out, you do," she threatened darkly and turned to lead the prancing horse back to Jinny.

"D'you see that?" Marlene demanded when she reached the gate. "Had to give him a bat on the nose."

"I saw," said Jinny, who had been watching helplessly. "I told you not to hit her. She's scared of being hit because of the circus."

"Garn," said Marlene. "He ain't scared. He's having you on, he is. Any road I didn't hit him, just gave him a bit bat. Cheek of him snatching at me sugar lumps."

"I told you you'd be better with a scoop of nuts," said Jinny, opening the gate, but Marlene wasn't listening.

"What's next?" she demanded. "Going at him with the brush, ain't it? Keeping all them hairs lying nice and flat. Then on with the saddle and that's me set for the riding. 'Spect I'll be proper good today."

An hour later Marlene wasn't feeling so confident.

"Up, down. Up, down," chanted Jinny as she ran at Shantih's side.

"Eh, that were awful," lamented Marlene when they stopped. "I just go bump, bump, bump, bump. I ain't never going to be much good until I get the hang of this, am I?"

Reluctantly Jinny had to agree.

"Come on then," said Marlene. "Let's have another bash."

"Wait till I get my breath back," gasped Jinny. "Here's Sue," she added, spotting Pippen's skewbald shape bumbling over the fields towards them. "Perhaps Sue'll know what we're doing wrong."

"Hullo," said Sue, opening the gate without dismounting and riding into the field. "You both look like the end of the world. What's wrong?"

"I'm trying to teach Marlene to post," said Jinny. "But I'm not doing very well."

"Took me weeks," said Sue.

"And me," said Jinny, remembering the hours she had spent bumping round Major Young's paddock at the riding school in Stopton.

"Well, I ain't got weeks," said Marlene. "Come on. Give us another go."

Jinny set off round the field again, holding Shantih's bridle with one hand, the other pressing Marlene's knee against the saddle and chanting, "Up, down. Up, down," to the rhythm of Shantih's stride, while Marlene bumped around.

"Do you want a try on Pippen?" Sue offered when they got back to her. "He might be steadier."

Marlene shook her head stubbornly. "Ain't the old horse, it's me," she said.

"Try holding on to the front of the saddle," suggested Sue, "and sort of push yourself up from your hands."

Next time round Marlene tried it. She was crouched forward trying frantically to push up at the right moment when Shantih tossed her head and caught Marlene a crack on the nose.

"S'all right," Marlene assured them, staunching the flow of blood with an inadequate paper handkerchief. "I'll have it stopped in a moment. I'll not bother getting off."

Jinny insisted that Shantih needed a rest and made Marlene dismount. Sue provided her with a bigger hanky.

While Marlene mopped at her nose Jinny made a hopeless face at Sue. She didn't know how else she could teach Marlene to post except by going on making Shantih trot and hoping that eventually Marlene's bumping would change into posting.

"That's it stopped," Marlene announced, sniffing experimentally. "Let's get back to me bumping. Can't go fast, can I, until we get this up and down business right."

They spent all afternoon in the field. Sue and Jinny taking it in turns to make Shantih trot round; but by five o'clock, although Marlene could control Shantih at a walk, her bumping was showing no signs of changing into posting.

"We'll try again tomorrow," said Jinny. "Shantih's had enough for today."

Marlene didn't argue but slid obediently to the ground. "I ain't no good, am I?" she said, looking despondently from Jinny to Sue.

"Of course you are," cried Jinny. "I told you, it took us ages to learn."

"Ain't never going to learn to go fast," despaired Marlene. "Better go and see how Bill's doing," she mumbled and limped quickly away from them.

"Come for a gallop on the sands," suggested Sue when Marlene was out of sight.

Jinny hesitated, then said no, for she knew there was just a chance that Marlene might be watching from a window and would see them doing what she dreamed of doing, going fast as flames, and Jinny was beginning to think that Marlene wasn't going to manage it in the five days she had left.

Next morning Marlene brought Shantih in and groomed her before she had her breakfast.

"Give us that bit longer for bumping," she said to Jinny.

Jinny supposed it would.

"We'll try up and down the path to the shore," Jinny suggested after Marlene had tacked Shantih up. "Perhaps that will be better. You'll have longer going straight. Maybe that's what was wrong yesterday, having to go round the field."

But going along the path didn't make any difference to Marlene's bumping, it only gave Shantih more scope for sudden shies, fly canters and head tossing. By the time they had been up and down the path a few times, Jinny knew it had not been a good idea to leave the field.

"It's your fault," she said to Shantih. "Why can't you trot smoothly and give Marlene a chance?"

"Eh, don't be blaming the old horse."

"Well, it is her fault," repeated Jinny. "We'll go back to the sea once more and then I think we'd be better in the field. And you calm down," she added severely to Shantih.

"Ready? Off we go. Up, down. Up, down."

Jinny had knotted a rope to the bit ring to make lead-

ing Shantih easier and when her horse shied at absolutely
nothing at all she tugged at the rope, spoke sharply to
her, feeling as irritated with her as she had with Bramble
when he was having one of his spooky days. Normally
Shantih could do no wrong in Jinny's eyes. On the surface she was annoyed when the Arab misbehaved, rearing
or bucking her off, but underneath Jinny thought up
excuses for her wild behaviour, and loved her so much
that it didn't really matter to Jinny how wild she was.
But now Jinny was thinking about Marlene, desperately
wanting her to be able to ride before she had to go back
to Stopton, and so much depended on Shantih.

"Trot on," said Jinny crossly as Shantih flung herself
sideways in a sudden canter. "How is Marlene ever going
to learn to post if you go on mucking about all the time?"
She gave Shantih's rope another sharp tug.

"Up, down. Up, down," Jinny chanted as they trotted
back to Finmory.

Sue rode up later in the morning to find Jinny holding
a glooming Shantih while Marlene pressed a paper hanky
to her bleeding nose.

"Knew you needed me," said Sue, handing up a larger
handkerchief. "What happened?"

"Same thing," said Jinny. "And Marlene was *nearly*
posting, weren't you?"

"No," said Marlene from behind Sue's handkerchief.
"I were just at me bumping."

"Well, you might have been posting in a minute,"
snapped Jinny, "if she'd been a bit more sensible. You
idiot horse."

The Arab swung away from Jinny, her ears pinned
back, her eyes rolling, as she pawed at the ground with a
front hoof.

"Behave yourself," Jinny told her. "You think you can
do what you like, don't you?"

Shantih tossed her head, jangling the bit and narrowly
missed hitting Marlene in the face for a third time.

"If I were you," said Sue, "I'd ride her in a martingale."

"I did," said Jinny. "When I had one. Clare Burnley
lent me one. She was better behaved with it on. It stopped
her getting her head up."

111

"Why don't you buy one? Can't be very expensive."

Jinny thought of the money in her tin box, of the lunge-ing rein she was going to buy with it. She saw herself standing in the middle of the field and Shantih cantering smoothly round on the end of her new lungeing rein.

"Don't think I could afford a martingale," said Jinny.

"Pity," said Sue. "I don't think Shantih tossing her head up the way she does helps Marlene to post. And it would stop her rearing with you."

Jinny groaned inwardly. If Marlene was ever going to go fast, she would have to control Shantih by herself and it certainly wouldn't help her if Shantih reared.

"Oh well," said Jinny, reluctantly abandoning the dream of the lungeing rein. "I suppose I could sell a few of my drawings."

"Would we need to go into Inverburgh to buy it?" Sue asked.

"Yes," said Jinny brightening at the thought. It was going to be a very hot afternoon and she was beginning to be a bit fed up with running beside Shantih, chanting her 'up, down,' refrain. "Might as well go this afternoon. If I can persuade Dad to run us to the main road we could catch a bus at two o'clock and there's one back at six."

Marlene said she would stay with the old horse and Jinny said she most certainly would not.

"Got to practise," Marlene insisted. "Ain't got much time left."

"We'll practise again this evening," Jinny promised. "And then we'll have a martingale and you can hold on to the neck strap."

"What?" said Marlene. Then, giving her nose a final dab, decided that it didn't really concern her. "Just have one more bump round the field," she said and gathered up Shantih's reins.

Jinny left Sue and Marlene to take off Shantih's tack and went in search of her father.

"Could you run us in for the two o'clock bus?" she asked.

Her father said he would and Jinny climbed up to her bedroom and reluctantly chose six drawings to take to Nell Storr. They had to be good ones. Nell knew the difference.

112

Jinny put the six drawings in a brown envelope and laid it carefully on her bed. She took down the cash box, pulled off the sellotape and took out the five one pound notes that were left in it. It didn't look much for months of saving, but Jinny had had to pay for Shantih's shoeing which had used up quite a lot of the money that Nell Storr had paid for her drawings.

"A pound each for six drawings," Jinny thought. "That's six pounds and five, that's eleven pounds. That should be plenty for a martingale."

Standing in her bedroom, eleven pounds had seemed hordes of money, but somehow, as they stood looking in the window of the saddler's shop, it didn't seem quite so much.

"Pretty expensive-looking," said Sue doubtfully.

Jinny agreed, but as far as she knew it was the only saddlers in Inverburgh.

"Should we go and sell your drawings first?" Sue asked.

"Let's find out how much a martingale will cost," said Jinny. "Perhaps I'll not need to sell them."

"Come on then," nagged Marlene. "We going in then? Got to have plenty time to pick a present for me mum. She likes something real nice does me mum. Proper fussy she is."

Jinny scowled at Marlene. At that particular moment she couldn't have cared less how fussy Mrs. Thorpe was.

"Shall I lead the way, seeing you're a bit shy like," said Marlene, pushing open the saddler's door. Jinny and Sue followed after her.

"Can I assist?" asked a slim young man, emerging from behind a glass counter.

Jinny was gazing entranced at saddles and bridles, horse rugs and numnahs, black jackets and breeches, and, best of all, hanging in a corner, a bunch of lungeing reins.

"We want to buy a what-do-you-call-it," said Marlene. "One of them things to stop me bumping."

The young man raised elegant eyebrows.

"We want to know how much a standing martingale would cost," said Jinny quickly.

"Pony size?"

"Arab size," said Jinny.

113

The assistant brought a standing martingale and laid it on the glass counter.

"Six pounds fifty," he said.

"Eh!" exclaimed Marlene. "For a bit belt!"

"We'll come back later," said Jinny.

"Certainly, Madam," said the assistant, putting away the martingale.

"Nell Storr's," said Jinny when they were out of the shop.

"Best be quick," said Marlene. "I've got to pick me mum's pressie."

But Nell Storr wasn't in her craft shop. She was away for a week. The girl behind the counter offered to keep Jinny's drawings until Nell came back but said that only Nell herself could pay Jinny for them, so Jinny said that was no good and kept her drawings.

Jinny stared gloomily across the road. Now that she couldn't afford to buy it a martingale seemed the most important thing in the world; the only thing that could ever teach Marlene to post.

"If we'd known I could have lent you the money," said Sue.

"Well, we didn't know, did we?" snapped Jinny.

"It don't matter," said Marlene. "Bloomin' well too much money. I'll just look for something for me mum and then we'll get back to me trotting."

"How about something from Nell's?" suggested Jinny.

Marlene regarded the pottery, glass, wood carvings and woven goods that filled the craft shop window.

"Naw," she said disdainfully. "Me mum likes pretty things, not that junk."

An hour and six ice creams later, Marlene found a pawn shop.

"Eh, we'll get something here," she cried. "People have to pop right pretty things sometimes."

The dirty window was filled with old clothes, watches, vases, jewellery, ornaments and all the other belongings that people had brought to the pawn shop, borrowed money on and never bothered to buy back.

"That's proper pretty," said Marlene, pointing to a small china posy of flowers. "She'd fancy that."

Jinny and Sue followed Marlene into the pawn shop.

Jinny looked round curiously at the clutter of abandoned possessions.

"It's all rubbish," said Sue.

Jinny nodded but she supposed that all the things her family owned would look much the same if you brought them here.

Marlene bought her posy bowl from a toothless young woman.

"Right bargain for fifty pence," she said, carrying it proudly out of the shop.

"It's a bit dirty," said Sue.

"Give it a right scrub up and it'll be real nice. Bet you'd have paid five pounds for it in one of your fancy shops. Saw one of those things we were going to buy. Be cheaper in there."

"What things?" said Jinny. "A martingale? In there?"

"Don't believe you," said Sue flatly. "You wouldn't know what a martingale looked like."

"Just seen one, ain't I? Come back in and I'll show you."

"Let's see that leather belt thing," Marlene said, pointing it out to the woman in the pawn shop.

"Would it be this you're meaning?" the woman said and laid a standing martingale on the counter.

"Wherever did that come from?" Jinny demanded in amazement.

"Came with a job lot from a sale," said the woman. "Lot of old junk out of the stables. Had to take it to get a chest our Jim had his eye on."

"It's not really a martingale," said Sue critically. "Only a bit of one. Someone's made up the neck strap from two stirrup leathers."

"Oh, but it would do," gasped Jinny. "It would be fine. How much is it?"

"One pound and fifty pence," said the woman. "Beautiful leather, it is."

Jinny still hadn't recovered from her surprise by the time she was standing in the stable fitting the martingale round Shantih's neck. She had cleaned it thoroughly and it seemed perfectly good. It was, thought Jinny, a bargain.

"Eh, this is it, ain't it?" said Marlene, as Jinny led

115

Shantih down to the field. "I'll be able to do the up and down now, won't it?"

"At least she'll not be able to bash you on the nose," said Jinny, tightening Shantih's girth and holding her while Marlene mounted. "Walk her to the hedge and back by yourself and then we'll trot."

Jinny watched as Marlene rode Shantih away from her. She sat very straight in the saddle, Jinny's hard hat firmly on her head, her heels pressed down, her elbows tucked in. Marlene was in charge of Shantih. She wasn't going to let any old horse boss her.

When they reached the hedge and Marlene turned back to Jinny, Shantih broke into a jog. Instantly, Marlene had checked her and brought her back to a walk.

"Grab hold," said Marlene to Jinny, "and off we go."

But by the time they were half way round the field both girls knew that the martingale wasn't going to work a miracle with Marlene's posting. Clutching the neck strap, she continued to bump.

As they walked back to Finmory through the summer dusk Marlene said, "It's me leg, ain't it? I ain't ever going to be able to do anything but bump."

"Don't be daft," said Jinny loudly, because she had been thinking the same thing herself. "Of course you'll be able to post. It takes time to learn, that's all. Of course you'll be able to do it."

"Some hopes," said Marlene.

"And you're doing really well controlling her and riding her."

"Riding?" exclaimed Marlene in disgust. "You can't ride when all the old horse is doing is crawling round. I don't call that riding, I don't."

They weren't any more successful the next morning, although both Sue and Jinny had spent all morning making Shantih trot round the field. Marlene went on bumping.

"While we're getting our breath back," said Sue, "try standing up in your stirrups."

Marlene did so.

"Now sit down and stand up. Go on, do it several times."

"Now," instructed Sue, "don't sit down in between,

hardly touch your seat on to the saddle and stand up again quickly."

Marlene tried but each time she sat down with a flop and had to reorganise herself into standing up.

"Don't *sit* down," said Jinny. "That's why you get bumped."

"Can't help it," said Marlene. "I ain't trying to get bumped am I?"

Ken appeared at the field gate.

"Eh," cried Marlene, all her attention riveted on Ken, "he ain't got our Bill with him." She swung Shantih round and urged her to the gate.

"Where's our Bill?" Marlene shouted as Shantih trotted forward.

"Make her walk," yelled Jinny as Marlene bumped precariously from side to side.

And then, to Jinny's and Sue's delight, Marlene was posting. She went up too far and came down with a flop but she was most definitely and decidedly posting.

"She's done it," cried Sue.

"Look at me," Marlene yelled. "I'm trotting proper. I can do it!"

Sue on Pippen led the way round the field and Marlene trotted behind her, posting most of the way. She returned to the gate, her face glowing scarlet with effort and success.

"Couldn't do it before," Marlene told Ken. "Right down in the dumps I was. Thought it were me leg mucking things up. Here, I'll do it again. You watch me."

Marlene and Sue trotted round again. This time Marlene posted all the way.

"How were that?" she demanded triumphantly. "I'm doing proper good now, ain't I?"

"Nearly as good as Bill and his pots," said Ken. "Come into the pottery after lunch and he'll give you a demo."

Marlene clapped her hand to her mouth.

"He went right out of me head with all that posting," she admitted.

Sue stayed for lunch and afterwards they went into the pottery.

"Bit squint, that one," said Marlene, looking critically at Bill's pots.

"Ain't easy," said Bill. "Watch this." He sat down at

117

the wheel and began to shape a pot out of a lump of wet clay.

"How's that?" he asked when he had finished.

"Smashing," said Jinny. "You've learned jolly quickly."

"Our Bill was looking right pleased, did you notice?" Marlene asked as they went back to the field.

Jinny said she had.

"You sit there and watch us," Marlene said as she mounted Shantih. "Sue and me'll have a bit trot round."

Jinny sat on the gate and watched as Marlene trotted round the field behind Sue. There was no doubt about it, Marlene had learned to post.

"Shall we have another go after tea?" suggested Marlene when Sue said it was five o'clock and she would have to go.

"No," said Jinny. "Shantih's had enough for one day."

"Tomorrow then," said Marlene, dismounting.

Jinny took Shantih's reins, rubbed her hand down her horse's neck, straightening her mane," said, "Yes. Tomorrow." Then she took Shantih into the stable while Marlene went to see how Bill's potting was getting on.

"You're being very well behaved," Jinny said to Shantih as she watched the Arab eating a small feed of oats and nuts. It might be the martingale that was stopping Shantih rearing, but in the whole afternoon of walking and trotting about the field Shantih had only bucked once.

"Expect you like having Pippen for company," said Jinny, but she knew that it couldn't only be that. Shantih had often had the Highland ponies with her when Jinny had been trying to school her before. Reluctantly Jinny had to admit to herself that it must be something to do with Marlene. It wasn't that Marlene knew anything at all about how to treat horses, just that when her mind was set on a thing there was no room in it for anything else. When Shantih had tried to buck, Marlene had slapped her hard on the shoulder and told Shantih to stop his old nonsense, that if he started that mucking about she'd be bumping again. Shantih had given another protesting hitch of her quarters and trotted on.

They all spent the next afternoon on the shore. Mr. and Mrs. Manders, Mike and Petra, Ken and Bill, brought down a picnic. Sue's parents joined them. Jinny spent her

118

time keeping an eye on Marlene and Shantih, watching anxiously as Marlene rode Shantih about. Tomorrow was Friday and then Saturday, when Marlene and Bill would go home to Stopton. Jinny didn't want anything to happen to spoil Marlene's confidence before that.

The afterglow of sunset turned sky, sea and wet sands into a glowing sapphire. We must be breathing blue air, Jinny thought. Sue and Marlene were walking the horses at the water's edge and the spray from their horses' hooves glittered ice blue, diamond, aquamarine. They were held in a jewelled paperweight of sky and sea.

"Home," said Mrs. Manders, beginning to gather up the remains of the picnic, and arranging with the Hortons to come up for supper on Saturday evening.

"Marlene will be in Stopton then," Jinny thought. "Everything will be the same for us, but not for her."

Mr. and Mrs. Horton began to walk back to their tent. Jinny's family, Ken and Bill, wandered raggedly back to Finmory.

"Don't be long," Mrs. Horton called to Sue.

"Coming now," replied Sue and turned Pippen to follow her parents. Shantih went with Pippen. Jinny ran over the sands towards them, took Shantih's bridle to turn her back to Finmory.

"Eh, let's go with them," pleaded Marlene. "Just along a bit and then I can have a last trot back."

"O.K.," said Jinny and walked between the two horses. She felt soaked through with the day's sunlight, warm and contented. She glanced at Marlene sitting very correctly on Shantih and thought that tomorrow Marlene could have a canter. If Sue rode with her, Shantih would behave, would stop when Pippen stopped. Jinny thought Marlene would manage.

Sue rode off to her tent and Marlene turned Shantih round and began to trot back. Jinny ran beside them.

"Got the knack of that posting now, ain't I?" Marlene asked as they walked up the path to Finmory.

Jinny agreed that she most certainly had.

"Reckon I'm good enough now, ain't I?" demanded Marlene.

There was a tense, strained quality in her voice that made Jinny look up at her.

119

"Good enough for what?" asked Jinny.

"You know," said Marlene. "To go fast."

"Yes," said Jinny. "You can have a canter with Sue tomorrow. I was thinking about it. There's a good canter on the moors. We can go up there tomorrow. I'll wait at the end and you and Sue can gallop up to me. Shantih's bound to stop. She knows that bit. She'll stop when she reaches me."

"Eh no!" exclaimed Marlene. "I don't want you lot there. Just me and the old horse, that's what I mean."

"But you can't," said Jinny. "You couldn't manage Shantih by yourself."

"I could that. We get on right good. I don't put up with none of that nonsense you have."

"Yes, but . . ." began Jinny, then changed what she had been going to say into, "We'll see tomorrow."

She didn't think she could possibly explain to Marlene the difference between riding Shantih by herself and riding Shantih with herself and Sue looking after her.

"Really Marlene knows nothing about controlling horses. Most of the time she doesn't even notice what Shantih's doing," Jinny thought.

"That's fixed up about me riding," Marlene said, before she went to bed. "I'll take him down to the sands and have a bit ride on him tomorrow, by myself. That's it, ain't it?" and she was through the door before Jinny had time to protest.

"Could she manage Shantih by herself?" asked Mike doubtfully.

"Of course not," said Jinny. " 'Course she couldn't. She's just talking nonsense. Of course I shan't let her gallop Shantih by herself."

CHAPTER THIRTEEN

In her dream, Jinny was running through Stopton streets, chasing Marlene and Shantih. The faster Jinny ran, the faster Marlene galloped Shantih away from her. "Stop!" Jinny screamed. "Stop! She's mine!" But Marlene only laughed and rode faster than ever between the roaring traffic. "Stop!" screamed Jinny again and woke herself back into her own bed at Finmory.

She lay, the dream still vivid in her mind. It was daylight, early morning blue. Jinny got up and looked out of the window to make sure that Shantih was still in her field.

The Arab was grazing peacefully by the far hedge. Being herself in the field, untroubled by humans. Perhaps Ken was right, Jinny thought, when he said that horses should be left alone to be horses; that they didn't need humans to ride them.

Shantih flicked her tail, lifted each foot in slow, deliberate steps as she grazed along the hedgerow. Jinny hesitated, unwilling to break into the secret horse world in which Shantih moved. Not calling her name, not yet, but knowing that in a minute or two she would, just for the joy of seeing Shantih look up and know her.

But before Jinny had time to open the window and call down to her horse, something startled Shantih. She jerked her head up, ears pricked, neck arched. From her window, Jinny couldn't see anything that might have disturbed her. She thought that it might be Ken and Kelly out for an early morning walk, or Mr. MacKenzie taking a short cut down to his fields by the sea.

Then Jinny saw who it was. Marlene was standing at the field gate. She had Jinny's hard hat on her head, Shantih's halter in one hand and a sugar lump on the other.

"Well," thought Jinny, "of all the cheek. She's going to ride my horse. Good job I saw her."

Jinny lifted her hand to open the window, to shout at Marlene and tell her to leave Shantih alone; but somehow she couldn't do it. She watched as Marlene limped across the field, saw Shantih take a few strides towards her, then wait. Marlene fumbled with sugar lumps and halter and although Jinny couldn't hear her she could see her mouth moving as she talked to the horse.

Confidently, Marlene led Shantih back to the gate, manœuvred her through it and closed it behind them. Shantih pranced at the end of her halter rope, fretting to reach the stable, but Marlene paid no attention to her

121

impatience. She checked that the gate was shut and then led Shantih out of sight.

"I'll go down to the stables," Jinny thought, scrambling into her clothes. "Stop her there. Go with her if she wants to ride."

Jinny ran lightly through the garden and down to the stables. She hesitated at the stable doorway. Inside she could hear the sounds of Marlene grooming Shantih.

"Come on, now. Stand still when I'm brushing you. Got to get you right shiny. Can't have you looking a mess. Not when we're going galloping. Got to be all sparkling, you have."

"Go in and stop her," Jinny told herself. "You know she can't manage Shantih. She could fall, jam her foot in a stirrup, be dragged. If Shantih got a fright, Marlene wouldn't know what to do. Anything, anything could happen to them. She doesn't mean to go back to the field."

Jinny knew quite certainly where Marlene meant to ride. She was going to take Shantih down to the shore and gallop her over the sands.

"She won't be able to control her," Jinny thought. "Won't be able to stop her." For Jinny knew how Shantih could become so excited that unless you stopped her she would go plunging over the boulders that made a barrier between the fields and the sand. To cross them safely you had to bring your horse to a slow walk. Even to trot through them was dangerous.

"Go on in and stop her," Jinny told herself.

But Jinny couldn't; couldn't make herself march into the stable and spoil everything for Marlene.

Jinny knew that it was what she would have wanted to do if she had been Marlene. If she had had to leave Shantih tomorrow and go back to Stopton, Jinny would have wanted to gallop by herself over the sands of Finmory Bay; to be alone with Shantih, sharing the ecstasy of galloping together—the freedom, the joy. To hoard the moments in her mind so that she would always have them there, to bring them out, to re-live them during the black times.

"Eh, you look proper nice," Marlene told Shantih. "Now for your bridle and the martingale thing. Watch

122

that big tongue of yours, I ain't made for licking. You put this in your mouth, that'll sort you out."

But if Marlene fell off . . . If Shantih hurt herself . . . Jinny *had* to stop her, couldn't take the risk of letting Marlene harm Shantih.

Jinny took a step towards the stable door. She had to go in, had to stop her. "Be sensible. Be responsible," she told herself. "You know best."

Marlene's white, pinched face swam into the front of Jinny's mind, as she had seen it reflected in the shop mirror, as she had looked when she had realised that Jinny knew the truth about Bill.

And Jinny knew that she couldn't do it. She couldn't bear to stop Marlene, couldn't bear to go into the stable and spoil it all.

"But Shantih . . ." thought Jinny, yet it made no difference.

"Now your saddle," said Marlene. "And heave ho the old belly band."

Jinny bit hard on the knuckles of her clenched fist, flung herself away from the stables, left Shantih to Marlene, and went running as fast as she could through the garden and up the hillside behind Finmory.

Not looking back, Jinny climbed steadily until she was sure that she was high enough up to be able to see the sands and the path leading down to the bay. Then she turned, crouched down by a boulder and picked out the grey stone stable buildings.

Marlene was leading Shantih into the yard. They were tiny, puppet figures—a girl with a lame leg and a chestnut Arab, her mane and tail blown out by the breeze, lifting her white legs impatiently high as she danced out of the dark stable doorway into the sunlit yard.

Three times Marlene tried to scramble up into the saddle and three times Shantih sprang away from her.

"Don't hold the reins so tight," Jinny thought. She itched to be there in the yard, to put out her hand and hold Shantih still for Marlene. "Don't dig your toe into her side."

Then, at her fourth attempt, Marlene made it, and was sitting in the saddle, while Shantih plunged forward and trotted down the path to the sea.

123

A kind of stillness came over Jinny as she sat, remote and high, crouching by the boulders, her eyes held to the figures of the girl and the horse. No matter what happened Jinny couldn't have taken her eyes away from them. If Shantih went mad, raced, runaway crazy over the sands, Jinny had to watch it happening. By turning away from the stable doorway, she had said, "Yes." Had allowed this to happen and now she could only watch. Had to watch.

Shantih went trotting out, her neck arched, the sea breeze winnowing her mane, her white hooves flashing over the short grass. Marlene sat posting deligently, sitting very upright, looking straight ahead. When they reached the ridge of boulders, Marlene steadied Shantih to a walk and she picked her way through them, clipping and stumbling in her haste to reach the shore.

Then they were on the sands. Shantih gave a half rear, leapt forward and raced away. She stretched her neck low, thundered the beat of her hooves against the glimmering drum skin of the wet sands. The track of her hoof prints flared out behind her.

For a minute Marlene lost her balance, was thrown forward over Shantih's withers but somehow, her hands grabbing at the neck strap, her knees held against the knee rolls, her feet wedged crookedly in the stirrups, she stayed in the saddle.

And although Marlene was still crouched over Shantih's neck Jinny knew that she wasn't going to come off. She had found her balance against the speed of the horse. Her hands low on Shantih's neck, her knees pressed into the knee rolls, Marlene was looking straight ahead as Shantih stormed the white brilliance of sea dazzle and gleaming sands. They went like flames, the flickering, burning, chestnut mare and the brightness of her rider laughing aloud into the silence of the morning. No longer lame.

As the Arab flew over the beach towards the first black shards of rock at the far side of the bay, Marlene was completely out of control. Tight as a limpet she clung on to the horse's back as they swerved between the rocks.

When they reached the cliffs and Shantih could gallop no further, she skidded to a violent halt, flung up her head

124

and in a split second had plunged round and was galloping back across the sands to Finmory. Marlene lost a stirrup, slipped dangerously to one side but somehow managed to stop herself falling off. In one hand she clutched reins, martingale and a lump of mane, while her other hand was clenched on to the pommel of the saddle. She was crouched over Shantih's withers but her eyes were bright with excitement and her face open and laughing with sheer delight.

Yet still Jinny didn't move. She sat hardly breathing, her long hair shielding her expressionless face as she watched this stranger riding her horse.

Before they reached the barricade of smooth pebbles Shantih broke into a ragged trot. She clattered her way through the stones at a walk and Marlene was able to push herself upright in the saddle. She found her stirrup and fumbled to reorganise the lassoos of reins, so that by the time they reached the path Marlene was in control again.

Alert and gay, Shantih trotted back to Finmory. Marlene posted. She had done what she had set out to do. Not once did Marlene look back at the sea.

Jinny saw Marlene reach the stable yard, drop down from Shantih and take her back out of the sun through the dark doorway.

Jinny had no words for it but she knew that something had changed. By her own choice she had let Marlene ride Shantih, had shared with this girl, whom she hadn't liked much, her most secret possession—what it was like to gallop alone on Shantih. The part of Jinny that clutched tight and hard on to anything that belonged to her had released its hold, just a little bit. She jumped up from the hillside, stretching her cramped legs as she went leaping down the hill. Her hair blew out behind her, her feet found their own way. Her arms outstretched to keep her balance, Jinny half ran, half flew down to Shantih and Marlene.

By the time Jinny reached the stable Marlene had taken Shantih's tack off and was leading her out to her field.

"You just up?" she asked Jinny.

"More or less," said Jinny.

"Eh, we'd a right proper ride. It were real great it were.

Me and the old horse, just us two on the beach. And whee! We didn't half gallop."

"Good," said Jinny. "I'm glad." And she meant it.

Later in the day when Jinny asked Marlene if she wanted to ride Shantih in the field, Marlene shook her head.

"Ain't got time," she said. "Got me packing to do."

"Don't be daft," said Jinny. "All you've got is that tartan shopper and that's been packed all the time you've been here."

Marlene grinned. "Got to be ready," she said.

"Don't you want another ride?"

"Naw," said Marlene. "I can ride now, don't need no more learning, do I? I got me own things to see to."

In the afternoon Marlene checked to see that Bill was still working in the pottery, then went off by herself. Jinny didn't see her again until teatime.

"Where were you?" Jinny asked her. "I couldn't find you anywhere. Sue's mother was teaching me how to play the guitar but there's not much hope. I can't hear the difference in the notes. What were you doing?"

"Minding me own business," said Marlene. "But I'll show you when I've got it fixed up."

The evening was overlapping, evanescent shades of grey, the sea a distant snail trail glimmer, the last of the day drained out of the sky. Jinny was sprawled in an armchair, half reading a book, half holding back the thought that first thing tomorrow Bill and Marlene would be going back to Stopton.

"Psst!" said Marlene, appearing at the side of Jinny's chair. "Come on out with me. I've got something to show you."

"But it's nearly dark," said Jinny. "Can't you show me here?"

"Got me mum's torch," said Marlene. "Come on."

Jinny followed her out to the stables.

"Now," said Marlene, opening up the plastic carrier she had been holding. "Listen right careful so you understand." She emptied twenty or thirty small knobbly parcels on to the tack room table.

"What on earth are they?" demanded Jinny.

126

"Sugar lumps, of course," said Marlene. "For the old horse. To say thank you, like. He can't half gallop, he can't. Eh . . ." Marlene's black eyes sparkled in the torchlight as the thrill of her morning's gallop filled her memory. "It were right proper good. Now you listen careful. I've done them up for him. One for each week. Don't want him having rotten teeth."

"Is that where you were this afternoon?" Jinny asked. "Buying these?"

"At Mrs. Simpson's. She gave me a right sinker, she did."

Marlene arranged the bags in rows. "Last him for ages, them will. Come on and we'll give him one lot now."

The torch turned the grey light into darkness so Marlene switched it off, and they walked together to where Shantih waited by the gate.

"That's your lot," Marlene said when Shantih had crunched her way through the last sugar lump. "Bet you don't meet anyone as soft as me for all the rest of your life. This has been your lucky summer, this has."

Jinny heard the catch in Marlene's voice, heard her swallow hard.

"You'll come back," stated Jinny.

"No chance," said Marlene.

She laid her hand with its bitten nails against Shantih's flat-boned cheek, straightened the silky fineness of Shantih's forelock, and held out her hand letting Shantih lip at her palm.

"You ain't a bad old horse," she said, and with a last rub at Shantih's velvet muzzle, Marlene left her and walked back to Finmory.

"But of course you'll come back," insisted Jinny.

"I'm only here with Bill. We won't neither of us be back."

"You'll come back even if Bill doesn't want to. We want *you* to come back. Dad will write to your parents. Next Easter or next summer, you'll see."

But there was a hollowness about Jinny's assurances. They both knew it couldn't be certain. Marlene would go back to Stopton tomorrow and probably they would never see each other again.

They stopped outside the back door. Marlene looked

round the darkening garden and up to the high reaches of the moor.

"You ain't half spoilt, you ain't. Having all this."

"I know," said Jinny.

"It's not the horse, or living here. I'd be right bored here after a bit. Like me fish and chips, I do. It's your family. Your Mike, he ain't never going to go pinching stuff. And your Dad, he doesn't go off much does he?"

"No," said Jinny, and she struggled to find words to tell Marlene that she knew how spoilt she was; knew she had far too much, but just now there was nothing she could do about it. She had to go on being Jinny Manders.

Suddenly Jinny grabbed Marlene's hand.

"Come on," she said, hurrying her indoors and up to her room.

For a second Jinny stood staring at her competition painting, trying to fix it forever in her mind's eye. It was only about six months since Jinny had painted it but already Shantih had changed. When Jinny had drawn her for the painting she had been wild and free, roaming over the moors, part of the freedom. Now she shared her life with humans. Answered to her name. Knew Jinny.

Very carefully Jinny unpinned the picture. She rolled it up quickly, found the cardboard tube in which the magazine had returned it to her, and fitted her painting into it.

"It's your share in Shantih," said Jinny, holding the painting out to Marlene. "Your share in Finmory for always."

"That's your good painting," said Marlene. "I can't take that. It ain't right."

"Please," said Jinny desperately. "Please. It's the best I've got."

Marlene hesitated, then took it from Jinny. "Thanks," she said. "I'll keep it proper careful. Always."

Next morning Mr. Manders drove Bill, Marlene, Ken and Jinny into Inverburgh in time for the Stopton train. In the station buffet they made stiff polite noises at each other, Mr. Manders assuring the Thorpes that they must come back to Finmory whenever they wanted to. Any time during the school holidays, they had only to phone him and he'd meet them at Inverburgh. In the draughty,

128

echoing, morning station, waiting for the hands of the station clock to jerk round to the figures that would let Mr. Manders say, "Better be getting on to the platform," it sounded to Jinny more unlikely than ever that Marlene would come back to Finmory.

"Back to the la-di-dahs," said Marlene, mocking them. She was clutching her tartan shopper, thinking about Stopton. "Been proper posh staying with you lot."

Marlene handed the ticket collector the two tickets she had been holding in her hand since they left Finmory. She went first through the barrier.

Bill nudged Jinny. "Here," he said. "I left something for you with Ken." He followed his sister on to the platform.

"I am not crying," said Jinny as they drove back to Finmory because both Ken and her father couldn't possibly not have noticed that she was. She had reached the red-eyed, gulping stage.

"Bill made a mug for you," said Ken.

"He told me," said Jinny.

"He was really keen on the pottery once he got going," said Mr. Manders.

"Gave him the address of a mate of mine who has a pottery in Stopton," said Ken. "I'll phone him up in a week or so and if Bill hasn't got in touch with him, he'll look Bill up. See he gets going on with it."

"A chance for him?" said Mr. Manders hopefully.

"A chance," said Ken.

"But Marlene," said Jinny. "Why should she have to go back to Stopton?"

"Because she wants to," said Ken. "Her whole life is there. All the people she loves. She's O.K., is Marlene."

"Tough as old boots," smiled Mr. Manders.

But Jinny didn't think she was, not underneath. She remembered something she had heard Ken say once—the skin beneath the skull.

Mrs. Manders was baking when they got back to Finmory.

"Run over to the farm and see if Mrs. MacKenzie can give you some eggs," she said to Jinny, and without even bothering to protest that Mike and Petra could have gone, Jinny took the money and went.

She caught Shantih, put her bridle on, and rode bare-back along the track to the farm. It was odd to be riding without Marlene. She felt cold and empty inside, strangely lost without Marlene's company.

Why had Marlene had to go back to Stopton? Why couldn't she have stayed at Finmory, shared Jinny's family? Why couldn't it be like that? thought Jinny bitterly.

But she knew it would have been no use. Ken had been right. The people Marlene loved were all in Stopton and Marlene had to be with them.

Round a bend in the track came Mr. MacKenzie, driving his tractor. Jinny felt Shantih stiffen, and drop behind her bit as the tractor snorted and clattered towards them.

"Get on old horse! None of that nonsense," Jinny said, and she slapped Shantih hard on the shoulder.

"You're not to go jumping my gates," Mr. MacKenzie shouted at her. "Now I'm warning you, lass, I'll not be having it."

"It was an emergency," Jinny shouted back.

"Well, don't be having another one."

"I won't," said Jinny and rode on.

Then suddenly she realised that Shantih had passed the tractor without bucking or rearing. Her mouth spread into a wide grin, for that was exactly how Marlene would have ridden past the tractor, her mind fixed on where she was going, looking straight ahead.

"Eh," praised Jinny, clapping Shantih's neck, "that were proper good, that were."

"I'll write and tell Marlene," Jinny thought. "Tell her that she's taught me to ride." And Jinny flicked her hair back behind her ears, deciding to go and find Sue after she had got the eggs.

"Forward the eggs," thought Jinny, and laughed. There were weeks and weeks of holiday still ahead of her and Sue to ride with.

"Be right proper good," she said aloud. "Be right proper good, eh, old horse?" and Jinny let Shantih canter on through the bright morning.

Night of the Red Horse

First published in a single volume in paperback
in 1978 in Armada

CHAPTER ONE

"Again," said Jinny Manders. "I'm going round again."

Shantih, the chestnut Arab Jinny was riding, pranced impatiently, threatening to buck—her white stockings glinting in the grey evening, her red-gold coat bright. A wind gusted in from the sea, blowing back Jinny's long, red hair and fanning out her horse's mane and tail.

"Isn't it getting rather late?" said Sue Horton. "Mum will be wondering what's happened to me."

She glanced over her shoulder to where the Horton's yellow tent perched on the grass above Finmory Bay. Sue and her parents were spending their summer holidays camping at Finmory. At the last minute they had managed to borrow a trailer and bring Pippen, Sue's skewbald pony, on holiday with them. Now he stood, four-square and solid, his feet planted firmly on the ground and an expression of mild disapproval at the Arab's behaviour on his brown and white face. His rider was as square and sturdy as her pony. She was twelve years old, the same age as Jinny, with short brown hair, hazel eyes and an open expression.

"You've jumped her round four times already," said Sue. "You'll only sicken her."

"Not over these silly little jumps," stated Jinny, and before Sue could produce any more of her commonsense arguments Jinny had eased her hold on Shantih's reins, tightened her legs against her horse's sides and they were away, galloping at the first jump.

Shantih thundered up to the first pole. Yards in front of it she launched herself into the air and sailed over it in a wide, flowing arc. Jinny, sitting tight in the saddle, moved with her horse. A grin of sheer delight spread over her face as Shantih, gathering speed, flew on down the field, over the jump made from one of Mr. MacKenzie's cast-out sheep pens and over the third jump of two straw bales.

Turning to come back up the field, Shantih was going faster than ever. Her speed whipped tears from Jinny's eyes, made her laugh aloud. She could have gone on galloping and jumping Shantih forever. It was more exciting than anything she had ever known in all her life.

The last of the five jumps was made of wooden fish boxes piled precariously on top of each other. Shantih was galloping too fast to be able to time her take-off and Jinny knew nothing about such things. She only knew that, most of the time, all she needed to do was to sit on Shantih and her horse would jump anything. But this time Shantih took off too soon. Her front feet sent the boxes flying, and in a sudden panic Shantih was bolting round the field, her head low, her body tight and her hooves beating out a frenzied tattoo of fear.

It took Jinny four circles of the field before she was in control again.

"Well, surely that's enough," said Sue, as Jinny brought Shantih from a trot to a walk and rode her back to Pippen. "I told you she had had enough."

"Enough! Shantih would go on jumping all night. It's these silly jumps. If we had proper ones . . ."

"If that last jump had been fixed she would have fallen. Coming at it at that speed! Just stupid. You let her go too fast."

"I like her fast," said Jinny irritably.

Although Sue arriving with Pippen and lending her a saddle had been the best thing that could possibly have happened in Jinny's summer holidays, she couldn't help feeling that at times Sue was depressingly right.

"Almost as bad as Petra," Jinny thought. "As if an elder sister isn't enough." She sighed gustily.

"I'm going in anyway," decided Sue.

Reluctantly, Jinny followed her out of the field.

"Tomorrow," said Jinny, "we'll build some proper jumps."

"O.K.," said Sue, grinning, and instantly Jinny was sorry that she had even thought that Sue was in the least like Petra.

"See you tomorrow about ten," Jinny called back, as Sue took Pippen to their tent to give him a feed before she turned him out for the night in Mr. Mackenzie's field.

Jinny rode Shantih back across the fields to Finmory. The Arab walked out with her long-reaching stride. She was still excited after her gallop. Her neck was arched, her ears alert and her eyes wide to catch the least movement on the moorland that stretched about her, grey and barren in the late summer evening.

Lights shone from the windows of Finmory House, glowing warm and welcoming.

"Home," thought Jinny, and shivered with pleasure to think that home wasn't a flat in the city as it had been a year ago when the Manders family had lived in Stopton. Now, home was Finmory House, a grey stone house in the north of Scotland, standing between mountains and sea and surrounded by heather-clad moors. The only other house that Jinny could see was Mr. Mackenzie's farm, and beyond that it was miles to Glenbost village. Jinny loved it all— the space, the freedom and the silence.

In Stopton, Mr. Manders had been a probation officer. Now he was a potter, selling his pots to Nell Storr's craft shop in Inverburgh, and the author of a book about the slums of Stopton and the lives of the people there with whom he had worked. Almost an author, thought Jinny more truthfully. Her father had written the book and one publisher had turned it down but he had sent it to another. So far he had not heard whether they wanted to publish it or not.

Petra, Jinny's elder sister, was fifteen. Riding home, Jinny knew exactly what Petra would be doing. She would be playing the piano, practising the pieces for her music examination. Jinny could picture her, sitting very straight on the piano stool, wearing neat, smart clothes, for everything that Petra wore became neat and smart the second she put it on. She would be playing very precisely, her face concentrating on getting each and every note exactly right —as each and every hair of Petra's dark, short curls was always exactly right.

"We're not sisters," thought Jinny. "I'm a changeling. Petra couldn't possibly be my sister. At least I won't have to go to the same school as her, where they would always be telling me how wonderful Petra is."

Until now, Jinny had gone to the village school in Glenbost, riding there with Mike, her ten-year-old brother, on Punch and Bramble, two Highland ponies borrowed in the off season from Miss Tuke's trekking centre, and Petra had been a weekly boarder at Duninver Grammar School. When they all returned to school in September, Petra would go back to Duninver, but Jinny was to travel each day by school bus to the new comprehensive school at Inverburgh. It had been like a miracle when Jinny had heard that they were building a new school and that she would be able to travel there each day. She could not possibly have left Shantih at Finmory; could not possibly have gone to stay at the Duninver school hostel.

"I just wouldn't have gone and that would have been that." Jinny laid her hand on Shantih's warm, strong neck. "I couldn't have left you alone all week, could I?"

Shantih flickered her ears at the sound of Jinny's voice and flurried her nostrils in reply to the question.

Warm and sweet and sudden, love for Shantih filled Jinny. Once the Arab had been 'Yasmin the Killer Horse', beaten into a fury in a circus. Jinny had rescued her, made Shantih her own, tamed and gentled her.

"And now you can jump," said Jinny, "I must go on schooling you."

Jinny knew that Sue didn't consider what she had been doing on Shantih tonight as schooling, but then Sue only had Pippen. She didn't know what it was like to jump Shantih, to feel as if you had wings, so that all you wanted to do was to go on jumping, faster and higher, over and over again.

Jinny rode up to the stables at Finmory House. Once they had been broken-down, deserted outhouses, but now they were a feed house, tack room, two stalls that Punch and Bramble used, and a loose box for Shantih.

Mike was waiting for her.

"Where have you been?" he asked, opening the loose box door for Jinny. "You've been ages. They've been waiting for you since before tea."

Mike had short curly hair like Petra's and brown eyes. Jinny liked her brother. Even if he hadn't been related to her, Jinny thought, she would have wanted to know him. He was easy to be witl, not moody, always the same.

"Who?" Jinny asked, taking off Shantih's tack.

"Two people," said Mike. "Especially to see you. So buck up."

"Who?" said Jinny again, but Mike had gone. "Well,

whoever they are they'll have to wait until I've finished with Shantih," she thought.

Jinny tipped oats and nuts into the trough and stood watching Shantih eating her feed. When the horse had chased the last elusive grain of corn into the corner of her trough and swallowed it down, Jinny put on her halter and led her down to her field.

Punch and Bramble were at Miss Tuke's being trekking ponies again, so Shantih was alone. Jinny had thought that Pippen could have shared Shantih's field, but Mr. Mac-Kenzie had said the Manders' grass needed resting and Pippen would be better in his field. "I expect the Hortons are paying Mr. MacKenzie for their grazing," Mr. Manders had suggested, and Jinny had agreed that it was more than likely.

Shantih waited while Jinny gave her a sugar lump, then plunged away from her. She lay down to roll, her legs suddenly clumsy and ridiculous as she scrubbed herself into the grass. She surged upright again and instantly began to graze. For a moment longer Jinny leaned on the gate, watching her, hearing her cropping the grass and, in the distance, the slow rhythm of the waves in the bay.

"Dear horse," said Jinny and walked backwards up the path until Shantih's gold was only a grey silhouette in the grey evening.

"People to see *me*," Jinny thought, and she spun round and began to run up to the house, imagining that the committee who chose the show jumping team for the Olympic Games were waiting to see her.

"Of course, we do realise that you are not quite ready yet, but we like to select promising partnerships of horse and rider and start training them together for a few years before they actually compete in the Games. Can't guarantee you a place in the team, of course, but from what we've seen of your horse we think you've a pretty decent chance."

The sight of an unknown Land-Rover parked in front of Finmory brought Jinny back to reality. There really was someone in the house waiting to see her. Jinny had thought that Mike was only kidding her, wanting her to hurry up so that she would be in time to dry the dishes.

A loud woman's voice came from an open window.

"These Scottish digs can be rather amusing, but of

139

course when Terry was alive, most of our work was in Egypt."

Jinny didn't know the voice. It didn't sound like someone who would want to see her. Cautiously she went round to the side of the house and in by the back door.

Ken was standing by the sink, washing some stones he had collected from the beach. He had put the stones in a basin of water and was gazing down at them, meditating on them.

Ken Dawson lived with the Manders. He worked with Mr. Manders in the pottery, cared for the vegetable garden, which he had created and which fed them all with vegetables and fruit. "No need for all the slaughtering. The earth feeds us, if we'll only let it," Ken said. And with Ken to look after the garden it did.

Ken was eighteen—tall, bony, with straw-coloured hair growing long, past his shoulders, his green eyes calm in his weather-beaten face. Ken had saved Jinny's life and had helped her to rescue Shantih.

Mr. Manders had been Ken's probation officer in Stopton when Ken had been involved in a break-in to a warehouse. On the last day of his probation Ken had said to Mr. Manders, "I'd nothing to do with it." "I know," Mr. Manders had acknowledged.

After the Manders had come to live at Finmory, Ken had arrived with Kelly, his grey, shaggy, yellow-eyed dog, and offered to help. Now he was part of the family. "Just as well he found us," Jinny often thought. "Just as well for all of us." For Ken's rich parents wanted nothing to do with him. They sent him a monthly cheque through their bank. "So that they'll know I'm not starving," Ken said.

"Who's here?" Jinny asked, going across the kitchen to look at Ken's stones.

He handed one to her, holding it carefully between bony forefinger and thumb.

"A flint," he said. "You can see where it was chipped to make a sharp edge on it. Made in the Stone Age and now you're holding it." He laid it reverently on Jinny's open palm.

"I thought I heard you come in," exclaimed Jinny's mother, bursting into the kitchen. "Where have you been?"

Jinny gave the flint back to Ken. She knew from the tone

of her mother's voice that things more urgent than Ken's stones were about to overtake her.

"Jumping Shantih," Jinny replied, while Ken turned himself off from their raised voices and went on staring silently down at his underwater, shimmering stones.

"All afternoon and all evening?" said Mrs. Manders in obvious disbelief.

"Well, more or less," said Jinny, trying to remember anything else she might have done.

But her mother wasn't really wanting to know.

"You've to go upstairs straight away and tidy your bedroom. It is an absolute disgrace."

"Now?" asked Jinny in amazement. Remembering the strewn clothes, books, paints, paper and all the other things that were rioting over her bedroom floor, Jinny could quite see why her mother should think that it needed tidying up, but she couldn't imagine why she wanted her to do it now.

"This very minute. Two archaeologists arrived hours ago wanting to see your mural. Luckily, before I took them upstairs, I had the sense to look at your room. It is a shambles, Jinny. I wasn't going to clear it up after you so I told them they would have to wait until you came home. We're all on to our fourth coffee, so do you think you could hurry up?"

"I don't see why they should get into my bedroom . . ." began Jinny.

"At once," said her mother in the voice which Jinny didn't argue with.

Jinny raced up the wide flight of stairs, ran along the landing corridor to where an almost vertical ladder of stairs led up to her room.

When she had first seen it, Jinny had known that this must be her room at Finmory. It was divided into two parts by an archway. The window on the left looked out to sea—down over Finmory's wild garden to the ponies' field and on to Finmory Bay. Waking in the morning, Jinny would lean out and call Shantih's name, and her horse would look up and whinny in reply. The opposite window looked out over the moors and the high, rocky crags hustling up against the sky. It was in this half of the room that there was a painting on the wall which the archaeologists wanted to see. A mural of a red horse with yellow eyes that came

141

charging through a growth of blue-green forest branches laden with white blooms.

Jinny could see what her mother had meant about her room. It was worse than usual. Jinny gathered up armfuls of clothes and pushed them into drawers, stacked books into piles, collected pencils, felt-tipped pens, pastels and paints into boxes and tried to sort out the sheets of paper that lay like autumn leaves after a gale, covering everything.

The walls, too, were covered with Jinny's pictures—drawings, paintings, collages. They were mostly of Shantih and the animals that Jinny had seen on the moors—red deer, foxes, eagles, and the insects that lived their intense, secret lives in the same world as blind, gigantic humans.

Suddenly Jinny stopped clearing up. If the unknown archaeologists came up to her room they would see her pictures on the walls and Jinny hated anyone looking at her drawings. She wondered if she should make a fuss, go down and tell them that her bedroom was private.

"Jinny," called her mother, still using 'that' voice, "are you ready? Can we come up?"

Jinny pushed a last pile of drawings under the bed, captured a stray sock and hid it beneath her bedclothes and glanced quickly around. Her room was not perfect but it would have to do.

"Yes, O.K.," she called down, and waited, hearing footsteps and voices growing louder as they approached.

Jinny's mother came in first, looking round quickly to see if Jinny's tidying was satisfactory. She was followed by a large woman in a tweed suit, bullet-proof stockings and lacing shoes. Her white hair was cropped, her wrinkled skin a dusty yellow. A young man with pimples and thick glasses peered out from her shadow.

"This is Jinny," said Mrs. Manders. "Jinny, this is Mrs. Horgan."

"Freda," said the woman, holding out a powerful hand to Jinny.

Jinny grasped it, said how do you do—but already Freda was striding towards the mural.

"And Ronald," said Mrs. Manders, but the young man was trotting behind Freda, paying no attention to Jinny.

They both stood for a moment in front of the Red Horse,

142

their heads thrust forward, staring at it, then Freda gave a snort of disgust.

"Useless," she announced. "Totally useless. Obviously painted this century. Crude primitive."

"Waste of an afternoon," agreed Ronald. "No chance of an original underneath." And he scratched at the paint with his fingernail.

"Well, I like it," protested Jinny indignantly. "I like it very much indeed."

Secretly, Jinny was afraid of the Horse. There was a strangeness about it, a power. When Shantih had been trapped in the circus, and Jinny had thought she would never see her again, she had drawn a picture of the Arab galloping free on the Finmory moors and pinned it on the wall opposite the Red Horse and Shantih had come to Finmory. Jinny didn't really believe that the Red Horse could have had anything to do with bringing Shantih here, but then you never knew for certain about these things. You could never be quite sure about them.

"And it's mine," added Jinny, as if that settled the whole matter.

"Jinny," warned her mother.

"Now please don't get the wrong idea. I'm sure you're very fond of the old fellow, but we're looking for something else. Traces of a pony cult that we think might have existed in these parts. The Celts had many sacred animals—the horse, the stag, the dog, the boar and several others are all linked up with Celtic mythology. We're excavating a Celtic settlement at Brachan, about twelve miles from here. One of the locals told us there was an old painting of a horse at Finmory House. We pricked up our ears when we heard that. There's cup and ball markings on some of the rocks above Finmory. Wouldn't mind excavating here sometime. Definite links with the Celts. So we took a chance and came over. Decent of you to let us see it, but no interest."

"What's a pony cult?" asked Jinny.

"The Celts worshipped the Earth Mother, and one of the forms she took was the goddess Epona, goddess of ponies and foals. Not so long ago, about the turn of the century, a statuette of Epona was found quite close to where we're digging. A tinker found it, handed it in to a museum in Inverburgh. Still there. Utterly ludicrous, a

143

museum that size sitting on a valuable piece like that. Ought to be in London."

"I didn't see it," said Jinny. She had been to Inverburgh Museum with her teacher, Miss Broughton, and the other pupils at Glenbost school. "I was doing a project on horses and I'm sure Miss Broughton would have shown it to me."

"Oh, not *the* Inverburgh Museum. That's quite reasonable. The silly old joker who handed it in had to go poking down the back streets and give it to the Wilton Collection. Nothing but a dust dump and you cannot get them to part with a thing."

"Wish I'd seen it," said Jinny. She liked the idea of worshipping a pony goddess, or, better still, a horse goddess like Shantih.

"Are you interested?" asked Freda.

"She is if it's horses," said Mrs. Manders.

"Well, why don't you ride over? Your mother has been telling us about your horse."

"I'm not sure that I'll have time," said Jinny doubtfully.

"Can't promise to produce another Epona while you're there, but we'd show you round the dig."

"Could Sue come?" asked Jinny. "To ride with me?"

"Why not? Bring sleeping-bags, bunk down for the night and give us a hand the next day. Two ponies might bring us luck."

Jinny hesitated.

"It would be very interesting," said her mother.

"Broadening my interests," thought Jinny.

"Not tomorrow, but the next day?" suggested Freda, making it definite where Jinny had hoped it would remain vague. "Your father knows where the dig is. He'll show you where to come."

"Well . . ." said Jinny doubtfully, thinking of course-building and jumping Shantih, and how there was so little of the summer holidays left, and then school and probably masses of homework. "Well . . ."

But Freda was already out of the room, Ronald pattering behind her.

"So sorry to have troubled you," Freda said, standing in the doorway as she said goodbye. "One never knows, does one? Can't afford to ignore any clue."

144

She was sitting in their Land-Rover before she remembered about Jinny.

"See you on Saturday," she called, starting up the engine. "And your friend."

"It's not absolutely definite," Jinny explained to her father as they went back into the house. "She just mentioned that Sue and I could ride over and see the place where they're excavating. It wasn't absolutely settled. We're going to build more jumps tomorrow and it really depends on how long that takes."

"She invited you to stay the night," said Mrs. Manders. "I think you should go."

Mr. Manders brought out his Ordnance Survey map and laid it on the table.

"That's where they are," he said, "staying in the old schoolhouse at Brachan. And that's where they're digging." He traced with his finger.

"You could ride across the moors. You know your way to Loch Varrich. Ride along the side of the loch to there . . . and take that track that's marked right across the moors to Brachan."

"Well . . ." said Jinny, knowing that it was something that she was always talking about doing, riding further over the moors to a new part of the hills, further than she had ever ridden before. She supposed there would be walls for Shantih to jump. "I'll ask Sue tomorrow. Too late to go down to their tent tonight."

Lying in bed before she went to sleep, Jinny was thinking about show jumps. Behind Mr. MacKenzie's hay shed there was a discarded gate, and she was almost sure that he would never miss it. She would go over tomorrow morning and ask him if they could have it. They could paint it red and white and that would be almost as good as a real show jump.

Jinny remembered a chapter in one of her pony books that told you how to build a show jumping course. She got out of bed and went through to the other half of her room to look for the book.

When she had found it, she leaned on the windowsill, staring out at the moors. They were patched with gulleys of black moon shadow and plains of blue silver moonlight. The mountains were dense velvet against the clear, cold sky. Jinny stared out, fascinated by this strange moonlit world, remembering how she had ridden Bramble over the moors at night.

"What would it be like to take Shantih out on a night like this, to gallop and jump by moonlight?" she thought, and Jinny was riding Shantih out into the night. She felt the Arab plunge forward into a gallop, felt her rise over the stone walls as she came to them, while Jinny balanced easily in the saddle.

Then suddenly, bringing her back from her dreaming, Jinny knew there was someone in the room with her, someone who had crept up close behind her. She sprang round, ready to be furious with Mike or whoever else it was. The room was empty. No one was there. Only the yellow eyes of the painted Horse, luminous in the silver light, were staring directly at Jinny.

For a second she stood frozen to the spot, her fingers gripping into her arms, unable to move. Then she dashed across the room, dived into bed and lay curled under the bedclothes as if she was hiding from something, as if the painted Horse could come galloping out of the picture to find her.

CHAPTER TWO

Shantih kinked her tail and fretted to be off as Jinny, poised to spring on to her back, tried to make her stand still.

"Whoa, Shantih, whoa. Stand now." And Jinny leaped nimbly up on to the Arab. With a half rear, Shantih sprang forward, but Jinny was already sitting securely astride her.

"Oh, no you don't," she warned her horse severely. "Walk now."

It was early morning. Jinny wasn't quite sure exactly what time because, as usual, both her watch and alarm clock had stopped. It felt about the right time for Mr. MacKenzie to be finishing the milking, and that was a good time to ask him for anything you wanted. Later in the day he might be in the middle of doing something. He never looked busy and it wasn't easy to tell, when he was leaning on a half door smoking his pipe, whether he was in the middle of an important job or not.

Jinny let Shantih trot on along the lane to the farm. The morning air was crisp and sharp, a breath of autumn at the end of summer. Already the bracken was rust red on the hills, dried reeds were withering to flaxen, rowans were heavy with bunches of red berries, and here and there the trees were slashed with tints of autumn's orange and gold.

"Aye," said Mr. MacKenzie, pouring water from the churns he had been washing out, so that Jinny knew her timing had been right and he had just finished milking. "You'll be up to no good raging around the countryside at this hour of the morning. What are you wanting?"

Mr. MacKenzie lit his pipe and leaned against the byre door, willing to chat.

"I'm just out for a ride," Jinny said, avoiding the direct approach.

"I can be seeing that for myself. It's the powerful amount of jumping you're putting in these days. We'll be seeing you on the telly the next thing we know. Only you'll need to be putting the jumps up a wee bit, I'm thinking. Ewan was watching you the other day and he was telling me your horses were shying with you on account of him not being able to see the jumps at all, they were that wee."

The old farmer sucked on his pipe, spat, and twinkled out of the corner of his eye at Jinny.

"Remind me to give you the fifty pence," said Jinny. "For the collection."

"What collection would that be?"

"For Ewan's guide dog," said Jinny.

There was an equal silence between them.

"You're not to be touching it," said Mr. MacKenzie, staring out beyond Jinny's head. "It's a good enough gate and I'm not having it made into matchsticks by you two."

"What gate?"

"Och, I saw you round the back of the hay shed with the red and white stripes in your eyes."

"We wouldn't break it," said Jinny, admitting the possibility of turning the gate into a show jump.

"That you will not, for you'll not be taking it. There's two hen coops—be having those if you want."

"If," said Jinny, who had already noticed the hen coops, "We can get them to the field before they turn into dust."

Mr. MacKenzie had lost interest in the subject.

"Thanks anyway," said Jinny, "but I bet you never use that gate."

"Aye," said Mr. MacKenzie, stuffing the bowl of his pipe with his blunt, nicotine-stained thumb.

Jinny jumped back on to Shantih and was about to ride away when Mr. MacKenzie stopped her.

"What were they after?" he asked.

"Don't you know," cried Jinny in amazement, for no matter what happened at Finmory Mr. MacKenzie always seemed to know about it.

"I ken fine who they were—the fancy English with their spades digging up at Brachan. What I'm asking is what were they doing at Finmory."

"They wanted to see the mural on my wall."

"Now that is just what I was after thinking."

"How could you know it was there?"

"Because it was myself was there when it was painted."

"You?" said Jinny in amazement.

"Me," said Mr. MacKenzie. "And I'll tell you something else that not one of them would be knowing. They should have been looking for the stone. Not that they'd be finding it today."

"What *are* you talking about?" demanded Jinny.

"Seeing you're not everyone," said Mr. MacKenzie, "I'll be telling you. When I was a boy, every spring the tinkers would be coming to Finmory to be painting up the Horse. It was carved on a stone that stood just by itself inside the gateway of Finmory House. They'd be touching it up with a spot of the red paint where it had washed away during the gales and be giving it the yellow eyes again. My old grandmother would take me to watch them. There was the gossip that my grandmother had the tinkers' blood in her, but I wouldn't be knowing the truth of that."

"I've never seen a stone at our gates," said Jinny. She had dismounted again so that she could listen properly to what Mr. MacKenzie was telling her. "The Red Horse is painted on the wall of my bedroom, not on a stone."

"I'm telling you," said Mr. MacKenzie, "if you'd be listening. It was one of the toffs blew the stone up so he could be making the fancy flower beds. Said it was a pagan thing." He drew slowly on his pipe, then went on.

"When the tinkers had the word of the destruction, they were not for coming back in the spring as they had always done. Five years it was before we set eyes on them again. An old tink woman, and a lassie with hair as red as your own, came asking to speak with my grandmother. My father let them into my grandmother's bedroom. In a wee while she called my father in too. I was twelve at the time and fine I remember it all. When they came out, my father took the key of Finmory House, the toffs being away as usual for the winter, and they all went over to the house. I followed to see what they were up to and I went up with them to the servant's room—all dust and cobwebs it was. The old woman cleaned the wall, then she sat herself down in the dust and began her moaning and chanting while the lassie was painting the Horse on the wall, the same as had been on the stone."

"But why on my wall?" demanded Jinny.

"They would be having their reasons, I don't doubt. But that's the truth of it."

"So that was how it was painted," said Jinny. "I've always wanted to know."

"Aye, that's how it was, though I dare say it will have been touched up since then. The tinks have their own ways of getting into an empty house. It's few have heard that story from me and why I should be telling you I couldn't say."

"Because it's my bedroom now," stated Jinny as she jumped back on to Shantih. "And Sue and I might be riding over to Brachan to help them with their dig."

"You'd be better doing no such thing. What the Old Ones were at was their own affair and nothing to do with the likes of yourself, but there's some people who can't leave anything alone, and I'm thinking you are one of them."

"We're only going to watch," said Jinny.

"Aye," said Mr. MacKenzie.

As Jinny rode home, the scarlet Post Office van drove up

149

beside her and the postman handed up two letters to her. Neither was for Jinny. One was for her father and one was for Ken.

"You see," Jinny said to Shantih, "you are improving. You are much, much better. Only a month ago you'd have been all over the place if a van had come creeping up behind you like that."

Jinny took Shantih's bridle off and left her in her loose box. After breakfast she would ride her over to Sue's tent.

As Jinny went into the house she looked at the letters. Ken's was an airmail from Holland, and her father's was from the Education Committee. Uneasily, Jinny wondered if it might be about her. "They shouldn't be able to get at you during the holidays," she thought.

"Post," called Jinny, going into the kitchen where her family were gathering for breakfast.

"For me?" asked Petra.

"Nope," said Jinny, giving Ken his letter. "And one for Dad from the Education Committee. That might be about you, complaining about the noise you make practising when the rest of the hostel is trying to sleep."

Mr. Manders came into the kitchen and took his letter from Jinny, looking at it quickly just in case it should be from the publisher who had his book.

"Whee!" exclaimed Ken. "Listen to this. It's from Bob Schultz!" He looked round, his face lit up with surprise. "From Bob Schultz!"

"Sorry," said Petra, "never heard of him."

"You've heard of him, Tom?"

"No," said Mr. Manders.

"The potter. The only potter worth crossing the great water for. Saw some of his stuff in an exhibition in Stopton. Great stuff. Pots for the New Age. And the glazes he gets. Beautiful!"

"What's the letter about?" asked Petra.

"That's it. He's seen some of my pots, the ones Nell had at the Common Market exhibition. He liked them. Wants to meet me in London next week. If I'd be interested, he suggests I should go to Amsterdam for three or four months this winter to work with him in his pottery."

"Oh, great, Ken. That is good," said Mrs. Manders.

150

"It's what I need," said Ken. "To work with a master potter, and Bob Schultz is a master all right."

"But you can't leave us!" exclaimed Jinny. "We can't manage without you. *We* need you."

"Don't be so selfish. Of course Ken must go," said Mr. Manders.

"Thanks," said Ken. "When I come back I might know what I'm about."

Jinny turned her back on them, crossed over to the Aga. She couldn't bear the thought of Ken leaving. Not even for a few months. They needed him at Finmory. Jinny felt herself drowning in a black, unreasonable hopelessness.

"This toast isn't even pale brown," she said crossly, picking up a slice of toast from the toast rack, but no one was listening to her.

"I've to phone Nell about the arrangements for London," said Ken. "She's coming too."

Jinny scowled over her shoulder. "Did Petra make it?" she demanded, still messing with the toast.

Mr. Manders' letter was typed and official. When he had finished reading it, he held it out to Jinny.

"Really for you," he said.

"Me?" said Jinny, reaching out for it but not wanting it.

"Dear Mr. Manders," she read. *"We regret to inform you that due to unexpected delays in the building schedule of the new comprehensive school at Inverburgh, it will not be ready to accept the September intake. Your daughter Jennifer Manders will therefore be attending Duninver Grammar School as a weekly boarder. A place has been reserved for her at the school hostel and further details will follow in due course. We apologise for any inconvenience which this unavoidable change may cause."*

For a moment Jinny didn't believe it possible. She stood staring at the letter and heard her father telling the others what was in it. They all looked at Jinny.

"Why, oh why," exclaimed Mrs. Manders, "did this have to happen."

"Tears and temper," said Petra. "Fuss, fuss, fuss, until she goes—and when you get there you'll love it. There's colour telly in the hostel and a super games room."

151

"What about Shantih?" asked Mike. "If Jinny goes to Duninver, who is going to look after Shantih?"

"You will have to go," said Mr. Manders. "You must go to school."

Numb and cold, Jinny stared back at them. She could not believe it. She felt tears brimming in her eyes, her nose beginning to run. She wanted to run away, to dash upstairs and hide in her bedroom.

"Don't. Don't," Jinny told herself. "You mustn't run away."

She squared her shoulders, pushed her long hair back behind her ears, and looked her father straight in the eye.

"I am not going to Duninver School," she said. "I am not going to the hostel there. I am not leaving Shantih."

Jinny spent the rest of the day doing nothing but saying much the same thing over and over again. She was still saying it as she rode with Sue along the shores of Loch Varrich on their way to spend the night at Brachan.

"I am not going and that is all there is about it," Jinny stated fiercely.

"But you have to go to school," said Sue. "It's the law."

"Then they can put me in prison," said Jinny. "I don't care. I'm not going."

"You can ride Shantih at the weekends. It would be too dark to ride at night, anyway."

"I'd be with her," said Jinny. "I could talk to her. But it's not just that. There is no one to look after her during the week. Dad and Mummy won't even consider it. Petra's at the hostel, Mike hasn't time, and Ken is going off to this pottery place in Holland. So I HAVE to stay. I cannot go to Duninver!"

Sue didn't answer.

"Do you know what they said? That I'd have to find somone to take her for the winter. They even suggested Miss Tuke."

"If there's no one at home to look after her, you'll need to fix up something," said Sue.

"I've told you," snapped Jinny. "I am not going. I've thought of several possibilities—enough money for a private tutor, a nervous breakdown . . . That could last till March—or even longer."

"Oh, Jinny," said Sue, laughing.

"Well, I must find some way. I must."

Jinny gathered up Shantih's reins and sent her galloping over the moor, leaving Sue and Pippen far behind. She didn't stop until she had reached the head of the loch, where she halted Shantih and waited, watching Pippen's bumbling canter.

"Sue will be mad," thought Jinny, "but at least she didn't see that I was nearly crying."

Beyond Loch Varrich, the moorland rolled in waves to the far mountains. Stone walls, broken down by sheep and frost, ridged grey ribs through the heather. Except for the grazing sheep, there was no sign of any other life.

"You might have told me that you were going to gallop," exclaimed Sue indignantly.

"Sorry," said Jinny, meaning it.

"Oke," said Sue. "But tell me next time. This place is like a desert, a heather desert."

"I don't often ride as far as this," said Jinny. "So I don't really know the moor after Loch Varrich, but I should think this must be the track to Brachan. There isn't another one."

"Let's trot on," said Sue. "We don't want to be caught up here in the dark."

The track they were following wasn't much more than a sheep track. It wound its way round rocky outcrops and barricades of gorse; it skirted silent, quicksilver pools that lay hidden in the heather like patches of sky.

After they had been trotting for a bit, Jinny halted Shantih and took the map out of her pocket. She spread it out over Shantih's withers and found the Brachan track on it, then tried to decide where they were. But she couldn't see any landmark, all around them there was nothing to be seen but rolling moorland.

"What are those little marks?" Sue asked, pointing at the map.

"Marsh," said Jinny. "The track seems to go right through it."

"Well, that looks a reedy bit ahead now."

"If it is the marsh, we're almost at Brachan."

"About time too," said Sue. "You can feel it turning into evening."

153

Putting the map back into her pocket, Jinny knew what Sue meant. The afternoon light had faded from the sky, leaving it steel grey and heavy. The moorland was closing into shadow.

"Only about another half hour," said Jinny, trying to make her voice loud to fill the silence. "Less, if we hurry."

"Hope they remember we're coming," said Sue. "Perhaps they've forgotten about us."

"Not the happiest thought," said Jinny, letting Shantih jog on towards the marsh.

Soon the short, cropped turf changed into tussocks of reeds, and then into peat bog covered with a thin coating of half-dead, flaxen-coloured grasses. The horses' hooves sludged into the bog and came out with ominous squelching, sucking sounds.

"I wouldn't ride over this if the track wasn't marked on the map," said Sue, from behind Jinny. "I suppose it must be O.K.?"

Jinny made reassuring noises. She was standing up in her stirrups, balanced forward over Shantih's withers, taking her weight off her horse's quarters, and concentrating on following the track.

It was harder to follow now. The flat, peat bog had broken up into peat hags, each clod of peat surrounded by stagnant water. Shantih was picking her way across on top of the tussocks but twice her hind legs had slipped into the troughs between the peat hags. Her white stockings were black with mud and her belly splattered with gobbets of peat. She snorted unhappily through wide nostrils, wanting to swing round and gallop out of the bog.

"It's getting worse," said Sue, her voice sounding strained and high pitched. "Are you sure it's O.K. to go on?"

Jinny didn't answer. Mr. MacKenzie had once told her that it wasn't safe to trust maps that had been made several years ago; that one farmer changing the drainage on his land could affect the whole of the moor.

Quite suddenly there was no more track, only islands of peat bog surrounded by black, stagnant water.

"The track's stopped," said Jinny.

"Isn't that it over there?" asked Sue, pointing ahead.

"Might be," said Jinny. In the grey light she couldn't really see whether the track did go on or not. And even if

154

it was the track there was a stretch of bog to be crossed before they reached it again.

Shantih pawed the ground, sending up sprays of water, then half reared in her anxiety to escape from the bog.

"What shall we do?" Sue demanded.

Jinny scowled. She was furious with herself for being so stupid as to ride into the middle of a peat bog. It was exactly the sort of thing her father and Mr. MacKenzie were always warning her about.

"Even if we go back it won't be any better," said Sue. "We could easily get lost trying to find another way round."

Jinny could hear the sucking, squelching voice of the bog all around her. She brought out the map and looked at it again.

"This must be right," she said at last. "Brachan must be in the next hollow."

"Then we are almost there," said Sue. "We can't go back. It would be dark before we reached Finmory."

"We're going on," said Jinny, pushing the map back into her pocket. "I'll go first. You wait here until I reach the track—that is, if it is the track."

Jinny urged Shantih forward, forcing her to walk further into the bog when all the Arab's instincts told her it was not safe to go on.

"On you go," muttered Jinny between gritted teeth. "Walk on, get on with you."

For the first few strides the ground was no marshier than it had been when they were following the track.

"Seems O.K.," called Sue.

"Wait," warned Jinny. "Wait till I reach the track again." Even as she spoke, Jinny felt Shantih's front legs sink into the bog.

Shantih gave a high whinny of fear as she struggled to free herself. She reared up out of the peat like a water horse, splattering water and slime. Jinny's hands were knotted in her mane, her heels drummed against her horse's side. She felt the power in Shantih's quarters as she surged forward and sank again, her chest straining, her neck crested and a high-pitched, desperate whinny of fear stretching her nostrils.

Suddenly, as they fought to escape from the quagmire,

155

Jinny was sure she was being watched. Not by Sue and Pippen, but by something else. It was the same feeling as she had had that night when she had been alone in her room yet certain that someone else was there.

"Get on, get on," she screamed at Shantih, driving her on with renewed urgency.

For one terrible moment Jinny thought that Shantih was going to be sucked down into the bog. Then Jinny felt Shantih gather herself together for a final effort, plunge forward and this time she didn't sink so deeply into the mire.

In another four or five strides they had reached the track again and Shantih was standing on firmer ground. Her plastered sides were heaving, her head low as she fought for breath, but they were safe. Jinny fell out of the saddle and leaned against Shantih. She couldn't have stood by herself.

"I'm coming," yelled Sue, and Jinny watched helplessly as Pippen crossed the bog. Like Shantih, he plunged and fought his way through it, but his soup plate hooves stopped him from sinking into it as deeply as Shantih had done.

Jinny and Sue stared at each other, each seeing her own fear in the other's pale face.

"They'd have been excavating us," said Sue.

"Peat bogs preserve skeletons," said Jinny. "They'd not have dug us up for thousands of years."

They both began to laugh—high, hysterical laughter. It had been a near thing and they both knew it; the kind of thing you read about in the newspapers and can't imagine how anyone could have been so stupid.

"Come on," said Jinny, leading Shantih away. "Let's get on."

Soon they had left the bog behind them. Glancing back over her shoulder at its black, glimmering water, and white, bleached reeds, Jinny swore to herself that she would never ride through it again. They would find a different way to ride home.

They remounted and rode on, until, from the top of a rise in the moors, they saw the excavation, and, a little further down the hillside, the few stone crofts that made up Brachan. Staring down at the piled rubble and earth of the

156

dig, Jinny felt an uneasy coldness settle about her. They were disturbing things that belonged to the past, that should be left alone.

Quickly, Jinny turned Shantih towards Brachan. She could see the square shape of what must be the school-house. Smoke rose from its chimney, lights shone from its windows. There would be people and noise and warmth.

Hearing the sound of hooves, Freda and Ronald had come to the schoolhouse gate to welcome them and were suitably impressed by the state of their horses.

"What would your parents have said if you had sunk without trace? Still, as an archaeologist, one can't help feeling what a valuable find you would have been to the future."

"Thank you," said Jinny. "Thank you very much." She still felt chilled and uncomfortable. Not only because her feet were soaking and her jeans clinging muddily to her legs, but something else that she couldn't quite reach was troubling her.

Freda told them that a hot nosh-up would be ready when they were, and Ronald went with them to show them the field by the side of the school where the ponies were to spend the night.

When they went back to the schoolhouse, carrying tack and sleping bags, voices called to them to come in. Seven or eight people were sitting on the floor round a blazing log fire. Oil lamps were burning on the high windowsills. The bare schoolroom was softened with shadows. Freda introduced them, and a young man wearing a blue and white striped apron gave them mugs of soup and doorsteps of bread.

"Stew to follow," he promised. "Fifty-seven variety."

Jinny and Sue found a place on the floor and drank their soup. At first the others asked them questions about their ride and their ponies, but gradually the talk returned to the excavation. Jinny leaned back against the wall and thought about Shantih. "I'm not going to Duninver," she told herself. "I'm not leaving Shantih. They can't make me go." But tonight Jinny was too tired to be able to think of how she was going to stop them.

Before they settled down for the night, everyone went

157

out to the field to see Pippen and Shantih. Pippen was grazing, but Shantih was standing, alert and wary, looking over the moors towards the dig. At the approach of the strangers she flung herself away from them, tail and mane swirled and wild, her metal shoes glinting in the moonlight as she bucked. She turned back to face uphill again, her head outstretched as if searching for something on the moors that the humans couldn't see.

"She is Sleipner, the horse of Odin," said a young man.

"Or the horse of the Wild Huntsman," suggested someone else.

"She is the Horse worshipped by the Pony Folk," said Jinny.

"If you mean Epona," said Freda, "she is usually shown with ponies, not Arabs."

"Oh," said Jinny, not knowing what she had meant, hardly knowing what she had said.

The schoolroom floor was very hard indeed. Jinny lay in her sleeping-bag next to Sue and gazed at the dying fire. Already she was stiff and aching and she had only been lying there for about an hour. She was sure that she would never sleep; wished that she had never come.

Suddenly Jinny sat up. She was certain that she had heard Shantih neighing. She wondered if she should go out and take another look at her horse, but she didn't want to go out alone, not alone at night so close to the dig.

Jinny did not know much about the Celts, only that they had been a dark, magical people living in prehistoric Scotland. So long ago that Jinny's imagination could hardly reach them. And now, here at Brachan their houses and graves were being disturbed.

Jinny listened intently but she didn't hear Shantih again. She lay down, still listening. Gradually her eyes began to close, then she woke with a start. The yellow eyes of the Red Horse were staring at her through the glowing embers of the fire.

CHAPTER THREE

Jinny was back trapped in the peat bog. For as far as she could see, there was nothing but the black peaty water and the tussocks of dried reeds under a metal sky. At every step that Shantih took she sank deeper into the mire, until only her head and neck were visible. Then she would rear upright, her nostrils flared, her eyes huge with fear as she screamed her panic before she sank back into the bog. .

On and on they went, sinking and rising, filled with blind terror, both knowing that the horror was about to begin.

Suddenly red light flashed over the metal sky, and above the rim of the marsh came the Red Horse. He stood braced for a movement, its head turning arrogantly as it surveyed the bleak landscape through its yellow eyes. It stretched out its neck and breathed in the essence of all the creatures struggling in its mire. It plunged to and fro as if uncertain where it would find the thing for which it was searching.

Jinny knew that it was looking for her. She tried to urge Shantih on, but the bog was closing over her. She could not turn her head to see if the Horse was coming any closer, only scream at the pitch of her voice.

"You were screaming all night," Sue told her in the morning. "I kept trying to wake you but you wouldn't. What were you dreaming about?"

"The Red Horse," said Jinny, and she shuddered at the thought of her nightmare. "It was searching for something."

"Having bad dreams?" asked Freda, overhearing their conversation. "You won't be the first to have bad dreams on a Celtic dig."

"A woman I know," said a young man, "took home a Celtic stone head. She had to keep it in her house for two weeks before she could take it into the museum, and during those two weeks her husband, her son and herself all saw a small, dark man, dressed in skins, lurking in different places around the house."

"You mean really saw him?" asked Sue.

"She said that when she saw him it reminded her of television—real but not real."

"I believe that there are communities in Wales and parts of Scotland where they still follow the Celtic way of life, worshipping the Earth Mother in various forms," said Freda.

"Well, I think it's all stupid," said Jinny abruptly. "Why do you have to go digging things up?"

"Perhaps they won't leave us alone," mused Freda. "We think we choose to excavate, but maybe the buried things choose us to set them free, to return them to where they should be."

"Nonsense," muttered Jinny. "That's all rubbish talk. I don't believe a word of it." And she walked away, not wanting to hear any more."

After breakfast, Sue and Jinny were shown round the dig by one of the students. He showed them the circle of stones that marked the walls of the main house, the remains of the ring of posts that had supported the roof, and where they thought the fire pit had been. To Jinny it just looked like any other heap of mud and stones.

"I don't see how you can know," she said stubbornly, as if by refusing to believe what the young man was telling them she could stop it being true. "Haven't you found any skeletons?"

"No such luck. Buut we think the statuette of Epona was found round about here and we are hoping to find other evidence of horse worship."

"You won't find it here," stated Jinny. "You're digging in the wrong place."

"Is that a fact now?" said the young man, losing patience with Jinny. "What would you know about it?"

Jinny couldn't tell him. She didn't know herself.

"Just feels wrong," she muttered.

"A case of the second sight?" asked the young man, and went on showing things to Sue, who was being bright and asking intelligent questions.

Sue and Jinny spent the rest of the morning carrying buckets of earth from one place to another. It was not the least like Jinny's idea of an excavation. It was all far too slow for her taste, with lots of exact measuring and marking going on. She hated the place. There was a cold eeriness about it that made the skin creep on the nape of her neck.

"We'll need to go immediately after lunch," Jinny said to Sue.

"Wish we could stay another night," said Sue.

"Well, we can't," snapped Jinny. "Not possibly we can't." Jinny had no intention of spending another night in the schoolhouse.

"All right. Keep your hair on. I only said I wished we could."

"Well, I don't," said Jinny, scowling. "I wish we'd never come. I've more to do than waste my time here. Not like you. I've to teach Shantih to jump, and I've to sort out this mess about my school and I've my drawing. You've nothing to do compared to me."

"How do you know I've nothing to do?" demanded Sue, startled by Jinny's sudden attack. "You never did any jumping until I came."

"I was just going to start," said Jinny. "It had nothing to do with you."

"It had a lot to do with my saddle. Before I lent you my saddle you could hardly stay on Shantih, never mind jump her!"

Jinny grabbed up her bucket of earth and marched away from Sue. She tipped the earth out on to the pile of rubble and stared round at the people working on the dig. She hated them all. They thought of nothing except measuring and labelling and locking things away in museums. And what did Sue know about riding a real horse? She only sat on Pippen. Jinny scowled to herself, drawing her brows down and setting the corners of her mouth. She didn't want to stay. She wanted to go home *now*.

"Is this the first dig you've seen?" a girl asked Jinny.

"Yes," said Jinny.

"Fascinating, don't you think?"

"No," said Jinny.

A cloud shadow blowing over the bracken looked, for a moment, like the shape of a great horse, mane tangled, hooves upraised.

"Look out," yelled Jinny, jumping back, her arm shielding her face.

161

"Whatever's wrong?" asked the girl.

"I thought I saw . . ." Jinny's voice trailed into silence. The wind had blown the Horse away.

"Bet you it was a worm," teased one of the students.

Jinny opened her mouth to deny such a stupid suggestion, then thought it might be easier to let them think that. She smiled half-heartedly.

"A great big woolly one," mocked the boy, as Jinny turned away.

"We can ride down the path from Brachan to Morston and then along the road to Ardtallon, through Glenbost, and then home," Jinny told Sue, as she studied the map while they were eating their sandwich lunch. "It's longer that way, so we'll need to go at once, the minute we've finished eating. I'm not trying to get through that bog again."

"Not even with my saddle?" asked Sue.

"Sorry," said Jinny. "You're right. I couldn't jump without it."

Sue grinned, "And I can't jump with it because it gives Pippen a sore back."

"I'm jolly glad it does," said Jinny.

They said goodbye and thank you for having us to Freda, who said she was sorry they had to rush off and she'd be pleased to see them back any time."

"Not me. Never!" said Jinny as she ran downhill to the schoolhouse. "I'm not going back there. It's a foul place. I hate it. They should leave it alone."

"Well, I thought it was very interesting," said Sue, but Jinny didn't reply. She wanted to get back to Shantih as soon as she could, to be sitting astride her, trotting away from Brachan, away from the Celtic settlement, away from these people who didn't know what they were doing, disturbing hidden things.

They collected their sleeping bags and tack from the schoolhouse and walked over to the field. Pippen came bustling to the gate, but Shantih was still gazing out over the moors. Even when Jinny haltered her and led her over to the gate, she still went on staring out towards the dig, hardly paying any attention to Jinny.

"Ready?" asked Sue when they had saddled up and tied their sleeping bags to the fronts of their saddles.

Jinny had been waiting for Sue, watching the tiny figures working at the dig. She had become so intent, staring at the low stone huts, that she had hardly heard Sue's question.

"Are you ready?" repeated Sue. "Oh, do wake up, you're dreaming again." As Sue spoke, she led Pippen up to Shantih, meaning to open the gate and lead him through. "Come on," she said, reaching for the latch of the gate. "I thought you were in such a desperate hurry to get away." Shantih laid back her ears and glowered at Pippen.

"Get back," Jinny shouted, her voice deep with authority. "You have no right to bring a pony near the Horse."

"What?" exclaimed Sue in astonishment. "Whatever are you talking about now?"

"I don't know," said Jinny, as surprised as Sue. "I was staring at the huts on the moor, then I thought Shantih was going to kick and I said that."

"What huts? There aren't any huts on the moor."

"Up there," said Jinny, but the cluster of low stone huts weren't there any longer. Now Jinny could only see the trenches and heaps of earth where they were excavating. "But I saw them," she said in bewilderment. "They were there."

"Well, they're not there now. And for goodness sake stop shouting at me!"

Jinny didn't try to argue. She led Shantih through the gate and mounted quickly. Her horse shied, dancing sideways, her tail kinked over her chestnut quarters as she waited impatiently for Sue to shut the gate.

The path from Brachan twisted over the moor. Jinny urged Shantih into a canter.

"I'm never going back there," she swore. "It's a foul place. I loathe it."

Even when she reached the road, Jinny kept Shantih trotting on. The regular clip of the horses' hooves comforted her; the contact between the reins in her fingers and the bit in Shantih's mouth, the rhythmic strength of Shantih's stride and Sue riding beside her.

Jinny glanced back towards Brachan. She shuddered suddenly, goose over her grave. A cold fear clutched at her, for she knew that no matter how fast Shantih galloped, the Red Horse, moving with the speed of dream, must always be faster.

"Jennifer Manders," Jinny told herself severely, "stop this nonsense. That dig has nothing to do with you. You have got to find some way of stopping them sending you to Duninver. That is what you've got to do."

That evening, Jinny's parents tried to talk to her about what was to happen to Shantih while Jinny was away at school.

"Have you thought about what you are going to do with Shantih?" her father asked her.

"Thought of nothing else," replied Jinny. "But it is not going to happen because I am not going to Duninver."

"Oh, yes you are," said Petra smugly.

Mr. Manders pushed his splayed fingers through his beard,

"Then where are you going to go?" he asked, trying to make it sound like a reasonable question, although he knew from the expression on his daughter's face that she had no intention of being reasonable.

"Perhaps I could stay on for another year at Glenbost?" Jinny suggested.

"And let Dolina go on to Duninver without you?" asked her mother, naming one of the other pupils from Glenbost who was the same age as Jinny.

"I don't care where Dolina goes. I don't care if she goes to university, as long as I can stay here with Shantih."

"You do care," said Mike.

"I could do the lessons they'd be doing at Duninver. I could manage myself as long as they sent the books to me. Or I'd buy the books myself and work here at home. Oh, Daddy, please."

"Now you're being silly and you know it," said Mr. Manders sharply, cutting through Jinny's rising hysteria. "You MUST go to Duninver."

"I could have a tutor. The minister at Glenbost could be my tutor."

Mr. Manders ignored the suggestion.

"What we have to decide is what we are going to do with Shantih while you are away at school."

"How can you say that?" cried Jinny. "How can you say that? As if she was a car or a wardrobe or an old coat.

164

It's like saying what will we do with Mike when we leave Stopton. Shantih is us. She lives here as much as I do. She's one of us. One of our family. I'm not going to *do* anything with her."

"We're not suggesting you sell her. It's only for the winter. There is no one here who can look after her. She has to be stabled at night, you know that yourself. Do try to understand," pleaded Jinny's mother.

"You're wasting your breath," said Petra. "She is going to make a fuss. You won't stop her."

"I haven't time to look after her," said Mr. Manders. "Even if I knew enough, I still wouldn't have time. If I don't work we don't eat. And your mother certainly couldn't cope."

"You could if you tried," Jinny said to her mother. "I'd show you what to do."

"I couldn't, dear. I don't know a thing about horses. I could not do it."

"You don't need to ride her," snapped Jinny. "All you have to do is muck her out and lead her up and down to her field."

"Jinny, I couldn't. You know there's far more to it than that."

"Then Mike can look after her," said Jinny, abandoning all hope of her mother becoming horsy.

"No," said Mr. Manders. "He'll have his trekking pony to see to, his homework and riding to Glenbost. That is quite enough."

"Oh, please," said Jinny, making her brother look at her.

"Not likely," said Mike. "She's all over the place when she has one of her crazy turns. And I wouldn't have time for anything else all winter."

Jinny stared bitterly round her family. She thought of all the families she had read about in pony books who would have thought nothing of looking after a horse while their daughter was away at school.

No one had mentioned Ken. He would have looked after Shantih for Jinny. If he hadn't been going to this Dutch pottery place. For a moment, Jinny allowed herself to think that perhaps she could ask him not to go; plead with

165

him to stay. He could go in the summer. He didn't need to go now. But she knew she mustn't even think of it.

"So the only thing we've been able to think of," Mr. Manders was saying, "is to ask Miss Tuke to take her for the winter."

"No! She'd want to ride her and try to school her. She'd turn her into a trekking pony. Shantih is my horse."

"A little schooling would do her the world of good," said Petra.

"And you like Miss Tuke," said Mike, so that Jinny knew they had been discussing it while she had been at the dig.

"I'd drive you over to ride her every weekend," promised her father. "And if she was at Miss Tuke's you'd know that she was being well looked after. She's perfectly competent. Look how well she runs her trekking."

"Shantih's my horse. I can't let anyone else ride her and school her. I can't. Miss Tuke is O.K. with her trekking ponies, but not with Shantih. She's all shouting and bossing. She only knows about hitting and kicking and shouting, 'trek forward'."

Jinny's voice cracked on the edge of tears. She ran out of the room, through the hall and out of the house. Running as fast as she could, she raced through the garden and down to Shantih's field.

Shantih lifted her head from her grazing, ears pricked at Jinny's sudden approach, her dark eyes wide with surprise.

"They can't make me! They can't!" Jinny sobbed, flinging her arms round Shantih's neck and burying her face in her mane.

Miss Tuke was bossy and loud. She would sit on Shantih shouting, "trek forward", as she did with the trekking ponies, and by the spring she would have turned Shantih into another of her trekkers.

It was dark when Ken came to find Jinny. He stood at the field gate and Kelly came across the field to Jinny, greeting her with low, wuffing barks, pushing at her legs with his wet nose, gazing at her through his grey, shaggy hair—his eyes glinting in the dark.

Jinny followed him back to Ken and they walked back in silence to the house.

"Ask him if he'll stay. Ask him if he'll look after Shantih," said the voice in Jinny's head. But she couldn't She couldn't be so selfish.

She didn't go back into the front room where her family were still sitting, probably discussing how difficult she was being.

"Be easy," said Ken. "Listen to your breathing."

But Jinny couldn't hear him. She went on alone, up the wide staircase, the bannister rail smooth under her hand, along the long corridor, and slowly, step by step, up the steep flight of stairs to her own room where the Red Horse and the nightmare waited for her

CHAPTER FOUR

For the next two days, Jinny tried desperately to find some way of stopping them sending her to Duninver School.

She went to see Miss Broughton, who had been her teacher at Glenbost school.

"So you see, I can't go to the hostel. I can't," she finished, when she had explained the circumstances to Miss Broughton.

"It is maddening," Miss Broughton had agreed. "It all seemed to be working out so well for you—the new comprehensive opening up at just the right moment. I'm very sorry, but there is nothing I can do to change things."

"Couldn't I come back here for another year," pleaded Jinny.

"You certainly could not. A whole year stagnating when you're ready to go on to a new school with a proper Art Department. Think of the other children you'll meet and the new friends you'll make. You wouldn't want to listen to Dolina talking about all the new things she's doing while you were still coming here."

"Oh, I wouldn't mind. Truly I wouldn't mind," declared Jinny.

"You think you wouldn't now, but you would by Christmas time. You would hate it. Anyway, the Education Committee wouldn't let you stay here."

Jinny grunted in disgust. She supposed that she had better go and speak to the Education Committee herself.

She borrowed a matching scarf, handbag and gloves from Petra, put on her best skirt and jacket, and that afternoon she hitched a lift into Glenbost and caught the bus to Inverburgh.

"You want to see the Education Committee?" said the girl in the Education Offices, looking at Jinny suspiciously. "What do you mean?"

"It's about the new school at Inverburgh not being ready in time."

"Oh, yes," said the girl. "We've had a lot of complaints about that."

"Nothing like mine," stated Jinny. "I must see someone."

"Perhaps Mr. Scott would have a minute to speak to you," said the girl, lifting a phone on her desk.

"He'll see you now," she said as she replaced the receiver. "Come this way."

She showed Jinny into a room furnished with filing cabinets and a large desk. Behind the desk sat a fat man.

"Sit down, little lady," he said. "And tell me what's troubling your little head." So that Jinny knew at once that he wouldn't be any help. No one who called her a little lady could possibly be any use.

Mr. Scott fumbled with the papers on his desk while Jinny tried to explain why she couldn't go to Duninver.

"Dear me, we do have problems," he said when she had finished. "I think the best thing you can do is to go straight home and ask your father to explain to you why your education is more important than bumping around on top of your gee-gee."

Jinny stared at him in fascinated disgust.

"But one thing I can tell you, when the new term starts, you and all the other first-year pupils from your district will be attending Duninver School. There is no possibility of the school in Inverburgh opening in September. Gallop off with you now. I can't waste any more of my time over such rubbish."

Jinny sat on the bus going back to Glenbost, seeing

168

nothing, thinking nothing. A heavy certainty was squatting on her—the certainty that when the new term started she would be at Duninver School.

Back at Finmory she changed, caught up Shantih and rode over to the field where their jumps were. The wooden boxes were still scattered from the night when Shantih had smashed her way through them; the night when Jinny had still been going to Inverburgh School; when the only thing that mattered was building a better show jumping course; before the archaeologists had come to Finmory.

The thought of the Brachan excavation made Jinny gather up Shantih's reins and send her cantering round the field, for last night she had dreamed the same nightmare. High and clear, Shantih soared over the jumps, while Jinny sat tight in the saddle, concentrating her whole mind on her horse.

That night the dream was waiting for Jinny again. It seemed that the second she closed her eyes she was back fighting her way through the marsh, while the Red Horse reared on the edge of the skyline, questing the air with trumpeting nostrils, his metal hooves sundering the earth, his yellow eyes searching, searching, while Jinny screamed.

"You've the banana face," said Mr. MacKenzie the next morning, when Jinny went over to the farm to see him. "It's that jumping that's going for your liver. I was warning you for it."

"I'm sick with worry," said Jinny.

"Och now, I'm sorry to be hearing that. It'll be to do with the Inverburgh school, no doubt, and yourself having to be for Duninver with that fancy sister of yours."

"Yes," agreed Jinny. "That's exactly what it is. I don't know what I'm going to do with Shantih."

"I'm no surprised to be hearing that."

"If they make me go to Duninver, please would you take her? Just be Monday to Friday, really only Monday night to Friday morning. You'd only have to feed her and muck her out, put her in her field and bring her in again at night. I'd pay you for it. Please, please, Mr. MacKenzie."

"That I will not. I haven't the time to be carrying on with a useless brute like that one," said Mr. MacKenzie contemptuously. "Was I not telling you from the beginning that she was not the horse for the likes of yourself

169

to be having? That Pippen now, he's the horse for a lassie, not a wild beast like yon."

"Thank you," said Jinny. "Let your 'no' be 'no'. Enough." And, carrying Finmory's milk, she trudged back home.

Petra was practising. Jinny hung around until she stopped and asked what Jinny wanted.

"Does anyone from Glenbost or Ardtallon travel to Duninver each day?" Jinny asked. "Maybe someone whose father has a car and works there?"

"Why?" said Petra.

"I thought I could travel with them."

"You're not allowed to. You must stay in the hostel, it's a rule." Petra returned to her practising.

"No," said Mike, when Jinny asked him again if he would look after Shantih.

"Go on," said Jinny. "Please, please."

"I can't," said Mike. "It's not as if she's going to be sold or shot or anything desperate. Then it would be different. Miss Tuke will look after her well. It's not long since you were wanting someone to school her for you."

"*With* me not *for* me," said Jinny. "And now I'm teaching her to jump I can't have someone else riding her."

"No," said Mike.

Jinny went into the pottery and waited until Ken appeared. He sat down at the wheel and began to throw pots with quick, deft movements. Kelly lay, hearthrug at his feet, watching him.

"Do you really think you'll go to Holland?" Jinny asked, not looking at Ken.

"Anyone else but Bob Schultz and the answer would be 'no'," said Ken. "But I'll go for him. Heard him on the telly once. A plastic woman interviewing him and asking all the wrong questions. She said wasn't he afraid of running out of new ideas for his pottery and he stood up—he's a huge giant of a man, about six foot—and shouted, "Lady, my head is like a furnace, burning, blazing. My hands can't move fast enough to keep up with the ideas that come leaping through me."

"Oh," said Jinny politely. She didn't want to hear about Bob Schultz.

170

"So that's why I must go and work with him. The disciple approaches the master."

"When are you going?"

"Going up to London next weekend with Nell. Probably Friday. She thinks he'll want me for the winter. Says he often takes on an apprentice during the winter when he's at his pottery in Amsterdam."

Jinny picked up a lump of clay and began to mould it into different shapes. It wasn't a bit like Ken to be so enthusiastic about anything. Normally he said:

" 'Sitting quietly, doing nothing,
Spring comes and the grass grows by itself '."

so she knew that he must really want to go. It wasn't just a notion.

Jinny began to make her clay into a pony shape. It wasn't up to Ken to say that he wouldn't stay and look after Shantih for her. It was up to her not to ask. She gave her pony a shaggy mane and thick tail. When she had finished she found a corner on the windowsill and left him there.

Then she ran out to Shantih, saddled her up and rode her down to the bay. The Horton's tent was a bright square against the grass—but there was no sign of Sue or her family. On the sands, Jinny let Shantih gallop in wide circles, encouraging her to go faster, yelling into the sea silence, and, when Shantih bucked, encouraging her to misbehave. Then Jinny cantered up to the field where the jumps were and rode Shantih at them.

"Go on! Go on!" cried Jinny as Shantih flew over them. She jumped her round again and again. When she was jumping Shantih Jinny forgot about the Red Horse, forgot about Duninver School and the thought of Miss Tuke taking Shantih away from her. There was nothing but the flying speed of her horse.

In the afternoon, Jinny went up to her room and shut her door with a bang so that her family would know she wasn't to be disturbed. Even at the very top of the house Jinny could still hear Petra's playing.

"Thank goodness," Jinny thought, checking through her window to make sure that Shantih was safely in her

171

field, then flinging herself flat on top of her bed, "her exam is on Saturday, then we'll get some peace."

Mike was going to Stopton tomorrow to stay with a friend until the end of the holidays. Jinny thought he was mad.

"I don't really want to go," Mike had said.

"Then don't," said Jinny.

"But I promised I'd go back and stay with them. I didn't go last summer and I didn't go at Easter, and now his mother keeps on writing to Mum saying when am I coming and how much David is looking forward to seeing me again. I'd rather be here, but I suppose I'd better go."

"I wouldn't."

"Doesn't really matter," Mike had said. "It's only for a fortnight, and then we'll be back at school."

"A fortnight!" thought Jinny, and in a sudden panic she jumped off her bed, brought her cash box down from the top of her wardrobe and emptied its contents out on to the top of her bed. She was saving up to buy a lungeing rein for Shantih. Nell Storr bought her pictures and sold them in her shop, but really Jinny wasn't very keen on selling her pictures to Nell. Once Nell had bought them, Jinny never saw them again.

"Money," thought Jinny, counting out the eleven pounds that was in her cash box. "I'll need money whatever happens. If Dolina knows a farmer in Glenbost who would look after Shantih during the week I'd need to pay him, and I'd need more than eleven pounds."

She would need to do more drawings for Nell. Jinny swept the money off the edge of the bed into the cash box. Quickly wrapped it up again in its Sellotape and put it back on the top of her wardrobe. She found her drawing pad, pastels and paints, and, sitting down on the floor, she began to draw.

"Each drawing two pounds," Jinny thought. "Six drawings enough to keep Shantih for a week. *If* I can find someone in Glenbost who will keep her."

A lump choked in Jinny's throat. She blew her nose hard.

"Each picture two pounds," she told herself again. "Six pictures one week's keep. Twenty-four pictures, one month."

172

Jinny forced herself to go on painting as fast as she could. Nell had said that her customers liked the drawings of Shantih best, so Jinny painted Shantih—Shantih's head, Shantih grazing, Shantih galloping and Shantih jumping. If a bit of her drawing didn't look quite right, Jinny smudged it over. She drew grass round Shantih's hooves so that she didn't have to waste time with difficult fetlocks and pasterns; she painted swirling manes and tails to cover up necks that were too long or hocks that bent in an odd way.

All the drawings were hopeless and Jinny knew it. Even the ones that looked all right weren't of Shantih. They could have been any chestnut Arab. Normally, Jinny would have torn them all up and gone for a ride.

"They're very good," she told herself, arranging them in rows of weeks and months. "As good as lots of the pictures you see in shops. Better. Nell will never know the difference. She doesn't know anything about horses."

Jinny shuffled the pictures into a pile, not wanting to have to look at them again for they were all so bad.

She wandered through to the other half of her room, feeling gritty and cross with herself. Absorbed in her painting, she had forgotten about the Red Horse.

The glowing yellow eyes were waiting, glaring out at her. Jinny stood still, staring back at the Horse. It was a rough, crude drawing. The Horse's legs were too long. Its head was out of proportion to the rest of its body. But it was alive. It crashed through the branches straight at Jinny. The yellow circles of its eyes commanded her.

Jinny brought paper and pastels, and, kneeling on the floor in front of the Horse, she began to draw. Her hand moved, knowing by itself what to do, and on the paper in front of her Jinny saw her dream take shape—the peat hags sprouting their dead crowns of withered reeds, the black water and the metal sky, tight and suffocating as a killing bottle being pressed down on top of her. Then her fingers found the orange and red and yellow pastels— the fire colours—and the grey sky glowed with the coming of the Horse.

On the next sheet, Jinny's hand drew herself and Shantih struggling to escape from the black peat bog, the sky above them burning, molten.

173

On the third sheet of paper the Red Horse reared over the horizon, red-gold, burning, seeking. Its head was flung upwards, forelock blown back in the burning winds, yellow eyes flaming, as it searched for the thing it had come to find.

Kneeling on the floor, Jinny waited, unable to move. The pictures she had drawn held her captive.

Voices came from below. A woman's voice, loud and brisk, and then her father's voice shouting her name. Unmoving, Jinny swam towards the sound. She heard her father's footsteps coming along the landing and stopping at the foot of her stairs.

"Jinny! Jinny!" he called. "Come down. Miss Tuke is here to see you."

Jinny struggled to her feet. For seconds, the power of the Red Horse still held her—and then she broke free. She scrabbled the drawings of her dream together and hid them under the pile of drawings she was going to take to Nell Storr's shop.

"Jinny, are you up there?"

"Yes, I'm here," Jinny yelled back, and she went pounding downstairs to her father.

"What's Miss Tuke doing here?" she demanded. "Did you phone her? Did you?"

"No," said Mr. Manders. "I did not. You know I wouldn't have done that without asking you first."

"Well, why is she here?"

"To find out what trekking ponies we need for the winter. But now she is here we may as well take advantage of the opportunity and ask her about Shantih?"

"No," said Jinny.

"Only ask. There is no point in going on arguing about whether Shantih is to go to Miss Tuke's or not when Miss Tuke may not even be willing to take her."

Jinny followed her father down to the kitchen where Miss Tuke was sitting at their huge oak table having a cup of tea with Mrs. Manders.

"Didn't you hear us calling you?" asked Mrs. Manders. Jinny shook her head.

"What were you doing?"

"Drawings," said Jinny. "To sell to Nell Storr." She didn't mention the Red Horse, how it had come out of the

174

painting, making her draw her dreams, how it was still there on the edge of her mind, always there, waiting.

"Want to see you about ponies," said Miss Tuke. "Your mum tells me you won't be needing one. Off to Duninver to the school hostel. Quite a change from battling against the gales on Bramble. I hear it's utter luxury."

"I don't want to go," said Jinny.

"Who is going to look after that mad Arab while you are away?"

"It's rather a problem," said Mr. Manders. "In fact, we were going to get in touch with you and see if you might consider taking her for the winter?"

"Were you?" said Miss Tuke. "Now that's a thought. I always do stable one or two of my favourite Highlands so I have something to ride when the trekking is over. I was going to hang on to Shona this year, but I've had rather a tempting offer from a family who trekked with me for a fortnight and fell for her in a big way. Might be rather fun to have something like Shantih. Never had much time for Arabs. Fidgety beasts. But for a few months . . ."

Jinny didn't look up. She picked at the corner of the table, scowling.

"Of course I'd pay something towards her keep. We can't manage to look after her here when Jinny is away, so we would be most grateful."

"What has Jinny to say about it?" asked Miss Tuke.

"It's not going to happen. I'm not going to Duninver."

Jinny felt her parents and Miss Tuke smiling at each other, being adult and sensible.

"Wouldn't do the mare any harm to spend a month or two with a stronger rider," said Miss Tuke. "From what I've seen and heard of her, she has a will of her own. Gets the better of you more than sometimes."

"Not now," stated Jinny. "That's past. I'm teaching her to jump now."

"Would you consider it?" Mr. Manders asked.

"Could I have a ride on her? I've an hour to spare. My trekkers are morning and evening today."

"Certainly," said Mr. Manders. "O.K., Jinny?"

And somehow they were all out of the house and walking down the path to Shantih's field. Shantih looked up from her grazing, nostrils flurrying a welcome, and came

175

towards them with her exact, precise step. Jinny slipped the halter over her ears and led her back towards the stables.

"Hoy. Hi there," called voices, and across the fields came Sue, trotting on Pippin, and Mrs. Horton running behind her.

"Gosh me," exclaimed Mrs. Horton, out of breath as she caught up with them. "Need to do something about this flab."

"Oh, Mummy!" said Sue.

"All right for you young things. Wait till you're my age. It creeps up on you."

Mrs. Manders said she knew how it felt and that she too was being crept up on.

"A few weeks' trekking and you'd soon be fit again," said Miss Tuke.

"That's what we want to see you about," Mrs. Horton said. "We saw you drive past in your van. Pine Trekking Centre?"

"That's me," said Miss Tuke.

"Could we trek for a day this week?"

"Certainly. How would Thursday suit?"

"Very well. My husband and I haven't done any riding before, but with Sue having Pippen we're into horses, as they say, and we thought that before we go home this year we would have a shot at riding them."

"That's the spirit," encouraged Miss Tuke. "Two on Thursday. Full day trek."

"Three," corrected Mrs. Horton. "Sue is coming too. And Jinny?"

"It's too expensive," said Jinny. "I can't afford it."

"Jinny can ride Bramble," said Miss Tuke. "We'll call it a reunion. No charge."

"I don't know if I'll have time . . ." Jinny said, but no one was listening to her. They all took it for granted that she would go. Jinny supposed that it would be nice to see Bramble again.

"Thursday, then," said Mrs. Horton. "That's a definite booking. Hail or snow, we will be there."

Mrs. Manders, Mr. Manders and Mrs. Horton went back to Finmory while Jinny saddled up Shantih. Miss Tuke gathered up her reins and mounted. Her toe dug into Shantih, making the Arab spring away from her.

"Stand, you twister," bawled Miss Tuke as she struggled into the saddle. Her hands clutched at the reins, making Shantih fling her head into the air and Jinny wince.

"Tell you one thing," Miss Tuke shouted to them. "If I take her she'll stand to be mounted before I've finished with her. Never had a Highland yet that didn't learn that lesson. You couldn't have trekkers behaving like this."

Jinny wanted to shout back that it had been Miss Tuke's toe digging into her side that had made Shantih spring away, but, before she had time to reply, Miss Tuke was riding Shantih round the field.

Sue, Pippen and Jinny watched from the field gate, Pippen resting his blubber chin on the top bar, half closing his eyes.

When Miss Tuke trotted, she banged up and down on Shantih's back, her hands clamped heavily on the reins, her solid legs tight against Shantih's sides. There was no sweetness in her riding, no feeling for her horse. Miss Tuke might as well have been driving a tractor.

"All right to canter?" bawled Miss Tuke.

"Yes," said Jinny, because there was nothing else she could say.

Miss Tuke kicked Shantih into a canter, but instantly her hands pulled on Shantih's reins to slow her down again. Shantih battered round the field at a ragged, unbalanced trot.

"Canter, you idiot," yelled Miss Tuke, scarlet in the face as she held Shantih's mouth in a stranglehold and kicked her Wellington boots into Shantih's sides.

"She's not much of a rider," whispered Sue. "But she wouldn't be scared of Shantih."

Jinny had turned away. She couldn't bear to watch any longer.

"She'd ruin her," said Jinny bitterly.

"Of course, we'll need to discuss details," said Miss Tuke when she dismounted, "but if you do want me to take her I'd be quite willing to consider it. We'd have some good rides wouldn't we, old girl? Soon get some sense into your noddle." Miss Tuke clapped Shantih's neck with her broad, capable hand. "Must be off. See you both on Thursday."

177

"Come for a ride," suggested Sue, when Miss Tuke had driven away.

"Where to?"

"Over the moors?"

Jinny glanced quickly up at the moors. They stretched, flaxen, bronze and purple, to the far mountains. The after glow had faded from the sky. Light came from the rust gold bracken.

"Let's jump," said Jinny. "In the field."

"Oh no. Come for a ride."

"I want to jump."

"If you jump Shantih much more over those same jumps you'll sicken her for life."

"Won't."

"Well, I'm going for a ride." Sue turned Pippen and began to ride towards the moors.

For a moment Jinny hesitated, wanting Sue's company, wanting to be chatting and laughing together, the way it had been at the beginning of the holidays. Almost, she called to Sue to wait, almost, she sent Shantih trotting after them. But she didn't. She watched Pippen's skewbald quarters and Sue's straight, square-set back climb towards the moors, then she rode Shantih to the field where the jumps were.

Seeing the jumps, Shantih began to prance with excitement, tossing her head and clinking her bit. Jinny leaned her weight forward in the saddle, her knees tight, her feet braced against the stirrups, and Shantih surged forward. She soared over the jumps, her forelegs tucked in, close to her body, forelock blown back, her face hollowed by her speed, her eyes alight.

"Again," whispered Jinny.

She didn't want Shantih to stop. Wanted her to go on jumping, on and on. It was only when she was jumping Shantih, absorbed in the thrill of her pounding hooves and soaring leaps that Jinny felt safe, that she was able to forget the Red Horse. All the rest of the time it was there, haunting the edges of her mind, waiting for her to fall asleep so that it could come, brazen and terrible, charging into her dreams.

178

CHAPTER FIVE

Jinny cantered Shantih back to her field. She had been up since five o'clock, jumping in the field in the chill, early morning and now she was sure she was late. This morning, Ken and her father were taking Mike to Inverburgh to catch the Stopton train. Then they were taking a load of pottery to Nell Storr's craft shop. Jinny had to go with them. She had to get the money from Nell for her paintings and find out how many more Nell would be willing to buy.

Jinny took off Shantih's tack in her field. Not even waiting to see Shantih roll, she shut the gate and ran up to the tack room. She flung the bridle down and placed Sue's saddle carefully on a rack.

"Why someone doesn't give me a watch that works, I don't know," Jinny cursed as she ran up to the house. She felt tight and cross, as if she wasn't properly there. Last night her dreams had been worse. The Red Horse closer than before. Huddled under her bedclothes, Jinny had lain petrified, afraid of the painting on her wall, afraid of falling back into her dream.

"I'm coming with you," Jinny yelled to her family who were gathered at the front door, saying goodbye to Mike.

"Where have you been?" asked her mother.

"Jumping," called back Jinny, racing upstairs three at a time.

"We're going NOW," shouted her father. "We haven't time to wait for you."

"I'm ready," yelled Jinny.

In her room she snatched up the pile of drawings and turned to race back downstairs.

Mr. Manders was at the wheel, Ken and Mike getting into the car.

"Wait! Wait!" shouted Jinny, flinging herself through the hall and out of the door.

"You haven't had any breakfast," said her mother despairingly.

179

"And look at your hair. You haven't even brushed it," said Petra.

Jinny ignored them. She jumped into the back of the car with Mike and collapsed, gasping for breath.

"Didn't know you wanted to come," said Mr. Manders, driving down the road. "Another minute and we'd have been away without you."

"I thought you weren't even going to say goodbye," added Mike.

" 'Course I was," said Jinny. "I'll miss you."

"You will," agreed Mike. "You'll need to go for the milk every day."

"You'll need to do a fortnight when you come back," said Jinny.

"I'll need to do a whole term," said Mike. "You'll be at Duninver."

Jinny felt her blood run suddenly cold. It wasn't true. It couldn't be true—that Mike was going to Stopton and when he came back she was to go to Duninver, Shantih to Miss Tuke's.

Standing on the station platform waving goodbye to Mike, Jinny saw his departure as the first in a series of events. Now Mike had gone, all the other things must happen, like a row of dominoes all having to fall once the first one had been knocked over.

"Enjoy yourself," called Mr. Manders, waving. "Send us postcards."

Mike's head and waving arm vanished round the curve of the track. He had gone. Jinny walked, cold and miserable, back to the car. She curled into the corner of the back seat, wishing desperately that Mike hadn't had to go away just now. With the Horse so close she needed all her family to be with her, to make Finmory a safe place where she could hide.

"Joy to see you," Nell Storr greeted them, opening the doors of her shop so that Ken and Mr. Manders could carry in their crates of pottery. "Pile them up. Your shelves are nearly empty again."

Jinny helped to stack the pottery on the shelves, then she followed Ken and her father into Nell's office at the back of the shop. Normally, she would have been prowling around, looking at the carvings and weavings, the em-

180

broideries and silverware which filled the shop, but today she only wanted to show her pictures to Nell, to find out how much she would pay for them.

"Four orders for mugs and coffee pots. A woman at that phone number wants to know if you'd be interested in making a chess set for her with pottery pieces. And how do you feel about some Christmas things—hanging plates, Christmas bowls, candle holders?"

Nell Storr was wearing a black and purple velvet dress. When she moved, it seemed to flow around her like theatre curtains, Jinny thought. Her Afro hair was dyed orange, her lips painted to match her hair, and her long fingers knuckled with rings.

"Quite a turn up for the book, Bob Schultz liking your stuff," Nell said to Ken. "Seems he walked into the exhibition, more or less went straight over to the stall where my lot were on show, picked out your pots, asked where they'd come from and said he'd found his apprentice for this winter. Lucky you. Wouldn't mind spending a few months in his pottery myself." Nell raised her eyebrows in mock despair at the confusion of papers and samples in her crowded office.

"I'm going up to London on Friday for the weekend," she said. "You can drive up with me. Bob Schultz will be there, and we've to get in touch with him when we arrive."

"Great," said Ken.

"He wants to meet you before anything definite is decided. You don't need to worry, though—from what I've seen of him he is as silent as yourself. You'll get along."

Ken's slow smile spread over his face, lighting his eyes, lifting the corners of his lips.

"And he's a vegetarian."

"I guessed," said Ken, laughing.

But Jinny could only think that next weekend was Petra's piano exam; that Ken, her mother and Petra would all be away at the same time; that already Mike had gone.

"I've brought you some more drawings," Jinny said, when Nell had finished talking to Ken.

"Good," said Nell. "You have been busy," she added, seeing Jinny's pile of paintings. "I am honoured to have all these. Let's see them." Nell cleared a space on her desk.

Jinny spread out her paintings and drawings of Shantih.

181

She hadn't looked at them since she had finished them, and now, with Nell, her father and Ken all looking at them, Jinny realised how very bad they were. She laid them out quickly, trying to cover up the worst. The last three drawings were of her nightmare. Jinny hadn't meant to bring them with her. She had forgotten that she had hidden them under the others when Miss Tuke had arrived. She hid them behind her back and waited in the uncomfortable silence while Nell flicked through the paintings.

"You did these?" Nell asked at last.

"All of Shantih," said Jinny, trying to sound confident and enthusiastic. "You said they liked Shantih best, that you wanted more of her."

Still Nell didn't speak. She laid the worst ones back on the desk, then she looked straight at Jinny, lifting her eyebrows questioningly.

"They won't do," she said. "What went wrong?"

Jinny felt herself going red.

"I thought you wanted more of my drawings," she mumbled.

"Not this trash," said Nell. "I wouldn't sell them, even if I could."

"They're O.K.," said Jinny. "You have to buy them so that I'll have enough money to pay for Shantih."

"But I'm going to pay Miss Tuke," said Mr. Manders.

"Oh, not Miss Tuke!" snapped Jinny. "Shantih's not going to her. I'm going to find someone in Glenbost who'll take her."

"They've no magic," said Nell, shuffling the rejected pictures together. "No life. To create, you have to tear out your own heart and not expect to get it back. You haven't torn out a single hair for these. Let's see the ones you're hiding behind your back."

Reluctantly, Jinny produced the three drawings of her nightmare.

"Ah ha! Come on now," said Nell. "I'll buy these from you. In fact, I'll buy the one of the horse for myself. Fifteen pounds?"

"Nightmares?" asked her father, looking searchingly at Jinny. "We thought we heard you screaming in your sleep. Have you dreamed about this often?"

"All the time," said Jinny, and she bit into her lower lip to stop it shaking.

"Sue told me you were both nearly bogged down on the way to the dig. Is that what's giving you the nightmares?"

"Am I glad that horse chose you and not me. Can I have him?" asked Nell.

Jinny shook her head. Fifteen pounds would be no use to her. Who would look after Shantih for fifteen pounds? And she would never have enough time to paint real pictures of Shantih. Before she could paint the kind of pictures Nell wanted, Jinny had to see what she was going to paint clearly in her mind's eye; know it before she could paint it.

Ken was looking at the nightmare drawings, holding them carefully in his long, bony hands.

"The Horse in the mural?" he asked.

Jinny nodded.

"What mural?" asked Nell, and Mr. Manders explained, adding that she must come out and see it some time.

"You'll have seen the little statue of Epona?" Nell asked Jinny.

"Freda, the archaeologist at the dig at Brachan, mentioned her. Said the Celts used to worship her," said Mr. Manders.

Hearing the word Epona spoken out loud sent shivers up and down Jinny's spine. You shouldn't speak of a goddess like that, not out loud where anyone could hear you. She wanted to warn Nell but couldn't find the words.

"You haven't seen her? Oh, but you must visit the Wilton Collection. I'll take you now. Some rather nice pottery—and Jinny must see Epona."

"Yes," said Jinny. "I must. Let's go now."

Suddenly it didn't matter that Nell hadn't taken her drawings. To see Epona mattered more than anything else. Yet it wasn't like wanting to see something new, more like going back to Stopton to see one of her special places again, to go at once in case it should have changed.

"You really won't sell me the horse?" Nell asked. "I'll make it twenty."

"No," said Jinny. She needed her drawings. Somehow, to have drawn her nightmare gave it less power.

"Sorry I can't take the others."

"Doesn't matter." Jinny tore her other pictures into pieces and dumped them into Nell's wastepaper basket. "I knew they were no good."

"Going out for an hour," Nell called to her assistant, and led the way out of the shop.

"Only five minutes," she told them. "We don't need to take the car."

"You'll love the Wilton Collection," she said as they walked along. "Belongs to an old boy, ninety odd he must be now. All things collected by himself and his two brothers. Some very valuable stuff. The big museums are always on at him to let them take over his collection. Saying it is inadequately protected and that sort of guff. But no one ever seems to steal it. Just the opposite. You're always reading in the local paper that someone or other has died and left things to the Wilton."

People in the street turned to look at them—Nell in her flowing gown, Mr. Manders, balding with his red beard, and Ken, bleakboned as if he had been washed by the tides.

"Next time I shall be riding Shantih." The thought came into Jinny's head as if a voice had spoken it, a mad thought, for how could she ever ride through the Inverburgh streets, which were crowded with double-decker buses, cars, vans and lorries?

Nell turned down a side street where the high tenement buildings had an indrawn grace. She stopped by a plaque that announced The Wilton Collection—Open To The Public Monday to Saturday, 9 a.m. to 7 p.m. Admission Free.

Nell pushed open the outside door and they all climbed up a wide staircase to a long corridor. On either side of the corridor were glass exhibition cases, and on the walls were shelves of vases and pots. There was no sound. The thick walls absorbed all the noise of the Inverburgh traffic. For a moment they stood in silence, surrounded by the watching objects.

"George must be having his cuppa," said Nell. "He usually is. I'll introduce you later. Quite a character. Been caretaker here for fifty years."

She walked on. "Now for Epona."

They followed Nell into one of the three rooms leading

184

off the main corridor. The windows were stained glass, colouring the dusty light. The display cases around the room were old, made of dark wood and thick glass. Nell led the way to a case in the corner.

"Here she is."

Jinny had crossed the room with Nell, her throat and mouth suddenly dry and her heart lumping and thumping. Her mind felt like a kite pulling away from her body so that she seemed to be looking down on the room. It was a giddy, slipping feeling, making her hold on to the display case with both hands.

The statue of Epona was about six inches high. A woman with a round head, and wearing a long, sweeping dress, was seated sideways on a heavy, native pony. In one hand she held the reins and in the other a round fruit. There was no detail in the statue, only the simple shapes. The woman, the thickset pony and the fruit in her open hand.

Jinny stood without moving, hardly breathing. Vaguely she heard the others saying that they were going to look at some pottery as they left her alone.

The woman, the pony and the fruit.

Jinny felt the edge of the case move under her grasp. The wood round the lock had decayed into dry tinder. Jinny forced the lid of the case open. The lock lifted out of the rotten wood. She saw her hand reach into the case and lift the pony goddess out. Jinny held it in her open hand. From a corner of the ceiling her mind watched and recorded. The little statue seemed to pulsate with a beat of stored energy. It seemed to grow and swell, dwarfing Jinny. Words long forgotten, long buried, struggled to be heard again.

Voices came from one of the other rooms, footsteps crossed the corridor. The others were coming back. For endless seconds, Jinny couldn't move her arm, couldn't make it put Epona back into the case. It seemed certain that they must find her holding it. At the last possible moment Jinny broke the spell, forced herself to return the statue to its case and close the lid.

The others came into the room. Loud and violent they came straight towards her. Jinny turned to face them. Words came out of her mouth in a voice that was her own and not her own.

185

"Not one," she said, "but one."

"Surely you must know what you meant," persisted Mr. Manders as they drove home. "When you say something you must know why you've said it."

"But I don't," said Jinny miserably. "I just say things. I don't know I'm going to say them."

" 'The kraken waketh'," quoted Ken, which didn't seem to make much sense either.

"There's a letter for you," Mrs. Manders said to her husband when they reached Finmory again, but Mr. Manders had seen it the second he had walked into the room—a long, white, foolscap envelope lying on the sideboard. He picked it up quickly. It had a typed address, a London postmark. It might just be from the publishers who had his manuscript. He tore it open and pulled out the letter.

"Someone wanting info on one of my Stopton boys," he said, putting the letter down and going to make himself a cup of tea.

"Next time," said Mrs. Manders.

"But they've had it for ages," said Jinny. "Weeks and weeks. I'd phone them to find out what's happening to it. Maybe they've lost it."

"I'll write in another fortnight," said Mr. Manders. "I have the date ringed on my calendar when I give in and write to them."

"At least you would know," said Mrs. Manders.

"Better to travel hopefully," said Mr. Manders.

Jinny heard Sue riding up to the back door, and went out to see her.

"Hi! Smashing day," said Sue. "What are we going to do?"

"Nothing special," said Jinny warily. What she really wanted to do was to stay at home, safe and secure in Finmory with her family round about her.

"Come for a ride," begged Sue.

Jinny shook her head. She didn't want to go out on to the moors. Even the moors round Finmory that she knew well weren't safe when the Red Horse was looking for her.

"Oh, please. It's so much better when you come. I can

186

have a gallop when you're there. When I'm alone I'm always sure I'm going to break Pippen's legs."

"Let's jump," said Jinny.

"Mr. MacKenzie says you've been jumping already this morning."

"Trust him to see me," said Jinny in disgust.

"You can't jump again. Not so soon. You really will sicken her. Come for a ride. I only have nine more days left."

Jinny was shocked. She couldn't imagine life at Finmory without Sue. The summer holidays had been going on forever. Sue and Pippen had always been there.

"So please, please, please, do come for a ride."

"Oh. O.K. then. After lunch."

"I feel," Jinny announced to her family at lunch, "as if fate is against me. As if all the worst things are zooming straight at me."

"Do you want more pie?" asked her mother, and even Ken was talking to her father about shops in London where they could buy things they needed for the pottery.

"Where do you want to go?" Jinny asked Sue when they had both mounted.

"To the standing stones," said Sue, and began to ride Pippen along the path to the moors.

Jinny opened her mouth to shout after her, to tell her that she wasn't going near the stones, but she couldn't make a sound. She tried again as Shantih trotted after Pippen, but her voice croaked in her throat.

Waves of moorland flowed out behind them as they rode towards the stones. The mountains were metal ridged, sharply defined against the sky. Sue was chatting about cavalletti but Jinny wasn't listening.

The jagged teeth of the standing stones came into sight over a rise in the moorland. Jinny felt as if they were waiting for her, drawing her towards them. Shantih was playing up, shying and fretting, refusing to walk. Jinny sat down hard in the saddle, forcing her to walk on.

"What's got into her today?" said Sue, watching Shantih's antics from the safety of Pippin's broad back, his steady plod.

A heron flew up from one of the pools in the heather.

187

Shantih reared straight up, stood poised on her hind legs. Jinny clutched at handfuls of mane. For a moment she was certain that Shantih must overbalance and fall. She heard Sue scream, and the harsh craak of the heron, then Shantih had touched down again, half reared, and thrown herself forward into a flat-out gallop.

By the time Jinny had managed to stop her, they were almost at the standing stones. No longer were they teeth in the distance, but towering blocks of stone, standing in a broken ring, crowning this height of the moor. Shantih's mouth was white with froth, her chest foam-flecked, and her sides darkened with sweat. She stood shaking, her head down, as Pippen came trundling across the heather to reach them.

Suddenly Shantih threw up her head, ears alert, eyes wide. She whinnied, but she wasn't calling to Pippen, she was calling to something behind the stones.

The low sun shone directly between two of the upright stones, blinding Jinny. Its light glistered on Shantih's eyeballs as she stood, tense and tight, her neck arched and hard. Sitting on her, Jinny knew she had lost all control over her horse. Shantih had forgotten that there was anyone riding her.

Shantih whinnied again, a clarion blast of noise. The sound rolled over the moors. The echoes died, and in the silence that followed Jinny heard the thunder of hooves coming from behind the standing stones. She felt the ground shudder with their impact, felt the moment of indrawn breath before the terror burst upon her.

And in that moment Jinny had pulled Shantih's head round, sawing at the bit, kicking her heels in her horse's sides, cracking the slack of the reins against her neck and screaming at the pitch of her voice. Anything, anything to escape from the hooves that were thundering down on her from behind the black of the standing stones.

Shantih saw the reins flap against her neck. Almost forgotten memories of the circus, and the ringmaster's whip, stirred in her memory. She flung herself away from the whip, away from the reins. The movement was enough to allow Jinny to make contact with her horse again. She urged her into a furious gallop away from the stones.

When Sue eventually caught up with them, Jinny had

dismounted and was leaning over Shantih's withers, her face hidden.

"What on earth was all that about?" demanded Sue.

"Didn't you hear it?" cried Jinny, looking up so that Sue could see her white, panic-stricken face. "Didn't you hear the hooves?"

"No. Only you galloping off like a lunatic."

"Didn't you hear them coming from behind the stones? The hooves?"

"No, I did not. You must have heard Pippen. There must have been an echo or something that made it sound as if his hoofbeats were coming from that direction."

Jinny remounted slowly. Her whole body ached. Her head throbbed.

"I know what Pippen sounds like," she said. "It wasn't Pippen."

CHAPTER SIX

"Now, you will be sensible and tell Miss Tuke that you'll be pleased to accept her offer," insisted Jinny's mother.

Jinny was waiting for the Hortons to arrive and collect her for their day's pony trekking.

"You could look after her if you tried," said Jinny reproachfully. "I'd show you what to do, and, if anything did go wrong, Mr. MacKenzie would come up and sort it out."

"Oh, Jinny, be sensible. I could not look after Shantih. I know absolutely nothing about horses, and, although you never seem to notice it, there is a lot of work involved in keeping this house going. Miss Tuke is the ideal person to take her. There is no other solution."

"There are always other ways. It's just that we haven't thought of them yet," stated Jinny, straining her ears for the sound of the Hortons' car.

Mrs. Manders sighed. "Do you always have to be so difficult?" she asked.

Jinny didn't reply. She was thinking the same thing about her mother.

189

"Now, do tell Miss Tuke that you want her to take Shantih for the winter."

"There's the Hortons," cried Jinny in relief, jumping up and running out of the kitchen.

Mrs. Manders stared after her. "If only the school at Inverburgh had been ready to open on time or I knew about horses," she thought. "And she's looking like a ghost, having these nightmares every night."

"Oh, Jinny, Jinny, Jinny," Mrs. Manders said aloud to the empty kitchen.

"Hi," said Sue, opening the car door.

"Low," said Jinny, climbing in beside her.

"You do look pale," said Mrs. Horton, inspecting Jinny. "If you were Sue I'd say you were sickening for something."

"I'm just low," said Jinny. She hadn't slept much the night before. Not sleeping made it impossible to dream, and if she didn't dream, the Red Horse couldn't reach her. Jinny had spent the night sitting up in bed, reading. She had balanced two magazines on her head so that when she dozed off they fell down and woke her up again.

When they reached Miss Tuke's yard, six Highland ponies were standing tethered to a bar. There were three duns, one bay, one steel grey and one black pony.

"Bramble!" cried Jinny, and she was out of the car almost before it had stopped. She ran across the yard to the black pony. "Bramble," she called. "There's the good pony. There's the good Bramble."

The black pony turned his head, pricked his ears through his heavy forelock, wiffled his nostrils, uncertainly and knitted his brows together. He still wasn't sure who it was.

"Bramble," called Jinny again, and the pony was certain. He whickered, flurries of sound to welcome Jinny.

"He knows you," boomed Miss Tuke, striding across the yard. "I've never seen him do that to anyone except myself. Pity you'll not need him again this winter. He must have enjoyed being with you."

Jinny threw her arms round Bramble's neck. After Shantih, he was broad and bulky. Even his lips, fumbling at her hand for titbits, seemed rubbery and huge after Shantih's delicate lipping. Jinny ran her hand down his

190

neck and over his back, and suddenly she was back to last winter, riding Bramble home from school, feeding him and grooming him.

"Dear Bramble," said Jinny again. "You would have been coming back to Finmory if only they'd finished the bloomin' school in time."

Miss Tuke was welcoming the Hortons.

"Glad to see you haven't changed your minds," she said. "You don't need to worry about a thing. All my ponies are patent safety. Absolutely guaranteed to look after the rawest recruit."

"Not raw yet," said Mr. Horton, "but I dare say I shall be before the day is over."

"Mr. and Mrs. Cunningham," said Miss Tuke, introducing a young man and woman.

"Tim and Marigold," they said, introducing themselves.

Two other ladies joined them. One was very fat, with iron grey hair and glasses. She introduced herself as Brenda, and her companion, who was round-shouldered with a vacant, worried expression, as Pam. All four were beginners who hadn't ridden before their trekking holiday.

"Normally," said Miss Tuke, "it is my unbreakable rule that every trekker has to groom and tack up their own pony."

"Then we will not be leaving this yard," declared Mrs. Horton. "I could never put that bit into a pony's mouth. Their teeth are so obviously built for biting."

"Oh, Mummy," muttered Sue.

"But," continued Miss Tuke, "since Mr. and Mrs. Horton are only with us for the day, I shall permit their daughter to help them."

"Now," she said, "let's see—Marigold, Brenda and Pam, your mounts are in their boxes. When you've got them tacked up I'll check them for you. Tim, Beech for you." Miss Tuke pointed to the bay pony that was tied to the rail.

"Mr. Horton, Fergus for you." She showed Mr. Horton the biggest of the dun ponies. "He is one hundred per cent shock-proof. Compared to Fergus, your favourite armchair is dynamite."

Mrs. Horton was to ride Meg, the smallest of the duns, and Sue was to have Shona, the third dun.

191

"She'll nip you if she gets the chance," Miss Tuke warned Sue. "Too much darling pepperminting has been going on with her ladyship all summer. But she's a good ride. You'll enjoy her."

Miss Tuke handed out dandy brushes, telling them to pay particular attention to where the saddle and girth would go.

"Have you seen my stables?" Miss Tuke asked Jinny.

"No."

"Have a quick sortie round now, if you like."

Jinny would rather have gone on grooming Bramble. She paused, trying to think of some way of saying 'no' politely, but Miss Tuke was already marching across the yard.

"She only wants me to look round her stables so that I'll think they would be all right for Shantih," Jinny thought rebelliously, as she trailed after Miss Tuke.

"This is my tack room," said Miss Tuke.

In spite of herself, Jinny was impressed. There were rows of saddle racks on the walls, each with a place for a bridle underneath it and the name of the pony to whom the tack belonged. There was a saddle horse, buckets, and a basket filled with tack-cleaning equipment. One wall was covered with the certificates Miss Tuke had won with her Highlands.

"And this is my feed house."

It was as spruce and polished as the tack room. There was a neat row of feed bins, buckets, with the ponies' names written on them, hanging from hooks, and a sleek tabby cat licking her paws as she watched for mice.

"I have three boxes and six stalls," said Miss Tuke, showing them to Jinny.

The boxes were occupied by a grey Highland, a skewbald, and a chestnut pony with a wall eye. Each pony had its attendant trekker working on it with a dandy.

"If you decide to let Shantih come here for the winter, she would have one of these boxes and probably a Highland next door to her for company."

Jinny said nothing. She stood looking round the stabling. The floors of the boxes were well brushed, troughs scrubbed out, the woodwork freshly painted, but it wasn't the place

192

for Shantih. The only place for Shantih was at Finmory, with Jinny there to look after her.

"It won't happen," said Jinny. "I'm not going to Duninver. I can't leave Shantih."

"Let me know if you change your mind," said Miss Tuke. "I've taken quite a shine to her. Stir up my middle-aged bones having her here."

Jinny didn't want Miss Tuke to have taken a shine to her horse. She didn't want Shantih stirring up middle-aged bones.

"He will not stand still while I fasten his girth," shrilled Pam. "He is being a very naughty boy this morning."

Miss Tuke went to her aid, and Jinny returned to Bramble.

Already, Bramble was beginning to cast his summer coat and grow his dense winter one. Jinny swept her dandy brush down his strong neck and powerful shoulders and over his broad back. The familiar movements comforted her. So many mornings before she had set out for school she had groomed Bramble. She left his tail to the end. The hairs were coarse and wiry compared to Shantih's silken tail. Jinny felt she could have gone on trying to brush it out for hours without making much difference to it. Eventually she gave it up as a bad job and went to find his tack.

The yard was loud with voices.

"Darling, I cannot put that lump of metal into any creature's mouth. I am sure they can't like it," pleaded Mrs. Horton.

"Whoa there, Tiger," cried Tim, as Beech whisked her tail. "Got to be firm with them," he informed Mr. Horton. "Let them know who's in charge." Tim jumped hastily backwards as Beech shook her head.

"It's the size of this fellow that's worrying me," confided Mr. Horton. "Do we ancients climb up steps, or is there a hoist to lower us into the saddle?"

"You spring, Daddy," said Sue, tacking up Fergus for her father.

"I have not sprung anywhere for years," said Mr Horton. "I wonder might it be a better idea if I follow you in the car?"

"How are we doing?" asked Miss Tuke, distributing

193

packed lunches in waterproof bags to be tied to the saddles. "Getting on with it? Good, good. Jinny, would you saddle up the grey for me while I get the ladies on board. She's only four. Misty's her name. I'm riding her myself for a few treks this summer. She's still full of the joys, quite a handful. Only hope she's settled in by next year."

When they were all mounted, Miss Tuke cast her experienced eye over her trekkers, untied Misty and heaved herself into the saddle. The young pony jumped back as Miss Tuke's weight banged down on her back.

"Stand still, you little varmit," Miss Tuke shouted as she jabbed the pony in the mouth to stop it going forward while she hit it behind the saddle.

"Rattle up their ribs," she announced. "Always have a stick handy when you're riding a youngster."

Jinny watched in silent despair. Would Miss Tuke always have a stick handy when she was riding Shantih? If Miss Tuke tried to hit Shantih, the Arab would panic, but Miss Tuke would fight back. Jinny's heart sank as she watched Miss Tuke's heavy hands and her solid dead weight in the saddle. She would treat Shantih as if she were a trekking pony—shouting at her, hitting her, thumping down on her back and yanking at her mouth. No matter how smart the stables were or how spotless the feed house, Jinny knew that Shantih could never, never come here.

"Everybody fit?" Miss Tuke called. "Good. Mrs. Horton come in front beside me. Mr. Horton and Tim behind us. Marigold and Pam next. Brenda and Sue behind them. Jinny, you and Bramble are our rear guard. Pick up the drop offs and keep them all moving."

"O.K.," said Jinny. "We'll do our best."

"We're going to the white sands," Miss Tuke told them. "Bit further than we usually go, so let's hope the weather will be kind. The view is superb but the sands are mostly mud-coloured."

Miss Tuke rode Misty out of the yard and Mrs. Horton's pony fell in beside her.

"Here we go," said Tim. "Wagons roll. Keep Fergus up with me. He's Tiger's buddy."

The three ladies, rather bunched together, their ponies glowering, went through the gate next, then Sue and Jinny.

The track from the yard led through Forestry roads, then

194

wound over hills that were grassy and more rolling than the moors around Finmory. Jinny smiled to herself. It was good to be riding Bramble again, to feel his steady stride and have his strong neck reaching in front of her.

"You are a good pony," Jinny assured him, burying her hands in the warmth of his shaggy mane.

In front of them, the other trekkers bumped happily along. Brenda had her skewbald well under control. In spite of her fat she seemed to know what she was doing. Pam's chestnut had her well under control. Every now and again he stopped to restock with mouthfuls of grass.

"Let's try a trot," called back Miss Tuke. "Reins in one hand and a good tight hold on the front of the saddle with the other. Right? Good. Trek, trot forward."

The ponies knew Miss Tuke's command. "I expect they trot here on every trek," thought Jinny, watching the riders bumping about. "Bet the ponies would know where to trot even if there was no one riding them."

"Hold on there," encouraged Tim, as Mr. Horton swooped dangerously to one side.

"Don't worry, I'm well anchored," Mr. Horton assured him. "I'm holding the saddle with both hands."

"Going to walk again," called back Miss Tuke. "Walk now." But the ponies, hearing the shout, were already walking.

Jinny knew that, normally, trekking would have bored her to death. She couldn't have bothered with so many beginners, would have wanted to canter and jump, but to-day she was glad they were all there. She wanted to be with a crowd of people, to be doing things together. The Red Horse could not reach her here. She was safe with the trekkers.

They had been riding for about two hours when the far glint of the sea came into sight and the track began to lead downhill.

"Lunch in half an hour," called back Miss Tuke.

When they reached the shore, they tethered their ponies to stobs in the ground.

"There's a sheltered spot over here," Miss Tuke told them, when she had checked that all the ponies were safely tied up. "We can get behind those rocks. 'Fraid there isn't going to be a view today. You're out of luck."

Black clouds were massing over the grey sky, and the waves rolling up the beach were white with foam.

Crouching in the shelter of the rocks, they ate their sandwiches and drank hot soup in paper cups from a thermos Miss Tuke had brought with her. The trekkers compared moments.

"Did you see Beech leap when that sheep got up suddenly?" asked Tim. "I thought he was going in to the attack."

"We call it shying," said Miss Tuke. "She was having you on. She has met a sheep before."

Pam asked what she should do to stop her pony grazing but no one heard her. Mr. Horton said never again, and Mrs Horton said she was enjoying it and would be having shots on Pippen when she got home.

"We won't waste too much time here," said Miss Tuke, brisking them up. "No point in hanging around when there's no view. Think we're in for a soaking and we've a fair bit to go."

"Mercy, woman," said Mr. Horton. "Let me have a few more moments of earth-bound bliss before I go into orbit again. I am an old man."

But Miss Tuke was worried about the weather, and chased them back to the ponies as soon as possible.

Quickly and efficiently she helped the trekkers to untie their ponies and tighten their girths, then she hoisted them into their saddles before they realised what was happening.

Despite Miss Tuke's haste, heavy raindrops were falling as they rode away from the shore.

"Into single file here," Miss Tuke told them in her foghorn voice. "Keep directly behind the pony in front of you. There are a lot of rabbit warrens here, so don't let them wander about. Pam, shorten your reins and sit back a bit. Don't let him graze."

Although the sky was black and louring, it still wasn't really raining—only heavy, single drops of rain. In front of Jinny, the trekkers were billowing into plastic macs and rainhoods, making a bright patch of colour on the bleak moor.

"Why can't we have a trot?" asked Sue, riding beside Jinny. "We'd be home much more quickly if she let us trot."

Jinny hunched her shoulders. "Expect it would be slower if one of them fell off," she said.

Really, she didn't care what happened to the trekkers. All the impossible things had come crowding back into her mind. It was not possible that in a fortnight Shantih would be at Miss Tuke's and she would be at Duninver School.

"What am I doing here?" thought Jinny furiously. "I should be riding Shantih. I should be finding someone in Glenbost who will look after her through the week. I should be making money. I shouldn't be wasting my time here."

Then Jinny glanced back over her shoulder, saw white mist wreathing between the moor and the clouds, mists sweeping over the heather towards them, white fingers reaching out to grasp them, ghosts rising. And Jinny knew why she was there—to be with other people, to be doing something safe and ordinary, to be where the Red Horse couldn't find her. She had been safe in the morning, had almost forgotten the Horse, but now, with the change in the weather, the Horse was close behind her, was all about her, seeking her out.

Suddenly the wind whipped a plastic rainhood off Marigold's head and sent it flapping down the line of ponies. Brenda grabbed at it and missed. Her sudden movement startled her pony, who leaped forward into the rear of Pam's pony. The rainhood blew into Meg's quarters. The terrified pony bucked and Mrs. Horton screamed and clutched.

"Hands down," shouted Miss Tuke, but her words were lost as the plastic rainhood came crackling and blustering straight at her pony's head. The young pony reared in fright.

Jinny urged Bramble forward, knowing that if Miss Tuke's young pony started playing up, all the ponies would become excited. At that moment a sheet of lightning flickered over the sky and, almost immediately, thunder crashed over their heads.

"Hold on to your saddles," instructed Miss Tuke, unable to do any more than call out instructions as she struggled to calm her own terrified pony.

Jinny saw Fergus charge forward with Mr. Horton clinging to the saddle, his plastic mac billowing out in the wind.

Tim and Beech were close behind him, and in a second it seemed that the whole trek was galloping over the moor. Jinny fought to hold Bramble back, to steady him, to stop him joining in the runaway.

The storm clouds burst open. Rain blew into Jinny's face, blinding her; the wind howled in her ears, deafening her, and Bramble fought to follow the others.

And then the plastic-coated trekkers had gone. Jinny shouted aloud, the sound she made came from the base of her throat, blood-curdling, haunting. Her heels drummed against her pony's sides as she urged him forward, forced him straight through the band of galloping riders. Again and again Jinny cried out, rallying those who followed her to ride faster. They crouched over their ponies' necks, the skins they wore were sodden with the rain, their long hair matted on their shoulders. Their wordless cry spread over the moors, flowed out behind them and Jinny was one of them. She rode with the Pony Folk.

"Jinny Manders. Come back here. Sto⍵ galloping. Stop it at once."

Miss Tuke's furious voice reached Jinny. Her hands gripped leather reins again, once more she was riding on a saddle. For moments she was lost, terrified, caught in the horror of not knowing where she was, who she was.

"Stop that galloping!"

Somehow, Jinny swung her pony back to the sound of the voice. The moor was dotted with loose ponies and trekkers lying on the ground.

"What do you think you're doing, forcing him on like that? You could easily have stopped Bramble."

Jinny rubbed her hand over her eyes.

"Where have they gone?" she demanded. "The Pony Folk?"

Jinny searched the moor for the dark galloping fury, the men crouching over the necks of their ponies, the beat and pound of their hooves.

"Where have they gone?" Jinny cried.

CHAPTER SEVEN

The next morning, Jinny was sitting in the back of their car, being driven home from Inverburgh to Finmory. The seat next to her father was empty, but somehow it was safer to be sitting in the back and better for talking to her father. She could say things to the back of his head that she couldn't have said if she had been able to see his expression.

"There must be someone around here who has a university degree and a teaching whatever-it-is-they-need. MUST be. Please, Daddy. We could put an advert in the paper and I could go to them every day for lessons. I'd learn more that way. Being the only one, I'd learn much more. But honestly it doesn't matter. Artists don't need to go to school. We only need to be allowed to draw and paint. That's all."

Mr. Manders' back remained utterly unmoved. Jinny knew that really he wasn't listening to her.

"Please, please try to understand. I can't leave Shantih."

"You won't be leaving her. I've promised to take you over to Miss Tuke's every weekend so you can ride her."

"She won't be mine anymore. Miss Tuke will ruin her, banging about on top of her. She'll not be the same. She'll think I've left her. How would you like it if you had to leave Mummy? Never see her all week? You wouldn't like that."

"Oh, Jinny, try to be sensible. Shantih is only a horse."

"How can you even think that?" demanded Jinny bitterly. If her father thought that, there didn't seem to be much point in going on arguing with him. Jinny stared despondently out of the car window.

"As if Shantih were any ordinary horse," she thought. To Jinny, Shantih was a golden horse, she dazzled in Jinny's imagination—a horse of the sun—and Jinny loved her more than she loved herself.

They had taken Ken to Nell Storr's, and Mrs. Manders and Petra to Inverburgh station to catch the Glasgow train. Petra's piano exam was on Saturday morning. Going to

Glasgow today, they would spend the night in a hotel and catch a train back to Inverburgh on Saturday afternoon.

Petra had been cool and confident, her case packed by Thursday morning, certain she had everything with her, not having to check over and over again the way Jinny would have had to do. Even her good luck black cat was neatly packed in its own little box. Not that Petra needed good luck; she was prepared, thought Jinny.

Nell Storr had been waiting for Ken, sitting outside her shop at the wheel of her sports car. Watching them drive off, Jinny had wished that she could have gone with them, that someone had seen her drawings and had wanted to meet her. She had wanted to escape from Finmory. Surely, if she had been driving to London, the Red Horse couldn't have followed her, and in the excitement of London she might have forgotten some of the things that Miss Tuke had said to her. Mr. Horton had twisted his ankle, Tim had broken his collar bone and Brenda had refused to get on to her pony again. Miss Tuke had held Jinny responsible for the runaway and Mr. Horton had been furious with her.

"It was the lightning that scared them and Marigold's rainhood," Jinny had protested.

"If you had controlled Bramble, as you could have done quite easily, none of it would have happened," Miss Tuke had insisted. "You knew I was riding a young pony. I could do nothing. But for you to go urging Bramble on, yelling like that and charging through them all! I am disgusted with you."

And there had been nothing more that Jinny could have said to defend herself. She couldn't have started to try to explain to Miss Tuke that while she had been galloping and yelling she hadn't been with the trekkers. She had been surrounded by the small dark riders, had ridden with the Pony Folk from the past, her voice mingling with their cries, Bramble's hoofbeats had been part of their long silent stampede. Even standing in Miss Tuke's yard when it was all over, the wild, hawk screams of the dark riders still filled her head.

"I *am* sorry," Jinny had said.

"Sorry won't mend Tim's collar bone or Mr. Horton's ankle," Miss Tuke had told her, and Jinny had said no more. There was nothing more she could say.

Mr. Manders parked the car in front of Finmory. They got out and went inside through the iron-studded front door. Standing in the hall, the empty house seemed suddenly menacing, with his high ceilings and shadowy corridors. Kelly came through from the kitchen and, for a second, Jinny didn't see him as a tail-wagging, welcoming dog. She saw a grey wolf skulking in the shadows, its yellow eyes fixed unblinkingly on her face. Jinny shrieked with sudden fear.

"Whatever is the matter?" demanded her father, and Kelly was dog again.

"Nothing," Jinny muttered, stroking Kelly, ashamed at being so silly.

Yet she was afraid. No amount of pretending that she wasn't could make any difference. In her bedroom, the mural of the Red Horse waited for her, and, outside the house, the wilderness of moorland waited for the darkness that would set the Red Horse free, to let it come raging into her dreams. All day they would be going on digging at Brachan, disturbing the things that had lain hidden for hundreds of years. Jinny shivered uncontrollably.

Now there was only herself and her father left. The others had gone just when she needed them most. Jinny clutched desperately at her father's arm.

"You won't go too?" she cried. "You won't leave me alone here? I can't stay here alone."

"Of course I'm not going," said Mr. Manders. "What is wrong, Jinny? What is upsetting you like this? It's more than being worried about Shantih, isn't it?"

Mr. Manders looked down anxiously at his daughter's pinched face, her panic-filled eyes. The weight of her long hair made her face seem sharper and more drawn than ever.

"Can't you tell me what's wrong?"

But Jinny couldn't. She couldn't start to try and tell her father about her dreams of the Red Horse, how, when she was dreaming, it was more real than being awake. She shook her head dumbly.

"You won't go, will you? Promise?"

"Is it likely?" said Mr. Manders. "Look, go and make us both a mug of coffee and then come into the pottery and decorate some tiles for me."

"I'm going to jump Shantih," Jinny said.

"Make the coffee first?"

"O.K."

Jinny went through to the kitchen. She filled the kettle and put milk and coffee into two mugs. A gull flew across the window. The sweep of its wings, the suddenness of its moving shadow, made Jinny spring back, her heart thumping.

"It's only a bird. It's only a bird. Stop being so silly. Stop it!" Jinny told herself. "It couldn't happen. I couldn't be left alone here because I wouldn't stay here. I'd sleep with Sue, or go into Glenbost and spend the night with Dolina, or to the MacKenzies. I wouldn't stay here, so it can't happen."

Jinny poured boiling water into the mugs, and was about to call her father when the phone rang— shrill, commanding. Jinny froze, the kettle still in her hand, as she listened to her father's footsteps hurrying to answer the phone. She heard him lift the receiver and give their number.

Jinny could only hear half of the conversation, but she knew at once from her father's voice that the phone call was something special. As he spoke, his replies grew louder and more excited.

"But I don't believe it! I absolutely don't believe it," he cried.

"How tremendous."

"Yes, yes. Of course."

"Certainly."

"At once?"

"Of course, I do appreciate the urgency."

"Could I phone you back? Yes, in about five minutes."

"Yes. Yes."

"I'll let you know at once, but, to be quite truthful, I still do not believe it possible."

Mr. Manders put the phone down with a bang. He came running into the kitchen, grabbed Jinny by the waist and danced her round the kitchen.

"It's my book," he cried as they whirled round. "They actually want to publish it. And not only that, they're rushing it through, bringing it out in three months!" Mr. Manders released Jinny and fell back spread-eagled into one of the kitchen chairs.

"Fantastic," cried Jinny. "Absolutely super. You're an author now. A real author!" She was fizzing over at her father's success. "Wait till Mum hears about it."

"There's only one thing," said Mr. Manders, and Jinny felt a cold clutch of fear tighten in her stomach.

"What?" she demanded, when her father paused.

"Well," said Mr. Manders, standing up and reaching for his mug of coffee, "all the rush is because there's a report coming out in three months about the problem of unemployed school leavers. A lot of my book is about this and they want to link my book up with the report."

"But that's good, isn't it?"

"They're hoping for a T.V. documentary based on the report and the solutions I suggest in my book. If they can get it fixed up it should make quite a difference to the money the book brings in."

"That's even better," said Jinny, still not able to understand what was troubling her father.

"The T.V. producer who might be interested in doing the documentary is having dinner with the publisher tonight, and they want me to fly up to London this afternoon so I can meet them all."

Jinny felt as if she was choking for breath. Her lungs had stopped working. She wanted to yell, "You can't! You can't! You can't leave me here alone!"

"Seems vital that we get in first with my ideas before anyone else gets wind of the project. I'd be back tomorrow—but what about tonight? You would need to stay here."

"Of course I can stay here," declared Jinny, her voice too loud, too high-pitched. "I'll stay with Sue, share her tent. Of course you must go."

Jinny saw relief smooth out her father's face.

"Are you sure you would be all right with the Hortons?" he said.

"Perfectly all right," replied Jinny. She was gulping down mouthfuls of burning hot coffee to stop herself crying. It had been so sudden. Yet somehow she had known it must happen. "I'll go and ask them now. I'm sure it will be O.K."

Jinny caught Shantih and rode bareback to the Horton's tent. It had happened. They were leaving her alone. All her family leaving her alone when she needed them most. Now there was no one left to protect her from the Red Horse.

203

Sue had seen her and came out of the tent to meet her.

"Hi," she said. "Have they all gone?"

"How did you know," demanded Jinny.

"Because you told me. Ken to London, and Petra and your mother to Glasgow."

"Dad's going too," said Jinny. "To London. He had a phone call from the publisher and they are going to publish his book."

"Good for him," said Sue.

"They want him to fly to London this afternoon to meet a T.V. producer."

"T.V. as well!" exclaimed Sue.

"So can I stay with you. Just for tonight."

"There'll be no one left at Finmory?"

"No, so please can I share with you?"

"'Course you can. I'll just tell Mum and Dad."

Waiting outside on Shantih, Jinny couldn't quite make out what Sue was saying, only hear the voices inside the tent.

"That's fixed," said Sue, coming out again. "They're dead pleased about your father's book. Say to give him their congratulations."

"Thanks," said Jinny.

"Come over when he's gone," said Sue. "We can jump."

"Will do," said Jinny, riding away.

For a moment she couldn't help thinking that there had been something odd about Sue when she had come back out of the tent. Normally when Sue spoke to you she looked you straight in the eye, but just now she had been avoiding Jinny's gaze.

"Maybe she doesn't want me," Jinny thought, but it didn't make any difference, she wasn't staying alone in Finmory. For the first time since they had come to live there, Finmory wasn't home. No one was left there now. Only the Red Horse.

"I can stay with Sue," Jinny told her father.

"Grand," said her father. "Thank you. I'll phone them and let them know."

"There's a flight leaving at three-thirty," Mr. Manders said when he came off the phone. "I'll be straight back to-morrow morning. I'll phone your mother and Petra from London. Tell them the good news."

204

Jinny nodded, trying to make herself smile, not wanting to spoil her father's success.

"It's so unfair," she thought. "Why has it to be like this? Why couldn't we all have been here? Why should it happen now? Why?"

And clear into Jinny's head came a picture of the dig at Brachan. She saw the scarred hillside, the archaeologists with their measuring rods and graph paper. All busy, but not one of them knowing what they were doing.

Jinny shook her head, trying to clear it. "What's wrong?" she thought. "Why do I keep getting mixed up? Seeing things that aren't there? Saying things and then not knowing what I mean. Perhaps I'm going mad. I'm so worried about Shantih I'm going mad, but nobody cares."

Again Jinny saw the dig in her mind's eye. This time, the archaeologist's had bland sheep's faces. They were passing some small metal object from hand to hand and their hands were like claws. As Jinny stood by the table in Finmory's kitchen, she saw the grey shapes of wolves coming out of the disturbed earth. Then, as the picture in her head grew clearer, she saw that they weren't wolves, they were the small dark men she had ridden with yesterday; men dressed in wolf skins, with the wolf masks pulled over their heads. They crept closer to the archaeologists and, behind them, the sky grew red.

At first Jinny thought they were going to attack, and then several of them turned and looked directly at her. The wolf heads they wore didn't cover their faces and Jinny could see their expressions quite clearly. To her surprise they were not savage at all, but gentle, almost sad, as if they were being forced to watch some tragedy and were helpless to prevent it happening. Then it seemed to Jinny that they wanted to speak to her but couldn't. As if they needed her help.

"Jinny, what is the matter?" demanded Mr. Manders. "You look as if you've seen a ghost. What is wrong?"

Jinny blinked her way back to the kitchen. Desperately she wanted to fling herself into her father's arms, to plead with him not to leave her alone, to tell him about her nightmares. But she couldn't. If she made a fuss he wouldn't go to London.

"Anyway, he wouldn't really understand," Jinny thought.

205

"No one else can help me. Whatever happens is going to happen to me."

So she only said, "Oh, nothing. I was day dreaming." And Mr. Manders, not wanting to interfere too much, didn't ask any more questions.

" 'Bye," shouted Jinny, waving to her father as he started up the car. "Good luck."

"Take care of yourself," called back Mr. Manders. "Go straight to the Hortons and I'll be back tomorrow as soon as I can."

"Will do," Jinny shouted back. " 'Bye."

She stood at the front door, watching the car disappear down the drive, stood listening until the sound of its engine faded into silence. She was alone.

Jinny shut the front door and stood in the hall. In the silence, the whole house seemed to be listening to her breathing. There was the creak of a door being pushed open, and Kelly came padding towards her. He lay down beside her, watching her from under his thatch of grey hair.

Jinny made a dash for the stairs, ran up them, raced along the landing and up the ladder of stairs to her own room. Taking care not to look at the Horse, Jinny found her canvas bag, stuffed a nightdress and a heavy sweater into it. She dragged her sleeping bag from the bottom of her wardrobe and ran back down to the bathroom. She added her toilet things to her canvas bag and tore down to the kitchen. She locked the back door, fumbling in her haste, feeling the eyes of the unseen watchers staring from corners and from behind closed doors. She sped back through the hall, grabbed Kelly by the scruff of his neck and bundled him outside. Turning, Jinny pulled the front door shut and locked it securely. She dropped the key into her canvas bag.

"There," she said aloud. "That's it. I'm not going back in there until everyone is home again."

Kelly had twisted free from Jinny's grasp. He sat and watched her running down the path to Shantih's field. When she was out of sight he settled down on the doorstep, waiting for her to come back.

206

CHAPTER EIGHT

Sue was schooling Pippen. She rode to the field gate when she saw Jinny approaching.

"Do you want to jump?"

"Yes," said Jinny in surprise. She had been expecting Sue to want to ride over the moors, or at least suggest that they should go down to the bay.

"Better change the jumps, then," Sue said, leaping off Pippen. "They could jump this lot backwards and still have a clear round, they know them so well."

"Let's build a proper course," agreed Jinny enthusiastically. Jumping was the only thing that might take her mind off the Red Horse. She slid to the ground and looked round at the tumbledown pile of the jumps. "We were going to do it days ago, before everything was messed up. Really, we need to start all over again. This lot have had it."

"We'll build a complete new course and then we'll have a competition over it," said Sue. "Take their tack off and let them graze while we course-build."

"Right," agreed Jinny, and began to loosen Shantih's girths. Then she stopped, and pulled them tight again. "I'll take my sleeping bag and things down to the tent first," she said.

"Oh, don't do that," cried Sue. "Keep them here. Don't go trailing down to the tent just now."

Jinny looked suspiciously at Sue. She didn't think a few minutes would make any difference.

"Look, hang your bag from the gatepost and stick your sleeping bag between the bars. There, that's O.K., isn't it? Now come on."

They took off their horses' tack and turned them loose. Shantih broke away from Jinny at a springing trot. She went straight to the corner of the field closest to the moors and began to race up and down the hedge, whinnying.

"She gets so excited," said Jinny, watching her horse in case she tried to break out. "Perhaps she remembers when she was shut in Mr. MacKenzie's yard with his Shetlands."

"She'll settle. She'll not leave Pippen," said Sue, watching her pony's placid grazing.

"Hope so," said Jinny as she stared at Shantih, thinking, as she always did when Shantih was misbehaving, how beautiful the Arab was. "Miss Tuke won't see it like that," thought Jinny. "Miss Tuke will make Shantih behave herself."

"Come on, let's move these first," said Sue, starting to haul the scattered wooden boxes into a pile at the side of the field. Jinny went to help her. "We want to build them with a good spread on them, and not make them any higher," said Sue, organising.

"Not too low," said Jinny. "Shall we have a double and a triple? Shantih's never jumped anything like that."

"Clear everything away first and then we can start from scratch. Plan it out properly."

They dragged the straw bales, bits of broken sheep pen, the heather-filled sacks, the four rusted cans, the poles and the wooden fish boxes into the side of the field.

"Shall we go and scrounge round the yard?" asked Jinny. "Mr. MacKenzie said we weren't to take his good gate, but we could have the hen coop. Expect there'll be other things we could take as well."

"Right," said Sue.

"Can we take the hen coop?" Jinny asked Mr. MacKenzie, who was turning over his midden.

"Aye," he said. "As long as you're putting it all back behind the hay shed when you've finished with your nonsense."

"When they choose me to jump for Britain and interview me on the telly, I shall mention your name," Jinny promised.

Mr. MacKenzie snorted. "Just be clearing the field, that will do me well enough," he assured her. "And where would your father be off to?"

Jinny explained.

"That will just leave yourself in the house then?"

"I'm staying . . ." began Jinny.

"Isn't that Shantih?" interrupted Sue. "It sounded as if she was trying to break out."

"It would not surprise me," said Mr. MacKenzie. "It's not the peaceable bone she has in the whole of her body."

"I can't hear her," said Jinny, listening.

"I did," said Sue. "Let's get back."

They hurried back to the field, carrying the hen coop, a broken deckchair and four more fish boxes.

Although Shantih was still trotting up and down the hedge, she didn't seem any more disturbed than when they had left her.

"Must have been wrong," said Sue, and Jinny wondered why she had been in such a hurry to get away from Mr. MacKenzie.

"Almost as if she didn't want him to know that I was spending the night in their tent," Jinny thought.

"Do you want to try a triple?" Sue asked.

"Oh, yes," said Jinny, going to help her.

"We'll start at this end," said Sue. "Go down that side first, over an easy jump, up the other side over a triple, and back down the middle over a big jump."

"Puissance," said Jinny, forcing everything else except the thought of jumping Shantih out of her mind. "Enormous jumps."

They made the first jump out of the hen coop and the heather-filled sacks. The first two parts of the triple they built out of poles, and the third part out of the deckchair, boxes and straw bales. The jump in the middle was built out of all that they had left.

"Not very professional," said Sue regretfully.

"Suppose not," agreed Jinny, "but it is pretty good. I expect all the top show jumpers have practice jumps at home that look something like these. I've seen photographs of them in books."

"Better school first," Sue said, when they were mounted again.

Jinny didn't want to be bothered. Reluctantly, she rode Shantih round behind Pippen as he trotted and cantered figures of eight.

Shantih was annoyed at being caught again and taken away from her hedge. She threatened to buck, hitching her quarters, shying suddenly and stopping stock-still to stare goggle-eyed across the moors, blaring out her trumpeting whinnies. Jinny knew that if Pippen hadn't been there in front of her, Shantih would have been bucking and rearing in earnest.

"Can't we jump now?" Jinny demanded. "All this messing about is driving Shantih crazy."

"Sorry. Shall I go first, in case you crash through?"

Jinny nodded, and Sue rode Pippen at the first jump. He cantered up to it and popped neatly over it, but despite Sue's aids he stopped at the first part of the triple.

"He always does that. He has to put his glasses on to make sure there really are three jumps. Now he'll jump it without any fuss."

Sue turned Pippen and rode him at the triple again, this time he bounced over the jumps like a rubber ball. He cantered round the top of the field and up over the heap jump with a neat bound.

Jinny had been struggling to hold Shantih back. Now she half reared, snatched at the bit and charged forward. Jinny couldn't hold her. It was all she could do to steer her at the first jump. Yards in front of it, Shantih sailed into the air, soared over the boxes, touched down far beyond them and, with her head low, hooves drumming, she went battering round to face the triple. Jinny knew they were going much too fast, but she didn't care. She wanted the speed, wanted to go even faster.

"Slow her down for the triple," yelled Sue. "Jinny, slow her down. Don't try to jump it at that speed."

Shantih rose at the triple as if it had been a single jump. Jinny had done nothing to try and check her. She sat balanced easily over her horse's withers, her knees tight against the saddle, her hands light on the reins. She felt Shantih's surprise as she rose over the first jump and saw the next jump so close to the first. She felt Shantih stretch herself in mid air trying to clear the first two parts of the triple in one jump.

"Go on, Shantih, go on," Jinny cried and then knew that Shantih couldn't possibly clear the first two jumps; knew they were going to fall.

Shantih's hind legs caught in the poles of the second jump, bringing her down. Jinny was thrown into the ground in front of the straw bales. She lay there helplessly, watching Shantih struggling to stand. Saw her surge upright and trot away with her stirrups dangling and her reins around her legs.

"You stupid idiot," cried Sue furiously as Jinny tried to

210

stand up, felt her head swimming, and sat down hard on the straw bales. "That was all your own fault. You didn't even try to slow her down. You were kicking her on. I saw you."

Jinny felt dizzy. She put her head down between her legs, knowing that what Sue was saying was true. She had wanted Shantih to go faster so that she could escape from the Horse.

"You should think yourself lucky that she hasn't hurt herself," said Sue.

Hazily, Jinny got to her feet, found her hard hat, which had come off, stuck it firmly back on her head and went unsteadily to catch Shantih.

"Now," said Sue, when Jinny had remounted, "keep her trotting and take her over the triple again. I've squashed it down a bit."

Still feeling decidedly hazy, Jinny rode Shantih at the triple. She kept her at a trot and Shantih leaped stiffly over the first part, then crashed her way through the other two jumps, scattering poles and straw bales about the field.

"Try again," said Sue, rebuilding the triple. "Canter her in a circle first."

This time, Shantih demolished all three jumps.

"If I let her gallop she'll jump them, now she knows there are three of them," said Jinny, hating to see Shantih knocking down the jumps.

"Have you ever ridden her over cavalletti?" asked Sue.

"You know I haven't," said Jinny crossly. "You know I never did any jumping until you came this summer."

The light was fading into the grey of late afternoon. Although Jinny was hardly conscious of it, part of her knew the day was beginning to die, the night was coming closer.

Sue laid four poles on the ground for Shantih to trot over. She mounted Pippen and rode over the poles herself to show Jinny how Pippen could trot neatly between the poles without touching them.

"Once she can do that," said Sue, "we'll put up a low jump after the last pole. That will teach her not to get so excited."

Shantih reared impatiently while Jinny tried to listen to Sue's Pony Club instruction. When Jinny did ride Shantih over the poles, she clattered them all and galloped off.

211

At first Jinny really tried to listen to Sue and do what she told her, but the early evening was growing darker. The massed bulk of the mountains were being swallowed up by the grey light. Stray drifts of mist breathed over the moor.

"I think she's had enough," said Jinny at last. "She's only making a worse mess of it every time we do it. I'll take her over to her field then come back to your tent."

"Oh no," said Sue quickly. "It's far too early for that. I'll ride Pippen over with you."

"But I've got my sleeping bag and things here," objected Jinny. "I thought you could take them to your tent for me."

"I'll take them with us on Pippen," said Sue. "No trouble. He won't mind." And before Jinny could stop her, Sue had fixed Jinny's sleeping bag on to Pippen's saddle and slung Jinny's canvas bag over her shoulder. "Right. Off we go," Sue said, riding to the gate.

When they reached Finmory, Jinny took Shantih into her box to feed her.

"I'll put Pippen in a stall," said Sue. "No point in standing here holding him. In fact, no point in waiting here while Shantih's taking years to eat her nuts. Let's go into the house and have a drink of lemonade."

"But I'm coming to stay with you," said Jinny, the panic she felt sounding in her voice. "You're not coming to Finmory."

"Of course," said Sue, "if you don't want to give me a drink of lemonade, that's O.K."

"It's not worth it," said Jinny.

"She'll be ten more minutes eating those nuts and I've spent most of the afternoon instructing you. I need a lemonade."

"We'll get it in your tent," insisted Jinny, willing Shantih to eat her nuts more quickly.

"But we're here now. Come on. Don't be so mean."

The last thing Jinny wanted to do was to go back into Finmory. It's grey stone walls looked menacing and gaunt against the backdrop of mist. The blank windows seemed dead and cold.

"Well, just say if you don't want to give me a lemonade," insisted Sue.

Jinny glowered at her. "It's not worth it," she said again.

"Oh, don't be so feeble. Come on now. We've plenty of

212

time. We don't need to go back to our tent until eightish. Stop being so mean."

"Shantih's nearly finished her feed. In fact, that will be enough for her."

"Then let's put them both in your field and have tea at Finmory."

Jinny wanted to shout, "No! No! No! I'm not going back to Finmory, not until all my family are there. I'm not going back again."

But she was too tired to go on arguing with Sue. She leaned against the box door and watched Shantih finishing off the remains of her feed. "Well, if you really want to . . ." she said.

"It'll be fun," said Sue. "Let's put them in your field and have tea at Finmory."

"Lemonade," said Jinny, "and then we're going to your tent."

They turned Pippen and Shantih out into the field, and Sue bustled Jinny along the path to Finmory.

"Pretend you've lost the key," suggested a voice in Jinny's head, but somehow she couldn't. She fished the key out of her bag and pushed open the front door. Kelly walked in at her heels.

"You are lucky," exclaimed Sue, "living here. Ours is a bungalow, in a row of bungalows all exactly the same. I'll bet there's not another house the same as Finmory."

But Jinny wasn't listening. She was too busy switching on lights to banish the shadows.

"I'll make the tea," said Sue. "What would you like? Scrambled egg?"

Jinny sat down at the kitchen table. Her head ached where she had knocked it when she came off.

"I thought you only wanted a lemonade," she muttered, but already Sue was breaking eggs into a bowl.

Jinny watched, her ears peeled for the least sound. The creak of a floor board, the squeak of a loose window frame, the stir of a curtain made the skin creep on the nape of her neck. She was listening for the sound of hooves, the brazen whinny.

"Grub up," beamed Sue, handing her a plate of scrambled eggs and tomatoes. "Eat up."

"Then we're going to your tent," stated Jinny.

Sue didn't reply.

"We are," said Jinny, and ate her scrambled egg between two slices of bread, the way she wasn't allowed to when her mother was there. Munching her sandwich, Jinny tried to imagine where her family would be at that particular moment, but to her dismay she had not a clear idea of where any of them were. They had all vanished.

"Isn't this super," beamed Sue. "The mist outside makes it even better in here."

Jinny was gulping down the last of her sandwich.

"Listen," said Sue. "Do let's stay here tonight. It would be a real adventure. Just us."

"No!" cried Jinny. "No! We're going back to your tent."

"There's no adventure in that. You can come and stay in the tent tomorrow night if you want to. But tonight we can be here. No one to tell us what to do. We can go to bed when we like."

"No!"

Sue looked carefully at Jinny. "What's wrong with you?" she asked. "First you don't even want to come back for a lemonade, and now, when we've the chance of a super adventure on our own, you want to go running back to my mum and dad. I think you're scared."

"Of course I'm not." Jinny hotly denied the accusation.

"You're a coward, Jinny."

"I am not!" cried Jinny, wondering how anyone could say such a thing, actually say it to another person.

"Then let's stay here."

Suddenly Jinny felt too weary to argue. A strange numbness held her there, made her unable to fight with Sue. It was like the moments in the dentist's waiting room when it was still possible to pretend that she was going to be suddenly sick, or dash out screaming, or just refuse to go into the surgery because she couldn't bear the drill. But she never did. She knew she had to have her tooth filled and she just sat there, waiting for it to happen. Now that she had come back into Finmory, she couldn't escape again. She just sat, elbows on the kitchen table, chin propped on her hands, listening to Sue's bubbling enthusiasm.

"We could make toffee and eat it hot, or have a midnight feast," enthused Sue. "Jinny, it'll be great."

214

But Jinny was drawn to something else that stirred in the house, something else that was waiting for her, that had known she would come back.

"You'll need to tell your parents that you're staying here," Jinny's voice was flat, the words difficult to put together.

"Well, actually," said Sue. "I don't need to, because they know. I didn't know how to tell you, but Dad's still pretty mad about his ankle, and he says he's hurt his back as well. He seemed to think it was you galloping past that made him fall off."

Jinny looked down guiltily, fiddling with her knife.

"It isn't that they didn't want to have you," went on Sue, "but there's not very much room in the tent, and when Mummy said why didn't I come and spend the night with you here, it seemed the best thing to do. And I did so want to stay at Finmory. I've always wanted to live in a house like this. You don't really mind, do you?"

In a way, Jinny wasn't surprised. In a way she had known that she had never had any choice. She had to stay at Finmory tonight.

Later in the evening, they checked on their horses. They were both in Shantih's field. Pippen was grazing—stolid, clockwork—while Shantih stood at the corner of the field closest to the moors. Her every muscle was tense, her neck arched and her head poised. As the girls approached, she flung herself away from them, stormed in a sudden gallop around the field, mane and tail streaming about her, and then went back to her watching, her frozen staring out over the moonlit moors.

Jinny shut Finmory's heavy front door. It creaked and groaned, its wood swollen by the mist. The key grated in the lock as Jinny turned it.

"There," said Sue. "That's us safe for the night."

Jinny could only think that if something was looking for her, now it would know where to find her.

By half-past twelve, Sue admitted to being tired enough to want to go to bed. They filled hot water bottles and drank final mugs of chocolate.

"Goodnight," Sue said, going into the spare room. "Sleep well. We'll do more cavalletti tomorrow."

215

"Goodnight," said Jinny. Tomorrow morning seemed thousands and thousands of years away.

She walked along the landing, keeping herself close and tight. Not looking at the shadowy doorways, turning her head away from the windows, clenching her teeth.

At Petra's bedroom door she stopped, and went in. It was all neat and tidy. Petra's white and pink bedspread, her flowered nightdress case, the pink frill round her dressing table, were all controlled and tame.

"I could sleep here," Jinny thought. "I'd be safe here. I could spend the night in Petra's room and I'd wake up in the morning and nothing would have happened."

But she went back out on to the landing and walked slowly towards the stairs that led to her room. The grey shape of Kelly padded behind her.

CHAPTER NINE

The Red Horse on Jinny's mural glowed through the silvery moonlight. Instead of avoiding the mural, as she had done on other nights, Jinny went and stood in front of it. Standing perfectly still, she looked quietly at it.

"Only a painting," she told herself. "Why am I afraid of it?"

Petra would say it was all a nonsense, that, as usual, Jinny had let her imagination get out of control. Jinny knew that it wasn't that. There had always been a strangeness about the painting, something that Jinny hadn't been able to understand.

She wondered who the tinker girl had been who had come to paint the Red Horse. "Here, in this very room," Jinny thought, "with Mr. MacKenzie a boy, younger than me, sitting watching her."

As Jinny stared, the Horse seemed to grow—its yellow eyes burning, its charging hooves pressed on the edge of movement. Jinny stood still, held by the power of the painting. She could not move, only wait for the horse to gallop from the wall.

Kelly stood up, came stiff-legged from where he had

216

been lying by the window, to stand beside Jinny. He pushed his grey head against her leg, licked at her hand. The spell that had held Jinny motionless was broken. The mural was only a painting again.

Jinny shuddered. She paused for a second to glance through the window at the streamers of mist, floating, diaphanous drifts of vapour, flowing down the mountains, breathing over the moors, then she flung herself through to the other half of her room and stared over the garden to Shantih's field.

Pippen was a black mass of shadow lying by the hedge, while Shantih was still staring out across the moors. The sea was quicksilver, chequered by the cloud shadows as they swept across the moon.

Jinny sat on the edge of the bed. She was afraid to sleep. It seemed that all the things that belonged to her everyday life were no longer important, were toys put away in a toy box, and whatever it was that she was waiting for was the only real thing.

"I'm not going to sleep. I'm not," Jinny told herself, but her eyes wouldn't stay open. She had to lie down on her bed.

"But not to sleep," she murmured, "not to . . ."

The black marsh sucked at Shantih's plunging hooves. Jinny's hands were knotted into her mane. The metal sky pressing down above them flamed scarlet as the Red Horse reared above the horizon. It stood, legs braced, crested neck arched, its head turning and turning as it searched the marsh with its flaming eyes. Shantih's struggles grew weaker. She no longer had the strength to try to escape. Jinny crouched close to her neck, shielding her face as the glare of its eyes beamed straight at her. The terrible whinnying of the Horse grew louder, more brazen. Jinny drowned in it.

She sat up. Heard the whinnying coming from the garden and sprang across to the window. To her dismay, she saw that Shantih had broken out of her field and was raking about the garden, crashing her way through shrubberies, rhododendron thickets and flower beds. Jinny grabbed her anorak from the back of a chair and, thinking only of what Ken would say if Shantih got into his vegetable garden, raced downstairs.

217

"I'll need a halter," Jinny thought, knowing that when Shantih was excited she had no hope of holding her by her forelock.

Jinny unlocked the kitchen door, tore down the path to the stables. Somewhere in Finmory's grounds she could hear Shantih plunging about, her strident whinnying shattering the moonlit silence.

The hook where the halters were meant to hang was empty. The last person to use them, probably herself, hadn't put them back in the right place. But Shantih's bridle was hanging from its hook. Jinny snatched it up and ran back into the garden.

"Shantih," she called. "Shantih." She stood still to listen.

Jinny heard the sound of Shantih's hooves and ran towards it.

"Steady the horse, steady," she shouted. "Come on then, Shantih."

The sound of hooves stopped. The silent night breathed back. Jinny stood still, feeling the silence prickling on the nape of her neck.

Then Shantih whickered with the welcoming tremble of sound that Jinny knew so well. Plunging her way through the dark blotch of rhododendrons, Shantih came galloping straight at Jinny. For a panicked moment, Jinny thought she wasn't going to stop, then, within inches of where Jinny stood, the Arab skidded to a halt. Her mane was twined with creepers, spiky with rhododendron leaves, her nostrils and eyes wild with her galloping. She stretched out her neck and rested her head on Jinny's outstretched hand.

Jinny slipped the reins over Shantih's head, eased the bit into her mouth and settled the headpiece over her ears. Shantih waited with her head low, accepting the bridle, as Jinny buckled the throatlash.

For a moment Jinny paused, standing against Shantih's shoulder, the thought wordless in her mind that she would go for a ride, gallop Shantih over the moonlit hills.

Jinny leaped and landed easily astride Shantih. She felt the horse warm and solid, comfortingly real.

"Where to?" whispered Jinny, and saw Shantih's ears

tickle with the sound of her voice, heard her nostrils flittering in answer. Jinny eased her fingers on the reins and Shantih broke into a trot. Without hesitating, Shantih took the track that led on to the moors. As they passed the black shape of Finmory House and climbed up over the rough, bracken-clad slopes, Shantih's trot changed into a steady canter.

At first Jinny tried to slow her down, tugging pointlessly at the reins. Then she remembered how Shantih had run with Mr. MacKenzie's herd of Shetland ponies. Often on moonlit nights like this they must have galloped for the joy of it over the open moors.

Jinny relaxed, let her horse gallop on, let herself be carried to wherever Shantih wanted to take her. She gazed over the dark waves of moorland, at the bulk of mountains cramped down on to the brink of this moonlit world, and up into the huge immensity of the sky. She was only conscious of her horse, taken up and carried by this pounding urgency. A grey shape flowed at Shantih's heels. Jinny saw him, had no words to say 'Kelly', but was comforted by his being there.

As she rode, a voice sang in Jinny—a high, sweet singing.

Loch Varrich was a sheet of unbroken silver, mist wreathed over its surface. The gnarled pines that grew by its shore were etched, black claws against the bright sky.

When they reached the head of Loch Varrich, Shantih turned to the right. Without hesitation she took the path that led through the peat bog to Brachan.

Through the trance that held Jinny powerless, she tried to turn Shantih, but nothing she did had any effect on the relentless speed of her horse.

"Have to go where she takes me," Jinny thought, each word thick in her mind as if her head was full of cotton wool. "Have no choice."

Jinny had no knowledge of time. She clung helplessly to Shantih's mane. Tired now, she jolted and slipped, longing to fall and lie in the heather. But something of the will that drove Shantih on forced Jinny not to give in. Somehow it mattered that she should stay on Shantih, that she should survive.

219

Water from the peat bog spurted diamonds under Shantih's hooves. Her speed sprayed water over Jinny's head. As Shantih came to the deepest part of the bog she slowed to a trot, then plunged and reared her way through it.

Once clear of the bog, Shantih galloped on, showing no signs of tiredness. The mists grew denser. Sometimes they seemed to be riding through drifts of cloud, sometimes only Shantih's head and throat were visible, moving, disembodied, in front of Jinny, and at other times Shantih's hooves splashed through waves of mist.

Shantih began to canter downhill, and Jinny realised dimly that they must have reached Brachan. The mist was like an icy blanket, clinging to everything. Jewels of moisture glinted in Shantih's mane and Jinny's long hair. It was so cold. Jinny had stopped feeling anything. She was only vaguely aware of where she was, of who she was. Only the will remained, the force that came from somewhere outside of herself so that she could not give way, could not sink back into unconsciousness.

A wind blew aside the curtains of mist, and, for a moment, Jinny saw the crofts of Brachan and the schoolhouse where the archaeologists were staying, then Shantih reared away from the buildings and began to gallop uphill. She stopped for a moment by the scarred hillside where the dig was in progress, then trotted away from it. She paused as if listening, then cantered on and stopped again. She stood with her head stretched forward into the sheeting, moving mists as if sensing something that Jinny could not see.

Jinny sat numbly on her back, waiting for her to canter on, but still Shantih stood without moving. At last Jinny slid to the ground. She tried to speak to her horse, but her lips were numb with cold and too clumsy for speech. She could do nothing but lean helplessly against Shantih. Kelly pushed at her knee, whining and clawing at her leg. Jinny lifted her face from Shantih's neck to look down at him.

"To have come all this way," Jinny said to the dog. His amber eyes gazed back at her.

Shantih began to walk steadily forward. No longer searching for a way, each stride sure and positive. Jinny

220

walked beside her, holding her reins loosely in her hand. She was no longer afraid. All her fears had gone. The certainty that filled her horse was with Jinny too. This was where she should be. It was right for her to be here.

Crossing the rough ground, Jinny's feet found their own way. She didn't stumble or trip but walked easily, as if she followed a path she knew as well as the path between Finmory and the stables.

Jinny had no idea how long she walked at Shantih's side. It could have been hours or minutes. There was only the present moment. The Horse moving with power and grace beside her. The pad of an animal loping at her heels.

The mists shimmered and flowed about them, then suddenly drifted apart, and Jinny saw that they had reached a hollow in the moor. It was completely circular, as if someone had dug it out of the hillside; a smooth cup with steep rocky sides. There was only one way into it—the path which Shantih was following.

At first, it seemed to Jinny that the ground was mounded with heaps of skins, then one moved, and Jinny knew they were human. They crouched close to the hillside, their long, matted hair and skin clothing making them look as if they were part of the earth, still rooted in it. Jinny smelled again the fetid, rancid stench she had smelled when she rode with the Pony Folk.

They had left a pathway between them to the far side of the clearing. Shantih followed it without hesitation. She looked straight ahead, her neck arched proudly under its garlands of white flowers and leaves.

At the far side of the clearing was a woman wearing long robes. Her white hair fell about her like a waterfall. Her face was brown-skinned and furrowed with deep wrinkles. Her eyes were a pale, washed blue. Behind her was a high block of stone. A fire was burning in front of the stone, and, as Shantih approached, the woman threw handfuls of dried leaves and flowers on to the flames. They flared up, blue green, and a heavy, sweet smell spread from the fire.

Jinny's hand held the rope of twisted creepers. The robes she was wearing made her movements stiff and slow. As she stood in front of the altar, her lips moved in a droning chant.

Two small statues were on the altar, one on either side of a golden bowl. One was Epona. The other, about the same size, was of a Horse. It's simple shape was made out of metal. The head was an Arab's head, the tail kinked over its quarters was an Arab's tail.

The old woman's hand moved again, sprinkling more herbs into the flames. The two statues grew huge. The Pony Folk moaned with a low terror. Jinny flung herself on to the ground, pressing her face into the earth to block out the fearful thing that towered above her. The Horse on the altar was the Red Horse, rearing above them all, while Epona, an apple in her outstretched hand, watched and waited.

"No!" cried Jinny. "No!"

When she lifted her head the mists had rolled back, blotting out all traces of the Pony Folk. Jinny stood up, still shaking, Shantih's reins clutched tightly in her hand. There was nothing to be seen but white, billowing mists.

Jinny climbed stiffly back on to Shantih. When her horse moved forward, Jinny almost fell. She twisted her reins round her hands and dug her fingers into Shantih's mane as they cantered through the mists.

The ride back to Finmory seemed to be happening to someone else, not to Jinny. As if she were in a safe place, watching another skinny, red-headed girl clinging to the back of a galloping horse; watching the horse plunging through the bog, the girl spread-eagled, her arms round the horse's neck; watching them by the shores of Loch Varrich, silhouetted against the silver water, and, at last, galloping over the moors to Finmory.

When Jinny slipped to the ground by Shantih's field she was trembling with exhaustion. It took her minutes to undo Shantih's throatlash. Her useless fingers wouldn't grasp the leather. By the time she had taken the bridle off and watched Shantih walk off into the field, tears were running down Jinny's face, her whole body shaking.

As she shut the gate, Jinny remembered that Shantih had escaped from the field. Maybe she had broken through the hedge and would get out again. But Jinny was too tired to check. Surely after her night galloping, Shantih would not break out again. She had joined Pippen and was grazing by his side. Even if she had been tearing round the field Jinny could have done nothing about it. She had to sleep.

Left foot, right foot, Jinny made her slow deliberate way to the stable and hung up Shantih's bridle. Right foot, left foot, she moved like a robot along the path, through the back door into the kitchen and up to her bedroom. She collapsed on her bed. Her eyes shut. Clearly, before she gave way to sleep, she saw the stone altar. The Horse alone on it, for Epona was locked in the case in the Wilton Collection.

"Where is the Horse now," she wondered, and sat up, as if there was something she must do about it, that only she· could do. Then she slumped back across the bed. "Tomorrow," she mumbled. "Tomorrow." And was asleep.

CHAPTER TEN

"Jinny! Jinny! Are you awake?" called Sue's voice from the foot of Jinny's stairs. "Come on. Get up. It's a smashing morning."

Jinny woke. For a moment she couldn't think who was calling her. Then she realised to her amazement that she was wearing her anorak and muddy shoes.

"Come on," called Sue again. "Get up."

"Right. I'm up," Jinny called back, thinking, "of course, it's Sue. She stayed for the night because they're all away."

"I'll start and make breakfast," Sue shouted, and Jinny heard her footsteps going back down to the kitchen.

Jinny sat on the edge of her bed. She couldn't think why she was still dressed. Then slowly the night's happenings came back to her. Piece by piece, like a jig-saw, they fitted together in her mind. The night ride, the mists, the Pony Folk, the woman with the white cascade of hair, the altar with the two statues on it. One had been Epona, the same statuette as Jinny had lifted out of the case in the Wilton Museum. The other of an Arab horse. Jinny sat staring

223

into space. Thinking about it, she felt as if she was falling backwards, slipping, falling.

She jumped off her bed.

"It must have been a dream," she thought. "I must have dreamed it. I must have heard Shantih in the garden before I undressed, gone down and caught her, come back here and fallen asleep at once. I couldn't have ridden to Brachan. I couldn't have seen the Pony Folk. They're all dead, hundreds and hundreds of years ago. Time is solid. You can't swim about in it. It must have been a dream."

Jinny checked through the window to make sure that Shantih was in her field with Pippen, then she hurried downstairs.

"Where are you going?" Sue demanded, as Jinny hurried through the kitchen.

"Just out for a minute," Jinny called back. "Just checking."

She hurried down to the stables. Shantih's bridle was hanging from its hook. Jinny took it down and inspected it. There was dried grass on the snaffle, but that could easily have been from yesterday afternoon. There was nothing about the bridle to tell her whether it had been used last night or not.

"If I did ride Shantih through the bog again, her legs will be muddy and peaty," Jinny thought suddenly. "That will prove whether it was real or not."

When Jinny reached the field, Shantih was standing by the burn, drinking. She stopped when she saw Jinny, and came to meet her, splashing through the mud at the edges of the burn. Her sides were plastered with wet mud where she had been rolling. Even if there had been dried peat on Shantih, Jinny couldn't have seen it now.

"But it must have been a dream," Jinny told herself as she walked back to the kitchen. It couldn't have been anything else. Jinny had taken a short cut up to the house through the dense shrubbery that was still hopelessly overgrown. A branch clung to Jinny's sleeve. She plucked it loose by its leaves. A sweet pungent smell filled her nostrils and, for a second, the Horse reared in terrifying power before her.

"You want to do what?" demanded Sue in astonishment.

"Ride over to the dig," repeated Jinny. She hadn't told

224

Sue anything about her dream, if it had been a dream. "I just want to see it again."

"But you said you never wanted to go back, never wanted to see any of them again. And you were so rude to them."

"You can be sure," said Jinny, eating the egg Sue had boiled for her, "that when you hear me say I'm never going to do a thing again, that's the very next thing I'll be doing. Things change."

"Your family will wonder what's happened to you if they get back and you're not here."

"We'll leave them a note," said Jinny. "But if we hurry we can be back before them. I don't suppose they'll be home before the evening."

"Say your father phones?"

"He'll only think I'm out with Shantih. He won't worry."

"What do you want to go back for?"

"I've told you. I just do. You don't need to come if you don't want to."

"I'll come," agreed Sue. "Perhaps it will take a few more ounces off Pippen. We're not going over the hills though, are we?"

Jinny hesitated. Last night Shantih had gone through the bog as if it was hardly there. She had hardly noticed it. But that had been a dream. This morning the bog would be real.

"No," Jinny said. "We'll go round by the road."

Their horses trotted out well, hooves clipping the tarmacadam, ears pricked, going steadily forward.

"Of course," Sue was saying, "you can't expect cavalletti to make any difference if you don't work at it. You must school every day."

"Not much chance of that if they make me send her to Miss Tuke's."

Sue's conversation rippled the surface of Jinny's mind. She answered Sue, hardly hearing what she was saying, just making the right noises to keep Sue chatting. Underneath, she was thinking of what she would do when they reached the dig. She knew that where the archaeologists were excavating was not the right place where the stone altar had been last night. Jinny wanted to see if she could find it again—the rounded hollow with its high stone sides and its straight path leading to the altar.

"Maybe Miss Tuke would school her over cavalletti for you?" suggested Sue.

"Shouldn't think Miss Tuke would even know what cavalletti are," said Jinny.

When they reached Brachan, they stopped at the school-house. Sue held Shantih while Jinny knocked on the door.

"No one in," Jinny said, coming back to Sue. "They must all be up at the dig. Shall we put them in the field or ride up?"

"Better leave them in the field. Now we're here, I expect we'll need to help for a bit, and I shouldn't think Shantih would fancy walking to and fro while you carry buckets."

"Right there," said Jinny, and they led their horses down to the field and took off their tack.

"Will she stay?" Sue asked, looking back anxiously at Shantih, who was trotting back and forward along the hedge and pushing at the gate. "She does fuss, doesn't she?"

"Perhaps if you could see what she can see you'd be making a fuss too. All depends how it is for each person. No one else can tell what it's like for someone else."

"Well, Pippen is in exactly the same field and he's settled down."

"That's what I'm saying," said Jinny. "The way Pippen sees the field tells him its O.K., safe to go on stuffing himself, but the way Shantih sees it tells her it isn't." Jinny dumped her tack in the porch of the schoolhouse. "I'll come down and see that she's all right at lunchtime."

"Well," said Freda, when they arrived at the dig, "nice to see you again. Come to give us a hand?"

"For a bit," said Jinny. "We wanted to go for a long ride so we thought we'd come here."

"Glad you did. Go and see Jerry. He'll be grateful for a bit of help."

Jerry was pink and specky. He was labouring to fill in one of the pits they had excavated.

"Very important to leave the site as you found it," he told them without much conviction. He pointed out a pile of rubble. "That's to go back in as well," he said, finding them a bucket each.

226

Jinny trudged back and forward, obediently filling her bucket, carrying it to the hole and tipping it in. Now that she was back at Brachan, the memory of her dream was vivid in her mind. She searched the hillside, trying to pick out any spot that looked as if it might have been the hollowed bowl where they had worshipped Epona and the Horse.

"But it isn't anywhere real," Jinny thought, trying to convince herself. "It was a place in a dream. I can't possibly find it here."

"Station break. Everybody out," yelled one of the students.

"Gosh," said Jerry, "am I glad of that. Say, what about you two? Wonder if there'll be enough grub."

"We brought our own sandwiches," Sue told him as they walked across to where everyone was settling down on the grass for lunch.

"I'm going back down to the schoolhouse to see if my horse is O.K.," Jinny announced in a general sort of way.

"What a shame," said one girl. "You should have gone before it was lunchtime."

"Do you want me to come?" asked Sue.

"Oh, no," said Jinny quickly. "I'll not be long. If she is still messing about I might give her a gallop to calm her down," she added, in case Sue might see her riding over the moor and think she had been deserted.

Jinny ran lightly over the hillside, picked up Shantih's bridle, and ran on down to the field where Shantih was waiting by the gate.

Jinny rode up the moors, keeping far enough away from the dig so that no one could call to ask where she was going. Sitting high on Shantih, looking down on the archaeologists, Jinny remembered how she had seen them as sheep, not knowing what they were doing, and she remembered the expressions on the faces of the Pony Folk, their wistful longing, their hopelessness. The way they had turned to look at her as if they were depending on her to help them. A choking, heady excitement flowed through Jinny as she felt Shantih's stride quicken and become more definite.

As she rode, Jinny searched the hillside for any hollow

227

which might once have held the altar to Epona and the Horse.

"It could be anywhere," she thought hopelessly. "It was so long ago. Probably the hollow is all filled in by now. I'll never find it. It was only a dream. You don't find dream places on a real moor." Jinny almost turned Shantih back down to the dig. But under all her commonsense doubts there was a certainty, a knowing that was more sure than anything else, that made her go on searching.

"Probably I wouldn't even know the place if I rode over it," Jinny thought, but she went on walking Shantih about the moor, all the time staring about her. With each change of perspective, Jinny searched for traces of the straight way that had led them over the moors and taken her through the Pony Folk to stand in front of the altar.

Suddenly Shantih stopped, her whole being electric and tense. She gave a shrill whicker, and, without any hesitation, began to trot out as if she was following an invisible path over the moor.

Shantih went on, straight ahead, flirting her nostrils, knowing where she was going, but still Jinny could see nothing ahead that bore any resemblance to her dream hollow. Shantih was pushing her way through the red-gold, rusty fronds of bracken. As they went on, the bracken seemed to grow higher and more dense, it's fronds parting like a bow wave as Shantih made her way through it. Jinny glanced back and saw that they had left no track through the red-gold sea. It had closed behind them, covering over all traces of their passage.

Shantih stopped. She stood perfectly still. Jinny closed her legs against her sides but Shantih refused to move. Impatiently, Jinny kicked her on. There was no sign here of the hollow in the hills, only the waves of bracken. Yet still Shantih refused to go forward. Jinny jumped to the ground, took her reins over her head and led her forward. The bracken was so deep that it reached Jinny's shoulders.

Normally, when Jinny had walked through bracken, the ground was rough and treacherous under her feet, but here she seemed to be able to walk as surely as if she were on the open hillside, and Shantih moved freely at her side.

Jinny stopped at the same moment as Shantih. She laid the palm of her hand on the chestnut's neck and looked

228

about her. They were standing in a hollow in the bracken. It was as if the land here had been scooped out, but no one would ever have been able to detect it unless they had come the way Jinny had come and stood where she was standing now.

Jinny shivered. Her skin prickled with a sudden charge. For the blink of an eye she saw the hollow as it had been when the Pony Folk had worshipped here, when the old woman had sprinkled her herbs on the flames, drugging their minds and making Epona and the Horse change into gods before their worshippers' eyes.

Hardly knowing what she was doing, Jinny knelt in the bracken. Its fronds closed her into a rust-red world. Blind, she stretched out her hands in front of her and dug into the mould with her fingers. Frantically she dredged the humus through her fingers, feeling bracken roots and stones, and the gentle texture of decay. Her left hand closed on smooth metal; fingered it clean from the mould.

Jinny stood up, and on the palm of her hand lay the small statue of the Horse. The craftsman or priest who had made it so many centuries ago had known that it was an Arab. There on Jinny's hand was the goggle eye, the wide nostril and the curved Arab face, the tail kinked high over the little statue's quarters.

Jinny stared at it. Shantih stretched out her neck and breathed gently over the statue. Moors and sky slipped away. There was only herself, Shantih, and this most precious thing, taken out of the darkness and standing now, on her hand.

Jinny's hand closed over it. She held it tight. The moors and sky were back—real, enclosing—bringing with them the thought of Sue, who would want to know what Jinny had been doing, and the archaeologists who would have to be told about her find; who would want to take it away from her.

Jinny shut her hand round the Horse, clutching it tightly.

"I found it," she thought. "They shan't have it."

Quickly Jinny looked over her shoulder, afraid that someone might have seen her find it, then laughed at herself—for who could possibly have been watching her on the empty moors?

For minutes longer she stood rubbing the metal with her finger, awed by the strangeness of her find. If last night had been a dream, then it had been a true dream. Yet how could it have been a dream when Shantih had known her way to where the altar had once stood?

With great care, Jinny wrapped the Horse in her handkerchief, then put it back into her anorak pocket and rode back to the schoolhouse.

"If I tell them about it they won't let me take it back to Finmory," Jinny thought as she rode. "They'll say it's too valuable, and take it away from me at once. But it was me who found it. I'm not meant to give it to them."

When she had returned Shantih to Pippen and the field, Jinny took the bridle back to the porch. Hidden in the doorway, Jinny took the Horse out of her pocket and unwrapped the handkerchief just enough to let herself see it again.

She could, if she chose to, run up to the dig and tell them all how she had found the Horse. They would praise her, ask her questions, each person wishing that they had found it instead of Jinny. When they locked it away in a museum they would put a label by it saying that it had been found by Jennifer Manders.

For a moment Jinny hesitated. She would like all those things, would enjoy being the centre of attention. If she told the archaeologists, she would be able to tell her family. When Petra came back from Glasgow, full of her undoubted success, Jinny would be able to tell her about the statue she had found. When Ken came back she could tell him about her dream and how Shantih had led her to where the bracken grew over the Celtic altar.

If she told the archaeologists. But Jinny was sure that she wasn't meant to do that.

Jinny started violently, sprang round, thinking she had heard someone move behind her. There was no one. Fumbling in her haste, Jinny wrapped the statue back in her handkerchief and put it in the bag with her uneaten sandwiches. She tied the bag back on to Shantih's saddle.

"You've been ages," Sue exclaimed when Jinny got back to the dig. "I was beginning to think that you'd gone home without me."

"I didn't mean to go so far," Jinny said. "Sorry."

230

"Come and do a bit more bucketing and then I think we'd better get back."

"O.K.," said Jinny, gladly setting to work again, not looking at anyone.

She worked twice as hard as she had done in the morning, hurrying between the pile of earth and the pit, which didn't seem to fill up at all, no matter how much earth was tipped back into it.

"Nearly three o'clock," said Sue, making Jinny start with fright. "You are jittery. Nearly as bad as Shantih."

"I didn't realise you were there," said Jinny lamely.

"Well, I have been here all day," said Sue. "But maybe you hadn't noticed. I was only saying that I thought it was time to go home."

They went to say goodbye to Freda.

"Nice to have seen you again," she said. "Only sorry we haven't been able to unearth a Horse god for you. Still, next year we're going to try over there." and Freda pointed to where Jinny had found the statue. "Their holy places often lay to the East of their settlements."

Jinny felt her face reddening. She stared down at her feet. "I'm not telling them," she thought. And she held her tongue between her teeth to stop herself blurting out the story of her find.

Several times on the way home Jinny nearly told Sue, but each time the thought of Sue insisting that they return the Horse to the archaeologists stopped her.

"I will tell her," Jinny thought. "I will tell her sometime."

"I'd better take Pippen back to his field," said Sue, when they reached Finmory. "Then I think I'd better drop in and see Mum. Will your father be back?"

"They'll probably all be back," said Jinny. "And if they're not, they will be soon."

"See you tomorrow, then," and Sue rode off.

There was no car outside Finmory. Mr. Manders wasn't back. Jinny hurried Shantih through her feed and turned her out. In the tack room she opened her sandwich bag and took out her handkerchief with the Horse inside it. She was desperate to see the statue again, but she didn't look at it in the tack room. Holding it carefully in her hand, she carried it into the house and up to her bedroom.

CHAPTER ELEVEN

Kneeling on the floor in front of her mural, Jinny unwrapped the statue. There was no possible doubt, it was the same one that Jinny had seen on the altar next to Epona. And it was an Arab. The dished face carried with an Arab's pride and arrogance was so completely different to the head and neck of the pony Epona was seated on. It couldn't have been chance. Epona was riding a native pony, while the Horse was an Arab.

Jinny set the Horse down in front of the mural. She went back to the opposite wall and sat down cross-legged on the floor, trying to see both the Red Horse of the mural and the Celtic Horse god. Kelly came padding upstairs, pushed open Jinny's door and lay down beside her, his forelegs outstretched, his nose placed exactly between his paws, his eyes gazing through grey thatch at the Horse.

"B.C.," thought Jinny. "It was made and worshipped before Christ was born." All the history she had been taught at school, the billion, trillion, zillions of people, all the mixed-up stories in Jinny's head of King Alfred's cakes, the Princes in the Tower, Henry V and Walter Raleigh, had all happened, if they had happened at all, while the little metal horse had lain in the ground above Brachan.

"Waiting for me to find it," thought Jinny. "They wanted me to find it, not those sheep-brained archaeologists."

Just for a second she remembered how the Horse had appeared when the old woman had sprinkled her herbs on the flames; just for a second the Red Horse reared into Jinny's mind, searching, questing the air for the lost thing it had come to find.

Jinny shuddered with terror. She didn't know what to do. She held the little Horse tightly in her hand, feeling it real and solid. She had found it, but she didn't know what to do next. Only knew that she would never give it to the archaeologists. "They would take it away and it belongs here," she thought.

Jinny heard the sound of their car stopping in front of

232

the house and car doors being opened. She wrapped the statue back in her handkerchief, brought her cash box down from the top of her wardrobe, dragged off its swaddlings of Sellotape and thrust the horse into it.

"Jinny, Jinny, are you in?" called her mother, as Jinny put the cash box back, jumped down from the chair and ran downstairs to see her family.

"How did it go?" she asked Petra. "Bet you were brilliant. A distinction. Bet you did."

"I don't actually know," said Petra. "They don't actually say, but I could tell they were pleased with me."

"Oh, super, super," enthused Jinny. "And are they going to film your book?" she asked, turning to her father. "Did they think it was the utter, utter best they've ever read?"

"They're certainly going to publish it," said Mr. Manders, "and things are looking good for the T.V. link-up."

"Great," said Jinny. "That is fantastic."

"Were you all right by yourself?" asked her father.

" 'Course I was. Sue came up. We'd a super time. Of course I was all right. We built a triple and I jumped Shantih over it and Sue's showing me how to ride over cavalletti."

Words frothed out of Jinny. She was so glad to see her family again, she could hardly stand still. No matter how exciting a time her father had had in London, no matter how successful Petra had been, it was nothing compared to Jinny's secret.

"You seem to have enjoyed yourself," said Mrs. Manders, looking at her flushed, excited daughter. "You're all catherine wheels."

"Expect it's jumping that horse," said Petra.

"Oh, yes," agreed Jinny. "She flies over the jumps—higher and higher. There is nothing Shantih couldn't jump if she wanted to."

That night, Jinny waited until all her family had settled down to sleep before she unwrapped the Horse statue. She didn't want to risk any of them coming into the room and seeing it.

Jinny sat on the floor, holding the statue. "From so long ago," she thought. "Who made you? What are you? And

233

now I've found you. You'll always stay here." Jinny clutched the Horse tightly in her hand.

The house settled into silence. The Red Horse glowed out of the wall. The yellow circles of its eyes glared down at Jinny. Lost in wonder at the Horse she was holding, Jinny had forgotten her fears. Now they came flooding back. The waiting presence of the Red Horse was still there. She jumped up, shaking the fear out of her head.

"No," she told herself. "Now I've found the Horse I don't need to be afraid any longer. I've done what the dreams wanted me to do."

Jinny lifted her hand to strike the mural, to reassure herself that it was only a painting, but she couldn't bring her hand down to slap it. She stood frozen with her hand upraised, then spun round, away from the mural and ran through to the other half of her room.

She got undressed and into her nightdress. Stood daring herself to go back and look at the mural, but her nerve broke and she sprang into bed, pulling the bedclothes over her head, the Horse still clutched tightly in her hand.

Outside, the night stillness was broken by a sudden tempest of hooves. It could only be Shantih galloping round her field. Yet it seemed to Jinny that the hoofbeats gusted over the roof, circled over the moors and waited there.

Jinny lay, tight and shivering, her knees tucked to her chin, straining to hear. Afraid that she would hear the hooves again, yet more afraid that she wouldn't hear them and the Red Horse would take her by surprise. Suddenly she was too tired to care. The need for sleep was a lead weight inside her head. In a moment of total terror, Jinny knew that she must sleep, and that in her sleep the Red Horse was still waiting for her.

Shantih was deep in the mire, already tiring, too weak to struggle much longer. The heat from the flaming sky burnt Jinny's lungs with every breath she drew. On the horizon the Red Horse reared. It swung its head to and fro, the beams from its yellow eyes searching over the black water of the bog. Then it focused on Jinny where she clung desperately to Shantih. Before, the Red Horse had been a mindless force of destruction, but now its will was sharpened and directed. It had found what it was looking for. It was looking for the statue that Jinny was clutching in her hand. With nightmare hooves, the Horse came galloping at Jinny. Clouds of steam rose around it until there was only the noise of its hooves and the glare of its eyes as it galloped at Jinny.

"Jinny, Jinny, wake up. You're dreaming. Wake up."

Her father's hand gripped her shoulder through the bedclothes, shaking her awake.

Jinny's head surfaced from under the blankets. She was drenched with sweat. For seconds she still struggled to escape, not knowing where she was.

"By goodness, that was some nightmare," said her father. "I thought I'd never get you out of it."

Jinny pushed her hair back from her face and sat up, taking care to keep the statue hidden. She couldn't stop shivering. The Red Horse had been so close.

"Whatever were you dreaming about?"

"I can't remember," lied Jinny. "I can only remember screaming."

"You were certainly doing that. Can I get anything for you?"

"No," said Jinny. "I might go down and make myself a cup of chocolate."

"Good idea," said her father. "Wake yourself up properly. You don't want to fall back into that."

When her father had gone, Jinny wrapped the statue up again and put it back in her cash box. She got dressed and went downstairs, where she found her favourite pony book about two girls in a Shropshire village who ran a riding school during their summer holidays. Jinny took it into the kitchen, stirred up the Aga, made herself chocolate to drink and a tomato sandwich to eat, then she sat down to read.

She knew the book as well as she knew the story of the three bears—bringing the ponies into the stables in the morning, trotting them bareback through the summer lanes; the grey pony borrowed from the milkman who won the local show jumping class, the thoroughbred given to them by Major Grant because he couldn't control it, and Midget the almost carthorse. Sitting crouched over the Aga, reading, the security of the story, wove a warm web round Jinny. No danger. No dreams. Only summer days filled with riding school ponies. They held back the terror of the Red Horse.

"Have you been up all night?" Jinny's mother asked, surprised to find Jinny setting the table for breakfast.

"Well, I'd a bad dream," said Jinny, not committing herself.

"You certainly had. What is worrying you? Can't you tell me? How can I help you if you won't tell me what's wrong?"

"I don't know how you even need to ask," said Jinny. "There's so many things for me to worry about that I have to make a list to remind myself of them all."

"You were bursting out all over when we came home last night. What was that about?"

"I told you—Shantih jumping so well. She could jump the sun," cried Jinny, flinging her arm in a wide, sun-clearing arc.

Mrs. Manders, realising that she was getting nowhere, stopped asking questions.

Jinny spent the day helping her father in the pottery. Sue came over to see if she wanted to ride.

"Thought you'd want to school," said Sue. "Trotting Shantih over cavaletti once isn't going to do her any good. You have to do it every day, go on teaching her."

"I'm giving her a rest day," stated Jinny.

"From what we've heard," said Mr. Manders, "Shantih is ready for the high jump at Wembley after the way she was jumping yesterday."

"Yesterday?" said Sue. "We didn't . . ."

Jinny dropped the sugar basin she was decorating. She didn't want her father to find out about their return visit to Brachan.

"Idiot child!" exclaimed Mr. Manders. "That was part of a set."

Jinny picked up the pieces, and Sue said if she wasn't riding that was that, and umbraged out of the pottery.

Jinny settled down. In the bright morning pottery, safe with her father beside her, Jinny could relax. With sure strokes she painted pots. Ken said it was dishonest to decorate other people's pots, but he wasn't there to make her feel guilty. Ken wouldn't be back until tomorrow.

At intervals throughout the day, Jinny escaped to her bedroom, took the statue out of her cash box and sat on

236

the edge of her bed, holding it, looking at it, then quickly hiding it away again.

After tea, Jinny went down to see Shantih. She leaned over the field gate watching her horse graze. The fields reaching down to the bay, the glimmer of sea and the jet jaws of the cliffs swam hazily in front of Jinny's eyes. She knew them so well, on so many evenings Jinny had stood where she was standing now, being content.

The air from the sea seemed suddenly less clear, as if a mist had blown in from the water. Jinny blinked her eyes, but the dense air massed and grew thicker. It towered in over the fields, rising in swirling clouds from the ground to the sky.

Jinny stared, mesmerised. Through the mist came the thud of waves breaking on the shore, the thunder of hooves. Jinny caught a glimpse of the Red Horse, monstrous through the mists, its yellow eyes glared straight at her. She screamed aloud, ran flat out, feet slapping, hair flying out behind her, as she bolted for home.

"Now what's wrong?" exclaimed her mother in exasperation, as Jinny slammed the kitchen door behind her and leaned against it, gasping for breath. "You look as if you'd seen a ghost."

"I thought I saw," began Jinny, but she couldn't go on. The terror that gripped her was her own private terror. She had to find her own way through it. If she told anyone else they would only make her give the statue back to the archaeologists, and Jinny knew that she must not do that.

"Saw what?"

"Oh, nothing."

"Then fold these sheets with me," said her mother, making the kitchen warm and safe.

And, for a moment, Jinny thought that all she had to do was to give the Horse to the archaeologists and all her life would be like this again. The fear that pursued her everywhere would leave her alone.

"No," said the voice in Jinny. "No."

"Pardon?" said Mrs. Manders.

"I was saying, 'no'," replied Jinny. "No to everything, because that's the way I feel."

Jinny sat pretending to read, knowing that soon her parents would realise how late it was and insist that she

237

went to bed. The thought of going to sleep, knowing that the Red Horse was waiting for her, choked in Jinny's throat. Perhaps she would ask Petra if she could put the camp bed up in her room and sleep there.

Shocked at herself for even thinking such a thing, Jinny pushed the temptation to the back of her mind. Petra would never forget it. She would always remember.

"That is eleven o'clock!" cried Mrs. Manders. "And you're still sitting here, Jinny. Go on, off with you."

At the door, Jinny paused. "Don't ask," she told herself. "Don't ask." Then she turned back and heard herself say to Petra, "Could I come and sleep in your room. Could I put the camp bed up? Please."

Jinny saw Petra and her mother look quickly at each other.

"Of course you can," said her mother. "I wanted to suggest it to you, but you know what you're like."

"I don't mind a bit," said Petra.

Jinny wanted to run and hug them. They had saved her from the Red Horse. Perhaps she would never need to go back to her own room, could always share with Petra.

"I'll help you put the camp bed up," offered Petra, and bustled Jinny out of the room.

"Really, you can stop being so silly," Petra was saying, her voice reaching Jinny through the darkness to where she lay stiffly on the narrow camp bed. "You'll enjoy living in the hostel. You won't actually have a room of your own until you're into third year. In first year there's three of you to one room, but the partitions make it almost as good as your own room. They don't mind a bit what posters you put up on your own bit of wall."

Even in the dark, Jinny could sense the tidiness of her sister's bedroom. The clothes she had taken off were hung up in the wardrobe, put away in drawers, or dropped into her pink plastic linen-basket.

"Of course, you have to be in by eight o'clock or get a late pass. Matron is pretty generous as long as you keep on the right side of her."

"Can you hear anything?" demanded Jinny urgently. Behind the irritation of Petra's chatter, Jinny was sure she could hear the beat of hooves. Or was it her own breathing?

"Your bedsprings twanging," said Petra. "You'll find the beds in the hostel are very comfortable."

The sound of the hooves came closer.

"Can't you hear the galloping?" Jinny cried desperately.

"What galloping? There's no galloping."

But Jinny could hear it. Her hand under her pillow tightened on the statue.

"Goodnight," said Petra. "Don't have any of your nightmares in my room."

Petra's breathing was controlled and even. She was asleep almost at once.

Jinny lay, tight under the darkness. The air about her reverberated with the thunder of hooves. The Red Horse was searching for its own. Jinny knew that she must sleep. The hoofbeats took away her will to stay awake. She could not think how she had been so foolish as to imagine that Petra's pink and white, sugar icing bedroom, her fashion magazines, her framed music diplomas, could ever hold back the force of the Red Horse.

CHAPTER TWELVE

Ken came home the next afternoon.

"Tremendous," he said. "I start in Amsterdam in the middle of September."

From the minute that Ken had received the letter, Jinny had been certain that he would go. "And maybe once he's with Bob Schultz, he'll meet other people, more like himself, and stay there. We'll hardly ever see him. He'll forget all about us," she thought.

Jinny sat, lost in her own miseries, while Mr. Manders told Ken about his visit to London and listened to details of Ken's arrangements to go to Amsterdam.

Despite her retreat to Petra's bedroom, Jinny's nightmare had been as vivid as ever, and now she was heavy with disgust at herself for being such a coward. Tonight she would sleep in her own room. It was true, you couldn't escape from things by running away from them.

"Did Kelly keep an eye on you?" Ken asked.

Jinny started back to her present surroundings and realised that there was only Ken and herself left in the room.

"Yes," she said in surprise. "How did you know?"

"Mentioned to him that you might need him."

"Oh," said Jinny, "did you?"

Ken stood up, stretching up on his toes, his arms above his head, spreading out his fingers.

"How's Shantih?" he asked.

"Fine," said Jinny, her voice polite and distant.

"Let's go and speak to her," said Ken, and with long, light steps he was across the room and holding the door open for Jinny.

Jinny hesitated. She nearly made an excuse not to go with Ken, for she knew that part of her wanted to tell him about her find; wanted to show him the statue. Ken had always known that the Red Horse on Jinny's wall was magic. The very first time he had seen it he had known that there was a strangeness about it.

It was only fair that Ken should share the statue, but Jinny was afraid to tell him. She didn't think that Ken would want to tell the archaeologists, but she couldn't be sure. And somehow she felt that she couldn't ask anyone else what to do. She had to find out for herself.

"Coming?" Jinny realised that Ken was waiting for her.

"Oh, er, yes," Jinny said, going out with him. "But I can't be long. I've to, er, well, I've to be . . ."

"You can't be long," interpreted Ken.

Jinny said nothing and they walked together down to Shantih's field.

"What's twisting you up?" asked Ken.

For a second, Jinny almost told him about her nightmares, her night ride back through time, the finding of the Horse and the continuing terror of her dreams. She so longed to be able to tell Ken that she had to bite her nails hard into the palms of her hands to stop the jangle of fear from bursting out of her.

"You look desperate," said Ken, as they walked across the field to Shantih.

"Of course I'm desperate," cried Jinny, barricading Ken out with words. "I'm worried crazy about Shantih. You all

240

think she's going to Miss Tuke's. You think it doesn't matter—that once I start school I'll forget all about her. Huh! Forget that someone else is feeding my horse; that someone else is riding her. Miss Tuke isn't good enough for Shantih. She can't ride. Not ride Shantih. You all think it will be O.K. if I see Shantih at weekends and have her back for ten days at Christmas. You all think that's fine. Well it's not. And it's not going to happen. I'll find some way of stopping Miss Tuke from stealing my horse. That's what it is. It's stealing."

Ken absorbed Jinny's aggression into his own silence. He ran his bony hand down Shantih's sleek neck, accepted her lipping caresses.

"Meeting Bob Schultz was like meeting someone I had known all my life," he said. "In the black days in Stopton I was so down that I couldn't even have hoped for a Bob Schultz. Couldn't even have wished for it to happen. It was all so black. But it has happened. I had to go through Stopton to meet Bob. 'Joy and woe are woven fine'. Be O.K. You'll see."

Jinny turned away quickly. "I've got to get back," she said, knowing that if she stayed another second she would tell Ken all that had happened.

That night, Jinny went back to her own room.

"I'm perfectly all right now," she assured her family.

"You screamed last night," said Petra. "It took me ages to wake you up."

"Then I wouldn't want to disturb you again," said Jinny, ungrateful because the cowardly part of her wanted to stay with Petra. But she wasn't going to give in to it a second time. "I'm quite O.K. now," she repeated.

Jinny didn't undress. She sat on top of her bed, her quilt wrapped round her shoulders, but, in spite of all she tried to do to stay awake, her eyes closed. She slept, and her dream came raging out of the shadows of her mind.

The Red Horse burned over the marsh, its yellow eyes beamed straight at Jinny where she lay over Shantih's neck. One of Jinny's hands was knotted into Shantih's mane, but tonight her other hand clutched the statue of the Horse. The Red Horse was closer than it had ever been before.

Kelly woke her. He had pushed open her bedroom door,

241

jumped up on to her bed and was clawing at her arm, licking her face and whimpering.

Jinny struggled free from her dream, sat blinking in the light, not knowing where she was. Then she cried, "Kelly," and clutched the dog to her, burying her face in his warm, shaggy coat. Normally Kelly never left Ken, and Jinny knew that Ken must have sent his dog to wake her.

Jinny reached her hand under her pillow and brought out the statue. She showed it to Kelly. The little Horse seemed more precious than ever. That she, Jinny Manders, should have been chosen to find such a hidden thing . . .

"Never," thought Jinny. "I'll never, ever, give it to them."

Kelly heard the hooves as well as Jinny. He sat suddenly alert, ears lifted, muzzle searching. The violent drumbeat of the hooves came down from the hills, seemed to Jinny to circle the house.

"It's not my imagination," she thought. "Kelly can hear them too."

Kelly jumped down from the bed, and stood facing the other half of Jinny's room. His hackles rising, lips drawn back, he stalked stiff-legged towards the archway.

"Kelly, come back. Come back here."

The dog ignored her. A snarl rose in his throat as he paced on.

Jinny sprang off her bed, the statue still clutched in her hand. She made a grab at Kelly's collar, missed, grabbed again. As her hand gripped his collar, Jinny was through the archway. The Red Horse in her mural was burning, glowing, its yellow eyes starting from its head. The hooves outside became the beat of its hooves as it galloped free.

Jinny crouched in the corner of the room, powerless to run back to her bed, or to dash downstairs to Petra or her parents. She clutched Kelly to her as the room was filled with the presence of the Red Horse. It was the Horse of the mural, the Horse of Jinny's nightmares, the Horse that had been waiting for Jinny behind the standing stones, it was Shantih as she had been when she had run wild on the moors, as she was when Jinny saw her as a horse of the sun —and also it was the small, still, metal statue that Jinny clenched tightly in her hand.

Somehow Jinny struggled to her feet and, dragging Kelly

with her, stumbled her way downstairs. She sat down at the table and buried her head in her arms. She couldn't go on like this. The terror of her nightmares was unbearable.

"Anything," said Jinny aloud. "I'll do anything if you'll only leave me alone."

But Jinny didn't know what to do.

"You have been up all night again, haven't you?" asked her mother when she came down the next morning to find Jinny dozing in one of the kitchen chairs, Kelly at her feet. "When did you last have a proper night's sleep?"

Jinny said nothing, because she wasn't sure herself.

"I'm having no more of this silliness," said Mrs. Manders. "You look so ill. I'm phoning up Doctor Thornton and we're going to see him."

"It wouldn't make any difference," said Jinny bleakly. "Not if I saw a hundred doctors, unless they could find a school for me at Finmory."

"I don't think that is all that's disturbing you," said her mother. "There's something else that you won't tell us about."

"Shall I help you with the breakfast?" asked Jinny, cutting off her mother.

After breakfast, Mrs. Manders kept finding jobs for Jinny, and it was nearly eleven o'clock before she escaped to her bedroom. She stood at her window, staring out to the bay, trying desperately to think what she could do to escape from the Red Horse. "There must be some way," she thought. "There must be. I can't give the statue to the archaeologists. I found it. It wasn't just chance. It's all connected with Shantih and my dream. I was meant to find it and now I've got to do something with it. I can't keep it here. I can't go on being afraid all the time. I've got to get rid of it somehow."

And suddenly Jinny knew what she would do. She would find a secret place on the moors, a safe place where she could hide the statue, where it would never be disturbed again, where no archaeologists would come prowling and digging. It would be back in the earth, buried safely as it had been for so many hundreds of years.

"I'm going for a ride on the moors," Jinny told her mother.
    "With Sue?"

"No, by myself. It might be quite a long ride, so don't worry about me."

"Don't do anything silly," cautioned her mother, but Jinny had already gone.

Jinny urged Shantih on up the moor. The statue was safe in her anorak pocket.

"It will need to be well out of sight of the house," Jinny thought. "Somewhere where even Mr. MacKenzie couldn't find it." And that was the trouble, for where was there on the moor that would be safe from Mr. MacKenzie's all-seeing eye? Jinny could just imagine him asking her what she had been doing, burying the wee horse on the moors when it should have been for the museum.

Then Jinny thought of the one place on the moor where Mr. MacKenzie hardly ever visited—the old quarry. Forty years ago, the quarry had been closed. Now its scarred sides were covered over with bracken, brambles, gorse and rowan trees, and if there hadn't been a barbed wire fence surrounding it, you would hardly have noticed it. It looked almost the same as the rest of the hillside. It would be the ideal place to hide the Horse. Jinny turned Shantih and began to ride towards it.

Jinny halted Shantih and stood looking down into the quarry. It was still possible to see the road that led down the side. Jinny could still make out the rusted metal rails where the trucks had run when they were working the quarry.

"Looks O.K. to me," Jinny thought. "If I could get down to the bottom of it there would be lots of places where I could hide the Horse and no one would ever find it. In a way it's quite like the hollow at Brachan. A million times better than being shut in a dusty old museum."

Once, the quarry had been wired off to stop anyone climbing down into it, but over the years the wire had grown brittle and rusted, the wooden posts had rotted away and no one had bothered to replace them. It would be easy now to get down into it.

Jinny looked round for a place where she could leave Shantih. There was nowhere at all. Jinny didn't want to risk tying her up by her reins. She would be too likely to pull back and break them.

The wire above the track down into the quarry was

broken and decayed. "Shantih could easily step over that," Jinny thought. "I could easily ride her down there. Then no one would see her. If I leave her tied up, Mr. MacKenzie would be sure to see her and come over here noseying."

Jinny rode Shantih to where the track sloped down into the overgrown depths of the quarry.

"It looks perfectly safe to me," she thought.

There was nothing in Jinny's mind except her urgent need to bury the Horse again. No thought of Shantih's safety or her own. The many times she had been warned never to come near the quarry were completely forgotten. She had never been told not to ride into the quarry for no one had even thought of her doing such a crazy thing.

"Walk on, Shantih," Jinny said, encouraging her horse to step over the broken, rusty strands of barbed wire.

Jinny rode between the rails, keeping to the middle of the track as it sloped steeply downwards. It was built on a high embankment, the sides of which were overgrown with a surging riot of bramble bushes, bracken and gorse, so that Jinny couldn't see the ground. She almost seemed to be riding along on top of the bushes.

Suddenly Shantih froze. There was something moving in the bushes just ahead.

"It's only a bird," Jinny told her, knowing that it certainly wasn't a bird. "It won't hurt you." But Shantih wouldn't move.

The disturbance in the bushes came closer. Jinny couldn't see what it was. "Maybe a sheep or a dog," she thought. And yet it didn't seem like either. It was moving too fast for a sheep and was too solid for a dog.

Shantih began to tremble. She made no attempt to run away but stood rooted to the track, shaking.

"Get on with you," Jinny shouted, as much to encourage herself as to encourage Shantih. Whatever it was in the undergrowth was coming nearer. "Walk on!"

Jinny caught a glimpse of a dark shape, a curved white tusk, a red-rimmed eye watching them. There was a grunting snort of fury and a black beast charged out of the bushes, straight at Shantih.

The Arab shied, throwing herself off the track to avoid the hurtling bulk. Jinny felt Shantih's hooves plunging into the mass of brambles, felt her fight to stay upright as the soft ground of the embankment gave way beneath her, and they fell.

Jinny was thrown out of the saddle, the reins plucked from her grasp as Shantih crashed down the side of the quarry, an uncontrollable mass of horse. At the bottom of the quarry she lay still.

Jinny threw herself down after her horse. She felt cold and detached. The need for immediate action took away all feeling.

In her fall, Shantih had trapped her hind legs under a heavy branch. Jinny tore at it. Lifted it a few inches, enough to let Shantih kick herself free. She snaked her neck and surged to her feet again.

Jinny snatched at her reins and led her round the enclosed space at the bottom of the quarry. She wasn't hurt. Sobbing with relief, Jinny collapsed on a block of stone, her legs fluid, her hands so worn out they could hardly hold the reins. She felt the hard lump in her anorak pocket. The statue was still there.

Jinny couldn't be certain, but she thought that the animal that had charged out of the bushes had been a black pig. The first time that Freda had come to Finmory she had said something about the boar being another of the Celts' sacred animals. But whatever it had been, it had not been a dream. It had been real enough to terrify Shantih. She could easily have broken her back in a fall like that. The power that had sent Jinny to find the statue of the Horse did not intend her to bury it back into the earth.

"Then what?" cried Jinny. "What am I to do with it?"

Her words echoed round the quarry. She took the statue out of her pocket and stared down at the little Horse where it lay in the palm of her hand. It looked so alone. Jinny remembered how it had stood on the altar next to Epona.

"Not one," said the voice in Jinny's head, the same voice that had spoken through her when she had stood in front of Epona in the Wilton Museum. "Not one, but One."

And, all at once, Jinny knew what the voice meant, knew what she must do. Couldn't imagine why she hadn't known all along. She must take the Horse to Inverburgh to the Wilton to be with Epona. Leave the Horse there, beside Epona, as they had been on the altar. Then Epona would no longer be one alone. Together they would be whole, be

246

One. This was why her dreams had led her to find the Horse; why *she* had found it and not the archaeologists who would have taken it away with them. This was what the Pony Folk wanted her to do for them.

"Tomorrow," Jinny said aloud. "First thing tomorrow morning I'll take the Horse back to Epona."

Her words echoed round the quarry, seeming to reverberate into a deeper voice than her own.

"The Horse with Epona. With Epona. The Horse with Epona."

And Jinny knew that she would have no more nightmares, would no longer be haunted by the brazen hoofbeats of the Red Horse. Now she knew what to do.

As Jinny led Shantih up out of the quarry, she felt as if a great weight had been lifted from her shoulders. She could breathe again, she could see again. She wasn't afraid any more.

When she got out of the quarry, Jinny remounted and rode slowly back to Finmory. "I'll catch the first bus to Inverburgh," she thought, then suddenly she knew that she couldn't just go by bus to Inverburgh. It wouldn't be enough for the Horse. There should have been a procession, but Jinny couldn't manage that. The best she could do would be to ride Shantih to the Wilton.

"Ride to Inverburgh!" exclaimed Sue when Jinny asked her. "Tomorrow morning?"

"I don't think I'd manage by myself. Shantih would behave herself better if she had Pippen beside her."

"But why?" began Sue.

"I can't tell you now," said Jinny. "But I will, honest I will."

Sue could tell from the state of Jinny's hair and clothes that she must have had a fall. Shantih, too, had bits of twigs clinging to her mane and tail, mud on her quarters, a long scratch on one of her white stockings. Yet Jinny seemed bubbling over with excitement, full of a secret that she couldn't share.

"Please," said Jinny.

"All right," said Sue.

CHAPTER THIRTEEN

It was very early in the morning when Jinny and Sue rode to Glenbost. The world about them was grey, without light.

"When we reach Glenbost we can go over the moor," said Jinny. "Over the top of the hills and down on to the Inverburgh road. Shouldn't think it's much quicker, but it cuts off a good bit of the road."

Glenbost was still closed against the night, no lights showed in any of the croft windows. Mrs. Simpson's shop was shuttered and dead. The junky, rusting cars piled outside the garage were in pools of deep shadow. A cat ran across the road in front of them, making Shantih drift sideways and Pippen prick his ears.

"Here," said Jinny. "It's this track, behind the church." They left the road and began to climb into the hills.

The statue was in Jinny's pocket. Once she had returned it to Epona, her part in the mystery would be over. Last night she had slept without dreaming. The Red Horse was satisfied. The mural on her wall was only a painting. She could not think why she had ever been afraid of it.

As they climbed, light seeped back into the world.

"Pretty steep here," said Sue. "Shall we lead them?"

"All right," said Jinny dismounting.

Shantih walked sweetly at her side, mouthing the bit, her walk relaxed and easy.

"This is how they brought them," thought Jinny. "Out of the darkness. The procession would be waiting down below to join them, but here in the hills the gods would be alone with the priestesses."

They reached the crest of the hills. The Inverburgh road lay coiled beneath them.

"Whee!" exclaimed Sue. "How about a breather?" She sat down on a comfortable rock.

Light from the rising sun arrowed across the moors. The rocks on the crest of the hills were rimmed with gold.

"Swear," said Jinny to Sue. "Swear on the thing you

248

love most, your most precious thing, that you'll never tell anyone about what I'm going to show you."

"Swear?" said Sue in amazement. "What do you mean, swear? What are you going to show me?"

"Think of your mostest thing then say, 'I swear,'" instructed Jinny.

Sue thought. "I swear," she said.

"Right," said Jinny. She felt in her pocket and brought out the Horse. She set it on one of the rocks and it was ringed with the sun.

"What is it?"

"I found it at the dig," said Jinny. "It's a Celtic Horse god. It should be with Epona. Her statue is in the Wilton Collection and I'm taking it there.."

"Fancy you finding it! Didn't you tell them?"

"They wouldn't have given it to the Wilton," said Jinny. "That's why I found it, so I could take it to Epona."

"It's an Arab," said Sue. "Couldn't be anything else. Maybe that's why you found it, because of Shantih being an Arab."

They sat in silence, watching the Horse until the light spread over the sky and the Horse had lost its halo of sun.

"Are you just going to hand it in to the curator at the Wilton?" asked Sue. "Won't they want to know where you found it and all that?"

"I'll manage," said Jinny, "if you'll hold Shantih."

"Do my best," said Sue.

"Remember," said Jinny, as she put the Horse back in her pocket, "you swore."

"To my grave," said Sue.

When they reached the Inverburgh road it was already busy. A vast yellow lorry roared past, making Shantih rear.

"Single file," said Sue. "I'll go first. Pippen doesn't mind it."

Keeping well into the side of the road, they made their way into Inverburgh. At first Jinny was tense, sitting stiffly, knowing that Shantih had never been ridden in traffic like this before; that if she got a fright and came down on the road she could break her knees, blemishing herself for life. A car transporter careered past, its twelve convict cars

249

clanking behind it, and Shantih cantered on the spot, her shoes scoring the road.

"If Pippen wasn't here she'd be away," thought Jinny, tugging frantically at Shantih's reins as she heard the rumble of another heavy lorry bearing down on them. "Steady, Shantih, steady."

The lorry roared past and Shantih shot forward into Pippen's broad rear.

"Oh, steady, you idiot," cried Jinny. A bubble of panic blew up inside her head as she fought to control Shantih. Her elbow banged against the Horse in her pocket and suddenly Jinny remembered why she was there. They were taking the Horse back to Epona. She shouldn't be crawling along like this. The Horse must be at the head of the procession.

Jinny squared her shoulders, relaxed her stranglehold on Shantih's reins and sat down hard in the saddle. She rode alongside Sue.

"Shall we trot for a bit?" Jinny asked. "I'll take Shantih in front. She'll settle if she can trot out."

Jinny let Shantih trot on, kept her moving forward, not letting her spook about.

"To take the Horse to Epona," said Jinny aloud.

The traffic grew heavier as they reached Inverburgh, but still Jinny kept Shantih trotting, fleet and red-gold, she gallanted through the city din and fumes.

"Which way?" asked Sue at traffic lights.

"I know my way to Nell Storr's shop," said Jinny. "Once we're there it's only minutes to the Wilton."

The lights changed to green and Jinny trotted on. Double-decker buses towered above them, motorbikes backfired, passengers in cars shouted and pointed, but Shantih paid no attention to any of them. She was all power and light, brilliant in the city grime. As she rode, Jinny was conscious of the Horse god in her pocket and of Epona waiting in her glass solitude.

"If they could only see them," Jinny thought, looking down at the scurrying pedestrians from her horseman's pride. "Not as they will be in their glass case in the Wilton, but the way they were when the old woman sprinkled her herbs on the fire. If they could only see them. If they only knew what we are doing."

They stopped outside Nell Storr's shop.

"Along this road," said Jinny, leading the way to the Wilton.

When they turned into the road where the Wilton Collection was they seemed to drop into a silent well. No traffic—even its noise was blown away over the high rooftops.

"About half-way down the road," said Jinny, and, looking ahead, she saw the plaque on the door of the Wilton.

"Shall I just hold them in the street?" asked Sue doubtfully.

"Along there," said Jinny, and they rode past the Wilton to where there was a rough patch of ground between two tenements.

"Even some grass for them," said Jinny as she dismounted.

"Don't be too long," warned Sue, taking Shantih's reins. "I'll yell for you if I can't cope."

Jinny hardly heard her. She took the Horse out of her pocket and held it in her hand.

"I shan't be long," she said, and walked slowly up the road to the Wilton. She pushed the door open, went into the hall and stood at the bottom of the flight of stairs. There was no sound in the building, no noises from outside. Jinny climbed the stairs. The long corridor was empty. Carrying the Horse, she went quickly, silently, to the room where Epona waited.

Jinny paused in the doorway, swallowing hard, then crossed to the case in the corner. She moved as if she was flying—a lightness, a certainty. The lid of the case lifted easily. Epona waited, small and self-contained – expressionless. Very slowly, Jinny put the Horse down beside her as they had been on the altar.

"Together," said Jinny, and, for a second, the vision flamed in her mind—the Horse in its awe and majesty, Epona with the fruit in her open hand.

Jinny closed the lid of the case, fitting the lock back into the rotting wood. When had the Horse and Epona last been seen together? Who had last seen them as she was seeing them now? Unanswerable questions built up in Jinny's mind.

Someone came into the room, came to stand beside

251

Jinny. She looked up quickly, afraid they might have seen her. It was an old man, not much taller than Jinny, with a mane of thick grey hair, a brown suit and a gentleness about him.

He stood looking down at Epona and the Horse.

"You brought it?" he asked Jinny.

"Yes," she said.

"He was right then, the man who brought Epona here. He said the Horse would follow."

"Who brought Epona?" demanded Jinny.

"One of the travelling people. You can call them what you please. Some call them tinkers, some still use the old name—the Pony Folk."

A cold shiver ran through Jinny. "How did he know I would find the Horse?" she cried.

"He only said it would follow. He didn't mention you."

"But it was me," said Jinny. "I dreamed the dreams. I rode Shantih to Brachan back through time and saved the Horse from the archaeologists."

"Enough that they are with each other again," said the old man calmly. "Tell me how it was."

Standing, surrounded by objects, the Horse and Epona together in front of her, Jinny told him of her fears, her nightmares, her dream ride and how she had found the Horse.

The man nodded, understanding, accepting. "We know so little," he said. "We are so lost that the gods must appear to us as beings of terror."

Then he turned, looking straight at Jinny, and said, "'Don't forget what has happened to you. Don't try and turn it into less than it is. Accept it as you accept the incredible miracle of food—apple blossom into apple."

Jinny remembered Sue, left with Pippen and Shantih.

"I'll need to go," she said awkwardly.

The old man nodded. He held out his hand to her. "I'm Jo Wilton," he said."

"This is your museum?" exclaimed Jinny in surprise.

"Sanctuary," said Jo Wilton and shook Jinny's hand. "The Horse and Epona are safe here. When I die my grandson will take over. He knows far more than I do. My sons stood on my shoulders. My grandson stands on theirs. He was born knowing things I could never even reach. They will be safe with him."

Jinny took one last look at the statues. They were together again. Her part was over.

"Goodbye," she said, "and thank you."

"Thank *you*," said Jo Wilton as Jinny ran out of the room.

She dashed along the corridor, hurtled down the stairs and half fell, half leaped into the open air.

"It's back," she yelled to Sue. She wanted to sing and shout and dance. She was free again. Her face was spread in an enormous grin. "I'm free! I'm free! I'm free!"

"Free or not," said Sue. "You have been ages. I thought Shantih was going to trample me underhoof."

Still exploding with laughter, Jinny took Shantih's reins and mounted.

"Were they pleased you took the statue in to them?"

Jinny considered the question as they rode along. Pleased was the wrong word. You weren't pleased about the air. It just was. The rightness of it was more than being pleased. "It belonged there," said Jinny at last.

They left the road and went over the hills to Glenbost. The sky blue, the air sharp. Jinny's mood was as high as the sky. Now there was nothing but light. Once Ken had said, "it's all luminous Love," and, riding back over the hills to Glenbost, Jinny knew it was true.

She let Shantih sail over the stone walls, loving her speed and her courage. She loved Pippen, bustling behind her, loved his steadfastness, his placid contentment. She wanted to tell Sue how it was for her. Kept saying to Sue, "Isn't it wonderful. Isn't it all so wonderful."

Glenbost lay huddled below them. As they rode down, the sun was high in cloudless blue.

"The day that Shantih escaped from the circus van was a day like this," Jinny said. "A blue day."

For a moment, Jinny thought that the two days were linked. Shantih coming to Finmory so that she would be there to find the buried Horse god. But how could that possibly be? Jinny shook back her hair, laughing aloud, for it didn't matter. It was enough to be riding Shantih over the open land.

"Jump this bit," Jinny called back to Sue, and cantered

Shantih at a level bit of wall. Shantih leaped and landed in a smooth, flowing arc.

"Oh, horse!" cried Jinny. "Oh, Shantih, Shantih, Shantih."

They rode past the church and into the village. Dolina was standing outside the shop.

"You'll have been having the letter?" Dolina called, her face glum and despondent as she came across to them.

"What letter?" asked Jinny. But almost she knew. It couldn't have been any other way. She had always known that it couldn't happen.

"From the Education Committee. It's not the weekly boarding we're for. Haven't they found the dry rot in Duninver School? The whole floor's falling in on them. They haven't the room for us. We're to be travelling to Inverburgh after all."

"Well," said Sue. "Thank goodness for that."

"Aren't you pleased?" she demanded, when Jinny said nothing, only sat on Shantih, staring at Dolina.

"I'll tell you this," said Dolina. "It's the better time we would have been having at the hostel. Clanging about in an old school bus all week. It's not me that would have been choosing that, I can tell you."

Jinny hardly spoke all the way back to Finmory.

"I'm into shock," she told Sue.

"See you tomorrow, then," said Sue. "When you've recovered." And she turned Pippen to ride down to their tent.

"Yes," said Jinny. "Yes, O.K."

She couldn't start and thank Sue for riding with her to Inverburgh, not just now. She would do that tomorrow. Tomorrow would be cavalletti and the freedom of the moors, no longer haunted by the terror of hoofbeats, the presence of the Red Horse. But today Jinny was still caught up in the wonder that she didn't understand, could only live.

Ken had been waiting for her at the foot of the drive. He came from between the trees, Kelly shadowing his heels.

"You know," he said, seeing Jinny's brightness. "You've heard."

"Yes," said Jinny. "I won't have to leave Shantih. She won't have to go to Miss Tuke's."

Saying the words aloud made it real. Jinny wanted to gallop and shout, send Shantih flying over the sands, soaring over the sun. All the things that had been closed against her were open now. Her new school, the Art Department, schooling Shantih, teaching her to jump, being able to speak to people again, not having to shut them out.

The Horse and Epona were together.

"Isn't it wonderful? Isn't it all so wonderful?" she demanded.

Ken laughed up at her. "I keep on telling you," he said. "If you'd only listen."